SWEET ABANDON

"Slade!"

He turned, and at the sight of her his face lit up. "Glory!"

She ran to him and his arms opened as she flew into their safe haven, exulting in the strength and warmth that immediately enveloped her.

"Glory," he whispered again, his warm breath caressing her skin as he stood and reveled in the feel of her. He gently adjusted his hold on her, bringing his thumbs together under her chin.

Glory instantly responded to his touch, tilting her head back, exposing the sweet vulnerability of her neck, offering her lips to him. She felt his grip tighten in her unruly tresses, binding her to him like velvet chains. And then his mouth was upon hers, fevered and hungry.

She moaned low in her throat and her arms went around his waist. Her small hands roamed over his back, caressing the hard muscles in his shoulders, pulling him closer, ever closer . . .

TEXAS GLORY
LAREE BRYANT

ZEBRA BOOKS
KENSINGTON PUBLISHING CORP.

ZEBRA BOOKS

are published by

Kensington Publishing Corp.
475 Park Avenue South
New York, NY 10016

First printing: November 1987

Printed in the United States of America

For my wonderful mother-in-law,
Oleva Bryant, and all the Bryants and
Moores of Cooke County, Texas.

ACKNOWLEDGMENTS

Special thanks to the ladies of Morton Museum and to Margaret Hays, for their help in compiling research material on Gainesville.

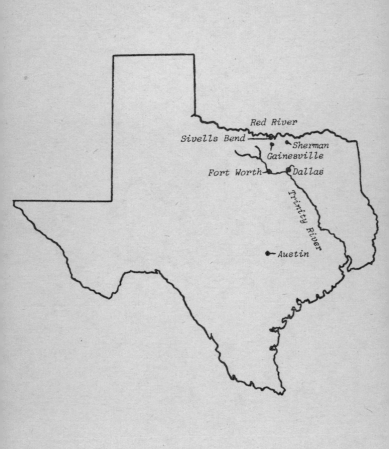

Foreword

As the hot winds of impending war raked the country, an inevitable sequence of events — local, state, and national — led North Texas, and Gainesville in particular, to the fateful fall of 1862 when bitter disputes over the issues of slavery, secession, and Union or Southern loyalty exploded in a tragedy unparalleled in history. In the area known as the "Forks of the Trinity," a small but forceful minority of rich pro-Southern slaveowners had settled on the rich bottom lands of the Red River, rising quickly to local and state prominence. But North Texas was also home to a very large number of die-hard Unionists.

Despite a rash of geographically scattered burnings, battles, and hangings, as the fifties became the sixties, Governor Sam Houston managed to ward off large-scale violence. But the state-wide referendum on the issue of secession held in February 1861 ignited the spark that would eventually set Gainesville and the surrounding counties ablaze in October 1862. Although Texas as a whole voted for secession

11

by a margin of 46,129 to 14,697, nineteen of Texas's 122 organized counties voted strongly against it.

Cooke County and seven other counties surrounding it (Grayson, Collin, Montague, Fannin, Wise, Jack, and Lamar) voted overwhelmingly against secession. A petition was circulated calling for the organization of a new state to seek admission to the Union. This might actually have been accomplished had those counties not been cut off geographically from the Union by the unsettled land known as the Indian Territory (Oklahoma). Disaster was inevitable.

To further add fuel to the fire, in April 1862 a Conscript Law was passed in Texas—something that no American government had ever done. All ablebodied men between the ages of eighteen to thirty-five years were ordered to serve in the military . . . except for those gentlemen who owned ten or more slaves. Thus, many of the poorer, Union-minded men were forced to serve the Southern cause while the rich slaveowners were exempt from such service. To a great many it was a flagrant move by the powerful "slavocrats" to avoid risking their own skins in a war being waged chiefly for their benefit. A regiment of one thousand men was raised from ten North Texas counties to protect the state's northern border against the expected assaults of the Union Army as well as against the renegade Indian bands that occasionally swept through on bloody raids. Strongly pro-Southern men were placed in charge of these troops, who were mainly pacifists or Union sympathizers. Tempers flared, resentment grew, and the seeds of a whirlwind were sown.

In response to the turbulent times, a clandestine organization called the "Union League" was formed, complete with secret passwords, grips, and signs. Claiming a membership in the hundreds, most of them believed that the goals of the League were to resist the Conscription Law and bide time until they could throw their loyalties to the Union Army when it arrived. But legend says that a few wicked men planned to use the deep-running emotions of the League's rank and file to rid themselves totally of Southern sympathizers in the area, killing all who stood in their way and thereby claiming the Unionists' riches and land-holdings as their own.

Still others believe that, when the existence of the League was discovered, certain devious slaveowners saw the opportunity to eradicate the dissenters to the Southern cause — and especially those who had been in contact with the capital at Austin concerning the unfair Conscription Law. A few perhaps saw a chance to amass even more power and wealth. Upon orders of the Southern leaders, the territory was placed under military law, and mass arrests began.

The residents were thrown into panic by the wild stories told by both sides — some perhaps false, others with more than a grain of truth to them. As the nation geared itself for Civil War, this small area of Texas was thrown into cataclysmic conflict over its own North-South issue . . . Abolitionist against "Secesh," father against son, neighbor against neighbor.

Sometimes even lovers were faced with the ultimate decision . . . their inbred loyalty or their love.

Gainesville, Cooke County, Texas
Summer 1862

Chapter One

"Glory, you daren't! Your pa will skin you alive."

Glory Kathleen Westbrook watched her father's imposing figure disappear through the doorway of his lawyer's office and then gave a dainty dismissing sniff at the alarm in her friend's voice. "Don't be such a ninny, Lydia."

Throwing one last quick glance over her shoulder, Glory hoisted the hem of her expensive blue gown a tad too much for proper decorum and scampered around the lavishly appointed buggy which only moments earlier had brought the two young women and Colonel Westbrook to the center of town. Safely out of her father's sight, Glory's pert little chin tilted at an even more determined angle. Resolve sheened her sherry-colored eyes as she passed under the broad, shaded gallery of the Foreman Hotel and across the dusty expanse of California Street. She hurried toward the bustling activity edging the courthouse square, pointedly ignoring her friend's warning.

15

"My, my, doesn't it all look just simply wonderful!" A saucy toss of her head set to bobbing the fluffy white plumes adorning the elegant little bonnet atop her head.

Glory's voice lilted with excitement, but Lydia Upton knew her friend far too well to attribute Glory's enthusiasm merely to the familiar sights and sounds of their home town. Her mind aswirl with what she was afraid were further useless protests, Lydia practically trod on her best friend's heels when Glory came to a sudden halt in the middle of the road to await the slow passing of a rickety farm wagon. A shake of the weary mule's head wafted the soft jingle of his harness on a gentle breeze.

Once across the broad, dirt-packed street, the two young women worked their way along the tangle of buggies and wagons lining the square for trade day. Face aglow, Glory hurried from one wagonful of wares to another. The warm summer air smelled of cabbages and onions, horses and hay, tangy wild plums, smoke and dust.

Smiling with delight at being home, Glory exchanged ebullient greetings with the owners of familiar faces along the way. Her musical laughter sounded often as she pertly answered questions or parried good-natured comments about how much she'd grown.

Despite the seemingly random path Glory was taking, Lydia knew they were ultimately headed toward the boardwalk that fronted the row of stores on the far side of the courthouse square.

"Glory—"

"Isn't it just the most glorious day? How lucky for

us that it didn't rain."

"Glory, I know what you're thinking. You'd better listen—"

"I would so hate to spend my first day back in town cooped up in the house. Actually, I was afraid I'd be stuck in the country all summer long. Papa said once that we might not use the town house at all this year. Well, I just about *died!* Can you imagine how boring it would be not to see everyone?"

"Everyone being Slade Hunter, I presume," Lydia muttered under her breath.

Glory totally ignored the caustic comment and again turned her attention to the intriguing sights and smells around them, her gaze raptly sweeping the sun-dappled congestion before her.

The one-story frame courthouse stood familiar guard at the east side of the square, its sturdy boardwork a bit more weathered than when she'd last seen it. The door on the side facing her was thrown open to the warm breezes of the day, and sunlight glinted off the two windows adorning the end wall.

She had forgotten the exhilaration of her home town on market day—a kaleidoscope of activities that seemed almost foreign after two years of parentally imposed exile to the genteel confines of one of the most renowned finishing schools for young ladies in the South.

"Glory, listen. You don't understand. Things have changed."

Glory turned toward her friend in exasperation, the braid-adorned hem of her blue skirt swirling about her slim ankles. "My goodness gracious, Lydia, why are you getting so riled up? All I intend to do is stop

17

by a store and purchase a spool of thread. What harm can there be in that?"

Small fists balled against her hips, Lydia endeavored to enlighten her tenacious friend regarding the realities of life.

"Humph! You can't fool me. I know what you really have in mind. And your pa will see through your ruse, too, if he catches you. He didn't much care for you being around Slade Hunter before he sent you away to that fancy school, and he's sure not going to like it now!"

"Papa's got no reason to dislike Slade—"

Lydia rolled her cornflower-blue eyes in annoyance. "Oh, no?" she asked, gentle sarcasm edging her voice. "What about the fact that Slade Hunter is still nothing but a small-time merchant?"

"What on earth has that to do with anything?" Glory asked, frowning.

"You know exactly what it has to do with everything," Lydia insisted. "Your pa didn't think Slade was good enough to come calling on the daughter of the county's wealthiest man before. I doubt that he's considered changing his mind in the past two years. Has it ever crossed your mind that Slade might not be interested anymore?"

Glory forced a brave smile to her face despite the violent lurch her heart gave at the disconcerting thought. "I suppose I *might* just find out the answer to that question if you'll let me make my purchase." She wondered if the catch in her voice was as obvious to Lydia as it was to her own ears.

Lydia rolled her eyes heavenward. "Lord, I feel trouble coming. All I can do is hope Slade's more sensible than you. If he's got a lick of sense, he knows your pa would never consider him a proper suitor."

"I can't worry about that now, Lydia." A sudden terrifying thought crossed Glory's mind. "He . . . he's not courting anyone else, is he?"

"Heavens, Glory, wouldn't I have already told you if he was? And if that was the case, I certainly wouldn't be so worried now, would I?"

Sweet relief flowed through Glory. "See there! I knew everything would be all right. He promised he'd wait for me, and he did."

"Glory, you've got to stop this foolishness. Things have changed since you left. You simply don't understand. It's not just the fact that your pa considers Slade beneath you socially. You've got to remember no matter how nice he is, he's still a Yankee—"

"He is not!" Glory stamped her small foot, showering red dust over her expensive black kid slippers. "Texas is his home. He's been here four years. He's not ever going back East."

"Listen to me, Glory. My pa says Slade's daddy voted against secession."

"What has that got to do with anything?"

"From what I've heard, Slade's pa and your pa have had harsh words about secession right here on the town square more than once! Your pa isn't likely to forget those arguments. Not now, not ever."

"What Mr. Hunter did has nothing to do with Slade. He's never cared anything for politics."

Lydia shrugged her shoulders. "Maybe he still doesn't. I don't know. But it won't change the situation. There's bad feelings in this town."

19

"Whatever are you talking about?" Glory stopped to stare at her friend in bafflement.

"Gainesville is as divided by the North-South issue as the United States itself! People like your pa and mine are on one side, and the Hunters and their kind are on the other."

"It won't matter—"

"It might matter more than you think," Lydia persisted. "You know how protective Slade's been of his father since Mrs. Hunter died. What if Mr. Hunter is against the relationship, same as the Colonel? Do you think Slade would choose you over his family?"

Glory's eyes clouded with confusion. It didn't seem fair. Why should anyone want to spoil what she and Slade might have? It was a totally foreign concept to Glory. Fulfillment of her childhood wishes had been the rule, not the exception. It was her birthright as the Colonel's daughter.

Heaven had always heaped its riches on Glory in double handfuls. There had always been so much of everything in her young life that sharing and giving came easily. She had been an endearing, sweet-tempered child whom people had been more than happy to pamper. And now, as a young woman just turned twenty, she possessed an enchanting beauty, a quick wit, and a charming personality. Life had always given Glory Westbrook everything she desired; why shouldn't it continue to do so?

For a brief moment she hesitated. Finally, she gave a small irritated shake of her head, sending the fashionable cascade of cinnamon brown curls at her nape dancing against her back. Then with quick determined steps Glory moved toward the street on the south side of the square.

Lydia gave a little yip of alarm and hurried to catch her friend. Reaching out, she tugged at Glory's arm, almost skipping to stay even with her.

"I know how much you used to care for Slade—" At Glory's cutting look, Lydia quickly amended her choice of words. "—How much you still care for Slade, but you've got to realize things are going to be even worse than before. Your pa will never allow it."

Even as the words left her lips, Lydia could see the familiar golden fire sparking in Glory's eyes. She recognized all too well the obstinance that had as children more often than not gotten the two of them in one scrape or another.

"Maybe. Maybe not," Glory replied softly. "But I *have* to see Slade. I thought you of all people would understand. Please don't make this any harder than it is, Lydia. I have to go, and there's simply nothing you can say that will stop me."

"Glory, all this war business has—"

"War!" huffed Glory, quickening her step once again. "Is that all anybody in this town can think about? That's all Papa and his cronies have talked about since I got home last month. I simply don't understand what all the fuss is about. The Yankees are far, far away. Why all the concern about what's happening hundreds of miles from here?"

"That's where you're wrong, Glory. There're things to worry about right in this town. My pa says we've got as many Yankee sympathizers as Confederates! Maybe more. Gainesville voted against secession even though the state as a whole voted for it. Everyone's *supposed* to be loyal to the Southern cause now, but there's a lot of folks hereabouts who haven't forgotten the people who voted against seceding from the Union."

"All that has nothing to do with Slade, with me. And even if it did, I'd still have to see Slade."

The determined tick of Glory's high-heeled slippers followed them down the boardwalk as Lydia scampered to keep up with her friend. Lydia knew there'd be no stopping Glory now.

Rounding the corner at Boggs Street and Commerce, Glory hesitated outside the entrance to Hunter's General Store as though at last questioning the intelligence of her actions.

For a moment a vision of her father's face passed before Glory's eyes. The knowledge that she was deliberately going against his wishes tweaked her conscience more than a little. She would have preferred an opportunity to win him over to her way of thinking, but she could think of no way to do so any time soon.

Glory's father was usually the epitome of the Southern gentleman, indulgent to a fault where his wife and three daughters were concerned. But on those rare occasions when he set his mind hard and fast on something, it was almost impossible to persuade him otherwise . . . and the subject of Slade Hunter was such a situation.

During her young life Glory had always managed to stay in her doting father's good graces. She had learned early that it was usually only a matter of approaching him at the right time in the right way. Even now, she naively believed that she could eventually find a way to sway him to her way of thinking concerning Slade—it would take time. Meanwhile, she'd just have to be careful not to let him find out what she was doing.

But right now she simply couldn't worry about such things. Not now, when Slade was so close.

Glory closed her eyes tightly and drew a long soothing breath deep into her lungs. Icy fingers clutched tightly around the drawstring cords of her fashionable reticule, she moved resolutely toward the shadowed doorway.

Lydia uttered one final syllable of protest and then snapped her mouth shut, knowing how futile any further plea would be. With a loud sigh, she resigned herself to standing guard for her friend. Slouching dejectedly against the rough log siding of the store's front, Lydia began to scan the street.

Slade Hunter heard the tap of heels across the store's broad plank floor just as he stretched high to set the first of an armload of tin buckets on the top shelf behind the main counter.

"Be right with you," he called without even glancing back.

Muted beams of sunlight seeped through the four small windows interspersed across the storefront, crisscrossing the interior with pale amber light before spotlighting the man perched on the stepladder. Butterflies battling in her stomach, Glory peered intently at the male figure.

At twenty-four, Slade had finally lost the youthful leanness she remembered so well. His white cotton shirt pulled tight across the broad expanse of his back as he reached to push the merchandise to the

23

rear of the shelf, and she noticed how much broader his shoulders were and the way the muscles roped and slid under the smooth brown skin of his forearms where his starched shirt-sleeves had been folded back.

Glory inhaled deeply, sweet memories assailing her mind. The small store smelled the same as it had on those long-ago afternoons—tart dried fruits, pungent leather, fragrant coffee beans, all underlaid with the clean crisp aroma of lye soap. A potpourri of merchandise filled the shelves and barrels and countertops surrounding her, but Glory had eyes only for Slade.

As Slade continued to bend and reach and stretch to stack the buckets, Glory's heart began an erratic little tickety-tickety beat, thudding painfully against her rib cage. Her mouth suddenly felt dry as the Texas prairie in July, and when she tried to swallow, her throat threatened to close in the most disconcerting manner. Her fingers nervously pleated and re-pleated the skirt of her gown. With rapt attention she watched the way Slade's raven hair brushed softly against the pristine white of his collar with his every movement.

Finally Slade stepped down from the ladder in one smooth motion, brushed the palms of his hands clean of dust, and turned toward his customer with a welcoming smile.

"Now, what can I do for you?"

"A spool of thread, please," Glory managed to answer in a voice not much stronger than a whisper.

In the fleeting moment before Slade's smile slowly dissolved into shock, Glory noted that the right corner of his pliant mouth still tilted a bit higher than the left when he smiled, and his eyes were the same startling clear gray that she had often dreamed of. But he seemed so much taller, broader, stronger. Her memories paled before the real man.

"Glory!"

The word escaped on a rush of breath as Slade drank in the sight of her. The slim, proud carriage of her body, now fully woman-rounded. The thick cinnamon hair, twisted in an elaborate knot under the ridiculous little frou-frou of a hat.

A flash of memory recalled a sun-kissed afternoon when he had plucked the pins from those tresses and then arranged the riotous curls reverently around her shoulders before running his hands through the silken strands. Her mouth still had that beguiling sultry look, the pouty fullness of her bottom lip as enticing as ever. The satiny heat of that mouth was as fresh in his mind today as it had been the afternoon her father had almost caught them kissing in the barn.

There were stains of crimson color on her high cheekbones, and Slade wondered if they were caused by the heat of the day or if Glory was experiencing the same almost suffocating delirium as he.

"I . . . I heard that you were back," Slade finally managed to say. No matter how hard he'd tried to prepare himself for her return, it hadn't helped.

Over and over during the last months he'd told himself that when the time came, he'd be able to look at her and see just another pretty girl, that the crazy gut-wrenching surge of emotion he'd always felt whenever Glory was near would have disappeared

25

. . . removed from his life by the grim knowledge of a world gone awry and the resultant undeniable futility of their young dreams. But every argument he'd built, every vow he'd made simply vanished like a puff of smoke in a whirlwind at the sight of her.

Glory smiled, the corners of her mouth trembling slightly. "Yes. I've been at the country house for several weeks." She gave her shoulders a little shrug, and her words tumbled over each other in her haste to fill the lull. "I'd almost given up hope that Papa would open up the town house this year. He's been so busy with things at Sivells Bend that he threatened to leave the family out there all summer. Thank goodness Mama finally managed to convince him otherwise."

Glory offered another tremulous smile, waiting restively for some clue to Slade's feelings. Was he glad to see her? It was so hard to tell. Despite his pleasant voice and friendly manner, he seemed to be holding himself in careful control. There was an almost guarded look to his eyes. And those tiny furrows of worry between his brows . . . had they always been so pronounced?

Slade's voice had sounded friendly. Of course, he had always greeted customers with a smile and a courteous word or two. . . . She would certainly not expect him to react in any other way. But hadn't there been something else? Almost a tone of eagerness? And the look that had filled his pewter gray eyes when he'd first seen her. Surely she couldn't have been mistaken—

Gold flecks flared in her eyes and the tip of her pink little tongue peeped out nervously to wet the corner of her mouth.

"Your mother . . . yes . . . uh . . . how is your mother?" Slade finally managed to free his mind from the strange lethargy that held it and leaped upon the last word that had caught his attention. He knew he was stammering, almost babbling, but he was grateful for anything that might fill the strange tingly silence between them.

"Fine, just fine."

Silence again.

"And your father?" Glory asked.

"A little better, I think. At least he's been showing some interest in something other than the store lately. I think he's finally quit grieving for Mother."

"I'm glad."

The steady tick of a clock filled another void. Glory nervously smoothed a wispy tendril at her temple. Slade cleared his throat, his fingers curling and uncurling against the rough fabric of his trousers. And they simply stood and looked at each other, each desperately searching for the proper thing to say.

"And . . . uh . . . your sisters, Mary and Helen?" Slade finally blurted. "How are they? It's been a while since I've seen them."

Glory laughed nervously. "They're fine. I was so surprised when I first saw them. They've grown so much. I expected the little girls I'd left behind. Now they're almost young women. It doesn't seem right."

"I know."

"Yes, of course you do. I almost forgot about Paula and Jeff. I probably wouldn't even recognize them. Let's see . . . they'd be — "

27

"Ten and thirteen now." Slade supplied the ages of his younger siblings.

"And Morgan? Where is he?" asked Glory, referring to Slade's older brother.

"Mostly he stays at the farm. You know him. He never did like the store. He's been . . ." Dark brows slashed downward as Slade searched for the appropriate word. ". . . oh, I don't know . . . kinda moody lately."

They continued to mouth the required pleasantries, the appropriate queries, the casual amenities, both of them unable to say what was really in their hearts.

Unable to bear the combination of cool words and heated looks any longer, Glory finally turned her confused gaze to the shelves that held a jumble of fabric and sewing supplies.

"Uh . . . my spool of thread?" She hesitated, hoping Slade would say something, anything, to continue the conversation, to prolong her visit. All she wanted was some small reassurance that he was glad to see her, that he'd missed her as much as she'd missed him, that somehow that shining, glorious feeling they'd shared before was still alive.

"Yes, of course." Slade flushed with embarrassment. *Was that all she'd come for?* Was she just trying to be polite? Was she simply making a duty call on an old acquaintance? Perhaps this was her way of letting him know that *her* feelings had changed. Maybe he had pined all these months for nothing . . . maybe she no longer cared. Something very akin to pain stabbed his insides at the thought.

Forcing himself to act as normal as possible, Slade

turned to fill her order.

"What do you need?"

"The large one," Glory replied, sadness tinging her voice at his evident desire to see her gone. She pointed toward the first spool of thread that caught her eye, not caring what color it was. With heavy heart, she watched his strong, long-fingered hand close around the spool and envied it his touch.

His back to Glory, Slade steeled himself, using the moment to bolster his fast-slipping composure. Finally he turned and reached toward her outstretched palm. Could she see how difficult it was for him to keep his fingers from trembling? Was she aware of how badly he wanted to touch her?

Slade's gaze never left her face, and because of that his errant hand almost missed its target. Glory watched as the tips of his fingers barely brushed against the soft skin of her forearm. Her heart leaped to her throat as Slade made no effort to break the almost imperceptible contact between them. Sparks of fire tingled up her arm as his fingers continued their slow path down her arm, across her wrist, and then toward the palm of her hand, his work-roughed fingertips softly, sweetly stroking the satin flesh with a butterfly touch.

At last his hand was poised over hers. It lingered there for so long that each could feel the heat from the other's flesh. Finally, Slade pressed the wooden spool into her palm, gently curling his fingers around hers as he did so.

Glory's heart capered and danced with hope at his touch. Reluctantly pulling her gaze from the giddy sight of her hand tucked snugly in his strong brown fist, she tilted her head and looked into the stormy gray depths of Slade's eyes . . . and into the silver reflection of all the longing and feeling and hope that filled her own heart.

"Glory, I—" His voice was a black velvet rasp in the stillness.

"Yes?"

"Glory!"

Glory was positive Slade was about to say all the words she'd dreamed of the last two years. So positive that it took her a moment to realize that her name was now being called by Lydia and that Slade was looking toward the entrance of the store with alarm in his eyes.

"Glory! I think I see your pa!" Lydia's wren-brown head poked quickly around the edge of the doorway and then disappeared again. "He's headed this way. You better get out here!"

Dejection flashed across Slade's face at Lydia's words. His hand dropped away from Glory's as if her flesh had scorched him.

With a ragged breath he told her, "You'd better go. It really would be best."

"But, Slade—"

"Not now, Glory," Slade pleaded, almost pushing her toward the store's entrance. "We don't have time. There's too much to say, too much to explain. It's too late. I'm afraid it's hopeless—"

Glory whirled to face him. "It's *not* hopeless!" she cried.

Slade stood frozen for a long moment and then suddenly his strong fingers gripped Glory's shoulders, two years of pent-up emotions naked on his

30

face as he roughly pulled her against him.

"Meet me tonight," he pleaded. "After everyone's gone to sleep. Remember? At the clearing, under the elm tree. Just the way we used to do."

"Yes," Glory whispered fiercely. "Yes, of course I remember."

Lydia's frantic call sounded again.

"Go on," Slade gently urged, finally dropping his frantic hold on her. "It's better that you do. We'll have tonight—"

"Tonight," Glory affirmed breathlessly, her eyes large and luminous. "Yes, tonight."

Chapter Two

Snatching their skirts high, Glory and Lydia hurried down the boardwalk and then dashed across the street mere inches in front of a galloping team of horses. Face red with disapproval, the startled driver of the carriage shook his fist at the two reckless young women and shouted a few choice words to announce the foolishness of their behavior.

Lydia cringed inwardly at the well-deserved epithets, but Glory barely heard him. At this point the driver's anger was the least of her worries. She would far rather have faced a team of plunging stallions than her father's wrath.

Heaving a great sigh of relief as they safely reached the town square, Glory and Lydia made sure they were lost in the noisy crowd before the Colonel finished his leisurely stroll down the boardwalk and crossed the street in their direction. When he finally found them minutes later, Glory was able to play her role well enough, but it took a great deal more acting on Lydia's part to appear serene. Still nervous, Glory was quick to declare that they'd just sat down on the sun-warmed steps of the courthouse to rest their weary feet for a moment. In truth, both girls were trying to slow the wild hammering of their hearts after their narrow escape.

"Through with your business so soon, Papa?" Glory asked sweetly, her mouth turning up in the familiar smile that in the past had always drawn a positive response from her father.

Before she was knee-high, Glory had learned the fine craft of cajoling her occasionally bellicose father. Not that it had really taken much effort. Robert Westbrook had doted on his beautiful daughter from the moment of her birth. More often than not he'd been willing to overlook any childish pranks she might indulge in—frequently with an uproarious laugh and a few proud boasts about what "fire" and "spirit" his little girl possessed and how she was definitely a "chip off the old block."

So adept at it was she, that the Colonel had only rarely been irritated at his oldest child. However, the few instances when she had overstepped what few restrictions he placed on her enough to earn his disapproval had made her all the more determined to avoid another such incident if at all possible. After all, she adored her father in return and preferred to see him happy and proud of her. If this meant simply not mentioning a particular incident or shading a situation just a tad on occasion, well so be it. There was certainly no harm done, and both father and daughter were happier for her small harmless deceptions. It all made perfect sense to her.

33

But Glory was smart enough to know that the subject of Slade Hunter would precipitate one of her few failures. Therefore she was taking no chances. She would bide her time and eventually win her father's approval . . . inch by inch if necessary. Patience was the key.

"Thank you for bringing us to town with you, Colonel Westbrook," Lydia spoke up, training her gaze on the bourbon-induced patchwork of tiny red lines shading the Colonel's rather prominent nose rather than chance meeting his penetrating eyes directly. "It's been a most interesting afternoon."

At this prosaic statement, Glory almost dissolved into nervous giggles. She barely managed to turn the first sputterings of her laughter into a fit of coughing. Lydia threw her friend a withering look before glancing warily at the Colonel. Luckily, an acquaintance called his name, and he looked away at the exact moment of Glory's initial cough.

The girls exchanged grateful glances as the Colonel moved away to exchange a few words with the man. Smoothing their dresses nervously, they tried to appear nonchalant as they waited for his return.

A few more days as "interesting" as this one, Lydia thought as she struggled to maintain the proper insouciance, and she'd be prematurely gray-headed.

Colonel Westbrook finally finished his conversation and turned back toward the two young women. "Well, ladies, we'd best be getting back to the house. We're expecting a special guest for dinner and I'm sure your mother is all adither by now. Might not be a bad idea for you to apply some of that fancy finishing school education, Glory, and help her make sure the evening comes off splendidly."

"Yes, Papa," Glory managed to answer in a properly meek tone.

With a muffled "harummph" and a tug at his stylish waistcoat, the Colonel turned and swaggered his way back toward the carriage, the girls following obediently in his wake.

As the two young women followed a cautious distance behind Colonel Westbrook's tall, rather portly figure, Lydia managed to whisper, "Who's coming to dinner?"

Glory shrugged. "I don't know. Some stodgy old business acquaintance of father's, more than likely. Seems like there's always someone or other every evening — discussing this tiresome war thing, or the new militia, or politics. Lord knows what's going on tonight. Personally, I plan to plead a headache and escape to my room early."

"Tell me what happened with . . ." Lydia cast a wary glance at the Colonel's imperious back. ". . . uh . . . you know."

"Shh! Not now. Wait till we get home. We'll be able to sneak up to my room for a few minutes." Glory's eyes glowed like rich warm brandy, her happiness obvious. "But I will tell you that everything's going to be just wonderful!"

Glory, the eternal optimist, thought Lydia with a worried sigh and a small shake of her head, while fervently hoping that her friend was right.

After several more delays while the Colonel exchanged pleasantries or shook hands with acquaintances along the way, the three of them were once again ensconced in the gleaming buggy and headed for the baronial two-story mansion on Pecan Street which served as the Westbrook's town house.

Set amidst a thick stand of stately old oak trees on a three-acre lot, the classically designed dwelling had for many years been the cornerstone of Gainesville's social season. The architectural style and pristine condition of the white framework façade were substantial evidence of the graceful and moneyed lifestyle enjoyed by its inhabitants.

Spacious, high-ceilinged rooms had embraced the more affluent citizens of the town during countless balls and soirees over the years. The town's gentry often danced until the wee hours of the morning across the polished parquet floors which gleamed like old gold in the soft candlelight of the crystal chandeliers. Cool wide double verandas supported by twin rows of pillars opened onto lush lawns, interspersed with flowerbeds meticulously tended by two of the Colonel's slaves. The varieties of blooms were rotated and planted to ensure that from spring until early fall there would always be a sweet fragrance in the air. The elaborate grounds afforded guests with an enchanting view and a pleasant place to refresh themselves after an exuberant waltz or quadrille.

The lush furnishings and appointments for the house had been brought by sea to Galveston, or upriver to Jefferson, and then carried by wagon train overland to Gainesville. Only the finest china and crystal graced the long expanse of the cherrywood table and the marble-topped sideboards in the dining room, where on frequent occasions guests were served elaborate meals and fine wines.

Life had indeed been good to the Westbrooks.

"Tell me!" Lydia urged the minute the elegant brass-trimmed oak doors to Glory's room were closed.

Glory folded her arms across her chest as if to hug herself. Hands clasping her shoulders, she whirled about the large room until she was dizzy. When she at last fell upon the bed's pale pink satin counterpane in a heap of delicious happiness, Lydia quickly piled onto the high feather mattress beside her. Small lace-trimmed pillows tumbled to the floor as the puffy mattress tick billowed and dipped around them.

"He still cares!" Glory declared raptly, her voice squeaky with emotion.

"He told you that?"

"Well . . . not in exactly those words," Glory admitted, scowling at the small cloud of negativeness that Lydia's words threatened to cast over her happiness. But, being Glory, she quickly dismissed them from her mind, refusing to let her friend dampen her joyous spirit.

"Then what *did* he say?"

Bouncing to a sitting position, Glory arranged her bouffant petticoats more comfortably about her folded legs. "It wasn't exactly what he said, but the way he looked at me. You should have seen him. Oh, it was glorious! Just the way I'd dreamed about. If we'd just had a few more minutes—"

"A few more minutes," replied Lydia obliquely, "and your pa might have walked right down that boardwalk and into the store!"

"But he didn't, did he?" Glory smiled serenely, still contemplating the fruitful results of her escapade.

"Well, are you going to tell me about it or not?" Lydia prodded in exasperation.

"He asked me to meet him tonight. Down by the old elm tree."

Hands flying to her face, Lydia stared at her friend in alarm. "You wouldn't dare!"

"Oh, yes, I would."

"But what about your pa?"

"I'll be very careful. I'll wait until everyone is asleep and then I'll slip out and run like the wind. No one will ever know I've been gone."

Lydia shook her head in consternation. "I don't know, Glory. Maybe you better not. If you get caught, your pa will send all of you back to Sivells Bend and we won't have any time together this summer. Oh, dear! You've been gone so long and now you're going to go right out and do something foolish. I'll be stuck here in this town again and you'll be miles away."

Lydia's stricken look at such a thought was so comical that Glory dissolved in a cascade of silver laughter. "Don't be a goose, Lydia," she scolded gently, and promptly hugged her friend. "I promise I'll be careful. I certainly don't want to jeopardize my staying in town."

Lydia was still protesting when a light rap sounded on Glory's door. In response to Glory's invitation, the door opened and Mrs. Westbrook entered.

Glory's mother couldn't help but smile at the sight of the two chattering young women in the middle of the disarrayed four-poster bed, so reminiscent of the hundreds of hours the two had spent in girlish gossip as children. She had come to suggest that her daughter think about getting ready for the evening.

"And wear your new green dress, dear. It's so lovely. Your father wants you to look your very best tonight."

"Very well, Mother. But why all the fuss? What's so special about tonight?" Glory smiled at her gentle mother with fondness, thinking that she hadn't changed a bit during Glory's two-year absence.

Mrs. Westbrook had been a real beauty in her youth, and even after many years of marriage and the birth of three daughters she was still slim and pretty enough to turn her share of heads. Glory had inherited her mother's glowing apricot complexion and cinnamon hair, while nature had taken her father's dark brown eyes and lightened them to warm sherry for the daughter. The effect was startling, and more than one man had considered laying his heart at Glory's feet since she'd left her childhood behind.

It had also been said more than once that Glory had been born with a considerable share of the Colonel's strong personality, it having been evident since babyhood that she certainly hadn't inherited the quiet, unobtrusive nature of her mother.

At Glory's question, Mrs. Westbrook's slim fingers fluttered nervously at the throat of her expensive rose-colored gown. "Your father has invited an important gentleman to dinner. He'd like you to be specially pleasant to Mr. Harper, dear."

"Yes, Mother," Glory replied dutifully.

"I'll send Violet up to help you dress when it's time." Mrs. Westbrook paused at the door, her hand on the knob. She turned back toward the girls. "And Jacob will be happy to drive you home when you're ready to go, Lydia dear."

"Thank you, ma'am," Lydia replied, a bit surprised at being summarily dismissed by the kindly Mrs. Westbrook. She had taken almost as many meals at the Westbrook's table over the years as at her own. The Colonel's dinner guest must be a very special business acquaintance indeed, she finally decided, to precipitate such uncharacteristic behavior on the part of Glory's mother.

With one last fleeting smile, Mrs. Westbrook pulled the door open, and with a graceful swish of her satin skirt was gone.

Glory sat before her mirrored dressing table, clad only in sheer lace-trimmed dimity chemise and pantalets while Violet tried to tame her long tresses. Glory's hair, thick and almost waist length, balked as usual at being smoothed and confined into an appropriately ladylike upswept coiffure.

"Sit up straight, chile!" Violet lovingly scolded the young woman she'd cared for since babyhood. "You're gonna be the death of me yet. Hum-humm! Just look at this. More hair than what two women would know what to do with!"

40

Despite Violet's talented brown hands, little tendrils of honeyed cinnamon hair escaped to curl softly around Glory's face.

The mirror allowed Glory to watch the café au lait face of the tall, lean woman behind her. The corners of her cat-tilted eyes crinkled with amusement as Violet continued to fret and fume. She hadn't changed one whit during Glory's absence. It made Glory feel safe and warm and secure to be back in the care of the sometimes stern, always loving slave.

Violet and her husband Jacob had been a part of Glory's life since her earliest memories. Glory had been eight when their daughter Sara was born. Delighted with the appearance of what she was sure was a real live babydoll acquired solely for her own little-girl games, Glory had spent hours on end in the kitchen with Violet, almost constantly underfoot while she toted and played with the laughing chubby brown baby.

Sara had been one of the first people Glory had sought out when she returned. She'd been proud and pleased to see that the skinny little child she remembered had become such a pretty girl. Twelve years old now and almost as tall as her mother, Sara was not far from being a woman.

"All right, honeychile," Violet finally said, giving Glory's curls one last pat. "Now, which dress does my pet want to wear?"

"It doesn't matter to me, but Mother suggested I wear the new green one."

"Justly so," agreed Violet. "You'll be pretty as a picture."

41

Brows drawn together in a slight frown, Glory remarked, "I really don't see why we have to go to all this fuss over some silly ol' business acquaintance of Papa's. Heaven knows they'll sit and talk war or some such thing all evening and completely ignore the ladies anyway."

"Come on, honeypot," urged Violet as she pulled the emerald green dress from the wardrobe and laid it carefully on the bed alongside a billowy mound of petticoats. "Time's awasting. I can't help you with this pretty dress while you're sitting there like a lump of dough."

Glory reluctantly slid off the low stool, moved to the center of the room, and obediently raised her arms so that Violet could slide the first of many starched petticoats over her head.

"Watch yo' hair, chile. And stop fidgeting! You're gonna knock them curls plumb out of place if'n you ain't careful."

Glory heaved a small, resigned sigh and tried to stand motionless while Violet added still another petticoat and then at last settled yards and yards of green silk over Glory's voluminous underskirts. Violet's quick brown fingers moved like lightning as she adjusted the low bodice against the peachy smoothness of Glory's shoulders and then fastened the dozens of tiny silk-covered buttons running down the back of the gown.

Standing back, fists upon her slim hips, Violet looked her charge up and down. "Humm-humph! You look good as sugar candy," she finally declared. "Now, be a good girl and don't muss your hair."

"I won't."

"And don't you go getting your dress all rumpled before the party starts."

Glory rolled her eyes in good-humored acquiescence to the familiar litany. "Yes, Violet."

"You best be getting downstairs. The Colonel's guest should be here any minute. You know your papa don't like you to be late." She gave Glory a little pat on the shoulder and a very gentle push in the direction of the door. "Now, get on with you."

Still muttering under her breath about doddering old men and boring conversations, Glory swept through the wide doorway when Violet opened the door. Her gown swished pleasantly with each movement as she hurried down the long second-floor hallway.

Nearing the head of the grand staircase Glory heard a distinctive knock on the front door. From her vantage point above she paused to watch as Jacob progressed in his usual stately manner across the gleaming parquet floor. Within seconds the ornately carved double doors were thrown open to admit her father's guest.

Glory hesitated, one foot poised to begin her descent. Her eyes widened in surprise. The man wasn't what she'd expected at all.

Tall, slim, almost arrogantly handsome, Preston Harper III glanced with mild interest around the elegant entryway of the Westbrook home. Just then Glory shifted her weight, and the slight rustle of her gown drew the man's attention to the top of the stairs. Blue fire flamed briefly in his disturbing

Nordic eyes as his gaze slowly swept from the top of her head to the tip of the small black kid slipper reaching for the second step.

Never taking his ice blue eyes from hers, he lifted an expensive top hat from sculptured pale gold hair and handed it to Jacob. Then a long, slender finger rose and stroked languidly across the trim, tawny mustache, just a shade darker than his hair, that rimmed his full upper lip.

Glory felt an uncomfortable flush rise, climbing from the fashionable show of cleavage above the emerald bodice of her gown, up her slim throat, and finally across her high cheekbones. Her fingers fluttered against the polished walnut banister and she had to consciously tighten her hold on the warm wood to keep her hand from creeping protectively to her bosom.

Perplexed at the strange discomfiture the man's appearance had caused, Glory forced a small, nervous smile. Then, with her composure held under tight rein, she continued her journey down the sweeping staircase toward the figure waiting at the bottom of the stairs.

What was it about the man that bothered her? His smile was perfectly proper and respectful, showing just a hint of even white teeth. He even gave a gentlemanly little half-bow as she neared him.

"Miss Westbrook, I presume?" he inquired in a slow, cultured drawl.

"Y-yes," Glory confirmed, still unsure of what was upsetting her.

He moved forward, politely offering Glory his

hand to steady her last step. "I'm so delighted to make your acquaintance. Your father has spoken of you so often this last year."

But before Glory could respond, her father's boisterous voice rang out. "Preston! Good to see you. Come in, come in." The Colonel stood just inside the wide doorway of the parlor, a heavy crystal glass of his favorite bourbon in one hand, a long black Havana cigar in the other. "Glory, show our guest in, dear," he instructed, the hand holding the cigar beckoning them inward, heavy blue smoke following each movement.

"Robert, how nice to see you again," Harper replied, standing his ground at the foot of the staircase, hand still outstretched, waiting for Glory to accept his help.

Noting her father's obvious enthusiasm in greeting his guest, Glory pushed away her disquieting thoughts about the cool blond man and placed her hand in his.

What could possibly be wrong with her? Perhaps it was simply that she'd been expecting one of her father's usual cronies, she told herself. After all, most of her father's friends were a bit older . . . this man couldn't be more than thirty. And she was still giddy from seeing Slade.

Of course. How silly of her. That's all it was.

"Thank you," Glory murmured politely as Harper tucked her hand into the crook of his arm. Her nervous fingers curled against the immaculately tailored fawn-colored cloth as he escorted her into the parlor. He was quite tall and his legs were long and

45

lean. But he slowed his stride so that Glory wasn't pushed to keep up with him.

Mrs. Westbrook was already settled in her favorite wing chair, her dark gown glowing sapphire blue in the soft candleglow of the overhead chandeliers. Glory's two younger sisters shared the small medallion-backed settee to the side of the unlit fireplace. The Colonel waved Glory toward one end of the long red velvet sofa and then urged Preston to "make himself comfortable." Although there were several other chairs available, Harper chose the other end of Glory's sofa.

"You've met the missus before, Preston. And these two scamps," the Colonel said, pointing at the giggling adolescent girls, "are my two youngest daughters, Mary and Helen."

The two pretty little girls, dressed in similar gowns of pale lemon yellow and petal pink, bobbed up, curtsied politely, and then quickly sat back down again. Younger versions of Glory, they watched with large luminous eyes while the adults settled themselves, occasionally exchanging whispered comments behind small hands. It was clear they were a bit in awe of being allowed in the parlor with the adults.

"A little something before dinner, Preston?" asked the Colonel, hefting his own glass slightly to clarify the question.

"Why, yes, thank you."

"And what about you, Glory? A small sherry, perhaps?"

Glory looked with surprise at her father. Wine was usually offered to her only at weddings or holidays.

46

The Colonel set his own glass down on the table beside his chair and headed toward the elaborate sideboard against the far wall. Surprisingly, he stopped his traverse across the spacious room to bend and pat Glory's hand lovingly.

"You're quite grown up now, my dear," he said with a deep chuckle. "I believe you can have a glass of wine if you so choose."

"Thank you, Papa. I believe I will," Glory replied, smiling fondly at her beaming father. Actually she cared little for the taste of wine, but she hoped a glass might soothe her slight nervousness.

Selecting from an array of crystal decanters, the Colonel quickly filled another goblet with vintage bourbon and a delicate wineglass with a splash of sherry.

He turned and raised a bushy eyebrow at his wife. "A refill, my dear?"

When she declined, he replaced the stopper and returned the decanter to its place on the polished surface of the sideboard. Cigar clamped between his teeth, Colonel Westbrook turned and carried the two glasses back across the room, stopping to hand one to his daughter and the other to his guest.

"Thank you, Papa." Glory took a small sip of the sweet liquid and watched her father settle back in his chair, trying her best to concentrate on the continuing conversation. But it was simply too much effort to pretend interest in the talk of slaves and crops, business and war.

As the monotonous subjects continued to swirl about her head, she finally forgot the disquieting figure sharing her sofa and her thoughts wandered back to Slade. A tingle of anticipation trilled through her veins when she contemplated their coming meeting.

Surely, she thought, when they had a little time to themselves, when no one was there to disturb them and no chance of her father showing up unexpectantly, Slade would at last admit how he felt about her. Things hadn't changed at all in the last two years. He'd wanted to kiss her this afternoon. Glory was positive of that. And she'd wanted him to . . . desperately.

She was sure that all the war business Lydia had talked about was just so much smoke. Given enough time, it would all dissipate and things would be back to normal.

After all, what did North and South mean here? They were all *Texans* now, weren't they? Regardless of past differences, the citizens of the state would be compelled to work together from now on. They could little afford the division of effort that clinging to those old ideas would cause.

And what did it matter that Slade's family was poorer than Glory's? The Colonel was one of the richest men in the state. There had always been more than enough money for the family . . . money to buy anything they desired. Why, many times Glory's father had assured her that he would make sure her future was secure, that she would never want for anything.

Naturally, she assumed that meant a sizable dowry when she wed. The Colonel had always been generous with his family. They had only to hint at wanting something and it was promptly provided. And as a child, the nursery had been filled to overflowing with toys of all kinds. Glory had twice the gowns of anyone else she knew. Her father had done everything he could to ensure her happiness as she grew up.

Money—or the lack of it—had never been a problem in her young life. She was innocently positive the Colonel would take care of things, as usual. Glory was quite sure that once she convinced her father of Slade's importance to her future happiness, he would provide her and Slade with all they needed to begin their life together.

Glory was contemplating whether they would choose to buy into Mr. Hunter's present store or perhaps establish a new one all their own when Preston Harper's soft voice broke through her musings.

"W-what?" she stammered, looking up at the figure hovering above her, slightly embarrassed at being caught daydreaming. "I'm sorry. I'm afraid I didn't hear your question."

Preston turned on that same lazy smile Glory had noted from the top of the stairs. "Dinner has been announced. I simply asked permission to escort you to the table."

Glory looked around and noticed that the rest of her family had risen and were already moving toward the dining room.

"Oh! Yes . . . yes, thank you."

She rose quickly and took his proffered arm. Just a touch ashamed that she had been so blatantly ignoring a man who was obviously her father's friend, she vowed to be more attentive and gracious to him for the rest of the evening. Such magnanimity was not difficult under the circumstances, for her thoughts of Slade and their future together had put her in a lovely rose-colored mood.

In the dining room, Mrs. Westbrook indicated that Preston and Glory were to sit on the far side of the table, between the Westbrooks and across from Glory's younger sisters. Once around the table, Preston was quick to pull Glory's chair out and seat her with tender concern. She smiled her thanks and then reached to pull the heavy linen napkin from its embossed silver napkin ring and lay it carefully across the lap of her elegant dress.

The wide, almost luminous surface of the highly polished cherrywood table was set with willow-patterned china, rows of heavy ornate silver bracketing each place setting. A crystal bowl of fresh multicolored flowers was centered on the table, double candelabras with fat ivory candles on either side. Wearing prim turbans and stiffly starched aprons that glowed starkly white against the chocolate texture of their skin, two servants circled the table on silent feet, offering an astounding variety of food, filling wineglasses, removing plates as each course was consumed.

Mrs. Westbrook tried to steer the conversation away from such depressing subjects as war or politics during the course of their meal, prevailing upon Mr. Harper to tell them about the new home he was building not far from the Westbrook's plantation at

Sivells Bend. Glory was not too surprised to hear that many of the man's plans mirrored the Colonel's past accomplishments.

No wonder Papa likes him so well, she thought, they're as alike as two peas in a pod.

She smothered an amused smile when she again caught her younger sisters casting calf-eyes at their handsome dinner guest. Yes, she supposed he was quite good-looking—if you liked his type. But her heart was too full of sable dark hair and clear gray eyes to appreciate the attributes of any other man, no matter how handsome.

The large hand of the ornate wall clock ticked its way to the top and the clock chimed the hour. Pinpoints of reflected light flickered in Glory's eyes as her gaze perused the gold Roman numerals spaced around the face of the timepiece. How long until she'd be with Slade? Two hours at least. Perhaps three. It seemed like forever. Each successive minute seemed to drag longer than the one before.

As her father called her name, Glory pulled her gaze from the clock and reluctantly rejoined the conversation. "Yes, Papa?"

"I was just explaining that Preston and I have done a lot of talking . . . getting to know one another . . . since he moved to Texas last year. I've found him to be one of the finest men I've met in a long time—"

"You flatter me, Robert," Harper said in that low, slow drawl of his.

"Poppycock," the Colonel replied with a wry grin toward the man. "No need to play modest with me, my good man. You forget just how well I know you."

He took a small sip of bourbon, rolling it appreciatively over his tongue before letting it slide gently down his throat. "As I was about to say, Glory. Preston and I have done a lot of talking. He has confided in me that his dearest wish, now that his new home is almost finished, is to find a bride to share his happiness."

"How nice, Papa," Glory said, her mind a million miles away.

"I'm glad you feel that way, my dear. I think very highly of Preston—he's become almost like a son to me. That's why I've given him my permission to call on you, with the hope that I'll soon have the great pleasure of seeing the two of you wed."

Chapter Three

Wed!

The word echoed in Glory's mind, cruelly jarring the sweet thoughts of life with Slade right out of her head. Her fork clattered alarmingly against the edge of the fragile china plate as her fingers suddenly began to tremble.

Her father couldn't possibly be serious! But one look at his beaming face destroyed all hope that she'd misunderstood him.

Wed! Glory's mind cried again, and she almost choked on the bite of food she was chewing. Pressing her napkin against her lips, she barely succeeded in suppressing a fit of coughing. She managed to swallow, and then gulped for air.

Glory's startled gaze then flew to the man beside her. Preston Harper looked cool and composed, the hint of a smile playing on his lips as he raised his glass to her and inclined his regal head. He tilted the goblet slightly and the candle flame glinted on the crystal rim, catching the light like a prism and

53

throwing back lovely, glittering rainbows of color that speared into her dazed eyes.

"I believe a toast is in order," Preston murmured. "To the future."

"Wonderful!" The Colonel's voice boomed out as he, too, raised his glass.

Aquiver inside like a small trapped animal, Glory watched in shock as her mother's glass was also lifted. Then Mary and Helen, amid barely stifled giggles, daringly lifted their small water goblets to join in the adult festivities.

Five pairs of bright eyes bored into Glory's.

Five expectant faces awaited her reaction.

Except for the steady tick of the clock, the room was silent as a tomb. Glory felt certain the others could hear the sickening thud of her heartbeat. Her skin felt dry and brittle, like an autumn leaf waiting to be crushed into ashes by the slightest touch. How could they not see her dismay at this dire pronouncement?

But the five smiling people surrounding her continued to look at her with nothing but delighted anticipation. Her mind raced, searching, testing, discarding protest after protest. No. Now was not the right time. If there was one thing she knew, it was that her father would never brook public disobedience. And right now, Preston was his "public." She dared not embarrass the Colonel or his friend by blatantly refusing to accept Preston's suit.

It would be far shrewder to pretend to go along with their aspirations at this point. Later, in kindly fashion, she could make Preston aware that she was not interested in marrying him. Perhaps she could even play her part well enough that he himself would become disenchanted with the idea.

Yes! Of course. That would be even better.

She'd act whatever role she had to to make Preston change his mind. After all, he seemed nice enough. It shouldn't be too difficult to allow him to call for a little while — just long enough to find out what temperament and personality he desired and expected in the woman he planned to wed. And, whatever it was, Glory swore she'd have him convinced in record time that she was exactly the opposite. She'd make sure the dashing Mr. Harper would shortly have no desire whatsoever to wed the Colonel's daughter.

What a perfect idea! Glory brightened at the thought. A faint smile played on her lips. If her plan worked — and she was quite sure it would — Preston could save face, her father couldn't be angry at her for going against his wishes, and she'd be free to marry Slade.

Glory's tremulous smile deepened into the real thing, as all around the table crystal goblets were pressed to lips to complete the toast.

Moonlight poured through the open doors of the French windows that led to the gallery circling the upper story of the Westbrook house. Its luminous sheen poured pale silver over the high four-poster bed where an impatient Glory lay waiting. It seemed like absolute hours since the disturbing evening had finally ended and Violet had come to the room to undo the tedious rows of tiny buttons down the back of Glory's dress and help her into a cool cotton nightgown. The familiar sounds of the occupants settling down to sleep in the night-shrouded house were just now beginning to cease.

Glory heaved a sigh and twisted nervously in her bed, holding her breath when the bedframe protested her restless movements. Knowing she had to be quiet, she clenched her hands and forced herself to lie still again. The last thing she wanted to do was wake her parents. Very carefully she kicked back the smothering covers and pulled her gown to the top of her thighs, allowing the brisk breezes that occasionally drifted through the open window to cool her.

She counted slowly to one hundred, twisted her head so she could once again see the fat yellow moon still hanging low in the black velvet sky, and then counted to one hundred again.

Finally the house was quiet, save for the usual soft creaks and groans of the timbers. Surely everyone was asleep by now, Glory thought.

She eased to the edge of her plump feather mattress, one inch at a time, until she could carefully push herself upright and touch her toes to the still warm floor. Slowly, slowly she stood up and crept on silent feet across the room to the wardrobe, which before climbing into bed she had purposely left standing open.

With one quick movement she drew her nightgown over her head and heedlessly let it fall in a pale puddle at her feet. Standing nude in the warm summer air she thanked her lucky stars for the bright moonlight filling the room, for it allowed her to distinguish the rows of gowns hanging in the closet.

She finally pulled an almost-forgotten calico dress from the back of the wardrobe, choosing it not for its beauty but because it buttoned conveniently down the front. For a brief moment she considered the fact that she wore no chemise or pantalets. There'd simply been no reasonable way to retain custody of the garments with Violet standing over her, nightgown in hand. She thought about tiptoeing to the chest of drawers in the far dark corner of the room for fresh lingerie, but when she remembered how the top drawer squealed when she opened it, for safety's sake she rashly decided to forgo such amenities.

Slipping the pale blue dress over her head, she hurriedly settled it across her hips and with trembling fingers pushed the small buttons through their holes. The bodice was uncomfortably tight across her bosom, proof again of how much she'd matured in the last two years. For comfort's sake she finally left the top buttons undone, unintentionally allowing the edges of the soft fabric to frame an enticing vee of cleavage.

She bent to slide her feet into soft kid slippers and then tiptoed to the door. Pressing her ear against the wood, she listened carefully for any sign of life. All was still.

Slowly, with painstaking care, she turned the knob. Inch by tiny inch she pulled the door open until there was barely enough room for her to slip through the crack. Just as carefully she drew the door shut again, wincing when the latch clicked loudly in the silence.

She stayed pressed against the wall until her heart slowed its wild leaping and resumed its normal beat, and then she began to creep down the hallway toward the servants' stairs, which would take her directly to the kitchen and the back door.

Within minutes she was free of the house and, hampering skirts clutched high in her hands, she ran wildly across the Colonel's beautifully manicured lawns. By the time she reached the end of the tended grounds she had a stitch in her side and thankfully slowed down in order to work her way through the thick stand of trees that bordered the rear of the deep, sloping lot.

Twigs crunched under her feet as she wound her way along a barely discernible trail. The pungent aroma of cedar bushes mixed pleasantly with the perfume from the Colonel's prized flower beds.

On the far side of the woods an ancient elm spread its mammoth limbs over a small grassy knoll beside a little brook. The only sound was the soft sough of the wind through the treetops and the liquid gurgle of slowly moving water.

For a moment Glory was afraid that Slade hadn't come, but then he stepped from the deep shadows and into a patch of luminescent moonlight. Her heart lurched at the sight of his tall, dark silhouette and she called out softly.

"Slade."

He turned toward her, and at the sight of her his face seemed to light up brighter than the moon above.

"Glory!"

Her feet traveled the remaining yards between them as if they had wings. His arms opened and she flew into their safe haven, exulting in the strength and warmth that immediately enveloped her. With her high in his arms Slade spun around and around, their joined laughter filling the little glade with joy.

At last he stopped and lowered her until her toes touched the springy grass and their laughter died away in breathless anticipation. Reverently he moved his hands from the span of her waist. First he traced the curve of her rib cage, then the gentle slope of her shoulders and the slim column of her throat. Finally he stopped, cupping her face between his palms.

"Glory," he whispered again softly, his warm breath caressing her skin as he stood and reveled in the feel of her.

God, she was beautiful. The long run had left her slightly breathless, the soft, shadowed valley between her breasts rising and falling in an innocent siren's call. The night wind had taken her long cinnamon hair and whipped it into wildly evocative tangles and curls that framed her radiant face before cascading down her back.

Slade thought he'd never be able to look at her long enough, or touch her as much as he needed to. There weren't that many hours left in his life.

He gently adjusted his hold on her, bringing his thumbs together under her chin, exerting just the tiniest hint of pressure. Glory instantly responded to his touch, tilting her head back, exposing the sweet vulnerability of her neck, offering her lips to him. Her eyes fluttered closed, the heavy lashes casting dark fans of shadow on the pale, silvered planes of her cheeks. His strong fingers slid gently along the line of her jaw and then across the sensitive skin behind her ears, evoking delicious frissions of feeling as he tenderly worked his hands into the mass of windswept curls.

She felt his grip tighten in her unruly tresses, binding her to him like velvet chains. And then his mouth was upon hers, fevered and hungry.

Slade's tongue grazed the seam of her mouth, teasing, tempting, tormenting. He licked at the satin lining of her lips, tasting her sweetness before skimming lightly over the ivory smoothness of her teeth. She moaned low in her throat and he hesitated for only a moment before his tongue plunged into her mouth with quick greedy strokes.

Glory's arms went around his waist, holding onto his strength for dear life. Her small hands roamed over his back, caressing the hard muscles in his shoulders, pulling him closer, ever closer. His arms surrounded her, his hands gliding over the smooth expanse of her back, past the beguiling dip of her waist. Finding the sweetness of her plump little bottom, he cupped her to him, pulling her up against the evidence of his desire, crushing her softness to his hardness. All the while, their mouths clung with wild abandon, tongues dueling with rapier sweetness.

Finally, almost sobbing for breath, he realized what he was doing and reluctantly pulled his mouth from hers. For a moment they stood quietly, just holding each other, then Slade forced himself to back away a few inches. When he again felt somewhat in

60

control, he reached for the small hand which had so recently rested against his heartbeat and raised it to his lips, pressing a tender kiss in its palm.

Lacing his fingers through Glory's, he gently led her toward the sheltering boughs of the venerable tree. Deep within the shadows, he lowered himself to the ground, placing his back to the gnarled trunk. Then he pulled Glory into the protective vee of his bent legs.

His arms wrapped tightly around the small trembling body. He cuddled her against his chest, whispering sweet meaningless words, brushing feathery kisses across her forehead and cheeks until the raging flames inside them cooled to banked embers.

Long minutes later, the crazy trip-hammer beat of their hearts began to slow. The ragged sound of their breaths softened and became almost normal.

At first, fear had stabbed through Glory when Slade had released her and moved away . . . fear that she'd been wrong about his feelings, fear that she'd lost him again somehow. But then he'd taken her hand. And now there was such tenderness and comfort in the feel of his palm cradling her head against his chest, his firm chin resting lightly against the top of her head, that the disquieting thoughts faded away. She snuggled against him, giving herself up to the utter contentment that flowed through her being.

She could have stayed thus for hours. But Slade finally stirred, turning her in his arms so that he could see her face.

"We have to talk, Glory."

"Do we?" she whispered, not wanting to break the

spell.

"Yes, we do. This is madness. Don't you know that?"

"No." She tilted her head back and appraised him with dark eyes. "I only know how I feel about you."

"Do you have any idea how angry your father would be if he knew you were here?"

Glory's mouth firmed resolutely. "I can get around Papa. I've always been able to. It'll just take a little time, that's all."

"Glory, Glory," Slade murmured, shaking his head remorsefully. "You simply don't understand. This isn't a child's game anymore. There's a war going on—"

"Damn the war!" she responded quickly, and then she blushed when she realized what she'd said. She drew a ragged breath and tried to still the anger in her voice. "It has nothing to do with us."

Slade looked at her dolefully. "It has everything to do with us, my dearest. No matter how we feel about each other, our lives are as different as day and night. There's no getting past that fact."

She watched his eyes—so sad, so resigned. Was it going to end . . . now? Before they'd even had a chance? No! She wouldn't, couldn't give up.

"Slade, do you . . . uh . . ." Glory stumbled over the brashness of the words forming on her lips. But it was now or never. "Do . . . do you remember what we pledged to each other that last night? Do you still care for me?"

"Oh, God!" Slade moaned, drawing her back against him. "Yes, heaven help me, yes I do. I still love you. I'll always love you. I thought I could forget you. I knew I should. For your sake, if for no other reason. But it didn't work. No matter how hard I tried, I couldn't make it happen."

"Slade—"

"Hush. Let me finish. It has to be said. I have nothing to offer you. Your life has been totally different from mine. I can never come into your world. And I can't ask you to leave yours for mine."

"But, Slade—"

"Glory, be sensible." Slade released his hold on her long enough to rake one agitated hand through his dark locks. "I have no right to ask you to give up everything you're used to . . . all the things your father has provided. You deserve a man who can continue to take care of you in the same manner. I can't do that."

Angered by the resignation in his voice, Glory flounced up and turned to face him. Kneeling between his legs, hands braced on the tops of her thighs, she tilted her head obstinately and glared at him.

"Do you think me such a spoiled child that I have to have everything handed to me on a silver platter?"

"No, but—"

"Then why do you say such hateful things?" she demanded, heedless of the hard ground under her tender knees.

"Because your father will never allow us to be together. Believe me," he said with a bitter little laugh. "He told me so in no uncertain terms—"

"Told you? When?"

Slade sighed and let his head roll back against the rough bark of the tree. "The day after he sent you away. He came by the store and . . . and expressed himself quite clearly."

Oh, yes. The Colonel had been *quite* definite in his opinion of Slade Hunter as a possible son-in-law.

Slade could still recall the stinging words, the way Westbrook's calculating eyes had looked him up and down like some vastly inferior specimen of humanity, the sound of his voice as he'd mockingly intoned Slade's humble background. There'd been no fire in the Colonel's voice. Only cold objectivity as he recited all the reasons why Slade could never make Glory happy. Yes, he'd poked and prodded at every nuance of Slade's self-worth. And, finding it sadly lacking according to his standards, Westbrook had dismissed Slade's every argument with haughty disregard.

And what was worse, the Colonel's visit had planted bitter seeds of doubt in Slade. In the ensuing days and nights after Glory's sudden departure, Slade had begun to believe what the Colonel said.

Now, two years later, Slade was still very much afraid that Glory's father had spoken the truth.

Glory's words intruded on his reverie. "But that was long ago. Things have changed since then."

"Yes, things have changed. They've changed for the worse. Now there are even more things to keep us apart. Not three months ago, my father and yours had a shouting match in front of the bank."

"That has nothing to do with us!"

"Yes, it does. Your father stands for everything my

father hates . . . everything I've been brought up to believe was wrong."

"What are you talking about?"

"All right," Slade declared. "If you want to have a political discussion right here and now, then I guess that's what we'll do." He glared at her almost belligerently. "Just like *my* father, I believe that it was wrong for Texas to leave the Union. And *your* father exerted all the political power he had to help push through the secession vote."

"For heaven's sake, Slade, I won't argue with you about that. I don't really understand all the issues anyway. You have a right to your beliefs. You may even be correct in some of your views. I know *I* certainly don't want this war to happen!"

"That's not all." It was obvious Glory was determined to thrash out every obstacle. Well, so be it, thought Slade. "I don't even know what I'll do if I'm called to fight for the Confederacy. Morgan has already been notified when to report to the militia. I'm simply waiting for my orders now. Oh, I'll go if I have to. I can defend our territory from Indian raids. I'm not afraid of fighting for a just cause. But what if the Union Army gets this far? I don't think I can turn a gun on a fellow American." He shook his head slowly. "I just don't think I can do it."

A shimmer of tears filmed Glory's eyes. "Do you think I would fault you for that?" She was filled with pride at the dignity and principles of this man. What more could a woman ask? A man of such honor was worth fighting for.

"And what about the slavery issue, Glory? I could

never accept slavery. There's still the undeniable fact that your father is one of the biggest slaveowners in the state."

Glory shook her head impatiently. It was such a stupid thing to argue about.

"But, you don't understand about slavery. It's not like the abolitionists say. You ought to know better than that. Our people wouldn't want their freedom. They're dependent on us. They're treated well, taken care of. Some of them are almost like members of the family. Why, just look at Violet and Jacob . . . and little Sara! How can you possibly think they're mistreated?"

"I didn't say that. But they're humans, not animals. They should have a say in their own destinies. No one on God's green earth should have the right to sell another human being."

"Papa wouldn't sell our people!"

"That's not the point, Glory. The fact is, he could if he wanted to. *That's* the problem."

"But that has nothing to do with us. We don't have to have slaves. I don't mind."

A sad little smile tugged at Slade's mouth. "Oh, my sweet girl, you couldn't possibly know whether you'd mind or not. They've always been a part of your life. How many slaves are at the house right now?"

"I don't know, maybe eight or ten."

"And even more at Sivells Bend?"

"Yes, of course . . . hands to work the fields. But what has that got to do with us?"

"You've been waited on and catered to all your life.

How could I ask you to give up all that you're accustomed to? It wouldn't be fair."

"Fair!" Glory bristled. "What's fair about this whole thing? You say you love me. I know I love you with all my heart. Would it be more *fair* for us to deny what we feel? Just how *fair* would it be for us to never be together?"

Her voice broke at the thought, and Slade's heart melted. All his resolutions, all his promises to end their relationship, to set Glory free, dissolved under the onslaught of her tears.

Slade swallowed hard against the lump that filled his throat. With a soft cry of defeat he gathered her to him. Pulling her across his lap, he wrapped his arms securely about Glory's slim body and buried his face in the wild silken tangles of her hair while she cried out all her fears and frustrations.

"Hush, my darling, hush," he whispered, gently smoothing the curls away from her damp face. He rocked her softly, all the while sprinkling tiny butter-fly kisses across her temples, along the sensitive line of her jaw, down the pert length of her tip-tilted nose. "I'm sorry. It'll be all right. I promise. Everything will be all right."

"Slade, Slade," she murmured brokenly. When the tears finally ceased, each breath was accompanied by a soft little hiccup. "Tell me . . . tell me—"

Her voice faded away, but he knew what she wanted to hear.

"We'll find a way, sweetheart. Don't worry. I'll take care of you. I'll make everything all right. Somehow. Someway."

Glory clung to Slade, soaking up the warmth of his body, letting his nearness melt away all her misgivings. She caressed the side of his face and then let her fingers trail slowly down his throat and across the expanse of chest exposed by his half-unbuttoned shirt.

The edges of her small, rounded nails seared like lightning across Slade's skin. He gasped abruptly and the sinewy muscles bunched and slid under the soft haze of hair beneath Glory's hand.

Intrigued with his reaction, Glory timidly slipped her hand beneath the fabric. She hesitated at the sharp intake of his breath but soon began trailing her finger slowly across his chest, luxuriating in the simple pleasure of his nearness. The crisp hair tickled her palm. The heat from his body radiated through her fingertips and stirred a fire in her blood.

Her hand stilled and pressed against the granite-hard wall of his chest, where she could feel the frantic beat of his heart. She raised her lips to his, innocently, guilelessly offering him her sweetness. The tip of her tongue peeked out shyly and tasted his mouth. She sighed softly. Slade groaned deep in his throat and stamped his mouth across hers.

Each touch, each movement, each small incoherently murmured endearment took them further and further from reality.

Unconsciously Slade twisted, slowly lowering Glory gently to the soft grass-covered ground. With one graceful movement he was lying beside her, one arm under her head, the other binding her close to him, their mouths still touching, blending, melding.

Kisses were peppered down her throat and then across the tender expanse of skin bracketed by the soft fabric of her bodice.

The delicate aroma of floral-scented bath salts assailed Slade's senses. He pushed his face closer to the tempting shadow valley and gave in to the sudden desire to let his tongue flick over the satin skin of Glory's breast. Ahhh! She tasted like sunshine and roses, like moonlight and magic.

Slade's fingers fumbled with the tiny buttons of her dress. They popped free with ease, as if eager to release her beauty to his gaze, to his touch. His hand trembled as he pushed one side of the restricting material away.

A small breeze stirred the tree limbs overhead. Moonlight flickered through the leaves, casting intriguing black and silver patterns over the bewitching blend of bare flesh, concealing, then revealing the heart-stopping tenderness with which Slade placed his hand on Glory's breast.

Intoxicated with the feel of her, Slade stroked and caressed the velvet flesh. Nothing in his life had prepared him for the tenderness, the passion, the all-consuming desire that enveloped him at this moment. He marveled at the resilient way her nipple swelled and blossomed against his palm. Cupping the underside of her breast, he pushed the delicious plumpness upward, thrusting the succulent coral-colored morsel toward his waiting mouth, exulting in the way it hardened at the first moist touch of his tongue.

"Slade!" Glory cried softly, threading her fingers through the thick strands of dark hair to pull him closer. "Oh, Slade."

His name was a sigh. She writhed under his ministrations. The full skirt of her simple dress slid upward and pooled across her thighs.

His teeth nipped gently at her nipple. His tongue stroked the fine textured skin. His lips suckled deeply. She moaned in protest when he lifted his mouth, then sighed with pleasure when she realized he had only stopped in order to push the bodice further out of the way so he could lavish the same sweet attention on her other breast. The gentle tugging of his mouth stirred a strange pulsing in the pit of her stomach.

Once again he claimed her lips.

Never ceasing the sweet plunder of her mouth, Slade curled his upper body away from Glory and reached to unfasten the few remaining buttons on his shirt. He hurriedly pushed it aside and rolled back toward her, his bared chest pressed hard against her breasts.

"Ahhh," he moaned at the precious feel of her softness beneath him. "Glory, Glory." His voice caressed her like black velvet. "Sweet heaven, I need you—"

Slade's heat burned into Glory. The exquisite sensitivity of her nipples was heightened to the brink of sweet agony as the fine hairs covering his chest rasped against her. Making small adjustments in their position, Slade nestled the long muscled length of one leg enticingly between Glory's. The coiled-steel flesh of his thigh brushed against her, pressing and retreating, pressing and retreating. Glory gasped aloud with pleasure.

Once again Slade shifted. As his weight gently settled over her, Glory marveled at how wonderful it felt, how infinitely sweet it was to have every possible inch of their bodies touching. The rough texture of his trousers against the tender flesh of her inner thighs was the most exquisite of feelings. Her hips cradled the heated length of his manhood. Instinctively lifting her hips to meet the thrust of his, she responded to the gentle pulsing pressure he exerted against her.

"Closer, Slade, come closer," she sighed into the honeyed warmth of his mouth.

Slade groaned deep in his throat. He shifted slightly. His hand skated down the length of her ribs, over gentle curve of hip, then inward to softly stroke. Glory gasped as his palm cupped her heated flesh through the fabric. His hand stilled as he gallantly waited for her protest.

Denying Slade never entered Glory's mind. She wanted his touch, needed his nearness, had hungered for him for so long. Arching her back, she pressed against him, exalting in the wild frissons of longing his gentle stroking evoked.

Joy flooded Slade's heart at her response. Slowly, lovingly, he pushed aside the tangled material of Glory's skirt. His senses reeled when he found nothing but sweet bare flesh underneath. The renewal of his gentle stroking summoned a sob of pleasure from her lips.

Slade murmured gentle love words against her lips as he discovered the secret delights of his love. She was satin. She was fire. She was everything he'd ever wanted.

"Love me, Slade, love me," Glory whispered.

"Oh, Glory, my sweet love," he groaned. One hand fumbled at the fastening of his trousers . . .

In the branches far above, an old owl frantically flapped his wings and hooted loudly before taking flight into the warm ebony sky in search of supper.

Slade's head jerked up in alarm as the winged shadow glided across the silvery face of the moon. The heated mists began to clear in his head, and a modicum of sensibility returned. He fought to still the thundering beat of his blood, to slow the ragged pace of his breathing. This wasn't the way things should be. Despite the burning in his blood, he knew what he had to do.

With the last ounce of willpower he possessed, Slade reluctantly pushed himself away from Glory.

Chapter Four

"What's wrong?" Glory asked, sitting up and looking around with wide, frightened eyes. Instinctively she clutched the gaping bodice of her dress over her heaving breasts.

Slade turned back toward her with a gentle smile. He patted her shoulder with infinite tenderness. "It's nothing, darling. Just an irritable old hoot owl. That's all."

Kneeling beside her, he took a deep breath to help cool the fever lingering in his blood, and then carefully smoothed her skirt down over her legs. His hands still trembled as he gently finger-combed her tangled hair. The springy curls clung to his fingers, the silken strands binding them just as his love for her bound his heart. His hands tightened momentarily in the vibrant mass, and then he pushed the last curl from her cheek and rose to his feet.

"Come on, my love," he said, offering her his hand. "It's time you got back home. It'll be dawn before long."

Almost shyly, Glory placed her small hand in his and allowed him to pull her to her feet. Embarrassment flashed through her as she remembered what they'd been doing mere seconds before. She ducked her head and began to fumble at the unfastened buttons of her gown.

"Here, let me help you." His long, slim fingers quickly finished the job.

There was such gentleness in his voice, such loving in his touch that Glory's discomfiture melted away. What did she care what the rest of the world might think? How could it possibly matter? Slade was her own dear love. Nothing in the world could be as wonderful as being with him, part of him. Their love made all things right.

Moonlight flickered in the sherry depths of her eyes, and Slade's heart constricted with emotion at the sight of her trusting gaze.

"I . . . I wish we hadn't . . . stopped," she said in a voice so low he could barely hear her.

He placed his hands carefully on her slim shoulders and held her away so he could see her face.

"One day soon, when things are right, we'll be together. When I finally make you mine, I want it to be the most wonderful time in the world for you. I want everything to be perfect."

"Oh, Slade." Glory gave him a trembly smile.

"When that time comes, there'll be no one to say we're wrong or foolish. But we have to be patient. There's a way to work all this out. I just know there is."

74

"Yes," Glory sighed.

"In the meantime, we must keep our wits together. We can't afford to antagonize your father. It'll take time to figure out a way to win him over." He gave a chuckle. "And my pa, too. I can't say he's going to be very happy when he finds out he's going to be related to the Colonel."

Glory's silver laughter joined Slade's.

"Come along now, like a good girl. It's time to get you home."

Glory placed her hand in Slade's and allowed him to lead her up the path toward her house. At the edge of the woods, he pulled her back into the shadows and they clung together for one last heart-stopping kiss. Then he watched her run lightly over the clipped lawn and disappear into the predawn darkness.

The fragrant aroma of hot chocolate tickled Glory's nose. Her sleep-fogged brain recognized the clatter-clack of the drapes being adjusted. Groaning her protest, she burrowed her head under the fluffy goose down pillow, shielding her eyes from the offensive brightness that flooded the room.

"Come on, child," Violet urged. "It's nigh on to noon. Have you forgotten that the seamstress will be here this afternoon to finish fitting your gown for the Upton's ball? And that nice Mr. Harper said he'd be here late in the afternoon to take you for a buggy ride. Now you best wake up, chile!"

"Mummmph, gabble, mumble," escaped from under the pillow.

Violet's deep-throated laughter rang out. "Ummum! Honeypot, you're gonna have to try that again. I couldn't understand one single word." She bent to tug away the rumpled sheet and then persistently shook Glory's shoulder.

Reluctantly Glory surfaced, rubbed small fists into her swollen eyes, and then stretched in delicious languor. Violet took the opportunity to fluff up the pillows and pile them against the headboard in an inviting mound. Glory slumped against them and reached to accept the steaming cup of chocolate that Violet offered. She cuddled the warm china in her palms and smiled in contentment.

With brown hands on her rounded hips, Violet eyed her young charge. The riotous halo of nutmeg-colored hair spilled over Glory's shoulders and across the snowy pillowcases. There was a golden inner glow to the peach-toned skin and a dreamy little sparkle in the sleep-misted eyes.

Violet frowned. This certainly wasn't the reaction she'd expected from Glory. As with most large households, gossip traveled fast among the servants. Especially gossip concerning such tempting tidbits as those overheard during dinner last night. Violet had been dismayed to hear that the Colonel was determined to marry Glory off to Preston Harper.

Oh, the man was good-looking enough, she supposed. And he was reportedly quite wealthy. But Glory had never in her life given in lightly to her parents' tour de force. There was no reason to believe she'd start now. Not that her papa would ever be aware of Glory's rebellion . . . oh, no. Glory was smarter than that. She was quite aware of how determined and stubborn the Colonel could be if crossed. Years ago Glory had learned to work her wiles in more subtle ways.

Having been privy to more than one of Glory's mutinous escapades in the past, Violet had come to her room that morning prepared to listen once again to the girl's usual mutterings and moanings about her father's manipulations. But here Glory was, all dreamy-eyed and smiling!

Violet shook her head in consternation. She had always suspected Glory to be in love with Slade Hunter. Could she have been so wrong? Instead, could Glory possibly be smitten with the man her father had chosen?

Well, far be it from her to question the whims of young ladies, Violet thought with a shrug of her slim shoulders as she exited Glory's room. If Glory was happy, that's all that mattered.

Glory barely noticed when the door closed behind Violet. She sipped slowly at the sweet chocolate and smiled to herself. Things had turned out even better than she'd hoped.

Slade *did* love her! And she believed with all her heart that they could work things out. Hadn't he promised to do so? It would take a little maneuvering where her father was concerned, but she was quite sure she'd eventually be able to convince him that her heart lay with Slade, not with Preston Harper.

Preston! Oh, dear! Glory had forgotten all about him in the excitement of being with Slade. And she'd also neglected to tell Slade about this additional stumbling block. She sighed loudly, and with a clatter set the cup back in its saucer.

Oh, well, it probably didn't matter, she decided as she slung her feet over the edge of the bed. It might even be for the best. She knew how badly Slade felt about her father's opinion of him. It would really be demoralizing to him to realize that the Colonel had already chosen another man to be her husband. Perhaps it was just as well that she'd forgotten last night to tell him about Preston. Slade certainly hadn't needed to hear that sort of thing then. There was no sense worrying about it now. She'd tell Slade about it the next time they were together.

Four hours later, just as Preston Harper was lifting the gleaming brass knocker on the Westbrook's huge, carved front door, Knox Coleman entered the Hunter's store.

"Howdy, Slade," Knox boomed. Well over six feet tall, broad-shouldered, heavy-bellied, Knox's voice was as imposing as the rest of him. His thick thatch of black hair and shaggy full beard gave him the appearance of nothing less than a huge, good-natured bear. "Anson here today?"

"Hello, Knox. Good to see you," Slade replied, moving around the counter to offer his hand to his father's closest friend. "No, he's out at the farm today. He and Morgan are trying to get the last few things caught up before Morgan has to report to the militia. You know, mend the hog fence, check the storage bins. That sort of thing. It's going to be kind of tough handling the store, the kids, and the farm with one less person."

" 'Magine so," Knox agreed gruffly, nodding his head hard enough to send his midnight-black beard bobbing against his chest. He pulled a large jack-knife from his pocket and pared off a sliver of chaw, popping the tobacco into his mouth with relish.

"What can I do for you? Need any supplies?" Slade questioned.

"Naw. Just came in to tell your pa something—" Knox stopped long enough to spit a stream of thick brown juice into a polished brass spittoon. His coal-dark eyes gleamed with sudden inspiration. "Say, Slade, you might be interested in what I was going to tell Anson."

Slade knelt to pry the top off a recently received packing case and pushed the splintery wood aside to expose a dozen hoes and shovels. He stopped his work to glance up at Knox. "What's that?" he asked politely and went back to his unpacking.

"There's going to be a little meeting tonight out at my house." Knox's gaze flicked quickly over the store's interior. "Ol' man Cranford working today?" he asked, referring to the elderly gentleman who often clerked at the store.

"Not today."

Assured that they were indeed alone, he continued. "Your pa's come out the last time or two. Thought you might want to drop by."

The gardening implements clanged against each other as Slade lifted them from the crate. "What kind of meeting?"

"Just a friendly little get-together. You know, some jawing about how we can get Austin to rescind the conscript law. That kind of thing."

Slade crossed the room and leaned the first load of tools against the corner formed by the wall and a tall set of shelves. "Oh? How do you propose to accomplish that?"

The clack of Knox's boots followed Slade across the plank floor. Slade retrieved a rag from under the counter and wiped the dust from his hands.

Knox tugged at his belt, hoisting his sagging pants up over his prominent belly. " 'Pears to me, if all of us that think alike about this secesh issue stick together we can do most anything we set our minds to."

Slade peered questioningly at the burly man. "I'm not sure I understand."

"Listen, Slade," Knox intoned, his eyes once again scanning the doorway. "You don't agree with what's been goin' on in this town, do you?"

"No, but—"

"You know your pa doesn't. And I sure don't. Matter of fact, there's a lot of us that feel pretty strongly about what's going on. More folks than you can even imagine. We got the right to protect ourselves and our families. And as decent law-biding American citizens, we owe it to our country to do something to help."

"Just how're you going to do that, Knox? Have you forgotten that Texas seceded last year?" Slade asked with a wry look at the older man. "Texas belongs to the Confederacy now, whether we like it or

80

not. You start raising too much hell and spouting loyalty to the Union and they're gonna brand you a troublemaker, sure as the world."

Knox raised one big ham-sized hand, palm out. "Whoa, boy. I ain't that dumb! Why do you think we're so careful about who we invite out to our meetings? We don't want anyone to get the wrong idea. And we sure don't want any bad feelings about all this. We're just looking for a way to protect ourselves if push comes to shove. And maybe a way to help the Union . . . now, I ain't talking treason, Slade!" Knox was quick to amend. "Just some peaceable means of showing our loyalties when the time comes."

"Well —"

"You think about it, Slade. Your pa's seen the light. He's joined up. I believe you'll feel just as strongly about the League as the rest of us, if you just give it a chance. Why don't you come on out and have a listen to what we have to say? Around ten o'clock tonight. How 'bout it?"

Slade knew his father had been spending a considerable amount of time at Knox's lately. Maybe he should look into the situation. At least, Slade thought, he'd be with people who thought the same he did. It was getting harder and harder to keep his mouth shut when some war-hungry rabble-rouser started spouting off about how the Confederacy was going to whip the daylights out of the United States.

Unconsciously his fingers massaged the bridge of his nose. He was tired . . . and desperate. Right now he'd try almost anything to help get this damn war

81

over and find a way to be with Glory.

"All right. I'll think about it," Slade finally agreed.

"Good boy!" bellowed Knox, slapping him on the back. "You remember how to get there? Just southeast of the Moore place."

"Sure, I remember . . . off to the left a little just as you get into the Cross Timbers. Right?"

"Yep, that's right. And . . . uh . . . Slade, be careful. Don't mention any of this to anyone else. Not a soul. We can't be too careful, you know."

"I won't," Slade assured him, ambling along behind the big man as he headed for the store entrance. Maybe a breath of fresh air would clear the cobwebs away.

Slade and Knox stepped onto the weathered boardwalk outside the store as a gleaming black buggy rolled by. Slade recognized the elegantly dressed gentleman holding the reins as Preston Harper. He didn't actually know the man—they traveled in very different circles. But what he'd heard about him from Joella Ashland, the owner of the Silver City Saloon, had convinced him he wasn't going to like Harper if they ever did meet.

Harper lightly flicked his whip over the gray velvet rumps of his prancing team. The expensive matched pair responded smartly. The shadowed figure beside him stirred and leaned forward slightly. Butter yellow sunlight speared through the gloom cast by the overhanging buggy top and illuminated the passenger's face just as she laughed in response to something Harper said.

What in hell! Slade's mouth fell open. What was

Glory doing out buggy riding with Preston Harper?

Knox's booming voice finally cut through Slade's shock-dulled senses.

"Uh . . . what?" His mind suddenly bedeviled with a thousand painful misgivings, Slade tried desperately to recollect what Knox had just said. What on earth had they been talking about? Something about tonight . . . oh, yes, that damned meeting! "Yeah, sure, I'll see you there," Slade finally muttered, while eyes as cold as winter rain watched the buggy roll down Boggs Street and turn left on Dixon.

Slade looped the reins of his horse over the limb of a prickly cedar bush and peered at the dark image of Knox's small house. Lamplight shone from the two front windows, small squares of beckoning yellow in the raven's wing night. Soft sounds surrounded him: the rustle of the wind through the trees, the restless movement of horses, punctuated occasionally by an equine snort and the jingle of harness. He heard the distant howl of wolves, which were still plentiful in this sparsely populated area of the Cross Timbers, the nearest neighbors being almost two miles away.

Hazy silhouettes could be seen moving beyond the wavy glass of the windows. Slade, his hand grasping the smooth leather of the saddle horn, leaned against the bay's warm flank and contemplated his predicament.

He didn't really want to be there. But curiosity about what his father was involved in and an even stronger desire to stay busy had prevailed. At least

83

here his mind might let go of the frantic questions that had plagued him throughout the long day.

Pushing resolutely away from Diablo's reassuring bulk, Slade plodded toward the house, his reluctant feet raising puffs of dust in the ill-kept yard.

The rough-planked door flew open at his first knock, and Knox's big bulk filled the opening.

"Slade! Good to see you. Come on in this house, fella," he fairly bellowed. "I'm sure you know some of these people." Knox's hand swept out, indicating a half dozen men hunched over the table in the center of the small room.

Heads turned, wary eyes appraised, small murmurs of greeting sounded in the thick silence.

"Come on, boy. Make yourself comfortable. Your pa couldn't make it?"

"Nah. He said to tell you he'd see you at the next meeting," Slade answered, still eyeing the men. He knew the majority by name or sight, but two of them were strangers. "Morgan had gone out earlier, and Paula wasn't feeling well. Pa didn't want to leave the kids by themselves."

"That's all right, we'll fill him in later," Knox said, nodding his shaggy head. "Make yourself comfortable, Slade." He drew another rickety chair up to the already crowded table.

A whiskey bottle and an assortment of glasses in varying degrees of fullness shared the scarred table-top with the lantern. Smoke hung heavily in the room, indicating evidence that at least some of the others had been talking for quite a while.

Knox poured a long splash of amber liquid into a

spare glass and pushed it in Slade's direction. "Here you go. A little something to take the kinks out," Knox declared jovially as Slade folded his long body onto the chair.

Slade downed the burning liquor with one gulp, hoping it would soothe the dull headache that was beginning to pound at the back of his head. God! What was he doing here? What he really wanted was to talk to Glory.

But that was impossible. What was he going to do, walk up to the Colonel's fancy house, beat on the door, and demand to speak to her? Not damn well likely! There wasn't a chance in hell that Westbrook would let him anywhere near her.

He slumped further down on the hard wooden chair. Maybe he should have tried earlier to sneak up to the back door. If he could have managed to get Violet's or Jacob's attention without rousing the whole household, either of them might have been willing to take a message to Glory.

Slade and the two Westbrook slaves had developed something akin to friendship over the last couple of years. They'd been Slade's best source of information about Glory while she was gone. The relationship had come about rather unexpectedly . . . beginning with small polite exchanges when the Westbrook servants were forced to shop in the Hunters' store for items unavailable elsewhere, then moving on to pleasant conversations about hunting and the weather and other amenities. Slade wasn't sure if the two had taken to him because he'd always treated them with dignity and respect, or if they were secretly in favor of his and Glory's relationship. Whatever the reason, over the ensuing months he had come to count them as more than acquaintances.

Or Lydia! Now why in hell hadn't he thought about contacting Lydia this afternoon? Surely she would have taken a message to Glory—

Knox's introduction of the two strangers as Johnny Dunlap and Curtis Simmons, both from Kansas, pulled his attention back to the present. Slade studied the two men. His curiosity piqued, he wondered what the two Kansans were doing in Cooke County.

Something about them made him think they could be up to no good, whatever it was. Both were hard-looking. Dunlap was lean and angular, with a jutting hawk nose and a frequent nervous smile that displayed crooked, tobacco-stained teeth. Simmons was considerably pudgier but looked to be all muscle rather than fat. Slade wondered absently how the man had acquired the faint white scar that raked down his face from his left eyebrow to just below his ear. Shaking each man's hand in turn verified the spring-coiled strength Slade had suspected at first glance.

"We've already explained what the League's about to these fellas," Knox said, indicating by a wave of his hand the four men whom Slade was remotely acquainted with. "I'll just give you a short run-down of what we aim to do. All right?"

Slade nodded his agreement. He really didn't care what Knox had to say. All he was doing was marking time, trying to fill his mind with anything but the worrisome thoughts of Glory and Preston Harper that had gnawed at him ever since he saw them whisk down the street in Harper's brand-spanking-new buggy. He simply could not come up with a reasonable explanation for what he'd seen. Glory couldn't possibly know the man . . . he'd moved to Texas after she'd been sent away to school. How on earth had he managed to talk the Colonel into letting him take Glory out riding so soon? And unescorted, too!

"Slade," Knox prodded. "Uh . . . you listening?"

"Yeah, sure," Slade said with a silent sigh. He shifted his weight and the chair protested noisily. "You've got my full attention." *That* was a lie, but Knox would never know it.

Knox flicked a quick glance toward the two Kansans and then began his tale. "The League was formed last year by a group of men who believe there is more we could do to help the Union than sit on our butts and take what's being shoved down our throats. Now, I'm not talking out-and-out insurrection," Knox explained quickly when he saw the beginning of a scowl on Slade's face. "Just hear me out on this."

"I'm still listening."

"Our political maneuverings mainly consist of taking a sacred oath to promote restoration of the Union and to come to the aid of any fellow League member who gets in trouble with the Confederate authorities, should it be necessary. We also vow to resist the conscript law wherever possible and, of course, not to take up weapons against the Union."

Slade folded his arms across his chest, listening with more interest than he would have thought possible, assessing the points as Knox ticked them off one by one. "I guess it sounds reasonable, but I don't quite see how you plan to accomplish all those things without some obvious confrontation with the authorities."

"Easy as pie, boy." Knox grinned. "Johnny can explain."

Johnny Dunlap shifted in his chair and crossed his arms on the table in front of him. The rumpled sleeves of his worn brown shirt pulled against the stringy, hard muscles of his biceps. "It's like this . . . all you gotta do is bide your time. If the Union army invades, any League members not already part of a unit will join the militia real fast. That way they can get ahold of a good supply of weapons. Once in battle they go over to the Union side. Simple, huh?"

Slade's eyes narrowed. "But wouldn't that be considered treason?"

"How can you even think such a thing?" Knox questioned quickly, his big fist thumping the table for emphasis. For a moment the lantern rocked precariously, sending patterns of shadow and light dancing over the strained faces of the men. "How could any self-respecting man fight against the country he owes allegiance to? And we all feel a loyalty to the United States, don't we? Even if we can't voice it out loud right now?"

"Yes, but—"

Knox quickly stilled Slade's protest. "If a man as fine as ol' Sam Houston can publicly refuse to declare loyalty to the Confederacy, I think we can be brave enough to do this."

"Right," Dunlap chimed in. "It sure ain't treason. We won't actually be doin' anything until the army gets here. Who knows what might happen in the meantime? We'll simply be prepared just in case they do." Dunlap's explanation sounded good. "This is the safest way to handle things."

"Besides, we're not dumb enough to forget that anybody who refuses to fight for the Confederacy is probably gonna wind up facing a firing squad," Curtis interjected. "Now, what kind of choice does that leave you with? Fight against your own country, face a damn firing squad, or do something positive about getting this country back together?" The patriotic speech seemed somewhat ludicrous coming from so disparaging-looking a man.

"Maybe it won't come to that," Slade declared hopefully. "Maybe the Union Army won't get this far and we'll never have to face the problem of deciding who to fight for."

Dunlap shrugged. "Could be. And could be that by that time we'll have enough members in the League so that we can settle this whole thing without bloodshed at all."

"Oh? And just how do you propose to do that?" Slade asked skeptically.

"If we can get two-thirds of the militia initiated into the League, then we can simply demand that all the arsenal supplies in the region be turned over to us. We could take control of this whole part of Texas and wait for the arrival of the Union Army."

Slade's mouth gaped open at the audacity of the plan. Could they possibly be serious? He scanned the eager faces of the men surrounding the table. It sure looked that way. But it wasn't the first time that men had had such thoughts. Slade remembered reading an editorial in a yellowed and torn copy of the *Southern Intelligencer* early last summer. It had expounded on a plan to create a separate state out of dissident counties if Texas seceded. Nothing had ever come of it when the state actually left the Union . . . but perhaps the scheme wasn't dead after all.

"Two-thirds of the militia in the League! That's a hell of a lot of people."

The scar on Simmon's face twitched faintly as he gave Slade a smug smile. "We've already got more members than you'd ever believe—"

"How many members are there? Who are they?" Slade questioned.

"Now, listen, boy," Knox intervened. "We can't give out that kind of information to just anybody. Nobody, but *nobody*, gets to know who the members are or how many of them there are unless they join up themselves. Are you prepared to take the oath of allegiance?"

"I . . . I don't know." Slade rose suddenly, causing the chair he'd been sitting on to scrape loudly against the rough plank flooring. Long fingers raking through dark locks, he paced the small room's perimeter. Finally he stopped and peered intently at Knox. "That's *all* we'd be obliged to do? There's not any more to this 'League' thing than that?"

"Nope," Knox quickly assured him. "All you got to do to be initiated into the first degree of the League is swear your loyalty. In return we'll give you the password and signs to use in determining who's a member and who isn't."

"You got to realize," Dunlap interrupted. "If you don't know the signs and passwords, then you and your family might not be safe if it comes to a showdown —"

"Showdown? I thought you said there'd be no fighting," Slade challenged.

"Now, now," Simmons soothed. "That's not precisely what Johnny meant. But if the Union Army does get this far, we need to know who belongs to our side. That's logical, isn't it?"

"Yeah, I guess so," Slade finally said. His mind was too full of thoughts of Glory to have complete understanding of what he'd just heard. It *seemed* to make sense . . . and if it would help protect his father and his younger brother and sister — Well, could he afford not to join up?

Besides all that, he really *did* believe that Texas should return to the Union. And, like he'd told Glory, he didn't want to fight against fellow Americans. He didn't want to have to fire a gun at fellow Texans, either. But he'd cross that bridge when the time came. God willing, this whole damn war thing would be over before he'd ever have to make a choice one way or the other.

So Slade agreed. And he and the other four men took the oath of allegiance to the League.

In return they were shown how to identify fellow members of the League by passing the fingers of the right hand slowly over the right ear. The answer to this sign was for the other man to pass the fingers of his left hand slowly over his left ear. The next step was to ask the man where he had got his horse or any other convenient article he had about his person. If the answer was "Arizona," then the man would be considered all right and could be trusted. If they met up with someone in the dark they could identify members by a special grip. A common handshake with the end of the forefinger pressed tolerably hard on the inside of the wrist would signify membership.

The initiation over, another round of drinks was quickly poured and downed. And then the men left the small house in the Cross Timbers and slipped away into the night.

Chapter Five

"I need to talk to you right away!" Lydia whispered to Glory the minute the Westbrook family entered the Uptons' home. But the sound of the door closing and the babble of distant voices drowned out most of Lydia's words.

Glory cast a questioning glance at her friend. She had just started to ask Lydia to repeat what she'd said when Mrs. Westbrook spoke up.

"Good evening, Lydia. Lovely dress, my dear. The color is just perfect for you," Glory's mother commented with a polite nod of her head. "Come along, Glory. We must go in and greet Lydia's parents."

"Oh, thank you. I'm so glad you like it," Lydia answered quickly. She had to keep Glory from following her parents! She was so rattled that she gave a small bobbing curtsy in Mrs. Westbrook's direction before turning back to her friend. "Glory! Dear me, I do believe you have a curl working loose. You must have lost a pin. Now, you come right upstairs with me and I'll get Maddie to fix it." She grasped Glory's hand firmly and began resolutely hauling her toward the staircase.

With her free hand, Glory patted at her curls. "I don't think so—"

"Yes, you have," Lydia declared again quite emphatically.

"Oh," said Glory, finally realizing that something was clearly amiss. She flashed a look of understanding at Lydia and quickly excused herself to her parents as the Westbrooks headed toward the already crowded ballroom.

Acknowledging her father's stern warning not to "dilly-dally" for too long with a deceptively meek "Yes, Papa," Glory hurried up the stairs after her friend.

"My heavens, Lydia. Whatever is going on?" she asked as they scampered down the hallway toward Lydia's room.

"Shh!" Lydia cautioned, nodding her head quickly toward the upstairs parlor, which had been set aside for the female guests to refresh themselves. A giggling trio of young ladies was just exiting the door.

"Glory!" one of the girls cried. "How nice to see you. We must make a little time for chatting later this evening. I want to hear absolutely *everything* about that fancy school you've been attending and what you've been doing."

"Yes, of course, Edith. I'm looking forward to it," Glory fibbed. She tolerated the girl's continued gushing with growing impatience. It was a good five minutes before she and Lydia managed to escape and continue their way along the hall.

"Mercy me, Lydia. Tell me what on earth is going

on!" Glory demanded the minute the door of Lydia's room was shut safely behind them.

Lydia turned to face her friend. Her expression was so serious it was almost comical. "I have a message for you from Slade," she explained in a theatrical whisper.

Glory's face lit up. "Well, what is it?" she asked breathlessly, her heart skipping erratically.

"He'll be waiting for you out by the gazebo as soon as you can get away. He said to tell you he'd wait all night if he had to!"

"Oh, my!" Glory was filled with a mixture of delight and apprehension. She wanted to see Slade more than anything. It had been almost a week since the night she'd met him by the old tree. There'd simply been no way to slip out since then without causing possible questions. But to see him here at the Uptons', and with her parents on the premises! That was cutting things a bit too close.

What could have precipitated his rashness? Was it just that Slade was desperate to see her? Glory smiled joyously at that thought. It bolstered her morale considerably and helped to whisk away the worries about her parents' proximity. Well, she'd just have to manage to get out without them missing her. It was going to be a warm night and people would be stepping outside frequently to take advantage of the cooler night air. All she had to do was make sure to choose a time when everyone else was busy inside.

"Tell me all about it, Lydia," Glory urged. "What did he say? How did he get in contact with you?" Anxious to confirm that she would look her very best when she saw Slade, she turned to survey herself in a cheval glass while Lydia explained how Slade had slipped a note to her that very afternoon.

Glory was well pleased with the image returned by the silvery mirror. Her gown was a confection of palest peach and rich cream. The sateen of her low bodice was secured down the front with eighteen tiny pearl buttons. The silk taffeta foundation skirt rustled seductively under a full overskirt of cream silk organza. The gown was overlaid, bodice and skirt, with raw silk Chantilly lace, delicate as gossamer. Flounced and adorned with froufrou, the top two layers of the skirt were caught up and held in place with peach-colored satin moiré ribbons gathered into bows. The colors hightlighted the delicate apricot tones of Glory's bare shoulders and brought out the cinnamon lights in her hair and eyes, presenting an altogether delectable picture.

Glory looked absolutely beautiful and she knew it. She could hardly wait to see the pride in Slade's eyes. *Soon, my love, soon.*

"You'd best stop your daydreaming, Glory," Lydia admonished when she ceased talking and caught sight of the faraway look on her friend's face. "Get your mind back on the present. You can think about Slade later. It's time we made an appearance at the ball."

Glory gave a sigh of resignation. Casting one last reassure-seeking glance at the mirror, she followed Lydia out of the room. The gentle rustle of taffeta and satin accompanied the two girls as they hurried toward the bustling ballroom.

The Uptons' house, while not as large and elaborate as the Westbrooks', was in its own right spacious and beautiful. At the moment, only soft background music was wafting from the corner of the ballroom where the musicians had been installed. The rest of the room was filled with dozens of milling people, the men mostly in striking black, the women in a veritable artist's palette of glorious color.

Glory spied her parents almost immediately. She tossed her head with slight annoyance at the sight of Preston Harper standing with them. Was there no escaping the man? He'd called at the house almost every day since that fateful dinner. And no matter how Glory played her part — coy or caustic, simpering or snooty — he seemed equally pleased to be in her company. She was beginning to fear that her plan wasn't as brilliant as she'd thought.

"Glory, how wonderful you look tonight," Preston murmured in his usual lazy drawl as she approached.

Glory found it hard to repress the sudden desire to snatch her hand back when he raised it to press a lingering kiss on her fingertips.

Preston was impeccably attired as usual, his black frock coat exquisitely tailored, the small ruching down the front of his pristine white shirt stiffly starched and pressed. The glow from the overhead chandeliers highlighted the shock of blond hair and turned his mustache the color of spun gold.

Any other woman would probably be thrilled to death to receive the attentions of such a handsome man. Glory fervently wished such were the case — that those icy blue eyes were scrutinizing any other woman but herself.

Something about Preston made her uncomfortable. It wasn't anything she could put her finger on.

Just a remote sixth sense, a tiny nagging feeling, of having been catalogued and pigeonholed in some convenient little niche without much thought being given to the *real* person involved. It was as if everything about their relationship was cut and dried, already decided . . . and perhaps it was in Preston's eyes since her father had already expressed his approval. But, even if Slade hadn't been in the picture, Glory's ire would have been raised at so cavalier a dismissal of her personal feelings on the matter.

If Preston really desired her for a wife, she thought a bit irrationally, he should be trying to win her acceptance, not blandly acting as if their engagement had already been announced!

"Why, thank you, Preston. How kind of you to say so," she managed to simper in return. She forced herself to smile up at him. Drat and double drat! She should have realized he'd be at the party. Just one more thorn in her side. Now she'd have to escape Preston as well as her parents!

The fiddle player pulled a long silvery note across his instrument. The crowd quieted and Mr. Upton called for the Grand March to open the dancing.

Preston led Glory through the lively procession and then claimed her for the waltz that followed. As he settled his hand on her slim waist, she analyzed her response to his nearness. He certainly didn't affect her as Slade did. There was no trembly sensation in her limbs, no quick blaze of fire in her veins, in response to Preston's touch. He was simply a handsome man with impeccable manners and evidently more than his share of riches — none of which made up for the fact that he wasn't Slade.

Several hours of dancing later, after no little whispered plotting on the part of the two girls, Preston was pressed into service as Lydia's partner and Glory was finally able to slip away.

The night air was pleasantly cool. Silver beams of moonlight cast barely enough illumination to allow Glory to make her way to the gazebo at the far end of the garden. Once she thought she heard murmured voices off to one side. She almost turned back but then she decided that, whoever it might be out there in the dark, they would not have a clear view of the place she and Slade were to rendezvous. Besides, this might be her only opportunity. She dared not postpone the meeting.

Glory rounded the end of a tall clipped hedge and the gazebo loomed in front of her. Pale moonlight bathed the small building, dark shadows from the lattice work making crisscross patterns on the floor.

"Slade?" she whispered, peering intently into the shadowed depths.

She had just hoisted her skirts and lifted her foot to mount the first step when a dark figure appeared out of nowhere, grasped her wrist, and pulled her unceremoniously into the velvet darkness behind the structure.

Brought up suddenly against the rock-hard wall of Slade's chest, her breath rushed out of her with a swoosh. In the space of a heartbeat his mouth was crushed against hers, grinding, burning, searing, as if he were somehow trying to brand her indelibly with his mark.

When he finally released her, Glory gulped for air. She stumbled back and stared up at him with large surprised eyes, feeling thrilled by the heat of his ardor but also slightly taken aback by his uncharacteristic behavior.

"My goodness!" she murmured, blinking twice in confusion when she noticed the dark scowl on his face. Was something the matter? This certainly wasn't the Slade she knew.

"Sorry," Slade finally mumbled. Dragging his hand through his dark disheveled hair, he turned and began to pace. A half dozen steps one way, a half dozen steps the other.

"What's wrong?" Glory asked, her mind imagining all sorts of disasters.

"Wrong?" Slade said. Sarcasm laced his voice. "Wrong? What could possibly be wrong?"

"I'm sure I don't know—"

"I'll tell you what's wrong!" he ground out. "It just might be the fact that I saw the woman who claims to love me out buggy riding with another man the very day after she made that extremely touching declaration! And what about the fact that I've spotted the same man's buggy at your house *three times* this week?" he finished with a growl.

"Oh," Glory said meekly, realizing at once how things must look from Slade's point of view.

"I suppose you're going to tell me not to worry about Preston Harper—"

"Precisely—"

"Just like I'm not supposed to worry about your father?"

"That's right."

"Damn it all, Glory! Do you have absolutely any concept of what hell this situation is putting me

100

through?" Slade's harsh voice rasped through the dark. He barely managed to hold the volume down to a grating whisper.

"Well, I think so—"

"You *think* so! Ha! Let me give you just a small sampling of what my week has been like!" He whirled and glowered at her. "How do you think I felt when I saw you out with Harper? *I* can't call on you and take you out for a ride! *I'm* forbidden the pleasure of walking through town with the woman I love on my arm. But that . . . that pompous, self-centered bastard has the Colonel's full blessings to squire you about any time he chooses! And unescorted, too!"

"Slade, please—" Glory tried to explain, but he was so caught up with his wounded feelings that he brushed aside her entreaty.

"This isn't going to work, Glory. I'm not made of stone, you know. I don't *want* you to be with another man!"

Glory stepped quickly to his side. Laying her small hand on his arm, she looked up into his anguished eyes. "Do you honestly think I want to be with anyone else?"

"N-no," he finally answered in a ragged voice. His shoulders slumped as the anger drained out of him. "Ah, Glory, Glory. What are we going to do?" He gathered her into his arms, tucking her head under his chin. His hands slid lightly over her arms, her back, in gentle loving strokes. "I can see no end to this madness."

Closing her eyes, she nestled closer to his chest, listening to the reassuring thump of his heart under her ear, breathing in the spicy male scent of him. "It *will* end, Slade. We just have to be patient."

"Patient," he repeated bitterly.

Glory raised her head and peered up at him. "You must understand about Preston—"

"Preston, is it? On first-name basis so soon?" He shook his head morosely.

"Stop that and listen to me!" she scolded. "Papa has this wild idea that . . ." She hesitated, all her previous fears concerning telling Slade about Preston running through her head. Well, there was no postponing it now. The issue *had* to be cleared up. She had to make him understand that she was only seeing Harper in order to keep her father happy and unaware. She drew a long breath and readied herself for the difficult task. "Papa has decided that I should marry Preston—"

"Marry!" The word exploded from Slade. He stared down at her incredulously. "My God! You've been away from home for two years and he's already talking about marrying you off to some . . . some stranger!"

Glory's gown rustled softly as she nervously stepped away from Slade. The situation was becoming more difficult by the minute. She plucked a blossom from one of the bushes framing the gazebo and twirled it restively between her fingers, trying to decide what line of reasoning to use next.

"Preston isn't a stranger to Papa. They've had some extensive business dealings the last year. He's very fond of him, actually."

"Oh, great!" Slade muttered as he slumped down onto the small bench behind the gazebo.

Glory quickly joined him on the small seat. Heedless of the flower that dropped from her fingers, she grasped his big hand in both of hers and cradled it to her breast.

"Listen to me! I don't care how fond Papa is of Preston, or anyone else. I love you! If I have to endure Preston's attentions in order to give us enough time to find a solution to our situation, then I'll do it . . . and gladly! He means nothing to me. He's a nice enough man—"

Slade snorted in disgust.

Glory rolled her eyes in exasperation and practically threw his hand back into his lap. "Honestly, Slade!" Hands on her hips, she glared at him. "You make me so mad! I can't help what Papa is planning. All I can do is work around it. I'll get rid of Preston soon enough. You just have to believe me."

Slade dropped his head into his hands, elbows braced against his knees. He was still for a long moment, as if wrestling with inner demons. Finally, he raised his head and gazed deep into her eyes.

"I do, Glory, I do," he assured her sadly. "It's just so hard for me to see you with him."

Once again he enveloped her in his arms, this time gathering her to him with exquisite tenderness. Their mouths locked in an agonizingly sweet kiss. Pulling her toward him, he shifted their positions until Glory's legs were draped across his and she was cradled against his chest. The cares of the world faded away. Ragged indigo shadows scudded across the crescent moon and the dark cloak of the night closed magically around them, creating their own small safe haven in the midst of the maddening world.

When Slade finally relinquished possession of her lips to trail tiny tender kisses across the slope of her high cheekbone, Glory breathed a deep sigh of contentment. Then he flicked the warm, moist tip of his tongue across her shell-like ear and she whimpered as white-hot heat seared through her veins. Her heartbeat continued to soar as Slade sprinkled burning kisses down her throat and across the beguiling swell of her bosom above the pale peach satin. His breath seared the tender flesh in the floral-scented valley between her breasts. Sliding his hand slowly up her midriff, he caressed the underside of the soft mound of her bosom, his thumb searching for the pearl that hardened and thrust urgently against the confining material.

Glory moaned softly and tangled her fingers in his midnight locks. Her body ached for his nearness.

"Glory," he groaned. "My sweet, sweet Glory. You fill my mind, my senses — "

"Glory!"

At the sound of her name being called, Slade's head snapped up.

"Jesus Christ! Not again! Who the hell is that anyway?" He glared at the dark garden between the house and the gazebo, where the offending voice was coming from.

Stiffening in recognition, Glory pulled away from Slade. "It's Preston," Glory replied in a voice filled with resignation. "I have to go. You do understand, don't you?" she pleaded.

"Sure," Slade answered, trying to make the tone of his voice believable. "It's . . . it's all right. Go on, before he comes any closer."

Glory reluctantly slid from Slade's lap. He stood up and tried hard to grin at her, but his smile was lopsided and a bit shaky.

"Don't forget, I love you," she whispered to him, quickly raising on tiptoes to brush a kiss against his lips.

Snatching up the hem of her gown, she sped around the side of the gazebo just as Preston stepped into the patch of moonlight in the clearing. The pale glow turned his hair silver-white.

"There you are!" he said. "I was beginning to get worried about you."

"Oh, Preston! I just got a little warm . . . that's all. I needed a breath of air and it was so pretty outside I just kept walking—" Glory prattled on, anxious to keep Preston's attention occupied while she moved quickly toward the light and noise of the house, luring him away from where Slade still stood.

Slade watched from the deep velvet shadows. Little by little, the warmth Glory had generated slowly slipped away, leaving him alone and strangely chilled in the warm night air.

Slade slid his hands into his pockets, his fists bunched against the fabric. Bitter resentment filled him as he watched the woman he loved walk away on the arm of another man.

Slade slumped low against the satin cushions of an overstuffed chair, his weight on his lower back, long legs thrust out in front of him. His legs were crossed at the ankle and the topmost booted foot swayed hypnotically, back and forth, back and forth, throw-

105

ing syncopated shadows on the thick wine-red carpet beneath his heel. An almost empty tumbler of whiskey was balanced on the flat expanse of his stomach slightly above the waistband of his form-fitting denim pants. The tense spring-coiled maleness of him seemed somewhat out of place in the very feminine surroundings of Joella Ashland's private suite above the Silver City Saloon.

In no mood to make the lonely trek home after watching Glory disappear with Harper, Slade had made his way to the one place he hoped he could find solace, seeking the noisy, frenetic atmosphere of the Silver City to drown his miseries. But, as the night wore on, the incessant shuffle of the cards and the click of the chips had become annoying rather than soporific. It had become harder and harder for him to keep his mind on the cards in his hand. The loud music and even louder voices of the boisterous occupants of Gainesville's finest saloon set his head to pounding. The melodic laughter of Joella's girls as they moved about the huge room, serving drinks, dancing with the men, flirting, or even occasionally disappearing with one of them up the small staircase at the back of the large smoke-filled room became increasingly irritating.

At Joella's whispered offer, he had gratefully thrown his cards on the table and stomped up the stairs alone, to sit and drink and brood in the solitude of the owner's elegant secluded chambers until she could slip away and join him.

Hours later, Slade barely raised his eyes when the latch of the door clicked and Joella slipped quietly into the room. Slim and graceful, she crossed the

106

room with quick, light steps, stopping only to lay her lacy fan beside the cut-glass whiskey decanter on the table by Slade's elbow and give his shoulder a small affectionate pat before slipping behind the gracefully carved screen in the corner of the bedroom alcove.

"Feeling better?" she asked.

"Yeah, sure."

Her cool green eyes scrutinized Slade's morose figure over the filigreed edge of the screen as slim fingers worked slowly to unfasten the tiny buttons down the front of her ruby red gown. Bending, she stepped from the dress, throwing it negligently over a nearby chair before sliding her arms into a soft wraparound dressing gown of blue-green satin.

Moving from behind the screen, Joella filled a small goblet with soothing wine and then curled into the cushiony corner of the sofa across the room from Slade. She tucked her slim bare feet up under her and uttered a weary sigh. It had been a long and tiring night.

"Want to talk about what's bothering you?"

Slade didn't even raise his eyes from their morose contemplation of the toes of his boots. "No, I don't think it would help."

Joella accepted his rebuff silently, continuing to study her friend as she took a sip of her drink. She could wait until he was ready to talk.

One of the reasons for the Silver City Saloon's prosperity was Joella's unwavering attention to every detail. There were very few nights when she couldn't be found downstairs until the wee hours of the morning, circulating among the customers, stopping here and there to exchange a teasing bit of conversation or inquire about the well-being of her steady customers. Her friendly but sophisticated demeanor not only kept the regulars happy but allowed her to keep a sharp eye out for those who might get a bit rowdy after one too many drinks or the occasional bad-tempered loser who might be tempted to take the anger incited by the turn of a card out on the girls.

Joella Ashland was a beautiful woman. She alone would have made a trip to the Silver City Saloon worthwhile. But Joella was also smart. She made sure her whiskey was the very best, the girls the prettiest, and the bartenders the most liberal in town when they poured a man's libation. The only man foolish enough to let Joella catch him watering the stock and pocketing the difference had been quickly run out of town, much the worse for wear after a few of her loyal customers got through with him.

Consequently, the Silver City's reputation had grown in the three years since Joella arrived in town and bought out ol' Dan Epperson. Weeks later, sparkling clean and thoroughly refurbished, the establishment had opened with a new name and new employees. The saloon was soon known far and wide as an honest and friendly place where men could gather to pass the evening in pleasant pursuit—be it whiskey, gambling, or the company of beautiful women.

Speculation had run wild for a good many months after Joella's arrival. Who was she? Where did she come from? How did she come by the large sum of money it had taken to buy Epperson out and spruce up the building? No one knew. It was evident from her refined vocabulary and regal bearing that she was well bred, well educated. This added further fuel to the flames of curiosity.

But how and why such a woman had wound up in a small frontier town stayed a mystery. Joella was as adept at avoiding personal questions as she was beautiful. Eventually the town's inhabitants grew weary of its unconfirmed conjectures and stopped asking the questions. Which suited Joella fine.

Joella set her glass on the ornate round table beside the sofa. With slim fingers she pulled the pins from her carefully arranged coiffure and allowed the long, golden curls to fall. She ran her hands through the heavy mass, massaging her temples, soothing the tender places where the heavy pins had lain against her scalp for hours.

And all the while she watched as Slade raised his glass and took another swallow before settling the crystal tumbler back in its place, only to repeat the action a minute or two later. Her fingers stilled and one corner of her mouth quirked up in a weary little smile.

"It's Glory, isn't it?" Joella finally asked. Her voice was slightly husky, as alluring as a kitten's purr.

Slade's moody gray gaze met hers as he gave her a sad crooked grin. "How did you know?"

A wry chuckle escaped Joella's perfectly shaped mouth. She shook her head slowly, the long, gold tresses swaying seductively against the shoulders of her robe.

"My, my, Slade. You do take me for such a simpleton. Glory's what brought you here in the first place—two years ago. Did you think I'd forgotten? All I had to do was take one look at that stormy face of yours tonight, and it was obvious. After all, what else could it be?"

"Am I really that transparent?"

"It wasn't too hard to figure out. Especially since I happened to hear from a . . . a mutual acquaintance . . . that she's back in town."

Slade's eyes narrowed. His hard intake of breath rocked the glass that was balanced on his stomach. "And who might that be?"

"Are we going to play games?" Joella asked in a lightly teasing voice.

"No. No games," Slade muttered, drawing his legs in and pushing his body upright in the chair. "I know exactly the son of a bitch you're talking about."

"I thought you might." Joella's head tilted upward as she watched Slade rise to his feet and begin to pace restlessly.

His laughter was edged with bitterness. "You're going to love this," he said with a mocking shake of his head. "Who do you suppose the good Colonel has picked to be Glory's dearly beloved husband?"

For once Joella's serene manner was shaken. "You can't be serious! Where did you get such an idea?"

"Oh, but I'm very serious. She told me so just tonight — "

"Ah," Joella said, nodding her head in understanding. "So that's what precipitated your visit. What an interesting situation. I'd heard that the Colonel and Preston had become thick as thieves, but I didn't suspect it had gone *that* far."

"Well, Joella, my dear, I know how much you'd like to see Preston Harper taken out of circulation, but I damn well don't want Glory to be the source of your relief."

"Quite understandable under the circumstances. Umm, I wonder what the Colonel would think if he knew that I had to threaten to call the law again to get his chosen heir-apparent to leave last night."

"What?" Slade's eyes turned the color of a stormy winter sky.

Joella gave a negligent flip of her hand. "The man is terribly ungracious when he's told no."

"Damn! You mean to tell me that bastard's squiring Glory about during the day and still pestering you at night?"

"I'm afraid so. He seems incapable—or unwilling—to believe that his money won't buy him everything he wants . . . including me."

Slade's long lean legs ate up distance as he circled the room time and again. "Dammit, Joella! What are we going to do about the bastard?" Wavy, dark shadows marched in tandem around the flower-strewn wallpaper as Slade continued his restless wandering.

"I'm not so sure that you can do anything about the situation. Colonel Westbrook's a very stubborn man. And if he's got his heart set on Glory marrying Preston—"

"But she loves me!" Slade protested.

"Does she think she can dissuade her father?"

"We really didn't have a chance to discuss it in detail. We were interrupted—by none other than the gentleman himself," Slade said in a bitter tone.

One shapely knee slipped between the edges of her dressing gown as Joella unfolded her legs and rose from the sofa. Her bare feet made no noise as she

111

crossed the luxurious expanse of Aubusson carpet on a path gauged to intercept her guest's restless wanderings. Hesitantly she placed her hand on Slade's arm to stop his pacing.

"Did you ever stop to consider that the two of them come from the same social level, that they might be far more appropriately paired than you think? Perhaps you're worrying about something that's totally beyond your control. Why . . . why don't we just forget about the both of them?" she asked in a soft voice.

Slade looked down at her hopeful face and felt sadness wash through him. He sighed and reached to run his fingers gently down the smooth flesh of her cheek.

"Ah, Ellie," he said, reverting to his own personal diminutive form of her name. "Sometimes I wish we could. But I can't do it. I can't—"

For the slightest moment, Joella turned her head, pressing her face against the warmth of his hand. Then, forcing a bright smile to her lips, she pulled away.

"Yes, I know," she said. "It didn't work the first time. It probably wouldn't work now. And why spoil a wonderful friendship in the process of finding out? You're right, of course."

Back stiff with barely concealed disappointment, she moved back toward her place on the sofa.

"Ellie—"

She ignored his plea. "Well!" she said with false brightness. "Perhaps we'd better move on to a different subject."

Slade ruffled the dark shock of hair falling across

his forehead with long, lean fingers. "Yes, of course. I'm sorry. I got so caught up in my own problems for the moment that I forgot everyone else's. I should have thought to ask sooner."

"It's understandable."

"Have you heard anything from Harris?"

"Word came this morning. They're going to try to bring two more through about three days from now. I was going to send word to you later today."

Slade took his place in the big overstuffed chair and filled his glass once again. Raising the glass, he took a long drink of the amber liquid. "Guess that means I'd better get ready for another midnight ride."

Chapter Six

Slade was grateful for the steady stream of customers who appeared at the store the next day. It helped keep his mind off the sleepless night he'd spent and the nagging headache he suffered from because of too much Silver City whiskey . . . but most of all, it helped dull his constant worries about Glory.

Knox dropped by in the late afternoon to tell him about another League meeting to be held at his house on Saturday night. "How about it? Can we count on you to be there?"

"I suppose so," Slade agreed, not so much because he wanted to attend the meeting but simply because it would fill his empty hours. He knew there'd be no chance to see Glory on that night . . . the Ladies' Auxiliary was planning a bazaar at the church to raise funds for the militia. Glory and her family were sure to be in attendance because the Colonel never missed the chance for a public appearance.

Slade could almost see him now. Strutting like a

peacock among the other attending dignitaries of the county—Bourland, Young, Hudson, Diamond—waiting for just the right moment to make a donation of suitable amount to inspire his constituents to proper awe.

The whole town was invited but Slade had no intention of attending. Not when he was positive Harper would be escorting Glory to the function.

Slade gave an irritated shake to clear his head of the disturbing picture and pushed away from the counter he'd been leaning against. Barely listening to what Knox was saying, his gaze swept the room, searching for something to do—anything to keep his body busy and his mind dulled with activity.

"Glad to hear it," Knox replied. "Dunlap and Simmons should be back by then. They've been scouting the area and talking with some of the outlying members. Once they return, we'll have a better idea of how many people we can count on in case of trouble."

"Fine, fine," Slade mumbled in answer to Knox's statement. After hearing the news, he almost regretted agreeing to attend the meeting. Personally, he hadn't cared much for the two Kansans, but he felt it wasn't his place to voice such misgivings. Knox knew the men far better than Slade did.

For lack of anything better, Slade shifted the barrels fronting the counter and swept beneath them for the second time that week. The store had never been so clean, so organized. What energy Slade didn't expend in the store, he applied to the needs of the farm.

Things were going to be a bit rough out there soon. Morgan had been ordered to report to his militia unit the first of September, just a matter of days now. That would make them short-handed out at the house. At thirteen and ten, Jeff and Paula were big enough to help in the fields and the barn but too young to be left at the farm alone for long periods of time.

The family had fallen into a comfortable pattern over the past four years, with Morgan mostly responsible for the farm while Slade ran the store with the help of Mr. Cranford. In the beginning, Anson Hunter had worked side by side with Slade, but as his wife's hold on life grew weaker, the elder Hunter had spent more and more time tending her. Her death had plunged him into a black depression that Slade and Morgan had begun to fear was permanent.

Much to the two older boys' relief, the head of the Hunter clan had recently shown some improvement in attitude. Slade couldn't help but wonder how much the gentle attention of Mrs. Stafford, the widow from the neighboring farm who kindly watched over Jeff and Paula when necessary, had to do with Anson's renewed interest in life. More frequently of late, Anson would take the two youngest children and spend an occasional day at Mrs. Stafford'ss — to repay her for watching the children by performing a few of the heavy chores, or so he said. Slade cared little what excuses his father gave for the visits as long as the elder Hunter's spirits continued to improve.

Toward the end of his mother's illness, Slade had

been lucky enough to hire Mr. Cranford to help out at the store. Ever cheerful and industrious, the debonair elder gentleman had proven his worth time and again. No longer did a particularly tedious, late-running day at the store force Slade to sleep on the cot in the small storeroom. Thereafter, he stayed over out of choice, not necessity.

Months later, the family's familiarity with Slade's occasional all-night absences proved invaluable on the rare nights when a message was received from Joella. The next relay post was just close enough that Slade could lead his charges to it and return before dawn. He'd suffered some long, sleepy days at the store, but so far no one had even suspected what he and Joella were up to. Slade intended to keep it that way.

However, tonight Slade knew he'd best get out to the house early and get a good night's sleep. There'd be no such opportunity tomorrow night if things went according to plan.

Prodding the flanks of his horse with his heels, Slade guided Diablo into the yawning black depths of the barn. The sudden loud rustling of hay in a far corner spooked the big bay and he nickered and crabbed sideways in the darkness. Slade tightened his hold on the reins; his hand automatically going to his gun.

"Who's there?" he called out.

"It's only me," a deep voice answered.

A tall form moved out of the darkness, stopping

long enough to strike a match and put it to the lantern hanging on a bent nail protruding from the back wall. A small golden circle of light blossomed in the shadows, leaving the rest of the barn veiled in hazy shades of gray.

"Morgan." Slade breathed a sigh of relief at the sight of the familiar figure and lowered his hand. "I thought you'd be in the house by now. It's too dark out here to still be working."

Morgan, a somewhat shorter, broader version of his younger brother, moved toward Slade. After Slade dismounted, Morgan reached to help him unsaddle his horse.

"I wasn't working . . . just sitting out here where it's quiet, so I could think."

"Kids giving you a bad time?" Slade asked, throwing the saddle over a rail. He filled Diablo's feedbin while Morgan rubbed the horse down.

"Nah, no more than usual. Paula's finally over that little touch of fever. They've just been restless. Pa finally threatened to eat Jeff's share of dessert if he didn't settle down and do his lessons."

Slade laughed. "I guess that convinced him. I know how much Jeff loves Mrs. Stafford's chocolate cake."

"Yep. It did the trick all right. You know, it's nice to see Pa and the kids cutting up again — acting like they used to."

"I know. It's been a long time."

"Since Mama died," Morgan said softly. "There, for a while, I didn't think things would ever be right again. The kids were so bewildered . . . and Pa,

118

withdrawing like he did."

"You still miss her, don't you?" Slade asked his brother.

"Ma? Sure, but I guess we all do." Morgan shook his head sadly. "Pa was so sure she'd get better when he got her out of that cold northern climate . . . so positive that Texas was the promised land."

"Except for the fact that it didn't help Mama, it's been pretty good for us here. Don't you think so?"

"Yeah, I guess it's been all right." Morgan draped a muscular arm over the top rail of the stall and looked at Slade with keen interest. "But don't you ever miss home?"

Slade looked up in surprise. "Not really. Oh, I guess I did at first, but this is home now. There are people here that I care about very much."

"Do you ever think what it would be like if we'd stayed up North? If Pa hadn't sold the store and spent most of the money on every fool quack doctor that came along trying to make Mama well? Or if we'd just come to Texas a couple of years sooner, with enough cash reserves to live like we did back home?"

Slade shrugged. "Why dwell on something that's over and done with? Something you can't change no matter what? Pa did what he had to do. That's how it is when you love someone. You do every damn thing you can to make things right for them. But sometimes it just doesn't work out the way you want."

Slade frowned, not liking the direction his thoughts were taking. It reminded him too much of the obstacles facing him and Glory. If he *really* loved her, would he fight for her? Or should he give her up?

Tormented once again with the same relentless questions, Slade moved restlessly about the barn. Morgan watched quietly as his younger brother took a piece of harness down and checked it, then stalked over to the corner and unnecessarily began restacking crates.

"No," Slade finally said as he tried to work off his frustrations. "I don't think about any of that. I just try to make the best of what we've got now."

"Well, I think about it."

Turning quickly, Slade gazed at his brother with sudden awareness. Why hadn't he noticed the weary look to Morgan's eyes before? And the thin worry lines etched along the side of his mouth?

"What's wrong?" Slade asked quietly.

Morgan strolled with deceptive casualness over to the far corner of the barn where the clean hay had been stored. He studied the tumbled pile intently, finally selecting a long, pale yellow blade and placing it in the corner of his mouth. Propping his hips against the low rail of the bin, he gazed at his brother. The end of the straw stem trembled slightly as he nibbled unconsciously at the portion caught between his strong white teeth.

"I'm going home."

"You're what?" The words exploded from Slade. "North? You mean you're going back North?"

"Yes."

"But why?"

Morgan jerked the hay from his lips and threw it to

120

the ground. "Lord, Slade, I thought you'd understand. We've talked about this often enough in the past. I've run out of time. You know I'm supposed to report to Young's unit pretty soon. But I'm not going to fight for slavery. I can't. If I have to fight, I'm going back and fight for what I believe in."

"Christ," Slade said softly, realizing that Morgan meant what he said. That soon he'd be gone and there was every chance in the world that they'd never see each other again.

"Does Pa know?"

"No."

"Are you going to tell him?"

"Not now."

"When are you going?"

"I guess when I pack up to join the unit. Instead of reporting in, I'll just keep going. No one will be the wiser. It may be weeks or months before anyone realizes I'm gone. If the family doesn't know, then they can't get in trouble later because of what I've done." Morgan shrugged. "It'll make things simpler."

Slade watched his brother with new respect. He had often wrestled the same demon. Would he have the courage to stand up for what he believed in if circumstances demanded? He knew he felt much the same as Morgan. He also didn't want to fight for an unjust cause. But he couldn't go "home." Texas was home to him now. Texas was where Glory was.

"Can I count on you to keep this to yourself?" Morgan asked.

"You know you can."

Morgan smiled and pushed away from the rail.

Throwing his arm around Slade's shoulders, he said, "Come on, let's go inside. Pa should have supper just about ready. And the kids are eager to see you."

Together they walked through the Indian summer warmth of the night toward the beckoning glow of the small frame house.

"Slade!" Paula let the silverware she'd been distributing around the table fall in a tumbled heap and ran to give her brother a boisterous hug. "We missed you last night."

"Well, I missed you, too," he replied, tugging playfully at the long black braids that lay on her thin shoulders.

Slade's heart gave a little lurch. She looked so much like their mother. Lord, when had she grown so tall? It seemed only yesterday when she'd barely come up to his belt buckle. Just another year or two and the little girl angles and awkwardness would be gone, giving way to the same willow-slender figure that their mother had possessed. Already he had noticed an occasional hesitation in her usual exuberant ways. The cheery youngster who'd always been eager to wrestle and romp was becoming more demure, and perhaps just a bit self-conscious of the changes her body was undergoing.

Contentment filled Slade as he gazed around the largest room of the house, always soothing and a haven of comfort to him. Unconsciously he compared the house with those belonging to their neighbors. The Hunters' home was furnished much nicer than most frontier farm houses because the family had brought many of their furnishings with them

122

when they moved to Texas. Therefore they enjoyed artistically crafted tables and comfortable uphol- stered sofas and chairs, while other farm families made do with rough-hewn plank furniture and rag- quilted cushions.

Reminders of the late Mrs. Hunter's touch were present in the lace curtains that covered the windows and in the framed photographs hanging on the wall. Her dearly loved knickknacks still graced the mantel- piece and occasional tables.

"How're things at the store, Slade?" questioned Anson Hunter from his place before the stove. He lifted the lid on a big kettle and gave the contents one last stir. The savory aroma of the stew — garden-fresh vegetables and seasoned meat in thick brown gravy — wafted through the room, setting Slade's mouth to watering.

"Fine, Pa. Need some help?"

"Nope. Everything's done. Jeff, you can get the biscuits out of the oven and put them on the table," Anson instructed his youngest son. The elder Hunter was tall and slim. His once jet-black hair had grayed considerably the last two years, further proof of his suffering since the death of his wife.

"Yes, sir." The tall, gangly youth discarded the stick he'd been whittling on and moved quickly to do his father's bidding. The familiar dark looks of the family had been repeated once again in the youngest boy.

"Get washed up, boys," Anson told his two oldest sons.

Slade and Morgan hung their hats on pegs by the

123

front door and then stepped to the kitchen area of the big room. Slade hefted the galvanized tin bucket and tilted it until clear fresh water gurgled out into a shallow blue-speckled porcelain basin. With neat, efficient motions the brothers washed their hands and splashed the dust from their faces. Morgan finished first. Pulling a soft worn square of cloth from the nail over the counter, he quickly dried and then passed the towel to Slade.

Moments later, the family was seated around the table, plates full of tasty hot stew. The pan of golden brown biscuits was passed from hand to hand, followed by a bowl of sweet cream butter and the crock of wild plum jam.

Slade paused in his eating to survey his family. What lay in store for the people dearest to his heart? Morgan would soon disappear from their lives to face the danger and uncertainties of war.

And what about Anson? Was he too caught up with the League? Should Slade try to discourage him from becoming so involved? No, probably not. Hopefully, his father's attention would turn more and more toward the farm next door. Lately Slade was tempted to credit Mrs. Stafford rather than the League for the spring in Anson's step, the cheery note to his voice.

The widow or the League, either or both, Slade didn't care. He just didn't want his father to lapse back into the bitter mood that had held him after their mother's death. There was really nothing to fret about. Mrs. Stafford was a sweet, kind woman, and the League seemed harmless enough. All their plans revolved around passive resistance to the secesh movement. If it gave his father something to believe in, then Slade had to approve.

Slade wasn't so sure about his own involvement with the League. His worries about Glory left him precious little enthusiasm to expend on meetings and mutterings. But he supposed he'd participate now and then; at least it provided him with a way to pass the time.

And what about Jeff and Paula? Except for the loss of their mother, life in Texas had been good for the family . . . at least until all this war business had started. What was going to happen to the kids now? They didn't have the firm convictions about slavery that their older brothers had. They were far too young to understand most of what was happening. But was this crazy war going to endanger them?

Would the fighting last long enough for Jeff to be called up to the militia? Was there any chance the government in Austin could be pressured to rescind the conscript law before Jeff could be affected? A lot of people in the state were upset about the law, and many of them had written letters or made personal trips to the capital to protest. Slade had certainly signed his share of petitions declaring opposition to the unfair law.

Paula's silvery laugh rang out in response to something Jeff said. Slade smiled as the familiar little dimples appeared in her cheeks. His heart contracted as he wondered who would take care of Paula if anything happened to the rest of them.

Slade dipped his spoon slowly into the cooling

broth. His head reeled. Heaven knew he had enough concern right here at home. And then there was Joella's crusade. And, last but certainly not least, Glory. He sighed softly and sat his spoon down beside his plate, his appetite suddenly gone.

Where would it all end?

Chapter Seven

"You better hurry up, chile. That nice Mr. Harper is here already," Violet admonished Glory as the girl continued to dawdle in front of the mirror.

"Oh, drat!" Glory moaned. She took one last sip of her cocoa and let the cup clatter back into the saucer. "It's simply too early for civilized people to be up and about. Whatever possessed me to agree to go with Preston?" She sighed loudly.

"It don't matter now, chile. You said you'd go and you're going." Violet stuck a few more pins among the upswept curls topping Glory's head and stood back to survey her handiwork. Her gaze met Glory's obstinate eyes in the mirror. "Now, you might as well get that look off your pretty little face, right now. You know what the Colonel will say if you don't hurry."

Glory rolled her eyes in exasperation. "Goodness gracious, Violet, I'm getting ready, aren't I? Quit fussing at me! Where is Preston, anyway?"

Violet's lips thinned. She crossed her arms over her

bosom and gave Glory a censoring look. "Mr. Harper is in the study, talking with your father. That'll hold them for a while. Them two always got their heads together talking about something! But it still won't give you much spare time." Her foot tapped a nervous tattoo against the polished wood floor. Glory recognized the familiar warning sign of the woman's waning patience.

Somewhat mollified, she cast a contrite look Violet's way. "I know. I'm sorry I spoke sharply to you."

Glory wasn't angry at Violet. She was perturbed with herself for letting the situation with Preston run on and on. She should have been able to put a stop to it by now. But nothing she said or did seemed to make the slightest dent in his determination. And her father kept going on and on about the presumed nuptial agreement. The fact that he would allow Glory to accompany Preston on an all-day outing unchaperoned spoke volumes about the Colonel's resoluteness that the two would wed. The whole thing was out of hand and for once Glory didn't know what to do.

Heavens above! Why had she committed herself to a whole day with Preston? It would take hours for them to travel to Sivells Bend, inspect Preston's reportedly fine new house, and return to Gainesville. She knew what he was trying to do. He'd dropped little hints often enough about the house being their future home. How like the man to be vain enough to think she'd take one look at the fancy dwelling and fall all over herself to set a wedding date.

Well, he was in for a big surprise. Seeing his lavish house wasn't going to change her mind one whit. She wouldn't want the man even if he lived in a castle.

Glory stood and let Violet slip a gown of royal blue sateen over her head. The full skirt snagged on the yards-wide hoop-supported petticoats and Violet bent to adjust the fabric.

Yesterday, when Glory agreed to the trip, it had seemed the smart thing to do. The entire day would afford her ample time to disillusion the indomitable Mr. Harper about her suitability as his bride. Now the prospect merely seemed tiresome. How much lovelier it would be to spend those hours with Slade.

Glory sighed again. Life was far too complicated of late.

"Glory . . . are you listening to me?" Violet's voice broke through her reverie.

"Umm? What?" Glory's eyes lost their misty glaze and sought the servant's stern visage. "What did you say, Violet?"

"I said you'd better take your umbrella. It's going to be warm out there. It'll protect your complexion. Don't want my honey chile to get sunburned or freckled, now do we?"

"No, of course not," she murmured. Glory glanced in the mirror, her attention automatically focusing on the faint dusting of pale gold freckles gracing the bridge of her nose.

She recalled an afternoon one long-ago summer when Slade had assured her how much he liked those self-same freckles. Then he had ever so tenderly brushed a kiss across each and every one before claiming her lips. Small shivers of excitement ran through Glory at the memory.

She gave herself an inward shake. Why dwell on

such matters now? It only made her more miserable. She might as well face what lay ahead and get it over with as painlessly as possible.

While Glory moped about the coming excursion, downstairs in the study Colonel Westbrook was imparting electrifying news to Preston Harper.

"Start at the beginning, Robert," Preston requested in response to the Colonel's opening remark, the threads of a bold scheme already forming in his mind. "Tell me everything that Bourland told you. Everything that happened, right from the first. Don't leave out one word."

Oratory being one of his favorite pastimes, the Colonel proceeded to tell Preston what his good friend James Bourland had imparted to him only last night. "You're aware of who J.B. McCurley is?"

"Not that I recall," Preston replied.

"He's a local farmer, but he also carries the mail from Gainesville to Denton."

"Yes, of course." Preston nodded his head, finally connecting the name with a vague remembrance of the man in question.

"A couple of nights ago, McCurley wound up at the hotel in the company of Ephraim Childs. Both had apparently been drinking. Childs made some comment about McCurley being 'a good Union man' and he asked him if he knew about a secret pro-Union organization in the area. When McCurley replied that he knew nothing about any such association, Childs offered to introduce him into this secret society and have his brother, Dr. Henry Childs, conduct the initiation."

"Interesting. Go on."

"McCurley claims Childs told him that this 'Union League,' as the organization is called, is spreading rapidly, with members throughout Cooke County and the surrounding area. He even alluded to a plan to seize the stores of gunpowder in Gainesville and at the arsenal in Sherman."

"Good Lord!" Shocked at the implication of this statement, Preston paused a moment to flick a speck of dust from his impeccable buff-colored linen trousers. "Then what happened?"

"McCurley told Childs he'd have to think about it. The next day he hightailed it straight to Hudson and, of course, Bourland."

"And what did those gentlemen have to say about the situation?"

"They persuaded McCurley to agree to the initiation. So McCurley rode out to Henry Childs' on the pretext of looking for some lost livestock. It didn't take him any time at all to get the conversation going in the right direction. Childs was more than willing to talk about the League. In very short course, McCurley took the oath and was sworn into the first degree—"

"First degree?" inquired Preston. "What does that mean?"

"I'm not really sure. Seems there're several steps of initiation. Childs hinted that each one makes you privy to more essential information regarding the League's plans."

"How soon can McCurley be initiated in those higher degrees?"

Westbrook shook his head. "Well, we have a little problem about that."

"What?"

"McCurley got scared about that time. He refused to take the next initiation steps. He made some haphazard excuse and left as soon as he could—"

"Damn!"

"I know. But at least he returned to Bourland's to tell him what he'd learned."

Preston shook his head. "Amazing story. How long has this conspiracy supposedly been going on?"

"They say a year or so." The Colonel pinned Preston with a sharp look. "How much truth do *you* think there is to what McCurley said?"

"I would presume there's a thread of truth to the tale. The organization must exist. Why would Childs, or McCurley for that matter, make up such a story? But as far as the alleged number of members . . . now that's a different matter. The count could be correct or it could be pure fabrication." Preston's voice was clear and concise despite the fact that thoughts of how to best use the information were swirling in his head.

As they spoke, Glory was reluctantly descending the staircase. Her small kid slippers made almost no noise as she crossed the wide hallway. Nearing the study she could hear the indistinct rumble of male voices. She raised her hand to knock on the door, but just as she leaned forward her full skirt brushed against the wooden panel, pushing it open a tiny crack.

"It really doesn't matter, does it? Either way, it appears to me that we may finally have those damn Unionists right where we want them."

Glory hesitated. The Unionists? Whatever was

Preston talking about?

"What are you suggesting," she heard her father ask.

"I do have an idea, but first tell me what Bourland and Hudson have in mind," Preston requested.

Hudson? Bourland? Glory frowned. They had to be talking about General William Hudson, the commanding officer of the district, and Colonel James Bourland, the man in charge of the Frontier Regiment.

She knew Bourland's name well. He was known to be a ruthless Confederate partisan, besides being one of the largest slaveowners in the county. Glory remembered Slade saying something about Bourland and some other planters manipulating the selection of delegates from Cooke County to the state convention on secession.

Glory could hear a rustling—probably her father rising from his desk to pace around the room, as was often his habit.

"Bourland's going to find someone else to infiltrate the organization—" The Colonel's voice lowered conspiratorially.

As Glory strained forward, trying to decipher the faint words, she lost her balance and stumbled against the door. It flew open and she stood framed in the doorway, face flushed, mouth open in surprise.

"Glory!" The Colonel's eyebrows were a dark slash on his furrowed brow. "How long have you been there, child?"

"Me?" she fairly squeaked. "Why, I just got here. Papa. I started to knock on the door. It . . . it must have been ajar because I'd no more than touched it

133

when it just popped open." She laughed nervously and smiled her most innocent smile.

"Oh. Ummphh! Well, come in, my dear, come in. Preston and I were just talking about the new cotton crop." The Colonel flicked a warning glance in Preston's direction. "We'll finish our discussion at a more convenient time."

"Of course."

Whew! thought Glory. Thank goodness they didn't suspect that she'd overheard part of their conversation.

Moving quickly into the room, she fretted over not having been able to learn more. Right now, very little of what she'd heard made sense. Unionists? Organizations? Suddenly all the intrigues and dangers of politics and war seemed much too close for comfort. It wasn't quite so easy to dismiss the war as being "something far away" when it might directly involve her hometown and the people she loved.

Drat! If only she'd had time to find out exactly what they were talking about. What in the world was Bourland planning? And who was infiltrating what organization?

How could she warn Slade if she didn't know if there was even anything to warn him about? She *had* to learn more. Tiny furrows of worry marred her brow as she remembered the dire tones of the overheard conversation. If this information had something to do with the Unionists, she had to be aware that it might mean trouble for Slade, too.

"Good morning, Glory." Preston's suave voice penetrated her worrisome thoughts. "You look extremely lovely this morning. Are you ready for our little excursion?"

Glory's mind whirled. No telling how long it would take her to discover the secret by eavesdropping on her father. He would certainly never tell her outright. But . . . what about Preston? Would it be possible for her to finagle any information out of him? Well, it was worth the effort. Perhaps this wouldn't be such a wasted day after all.

A forced smile tipped up the corners of her mouth, and she fluttered her long dark lashes in the most flirtatious manner her unwanted suitor had yet enjoyed. "Why, Preston. I'm so excited about our little outing, I can hardly bear it."

"Well!" Slightly surprised and more than a little pleased about Glory's unexpected enthusiasm, Preston drew himself up tall and straight, preening like a peacock, before offering her his arm. "In that case, my dear, let's be on our way."

Preston Harper's shiny black buggy rolled lightly along the narrow dirt road, easily devouring the miles between Gainesville and Sivells Bend, a small settlement to the north that had once been nothing more than the location of Simon Sivells's tiny store.

The victim of occasional bloody Indian raids, Sivells Bend had been alternately abandoned and resettled since its initial founding in 1850. By 1862, the community included a modest central cluster of homes as well as the grand plantations strung like a necklace of pearls along the banks of the Red River.

The Manion, Murrell, and Westbrook homes graced the steep banks overlooking the lower bends of the river. Preston's new house was located several miles past the other homes, between Sivells Bend and Horseshoe Bend. Other families, including the Overtons, Loves, Gaineses, and Burneys, lived across the river in what was actually Indian Territory.

Glory watched the powerful rump muscles bunch and slide under the sleek gray skin of Preston's matched pair of horses as the team maintained a steady pace across the gently rolling prairie land. All the while, her mind was searching for a way to turn the conversation in the necessary direction. If she could just get Preston to talking . . . talking about anything! . . . then perhaps he'd let something of importance slip.

Glory mentally squared her shoulders for the task ahead. Pasting a bright smile on her lips, she gave her small ruffled parasol a flirty little twirl and gazed up at Preston with rapt attention. "How much further, Preston," she questioned demurely. "I'm ever so anxious to see your house."

"It won't be long. Another mile perhaps. I had Pansey pack us a little picnic lunch. I thought it might be pleasant to eat on the front veranda. It's well shaded and should be cool."

"What a wonderful idea," Glory cooed. "You're so thoughtful."

A pleased little smile tugged at Preston's mouth. *She's coming around. I knew she would. It was just a matter of patience.* For the first time since he'd resolved to marry Glory Westbrook he began to feel secure about reaping the rewards he so desperately wanted.

Glory had been like quicksilver ever since that

136

night at dinner when her father had announced his somewhat premature blessings on their proposed union. Sometimes she seemed pliant enough, allowing Preston a quick flush of assurance that he could pull his plan off. Other times he caught a glimmer of such stubbornness in her that he worried about his ability to convince her to do as her father wished.

He'd known from the first that there would be obstacles to his plan. Winning Colonel Westbrook's approval had been only the first step. He still had to convince Glory to accept his proposal. Harper wasn't foolish enough to believe that the Colonel would actually force his cherished child to enter a union with a man she abhorred. He knew it would take time to woo Glory. After all, he was a veritable stranger to her.

Few young women would welcome marriage under such circumstances. Oh, arranged marriages were still common enough in Texas, but, for the most part, such young couples were usually at least familiar with one another before the wedding.

A healthy ego plus considerable past experience with women led Preston to believe in his eventual ability to elicit a positive response from Glory. He conveniently forgot that most of that experience was with women of considerably less social standing—not to mention sheer determination—than the Colonel's daughter.

Besides the usual barriers, Preston was still trying to decipher the key to Glory's personality. He often worried that he'd never discover what it would take to win her over.

He'd never met such a mercurial woman in his life.

One day she was a sweet woman-child, the classic picture of a simple-minded, butter-wouldn't-melt-in-her-mouth Southern lady; the next time she reminded him of the blue-stocking old maid schoolteacher back home, too educated for her own good. Occasionally she appeared to have all the makings to become a caustic, complaining harridan. It kept him hopping just to appear congenial to each of these changes in her personality.

Well, no matter. Preston was determined to weather any and all peculiarities Glory displayed. He was going to marry the Colonel's daughter, come hell or high water. With that marriage would come a great deal of additional wealth, which he would soon need after the vast expenditures for the new house. Such a union would also assure his enhanced social standing in the county.

It wasn't too soon to be thinking of the future. The Colonel was getting old. When the reins of power were passed, Preston was going to make damn sure they were placed in his hands.

"There it is," Preston said as the buggy rounded one last bend in the road and the almost completed house came into view.

Glory perused the imposing structure. Two stories of white-washed framework, surrounded by a wide veranda on three sides. Sunlight sparkled brilliantly off the glass windowpanes. Shading it with mammoth limbs, stately old oak trees surrounded the building.

Preston viewed the dwelling with pride. The finishing touches had yet to be completed, and delivery of the furnishings had been delayed because of the war.

Still, Preston hoped to be in residence by the first of the year. Now, if he could only convince Glory to agree to a Christmas wedding, all would be perfect.

"It's lovely, Preston," Glory stated truthfully. The house *was* beautiful, but she had no desire to share it with the man seated beside her. She would gladly turn down its opulence and grandeur for the simple loving atmosphere of Slade's frame farmhouse any day.

However, now was not the time to ponder such choices. She could little afford for Preston to become suspicious of her true feelings at this point. Not until she had an opportunity to ferret out all possible information about the Unionists and whatever Bourland was planning.

Worrisome thoughts plagued Glory. Bourland had a reputation for meanness. There was no telling what devilment he had in mind. She *must* discover if Slade would in any way be endangered.

There was one bright thought in her mind, a possible bonus to the situation. When she presented Slade with the information—information she had obtained for him while valiantly ignoring the possible risks to herself—wouldn't that prove how little she cared about the political differences that separated their families? What a splendid way to manifest her undying devotion to him!

She could almost picture the way Slade would respond . . . with grateful kisses and caresses, and small loving rebukes about her foolhardy but brave determination to venture into danger for his sake.

Preston looped the reins around the upright whip lodged firmly in its holder and stepped down from the buggy. He glanced at his passenger just as profound pleasure from her rather dramatic musings began to glow on her face.

When Preston reached an assisting hand toward Glory she continued to stare in blind rapture toward the house. He was quick to construe her entrancement as a sign that his excursion to Sivells Bend was indeed paying off.

"Come, my dear. Let me help you down," Preston prompted. He offered his hand again.

"What?" Glory said, rudely jolted out of her daydream. "Oh, yes. Of course. Thank you."

She rose, steadying herself against the edge of the buggy, and then allowed Preston to circle her waist and lower her to the ground.

A flash of disappointment filled her when she gazed upward into the face that was Preston's rather than Slade's. She quickly suppressed a frown and forced a coquetish smile as a reward for his aid.

From the space under the buggy seat Preston extracted a large woven basket. A snowy linen cloth covered the contents. Holding the handle with one slender-fingered hand, he grasped Glory's hand with the other.

"Come along, Glory. Before we have our meal let's see what the workmen have managed to do this week."

She allowed him to maintain his hold on her hand as she meekly followed him up the barely discernible path to the house. "I quite approve your design, Preston," she assured him, her voice sweet as molasses. "This is going to be a beautiful home."

"Why, thank you. By next spring this will all be

beautiful lawns and gardens," Preston explained, his gaze sweeping the tangled clearing surrounding the house.

"I'm sure everything will be perfect when it's completed. You have such impeccable taste," Glory forced herself to croon. She could almost see his chest swell in response to her honeyed words.

"Naturally I'm hoping for some suggestions from you, Glory. After all, some day this will be your home, too."

"Umm," Glory responded in a vague tone, adroitly sidestepping Preston's comment. She wasn't about to fall into his clever little word-trap by verbally agreeing to anything.

They climbed the steps leading to the broad, shaded veranda, and Preston bent to set the basket beside one of the fluted support columns.

"Shall we have a quick look at the inside before we see what delights Pansey has packed for us?"

"I'd just love to," Glory purred.

They made the rounds of the semifinished rooms, Preston pontificating on their future uses, Glory oohing and ahhing at proper intervals.

Back on the veranda, Preston dusted off the topmost step with his handkerchief before Glory settled on it. He chose a seat as close to her as possible.

Preston placed the basket in the small space between them. With deft fingers he unfolded the linen cloth and spread it out. A few more minutes and he had placed a bottle of wine and two crystal glasses on the cloth. Next he produced a variety of tasty tidbits, ranging from cheese to fruit to small flaky-crusted meat pies, from the basket's depths. Plates, ornate silverware, and a pair of crisp damask napkins followed.

Preston filled the plates with a small portion of each tasty treat. "Here you are, my dear," he said, handing Glory's to her. He filled the goblets and set hers at a convenient distance.

"Thank you, Preston. You must give Pansey my thanks for this lovely meal."

"I'll do that."

Glory knew that Preston presently lived in a rather small rented house in Gainesville, with only two servants in attendance. She gazed about the grounds but could see no evidence of permanent inhabitants. The slave cabins she had glimpsed through the back upstairs window had appeared only half finished.

"Where are the rest of your darkies, Preston?" she asked in a mildly puzzled tone.

"I've loaned them out to Bourland for the time being. His overseer will keep them whipped into shape until they're needed."

Glory frowned at his choice of words. Surely he didn't mean the statement literally, although Bourland did have a reputation for being harsh.

"I see," she murmured, not knowing what else she could safely say.

"Yes, until I'm ready to plant crops, they might as well be earning their keep somewhere else."

"Well, yes, I suppose that makes sense," Glory replied noncommitally.

"After all, this has been an expensive endeavor." Preston paused for a sip of wine. "I certainly don't need to feed more than a dozen mouths that aren't contributing to their own upkeep in some way. Besides, you can spoil slaves by giving them too much free time. Sets a bad precedent, you know. It's hard enough to get work out of them, as it is."

Glory wanted to protest that the Westbrook slaves had always worked willingly enough. Perhaps Preston expected too much of his people. She certainly couldn't visualize Slade having such a heartless attitude if he owned slaves. But, of course, Slade never would. A tiny frown furrowed her brow. Maybe there was more to what Slade said than she'd realized.

Glory'd never given it much thought before. Her family had always treated their people kindly. The slaves were well fed and well dressed. They received proper doctoring when necessary, and Glory had never known one to be whipped. It came as rather a shock to realize there might be people who possibly did not treat their slaves in the same kindly manner. The thought troubled her more than she would ever have expected, certainly more than it would have just a few short days ago.

Watching Glory take a dainty bite from a wedge of cheese, Preston felt almost intoxicated with self-satisfaction. The day was progressing splendidly. Glory seemed properly impressed by the house. He was sure he could soon press his suit and receive a positive answer to his proposal.

Preston was inordinately pleased with what he was about to accomplish. Luck was on his side and he had chosen well. Glory would make an excellent wife. Thank God, she had turned out to be beautiful and poised, as well as amply doweried by her wealthy father. She would make a "proper" wife who would run his home in a suitable manner and present him with offspring at regular intervals.

Love had nothing to do with Preston's determination to marry the Colonel's daughter. He would have done so no matter what she looked like. But he was selfish enough to be grateful that Glory was desirable as well as rich. Bedding her would be a pleasure. Young and healthy, she would bear him many fine sons. And if her response to his lovemaking proved disappointing, there was always Joella.

Once he had access to Glory's dowery, Preston was quite sure he'd be able to sway Joella to his way of thinking. He would purchase a small house at the edge of town—something quite nice—and install Joella there, where it would be convenient for him to visit often. And he'd have more than enough money to afford whatever luxuries she desired.

Preston felt sure he'd correctly interpreted her little game. All her coy little teasing was obviously aimed at making him want her more. Well, it had worked. Each day he grew more determined to have her. He vowed to make his offer so sweet she wouldn't be able to resist.

Surely by now Joella should be getting tired of struggling to provide for herself. With the war moving closer and closer, money in the county was apt to get harder to come by. Even the popular Silver City Saloon was bound to suffer financial setbacks sooner or later. Eventually, Joella would be grateful to accept an opportunity to be his mistress.

With Glory's imminent capitulation, Preston Harper would at last have access to everything he wanted.

And so the afternoon progressed, both of them

surreptitiously pursuing their prospective goals in a most unorthodox manner.

Glory flirted in her most charming way, continually trying to trick Preston into divulging more of what she'd overheard her father and him discussing in the study that morning. All the while her mind was aflutter with loving thoughts of Slade.

And meanwhile, Preston pressed his advantage whenever he could, seeking to convince Glory to become his wife. But even as the honeyed words of courting passed his lips, his mind was full of lustful thoughts of Joella.

Chapter Eight

Slade swung down from his horse as silently as possible. He left the lead lines of the two extra horses wrapped around his saddle horn and looped Diablo's reins over a small limb. On cat feet he crept toward the small deserted-looking shack, which was barely visible in the black velvet shadows of the night-shrouded woods. The crunch of his boots sounded alarmingly loud to him, and he concentrated harder on the careful placement of each foot.

Suddenly something rustled in the bushes off to the side and he stopped, standing stone-still for a long moment, hand resting tensely against the polished butt of his gun.

Some animal, he finally decided. A rabbit, maybe even a coyote. But not a man. No one had followed him to the meeting place.

The clouds shifted in the starless sky, and a fat half moon peeped out from behind its wispy curtain. Pale silver beams of moonlight speared through the gently swaying tree limbs, painting fairy circles of light at random intervals throughout the small clearing.

Once again Slade began to walk toward the gray

silhouette of the cabin, his movements slow and deliberate. A tendril of greenbriar vine snagged on his pant leg. "Damnation!" he muttered under his breath, and he halted long enough to disengage the wicked thorn from the fabric. Once free, he moved on.

Still several yards from the dark abandoned building, he stopped and emitted a low whistle — three soft notes, a long pause, and then two notes.

He waited.

Nothing.

He advanced another few steps and repeated the signal.

The answer finally sounded, almost undecipherable — low, shaky, fearful.

Slade closed the remaining distance to the shack. He edged up to the building, putting his back to the rough boards just to the side of the lopsided door. Carefully he twisted, reaching over to push the rotting plank panel open with his left hand, prudently keeping his right close to his gun. His heart kerthumped against his ribs when the long unoiled hinges screeched loudly in protest. He waited for the eerie sound to fade before speaking.

"Anybody there?"

No one answered.

"Come on out," Slade instructed in a low voice.

Small, shuffling noises sounded within. Slade waited.

"Come on," he prompted again. "It's safe."

Finally, two tense figures edged through the narrow opening.

"What are your names?" Slade queried.

"Ah's Elias, suh," the tallest man said with a nod of his woolly head.

"And I be called Moses," answered the other.

They were young, barely out of their teens, and obviously very afraid. They stood close together as if trying to draw strength and comfort from each other's bodies. In the wavering shadows of the clearing the whites of their liquid black eyes were large with alarm.

"Everything all right?"

"Yes, suh," they said again, heads bobbing to punctuate their answer.

"Seen anyone prowling about? Any sign of the militia?"

"Nah, suh, ain't seen a soul," Elias answered quickly.

"What about your master? Do you think he's got someone looking for you yet?"

"Don't know, suh. But we come a powerful far piece since we started out. Mayhap he can't track us this far." There was more plea than statement to Elias's last comment.

"Good enough." Slade expelled the breath he'd been unconsciously holding. "How long have you two been here?"

"Since last night. We been real quiet. Just stayed inside like that other man what brung us told us to do."

"You did exactly right. Are you hungry? I've got cornbread and bacon in the saddlebags. A change of clothes, too."

"Much obliged."

"Tonight you'll be at a safe house. You'll be able to

148

wash up, and even sleep a little more comfortably before you're moved on."

"That'd be mighty kind of you, suh," Elias replied.

"Well, we'd better get on our way. We have a fair distance to cover tonight. And I have to be back in Gainesville by sunup."

"Yes, suh, we's ready to go."

"Do you have anything you want to take with you?" Slade thought to ask.

"Nah, suh," Elias answered with quiet dignity. "Just what we got on our backs. We had to leave everything else behind—"

"Don't matter," Moses interjected with a shrug. "Didn't have much of nothin' anyhows."

"All right, let's be on our way."

The two runaways followed Slade across the clearing and through the woods to the three patiently waiting horses. Diablo snuffled a greeting when he smelled his master.

Slade paused long enough to dig the paper-wrapped food packets out of the saddlebags for the two hungry men, and then all three mounted up. Swaying atop their horses, the two hungry men tore the paper open and began to munch on the parcels' contents.

A lone owl hooted far off in the distance. Lacy gray clouds scudded back across the bright face of the moon.

Single-file, the trio of riders disappeared into the darkness.

Slade was bone-tired when he returned to Gainesville. The town was still shrouded in gunmetal gray shadows. Far off, at the very edge of the horizon, the tiniest smudges of rose and coral bespoke the impending coming of dawn.

With only the gentle thump of Diablo's hooves against the dirt surface to break the stillness of the dawn, he rode through the silent streets. Relieved to spot only an occasional glow of lamplight behind curtained windows, Slade let the breath he'd been holding seep slowly out. Thank God, it was much too early for most of the community's residents to be up. He'd make it to the Silver City Saloon long before people began to leave their homes and head for work.

Luck had been with him, and once again no one would be the wiser about his mission.

Minutes later, Slade secured Diablo to the hitching post at the side of the saloon and crept up the back stairs to Joella's private entrance. One soft tap on her door and it was carefully eased open. He cast one last searching look up and down the dark deserted expanse of Dixon Street and then slipped quickly inside.

The room was dark. Joella clicked the lock on the door and padded quietly to the center of the room, where she struck a match and lighted the small lantern on the table. She left the wick low, so that the room was still shadow-shrouded despite the feeble yellow flame.

"Everything go all right?" she finally turned to question, a worried look marring the ivory perfection of her brow. Both were oblivious to the fact that Joella wore only a thin silk wrapper over her lacy

150

nightgown.

"Yeah. No problems. I delivered them safely into Louis Jetter's hands. He'll shelter them for a couple of days . . . let them get rested up . . . before moving them on to the next house. With luck, they'll reach the North within a month."

Joella expelled a sigh of relief. "Thank goodness. I was worried about this trip. I know Bourland and Hudson have had the militia out patroling more frequently lately. I just can't shake the feeling that something's not quite right."

Slade frowned at the comment, his brows slanting down like the dark wings of a hawk in flight. "No one's let anything slip down in the saloon? No rumors? No hints about what might be going on?"

"No, not yet. Perhaps I'm being silly. Maybe there's nothing to be afraid of. I don't know. I just keep wondering if they've somehow got wind of what we've been doing."

"Well, at least it's over with for this time." Slade slumped wearily against the wall, passing a hand over his beard-roughened face. "I think we're still safe for now."

"Slade!" Joella exclaimed softly, eyes large with concern. "How thoughtless of me. Here I am, just prattling on and on, and you're worn out. I'm sorry. I should have paid more attention. That's a long ride and you've had no sleep. Do you want some coffee? Something to eat?"

"Nah. Right now all I want is a few hours of sleep. But I'm afraid if I lay down in the back room at the store I won't wake up soon enough. If I don't have the store open by the usual hour, someone might start asking questions. I sure don't want to raise anyone's suspicions by not following my normal routine."

"Of course not."

"I should have asked Cranford to come in early. All I need is for some busybody to show up this afternoon and find me dead-to-the-world asleep. That would certainly prompt some comments." Slade chuckled wryly at the thought. "And right now I'm too damned tired to think up anything even resembling a decent explanation."

"I know you are."

"Better get going, I guess." Slade pushed himself away from the wall and raised his hand, ready to set his dusty hat back on his head.

A determined look crossed Joella's face. "No. Wait. I can fix your problem. Come on." She crossed the room, the lacy hem of her robe swirling around her bare ankles. Clasping his hand in hers, she urged him along behind her.

"What are you doing?"

Joella pulled him through the wide doorway to her bedroom. Dropping his hand, she turned to face him, hands on her slim hips.

"You get in that bed, right now," she instructed, nodding at the sleep-tumbled four-poster she had just vacated.

"Nah, Joella, I'd better not—"

"You can stop protesting right now," she said with a perverse little grin. "There's no need to say a thing. Your 'virtue' is safe with me."

"Ah, Ellie, I know that. I just don't want to cause you any trouble."

152

"No trouble at all. Now pull those boots off and lay down. I'll make sure you're awake in time to get to the store. Now, listen here, Slade Hunter, don't you argue with me," she said sternly. Her eyes flashed dark green fire.

"Land sakes, woman, if you're going to be so stubborn, I wouldn't dream of it." A smile played at Slade's mouth. He leaned down and pressed an affectionate kiss on her forehead before tottering tiredly to the bed.

Sinking gratefully onto the feather mattress, he bent and pulled off first one scuffed boot and then the other. They dropped to the thick maroon carpet with soft twin thuds.

"Ahh," Slade murmured, stretching out full length on the bed. "My backside feels like it's been sitting in a saddle for weeks. Thanks. This feels wonder—" His eyes fluttered shut and a soft little snore escaped his lips.

Joella smiled fondly at the man in her bed. He looked almost boyish lying there against her pristine white sheets. An errant black curl dangled over his bronzed forehead. Long dusky eyelashes cast half-moon shadows on his cheeks, and coarse black stubble obscured the firm line of his jaw.

She fleetingly thought of crawling into bed with him, snuggling up to the long, muscular body, drawing warmth and comfort from his nearness. How wonderful it would be to wake up in his arms, instead of alone and lonely, just one time.

No. Better not. For a vast number of reasons, the least of which being the fact that she greatly valued this man's friendship. She lowered her head with a small sigh of regret, butter yellow curls swishing against the collar of her negligee.

"Being 'honorable' has definitely got its drawbacks at times," she muttered forlornly under her breath.

Resignation bathing her face, she crossed the few feet to the mahogany bedstead and carefully pulled the tangled covers from beneath Slade's legs. When she had worked them free of his weight, she pulled the sheet up over him.

With a deep sigh, Slade shifted slightly and snuggled deeper into the cushiony softness of the feather mattress.

Joella returned to the sitting room and quietly lowered herself into the big overstuffed chair beside the table. Slade's sleeping form was still visible through the wide doorway. She reached up and lowered the wick of the lantern. The flame flickered erratically and died, leaving the room in dove-gray shadow. Tucking her bare feet under the full tail of her robe, Joella leaned her head against the ivory crocheted antimacassar on the back of the chair and watched the gentle rise and fall of Slade's breathing.

A shower of small pebbles rained against Lydia's second-story bedroom window, softly clitter-clacking on the glass. When Lydia failed to respond, Glory repeated the act.

"Lydia, let me in!" she whispered loudly when the window was finally pushed open and a sleepy-eyed Lydia peered out the portal, blinking and shading her eyes against the early morning sun.

"Glory! What in the world are you doing?" she

called downward in a loud whisper. "Do you know what time it is?"

"Of course I do. Don't be a ninny. I need to talk to you. Please hurry up and let me in," Glory implored with an appealing look.

"I'm coming, Glory. I'll be right there," Lydia called down softly, recollecting years past and numerous other times when Glory had summoned her in much the same manner. Amusing memories tugged at her mind as she wondered what had induced Glory to once again travel the deserted back path between the two houses at such an early hour.

Lydia disappeared from the open window. Glory hiked up the skirt of her cocoa-colored dress and hurried to the Uptons' back door, arriving at almost the same moment Lydia clicked the lock.

"What's the matter?" Lydia questioned as soon as Glory was inside. She knew full well that Glory wouldn't be out at this time of day unless something exciting was going on.

"Shhh!" Glory placed a warning finger to her lips. "Not now. Let's get up to your room first."

Lydia's long white nightgown looked ghostly in the murky light of the stairwell as she ascended the stairs on silent, bare feet. Glory followed her, moving lightly on tiptoe, careful not to let the heels of her black kid slippers tap against the polished puncheon floor.

Once safely behind the closed door of Lydia's bedroom, Glory hurriedly told her friend what she'd overheard on the previous day.

Lydia's brow furrowed as she tried to decipher the portent of Glory's tale. "Umm," she murmured, tapping her finger against her chin. "Is that all?"

"All!" exclaimed Glory. "Good gracious! What more do you want?"

"But, Glory, you really don't know anything. You have no idea what Bourland's going to do—"

Glory cast an exasperated glance at her friend. "I told you, I tried to find out. I couldn't get a thing out of Preston." She flopped down on a corner of the bed and rolled her eyes heavenward. "Honestly, I simpered and cooed and clung until I wanted to scream. But it didn't do the least bit of good."

"Well, don't worry. I'm sure you'll find out eventually. You'll just have to be patient," Lydia advised in all seriousness.

"Patient" was a term that Glory was only vaguely familiar with. "Don't be ridiculous," she told Lydia. "I *have* to find out what they were talking about soon. I can't just sit around and wait. And whatever am I going to do about Preston? I'm afraid my little ploy was *too* convincing yesterday. Preston is talking marriage stronger than ever. Whatever shall I do?"

"Well, I'm sure *I* don't know," Lydia remarked, torn between mild feelings of amusement at Glory's theatrics and her long-ingrained awe of her best friend's uncanny ability to eventually extricate herself from the coils of any dilemma, no matter how dire the circumstances. "But I wouldn't worry about it too much if I were you. You always seem to manage somehow. I'm sure this time will be no different."

Glory sighed expressively. "I suppose you're right. I'll handle Preston somehow. Oh, well. I'll worry about that later. There are more important things to consider now." She gave a dainty, dismissing wave of her hand.

"See there," Lydia said. "You got all riled up over nothing. You could still be at home in bed . . ." Lydia smothered a big yawn. ". . . and so could I."

"Oh, no! We're not done yet." Glory jumped up and scampered to the other side of the room, pulling the door to Lydia's wardrobe open and beginning to rifle through the garments hanging there. "Which dress do you want, Lydia?"

"Dress? I don't need a dress now—"

"Yes, you do! We've got to get to the store and warn Slade. Regardless of how little I know at this point, I want to tell him about the conversation. He may be able to learn something himself, if he's aware that something's going on."

Vaguely familiar feelings of apprehension began to filter through Lydia. "I'm not so sure we ought to try that again. Remember, Glory, we almost got caught last time."

Heaven knew it would be bad enough if the Colonel did find out. But what if Glory couldn't work her usual magic in time to keep the Colonel from telling Mr. Upton what the two of them had been up to? Lydia's father had only recently admonished her about her behavior, sternly stating that Lydia was now far too old to get involved in any more of Glory's peccadilloes. Lydia hated to think how angry he would be that she had almost immediately disobeyed him.

"Heavens above, Lydia! It'll be safe enough," Glory declared, determination glowing in her sherry-colored eyes. "Papa had plans to ride over to Pilot Point early this morning. He's already gone. And

Mama's still asleep. I told Violet I was coming over here. She'll cover for me, if necessary. And you can have Mattie tell your folks that we've gone to my house."

"But, Glory—"

Glory yanked a pale green gown out of the closet and tossed it at her friend. "Will you please quit fidgeting? It's a perfect plan. They'll never check on us. And no one will ever know we went to town."

"Well—"

"Please, Lydia?" Glory pleaded. "Don't let me down now. Haven't we always stuck together?"

Lydia knew it was useless to argue. As always, Glory had but to instigate one of her wild escapades, and for reasons completely unfathomable, Lydia would routinely follow along. Reconciled to the inevitable, she pulled the batiste nightgown over her head and donned pantalets and chemise. Glory helped her put on a minimum number of petticoats and her dress.

"But what about Jacob? And won't your mama notice that the buggy is gone?" Lydia asked as she slipped the last button through its hole.

"We're not taking the buggy," Glory explained in a no-nonsense tone. "We can walk to town. It's only a few blocks. Mercy me! We could walk that distance any time. The only reason we take the buggy is because Papa thinks it's more proper and ladylike."

"Well . . . all right. I suppose that will work." Lydia slipped on a pair of comfortable slippers. If she was going to walk that far, she certainly wasn't going to wear her new higher heeled shoes.

"We really should hurry, Lydia," Glory urged fervently. "Come over here and let me help you put your hair up so we can get on our way."

Less than fifteen minutes later, the two young women were briskly wending their way down Pecan Street to where it intersected with Rusk.

"See, Lydia? What did I tell you? We haven't seen a soul. It's perfectly safe."

Lydia cast a quick glance up the deserted street. "But what about when we get to town? There's bound to be traffic on Dixon, or at least on Boggs."

"We won't go that way," Glory said with a determined nod of her head. "We'll go up Rusk and cut through the alley. It runs behind the stores for more than three blocks. It'll take us right to the back of Slade's store."

"Oh!" Lydia brightened considerably at this seemingly foolproof plan. "We can go in the back door! How clever you are, Glory." She shook her head in amazement. She had been afraid they would walk in the store's front entrance in brazen disregard of discovery.

The wide expansive lawns of the town's better houses gave way to smaller plots as they continued on their way. Another block, and hints of commerce were interspersed among the dwellings. Finally, Gainesville's market square stood only a block away.

"There!" Glory said triumphantly as she pointed toward the narrow entrance of the alley. "That's where we turn. Come on."

Without a shred of hesitation, Glory led the way into the shadowed narrow opening. Lydia gulped, plucked her skirts higher to avoid the foot-high weeds that grew along the sides of the alley, and followed her friend into the murky depths.

The alley twisted and turned its way along behind the stores fronting on Boggs Street. It was dark and deserted and dirty. Most of the buildings were of log construction. A few had back doors, others presented solid rough walls for the girls' perusal. Crates and boxes were stacked haphazardly behind some of the buildings, occasionally causing Glory and Lydia to have to pass single-file. Toward the end, they had to work their way around a pothole filled with greasy-looking water. Just ahead the alley intersected Dixon Street.

A few more steps and they were almost behind the last building. Even at this early hour they could see several horses hitched to the post at the far corner of the structure.

"Oh, no!" Lydia whispered in alarm as she came to a sudden halt. "We forgot where this leads, Glory. That's the saloon! We've got to go behind the Silver City Saloon to get out of the alley. Oh, dear, my pa'll skin me alive if he finds out I've been here."

"Shh! Don't take on so, Lydia!" Glory soothed. "No one will ever know. All we have to do is get across the street unseen and we'll be safe again. Then we'll only have to get past the Davenport Hotel and the dime store. Slade's place is right after that."

Suddenly, a low creak disturbed the quiet of their passage.

"What's that?" Lydia whispered in fright, dodging behind two barrels.

Glory quickly followed. They huddled behind the scant protection, hands clutching to bolster their badly shaken morale.

Pressing a finger to her lips, Glory warned in a shaky whisper, "I think it was just a door opening up there on that porch. Be still. They can't see us from here. We'll simply wait until they're gone."

The girls crouched behind the sheltering barrels, pressed tight against the rough-hewn wall.

Glory pointed at the sliver of light in front of them. "Peek through there and tell me what you see," she whispered in Lydia's ear.

"No! They might see us," Lydia protested in a tiny, squeaky voice.

"Fiddlesticks! Scoot back so I can see," Glory prompted. "How else will we know when the coast is clear?"

After they had carefully shifted places, Glory stood on tiptoe to peer through the slot of space between the curve of the barrels and the corner of the building.

"Can you see anything?"

Glory shook her head. "No. Looks like the door at the top of the stairs is open, but no one's come out yet."

"Oh, dear," moaned Lydia.

"Shh! Wait! I can see a shadow . . . someone's moving around."

Glory could feel the accelerated pace of Lydia's frightened breath warm against her back. She stood as still as she could, intently watching the landing at the top of the stairs. It was roofed and lattice-framed around two sides, making it hard to distinguish much in the shadows. Glory could barely discern two figures in the doorway. They were evidently talking, although she could hear nothing but a muted, indistinguishable murmur. Finally, the taller form moved toward the edge of the descending stairway — and into Glory's line of vision.

Slade! When the rush of surprise abated, Glory smiled with joy. What luck! She could hail Slade, tell him what was going on immediately. She wouldn't have to make the rest of the journey down the alley, wait at the back door of the store trying to get his attention, or worry about who might be inside.

Glory stepped from behind the barrels, hand raised in preparation to wave at Slade, who was still oblivious to her presence.

But then the second figure moved to the edge of the landing . . . and Glory's heart skipped a beat.

Early morning sunlight speared through the gloom of the alley to sparkle in the woman's long blond hair. An errant little breeze plucked at the hem of her thin, lacy robe. When she moved, the negligee gaped open, revealing the silk nightgown underneath. The pale rose color of the fabric tinted the woman's skin a pale pearly pink.

Glory knew immediately who the woman was. Not too long after her return to Gainesville, Glory had seen the beautiful blond woman ride by in a shining double-horse carriage. A question to her mother had prompted a horrified gasp and a sharp recommendation that Glory go see where her younger sisters were. Undaunted by her mother's refusal to assuage her curiosity, Glory had simply asked Lydia, who, thanks to the ever-present chain of gossip in small towns, knew of Miss Ashland's reputation.

Lydia, in a scandalized tone, had imparted all the shocking rumors about the Silver City Saloon and its

162

owner. Glory had thought Joella beautiful and mysterious, and all the more intriguing because of being "slightly wicked." But *never* in her wildest dreams would she have connected Slade with the woman.

Glory watched Slade's booted foot prepare to take the first step down the stairway that hugged the back of the building. Joella said something in a low voice, followed by silver-toned laughter. Slade grinned, turned, and hugged the woman quickly.

Once again Slade faced the alley. With a jaunty step he began his descent. Boots drumming rhythmically down the wooden steps, he finally raised his eyes and gazed directly into Glory's angry amber eyes.

Chapter Nine

They stood frozen in time and space, gray eyes locked with amber. Every overt implication of the scene, every subtle insinuation flashed instantaneously through Slade's mind. Sick at heart, he knew exactly what horrified thoughts were going through Glory's mind: shock, hurt, shame, anger, scorn. All these emotions and more flickered across Glory's ashen face in the length of a heartbeat.

And then Slade saw her gather herself for flight. No! He couldn't let her escape. He had to have a chance to explain.

Explain. How? He couldn't tell her why he'd come to Joella's. That might endanger the whole network. There were lives at stake. But what possible reason, except the truth, would Glory accept?

How could he explain the obvious camaraderie he and Joella shared? Friendship that, in Glory's accusing eyes, looked all the world like intimacy. A brotherly hug that could easily be misconstrued as one last indulgence in cupidity.

After all, who but a lover would be leaving the private chambers of a scantily clad lady at this early hour? Especially a lady whose reputation was shady at best.

Slade's small hesitation was his undoing. The last shred of Glory's disbelief dissolved. Smothering a sob, she whirled and raced blindly for the entrance of the alley.

"Glory!" Slade's cry echoed harshly in the restricted confines. "Wait! You have to listen to me. Please!"

Heedless of life and limb he clattered down the stairs, finally vaulting the railing and angling to the right to bisect Glory's path of escape.

Perceiving his intention she dodged to the left, fleeing toward a small stand of bush and briar at the edge of the narrow thoroughfare. Slade caught her just before she reached its thorny shelter.

The grateful thought flashed through his mind that the quarter-moon-shaped thatch of brush would at least offer a scant but effective shield from the street. Perhaps no one would witness the hysterical byplay after all.

"Glory!" Slade's hands closed around her arms, pulling her back.

"No!" she sobbed, tears finally cascading down her face. "Let me go!"

Oblivious to their two observers—Joella standing in stunned silence on the landing, Lydia peeking from behind the barrels with huge, bewildered eyes—Slade and Glory struggled.

"Stop it! Be still for a minute. You've got to listen to me," Slade pleaded heatedly.

"I won't! Let me go!" Glory twisted against his hands, turning, tugging, pulling, striving desperately to extricate herself from his grip. Slade's fingers bit into the tender flesh of Glory's arms as he tried to subdue her struggles.

Slade had no earthly idea what he would say even if he managed to persuade her to listen. He only knew that he had to try to soothe the hurt from her eyes, to temper the pain of betrayal she must be feeling.

He loved her. She loved him. That was the ultimate truth—the only truth that mattered. Dear God, if he could just get her to be still, somehow he'd make her understand. She *had* to understand.

Naively certain that, if the situation were reversed, he could never turn from Glory's embrace no matter how damning the evidence, he used his greater strength to quell her exertions enough to pull her into the encircling trap of his arms. Still twisting and struggling she battered his chest frantically with her small fists.

"Glory, sweetheart. It's all right, darling. It's all right." His voice was velvet soft, alternately pleading and soothing as he held the sobbing woman. "Hush, my sweet love. Hush," he crooned.

With that, Glory collapsed against him. Harsh racking sobs shook her body. A frisson of hope stabbed through him when she stopped fighting. He patted her, rocked her, held her as tenderly as a mother would a child.

Sweet Jesus! He'd done it! She was going to relent long enough to listen—to what he wasn't sure—but he'd think of something.

"Now, now, darling, it's over. Everything's all right." he murmured as her sobs became softer and farther apart. He cuddled her closer, basking in the beloved feel of her body, unmindful of the way her tears had soaked the front of his shirt. Pressing tiny, tender kisses against her temple, he continued to gentle her with his voice.

Physically and mentally exhausted, Glory rested against him, her eyes squeezed shut to close out the awful hurting memory of Joella in Slade's embrace. Deep inside her heart the pain she felt was like a raw wound. But the thought of being separated from Slade again after all the years of wanting and dreaming and hoping was a deeper pain, almost more than she could bear.

Utterly wretched, she assigned names to the conflicting feelings that flowed through her. A raging desire to hurt him as he'd hurt her. A fierce need to stay in his arms and let his familiar warmth ease the wrenching ache. A small, nagging thought that, for her own salvation, she should walk away and never see him again. A desperate desire to somehow put the awful moment behind them.

If only he would just give her time for the misery to abate, even a few short minutes to dull the pain's cutting edge, long enough for her to think straight again.

A tiny, almost infinitesimal ray of hope flickered deep in her breast. What if he asked her to forgive him? Would she?

And she suddenly knew, deep in her heart of hearts, that she would. She had loved this man for as long as she could remember; she knew she was condemned to love him forever.

Yes, of course, she'd forgive him. All he had to do was ask.

But right now, all she wanted was to get away from this awful place. She needed a chance to heal. Eventually she would be able to put the whole humiliating episode from her mind.

"Please, let me go. I . . . I have to leave," Glory entreated. She drew a long quavering breath and reached with trembling fingers to brush the dampness from her cheeks. "We'll—" It took supreme effort on her part, but she finally managed to say the words. "We'll talk about this later."

Relief flooded through Slade. "Of course, darling, whatever you say. Anything you want."

With her nerves strung so tight they almost hummed, Glory strove to pull the few remaining shreds of her dignity about her. Drawing a deep breath, she stepped away and tilted her chin in a heart-rending display of pride.

She almost managed to pull it off . . . until Slade raised a finger, tipping her chin and delivering a grateful kiss to her lips.

Horrified, Glory twisted her head. "Oh, Lord, please don't," Glory begged, her voice quaking. "I couldn't bear it. Not now. Not after you've just been with her—"

"Been with her?" Slade repeated in a stupefied tone. "You . . . you mean you still think that? But I haven't!" he denied vehemently.

Glory gaped at him in stunned silence. The terrible ache of betrayal and her sacrificial willingness to give Slade his asked-for forgiveness suddenly turned into a seething, mindless fury.

"How dare you?" she hissed, the spark in her tear-filled eyes flashing the fiery color of heated cognac.

She could have forgiven him almost anything. Anything but a bald-faced lie.

"How dare you deny what I've seen with my own eyes!" Wrath sizzled in her every word. "You . . . you lying bastard!" With that, she raised her hand and delivered a ringing slap to his cheek.

Shocked beyond words at the sudden turn of events, Slade could only stand silently, hand against his smarting face, as he watched Glory flee the alley.

Lydia emitted a startled squeak and finally overcame the lethargy that had held her frozen in place. Hiking her skirts almost knee-high, she dashed from her hiding place, throwing Slade a withering glance as she rushed past him in pursuit of her friend.

Glory's anger carried her all the way home where the whimsical fates saw fit to bestow one small token of pity on the suffering young woman. Miraculously, everyone in residence at the Westbrook mansion was busy somewhere else when Glory, with Lydia still dogging her footsteps, stormed through the front door and up the stairs to her room.

The resounding slam of her bedroom door caused curious glances among the servants in the kitchen, but when nothing further was heard they went back to their tasks, quickly forgetting the incident.

Upstairs Glory paced the room like an enraged lioness. "How could he? How could he?" she rasped over and over again. The only other sound in the room was the slithery sweep of her hem against the polished floorboards.

For once Lydia could only watch mutely, her usually quick mind unable to form the soothing words necessary to mollify Glory's anger. There was absolutely nothing she could say to take away her friend's suffering. No believable words to persuade Glory that she might have misconstrued the scene between Joella and Slade.

Lydia had witnessed enough to come to the same heart-numbing conclusion that Glory had reached. Slade was guilty. No doubt about it.

The high wave of rage that Glory rode finally began to ebb. The rosy splashes of indignity staining her cheeks at last began to fade. Her breath came in more normal cadence. Outwardly she appeared to be calming, perhaps even coming to grips with the situation.

But, inwardly, a hard knot of despair and hopelessness curled relentless fingers around her heart. How could she have been so foolish? What on earth had made her believe that she and Slade could have a life together—that he loved her now, that he had ever loved her?

She'd been behaving like a child, living in a fantasy that she alone thought possible. It was her own childish stubbornness that brought her to this misery. If she'd only listened to her father, she could have avoided all this heartache. Why had she been so blind?

Swallowing back the tears that threatened to overflow her burning eyes, Glory struggled to pull herself out of the morass of misery enveloping her. *Grow up*, her mind echoed again and again. *Grow up. See the world for what it is, not what you want it to be. Put your life to right. Act like an adult. Do what your father wants.*

Head up, shoulders back, she silently vowed to put the past behind her, to take those final reluctant steps into responsibility. And she'd start right now.

With one last gulp to vanquish all doubts, Glory sat down on the brocade-upholstered stool in front of the dressing table. Closing her eyes momentarily, she composed her thoughts and made the final decision.

With fingers that still trembled, she plucked out what few pins remained in her tumbled locks. Picking up a silver-backed brush, she began to draw it through her long cinnamon curls.

Confused and worried at Glory's sudden uncharacteristic calm, Lydia watched her finish the slow controlled strokes and then carefully lay the brush down on the polished dresser top.

Face devoid of emotion, Glory raised her arms and began to pile her long hair atop her head. "Would you help me put my hair to rights?" she asked Lydia in a calm voice. The chilling control of Glory's words frightened Lydia far more than her earlier ranting.

"Of course," Lydia replied quickly. She hurried to stand behind her friend and help with the tucking and turning and smoothing.

Glory quietly gave the task over to Lydia, simply sitting passively as the work was done, rousing herself only to pass opened pins as they were needed. Her reflection in the silvered mirror was composed, even somewhat remote. Only the uncommon rigidity of her spine and the faint telltale tick of a rapid pulse at the base of her throat confirmed that anything was amiss.

171

Lydia would have preferred that Glory scream and cry, even throw things as she had at times in their younger days — that at least would be more normal behavior for her friend. The peculiar dispassion Glory was presently displaying worried Lydia far more than the worst fit of temper would have.

"Thank you," Glory murmured when her hair was once again coiled and smoothed into a proper coiffure. She stood and, with slow and deliberate movements, unfastened the tiny acorn-brown buttons that ran down the bodice of her dress. Once finished, she stripped the dress over her head and dropped it in a heap on the floor. Each movement was slow and calm and deliberate.

"What . . . what are you going to do?" Lydia questioned in a quivery voice.

"Why, I'm changing clothes so that I'll be ready to greet Preston," Glory answered in a tone that implied her statement made perfect sense.

Lydia was totally confused. "Oh? You're expecting him to come by?"

"No. Not yet. But he'll come when he receives the message I'm going to send."

Suddenly alarmed at Glory's strange behavior, Lydia watched her friend with growing apprehension. Her fingers twisted together nervously. "Why . . . why would you want to send him a message, Glory?"

Head tilted bravely, Glory turned and gazed innocently into Lydia's concerned blue eyes. "Because I intend to accept Preston's proposal of marriage."

Lydia's stomach plummeted. "Oh, Glory! No! You can't do that! I don't care how hurt you are right now. Please reconsider! You're going to regret this —"

Glory shook her head decisively. "Oh, no, I'm not. Don't you see, Lydia," she said imploringly. "It's my only salvation. I've got to go on with my life. I've got to get Slade out of my mind. And I can't do it by myself. I need something else . . . a challenge, a new life to look forward to. Don't you see? Then I'll be able to forget Slade." There was desperation in her voice.

Tears formed in Lydia's eyes. She rushed to Glory's side and put her arms around her friend. "I know you're hurting, Glory, but please think about this. Wait, just a little while. Please."

"You must understand, Lydia. I realize now how wrong I've been, how foolish. Papa's been right all along. I have to do this. I have to. Preston is my only hope."

Although Lydia continued to plead, nothing she could say would change Glory's mind.

A message was penned on pale blue paper, placed in an envelope and sealed. Violet was summoned and given the communication. She in turn passed it to Jacob, who placed it in his pocket with plans to deliver it to Mr. Harper's place of residence when he made the trip to the market later that day.

Devastated by the turn of events, completely confounded as to how to rectify the situation, Slade agonized through the day's long hours. He longed to bar the doors and rush to Glory's house. The only thing that stopped him was the sure knowledge that it would do no good.

To compound Slade's misery, Morgan slipped

through the back door in the early afternoon to bid his brother good-bye. Supposedly, on his way to join his militia unit, Morgan had actually packed his saddlebags in preparation for the first leg of his trip northward.

The brothers stared at each other for a long moment, each lost in his respective thoughts. All Slade's weary mind could think of was the ironic fact that he was losing the two most important people in his life—all on the same day.

He couldn't stop Morgan from leaving, from going far, far away. He doubted that he would if he could. Physically, Glory was still heartbreakingly close, mere blocks away. But mentally, emotionally, she was farther from his reach than Morgan would ever be.

For the first time that day, Slade was grateful that the store was empty. He rounded the counter and embraced his brother, perhaps for the very last time.

"You take care of yourself, you hear?" Slade implored when he finally stepped back.

"Sure," Morgan replied, his voice as raspy as Slade's. "You, too."

"I will."

"And take care of the kids."

"You bet."

"I'm sure going to miss them."

"I know."

"Write to us. Surely some of the mail will get through."

"Yes, of course I will."

The brothers stood silently in the small, quiet store. There was nothing left to say.

Morgan raised one hand in brief farewell and

disappeared into the back room. Slade heard the creak of the back door as it was pulled open, the metallic click of the lock as Morgan turned the key from the other side. Then all was still.

Across the city in James Bourland's elegant study, three men discussed the portent of the recent discovery.

"Preston and I would like to hear what you've done since the last time we talked," Colonel Westbrook said.

"Well, after McCurley got skittish and decided he didn't want to have anything more to do with the League, I found someone else. Colonel Newton Chance is taking over."

"And what is he going to do?" Preston questioned.

"He has orders to gain the Childs brothers' confidence and swear allegiance to the organization," Bourland explained. "I told him to accept initiation into every damn degree they'll let him into."

His brow furrowed in thought, Preston considered Bourland's statement. "Wait a minute. Chance is a Southern officer. Do you really think he's the right man for such a job? After all, his strong convictions about secession are well known. Aren't you worried that Childs . . . and whoever else is involved . . . will be at least a little suspicious of this turn about in Chance's attitude?"

"Well, they weren't too discriminating when they told McCurley as much as they did before he was even sworn in." Bourland raised an eyebrow and waited for Preston to respond.

"That's true enough. It does appear that some of the League members are a mite overconfident about their security measures," Preston finally agreed.

"Right. The damn fools spout all that folderal about secret codes and passwords, and then get drunk and babble indiscriminately." Westbrook gave a sharp bark of laughter, then shrugged his black-clad shoulders and smiled sardonically. "We certainly can't be blamed for taking advantage of their stupidity, now can we?"

Bourland nodded in agreement. "Chance is a smart man. He'll get the information we need, if anyone can."

Preston's concerned cool blue gaze swung from one man to the other. "Fair enough," he finally said. "How long do you think it will take him to find out the whole story?"

"A few weeks, hopefully. Maybe a month. It's hard to tell. I don't want to rush things. If we push too hard, those League fellows might get suspicious and go underground again."

The Colonel nodded his agreement to Bourland's statement.

Bourland helped himself to another cup of strong black coffee. The delicious aroma wafted through the air. "Would you like some more?" he questioned his guests. Sun glinted sharply off the rounded silver surface of the pot. When they declined, he placed the pot back on its matching tray.

"We must remember," Bourland continued, "that the purpose of Chance's assignment is to find out as many names as possible. I'd like to know every single bastard that's involved with that damn League. Then we'll have some real leverage against them. Perhaps we can even put a stop to the constant barrage of petitions and letters that so many of the Unionists have been sending to Austin."

"Hell, yes!" the Colonel said sharply. "If we don't stop their messing around, they may eventually get the rules of the conscript law changed."

"Not if I have anything to say about it," Bourland declared vehemently.

"Well spoken, James," Colonel Westbrook agreed. "I'm sure we're all determined to keep the exemption clause for slaveowners in the law."

Preston waited patiently until the two men finished their tirade against possible revocation of the exemption. He was in complete agreement as far as the law was concerned. As the owner of twenty slaves, he, too, was exempt from the fighting if he so chose. He certainly didn't want a change in the law to endanger his privileged position. He had much more important things to do with his time than fight some stupid war.

"Is that the only way you've considered using this information?" Preston asked when Bourland and Westbrook finally fell silent.

Bourland's keen gaze scrutinized the younger man. His face was deceptively kind, belying the reputation he had for ruthlessness. "And just what else would you suggest we do?"

"Since fate has so fortuitously provided us with this information, what would you think of our using it to get rid of as many Unionists as possible?"

The cup Bourland had raised paused in mid-air. Without taking a sip, he returned it to the saucer. "How do you propose to accomplish that?"

177

Preston leaned back in his chair and waited for the full attention of the two men. "I believe we can use this information—regardless of what Chance finally manages to find out—to snare a good many of the Unionists in a trap of their own making."

"Go on," instructed Bourland, studying the cool demeanor of the younger man with great interest.

"Once we have enough information to lend a semblance of authenticity to our claims, all we have to do is plant enough rumors—"

"Rumors? What kind of rumors?" Bourland interrupted gruffly.

Preston smoothed a slim finger over his golden mustache. A hint of smile played at the almost hidden corners of his mouth. "What if the story got out about the League's alleged attempt to raid the arsenal at Sherman?"

"So?"

"And what if it was believed that the purpose behind that raid was to gain enough arms and ammunition to slaughter every man, woman, and child in the county who doesn't belong to the League?"

Stunned silence met Preston's statement.

"And," Preston continued, a satisfied smirk on his face, "what if the good citizens of Cooke County were told that the League has plans to rob and plunder and murder in order to secure the whole northern section of Texas for the Union? How do you think the general population—especially those loyal to the state and the South—would react to such threatening news?"

A thread of comprehension began to form in Bourland's mind. "Good heavens, man, there could be total panic!"

"Precisely," Preston said. "The good citizens of the county would be quick to take care of anyone they even remotely believed to be affiliated with such a plan."

Intrigued with the ramifications of Preston's scheme, Bourland leaned back in the big chair behind his desk and laced his fingers behind his head. "Yes. It just might work."

"Of course it'll work," Westbrook declared. "All we've got to go is scare the pants off the general public . . . those rumors will certainly accomplish that! We won't have to do anything ourselves; the local people will put a stop to all this Unionist claptrap soon enough." There was a decidedly wicked tone to the Colonel's chuckle. "Let the bastards spend the rest of the war in prison. At least they won't be causing us any more grief! Don't you agree, James?"

"Oh, yes. I certainly do." Bourland nodded his head sagely.

"Wonderful, gentlemen," said Preston. "I think the first thing we have to do is draw up a list of names. If we're going to go to all this bother, we might as well make sure that we get rid of as many thorns in our side as possible. I'm of the opinion that the first targets should be those who have the most respect and trust of the majority of Union sympathizers."

"I can think of half a dozen I'd like to see on that list right now," Westbrook muttered.

Preston continued his dialogue, an almost fanatical light in his pale blue eyes. "If we get rid of their leaders, the rest of them won't have the guts to stand

179

up to us any longer."

"Some of the people you're referring to probably aren't even members of this so-called Union League," Bourland commented.

"So what?" Preston leaned back in his chair, hooking the ankle of one long leg negligently over his other knee. "A few words in the right places and the general public will believe that the League has all sorts of evil plans up its sleeve. Including imminent plans for armed insurrection, bloodshed. A few more words, placing the blame on whomever we want to . . . and the town will be so piss-in-their-pants scared that they'll believe everything they hear."

"Goddamn!" Bourland boomed. "I do believe it'll work."

"Oh, it'll work, all right," Preston murmured. "As soon as you hear from Chance again, we'll begin to bait the trap."

Preston reined in his great black stallion in front of the modest frame house in which he resided. Quickly dismounting, he absentmindedly threw the lines to the young slave who hurried forward to greet his arrival. The stallion snorted eagerly as the gangling youth led him toward the stable in the back.

A warm breeze rustled the bushes lining the white picket fence as the sharp cadence of boot heels accompanied Preston up the flagstone walk. Hazy lavender shadows were silently forming, shifting, growing as twilight descended on Gainesville.

Preston's step was jaunty. Whistling an almost inaudible little tune, a heady sense of well-being radiated through him as he mentally reviewed the events of the day. How easily he'd been able to convince the two older men to go along with his brilliant plan! He chuckled softly as he opened the door.

"Evenin', suh." Pansey met him just inside the entryway and bobbed a polite curtsy at her owner.

"Good evening, Pansey," Preston replied expansively. He even flashed a smile in her direction.

"They's a letter come for you this morning, Mr. Harper. I put it on the little table in the parlor."

"Thank you, Pansey. You may call me when supper is ready."

"Yes, suh," the small black woman replied before turning to scurry back to her kitchen. She cast a puzzled gaze at Preston before the door swung shut, wondering at the reason for his uncharacteristically good mood.

Preston strode into the parlor. For once he didn't grimace at the sight, or compare the rather dowdy surroundings of his rented house with the elegance that would soon be his at Sivells Bend.

Three years ago, who would have expected him to have attained all this? Smiling, Preston smugly contemplated his recent accomplishments. Ah, yes. Preston Harper—black sheep of the family, disinherited son, the bane of the Charleston Harpers—now a respected wealthy man, and, if his luck held, soon to be married into one of Gainesville's most renowned families.

Wouldn't his family be surprised if they heard he'd landed on his feet after all? The money he'd managed to steal from the family strong box after that last horrendous scene with his father hadn't been an overly tremendous amount, but through shrewd investments, a quick hand at the card table, and a conscience that bent at will, he'd been able to amass more than ample funds to finance his new start on the frontier.

Texas was still wild, remote, a little uncivilized. The genteel family connections that grapevined through the old Southern cities did not extend to these far reaches of the country. A man could claim to be anything, anyone . . . and if he had sufficient funds to back his allegations, no one ever questioned him.

No, Preston thought to himself, he couldn't have chosen a better place. Luck had been with him from the first. And it certainly appeared he would have access to the Colonel's prodigious wealth long before his own began to play out. Perfect timing.

Stopping at the sideboard, he poured himself a large tumbler of whiskey, and then took his usual place in the room's most comfortable chair. Once settled, he tilted the glass and took a long drink, enjoying the spread of liquid heat through his veins as the expensive whiskey worked its magic.

Setting the glass down, he opened the carved cypress humidor on the adjoining table and withdrew a long black cheroot, which he placed in the corner of his mouth. A small blue envelope on a silver tray caught his eye. He lifted the letter and glanced at the writing. The penmanship was unfamiliar. It didn't look to be important.

Preston shrugged and negligently flipped the envelope back on the tray while he reached into a small enameled box beside the humidor. A whisk of his wrist and a match was ignited. He applied the flickering yellow flame to the end of the cigar, rolling its firm length appreciatively between his fingers while puffing. The pungent smoke filled his mouth. He savored the flavor a long moment before exhaling a hazy blue-gray plume into the air.

Leaning back, cigar in one hand, glass in the other, he smiled to himself. All in all, a most auspicious beginning to the plan, he mused to himself. Word would travel among the right people. If his plan worked—and he was quite sure it would—the slaveowning elite of the county would all owe him a debt of gratitude. His place in their ranks would forever be secure.

Preston continued to mull over the scheme they'd formulated that morning, sipping slowly at his expensive liquor. A fine gray ash formed at the tip of his cigar. As he flicked the residue into the crystal bowl atop the table, his hand brushed the envelope.

Might as well see what it was, he thought. He picked it up, turned it over, and slipped a long slim finger under the flap. One quick tug and the envelope was open. He withdrew the single sheet of paper and unfolded it.

Dear Preston,

Please do me the kindness of calling at your very earliest convenience. I have something to discuss with you.

Your devoted Glory

It took Preston only seconds to read Glory's gently

worded summons. A thrill of victory surged through him. Something of great consequence was about to happen; he just knew it. All clues pointed in that direction. He recalled Glory's considerably changed attitude on the previous day, her almost bold flirtatious demeanor. And now this sweet little love note.

Tapping the paper against his chin, Preston leaned back. Oh, he'd answer the beautiful Miss Westbrook's summons, all right. Just as soon as the supper hour was over he'd be knocking on the Westbrook's door. A wicked little chuckle escaped his lips.

Chapter Ten

Sara knocked lightly on Glory's bedroom door. "It's me, Miss Glory."

"Come in" came the faint reply.

Sara turned the knob and pushed the door open. The room was in semidarkness and Sara was surprised to see Glory lying catty-corner on her stomach across the bed, her chin propped on her clasped hands.

"What's the matter? You feeling bad, Miss Glory?" Sara asked, concern evident in her voice.

Glory sighed. "No, not really. I . . . uh . . . I just have a little headache."

"I can get Mama to fix you up something right quick. A little tansey or pasque-flower—"

"No, thank you, Sara. It's sweet of you to offer, but I'm fine, really." Glory sighed again, wishing fervently that a tonic existed that could cure her ailment.

Sara frowned. Miss Glory didn't sound fine to her. She didn't sound sick, really. Not sick in the body, anyway.

Sara tiptoed to the edge of the bed, her stiffly

185

starched calico dress rustling in the stillness of the room. She hesitated, mulling over in her mind the correctness of the words she was about to utter. "Miss Glory, be there some trouble? Can I do anything to help?"

Echoes of the past raced through Glory's mind. Fond memories of countless hours spent playing with a chubby brown baby. Helping Sara take her first wobbly steps. Teaching her patty-cake and how to count. Sneaking books down to their secret hideaway under the great staircase so she could share the wonderful stories and pretty pictures with Sara. The furtive thrill of teaching the small, eager child to read the elementary primers. So many hours, so much pleasure.

Glory studied the slim brown girl. The chubby baby of Glory's childhood was no more. Sara had grown tall and graceful during Glory's absence. The crisp white turban on her head highlighted the sooty lashes that fringed large black velvet eyes. Unblemished bronze skin was drawn tight over high cheekbones. Sara was going to be a lovely young woman very soon. But right now her pretty face was scored with lines of concern. Her troubled look warmed Glory's heavy heart.

Glory forced a reassuring smile and pushed herself upright, her silken dress whispering seductively as she slid to the side of the bed. Once on her feet, she put her arms around Sara's slim shoulders and hugged the adolescent girl.

"Thank you, honey. You're a dear to be concerned, but I'm all right. Really."

Sara wasn't so sure, but she wasn't about to argue

186

with her young mistress.

"Yes'm, Miss Glory. If you say so. Oh!" A small pink-palmed hand flew to her generous mouth. "I almost forgot what I come for. That Mr. Harper, he be in the parlor right now. He's waiting for you."

Glory's stomach did a slow roll. She took a deep breath and did her best to look delighted at the news.

"Th-thank you, Sara. Would you make sure Mr. Harper is comfortable? Tell him I'll join him in a few moments."

"Yas'm."

The slight slave girl cast one last speculative look at Glory's wan face before silently exiting the room.

Glory patted her hair, smoothed her dress, and then, with great reluctance, finally approached the door leading to the hall. Squaring her shoulders, lifting her chin bravely, she turned the knob and began the long walk to the parlor.

Downstairs, Preston stood gazing out the French doors that opened onto the veranda. There was actually very little he could see, for night had at last descended on the town. In truth, his thoughts were turned inward as he again congratulated himself on the day's accomplishments . . . and speculated on the possibility of this visit ending in still another—perhaps even more important—victory.

Stopping just inside the doorway of the parlor, Glory studied the figure across the room. The soft glow of lamplight illuminated Preston's burnished locks as he gazed out into the darkness. Glory took advantage of the small reprieve to gather her wits about her.

Why, oh why, she fretted inwardly, didn't her

stubborn body react to Preston's presence as it should? Why didn't the sight of him set her heart thumping in crazy cadence the way Slade's presence did?

This man would some day be her husband. She should be pleased to see him. No, more than that . . . *thrilled* to see him. Her heart should flutter at the sight of the tall masculine body, the smooth golden hair, the strong slim hands clasped behind his back.

Those hands . . . slim, pale, smooth . . . so unlike Slade's. When she married Preston, those hands would touch her as Slade's had.

Glory repressed a small shudder, silently assuring herself that all that would change once they were married. She'd forget all about Slade.

Despite her best intentions, the blood quickened in her veins as memories assailed her. Liquid warmth spread through the pit of her stomach. Her nipples pebbled in sweet agony as she remembered Slade's tender ministrations. The times she and Slade had been together had made her only want more. Each fiery kiss, each satin stroke had been met with matching ardor. It had been natural, wonderful, right.

Surely, sweet heaven, *surely* it would eventually be that way with Preston. After all, she'd really never had a chance to respond to him under the proper conditions. The closest she'd been to Preston was when he'd taken her in his arms to dance. That hadn't been unpleasant, had it? she chided inwardly.

No. Not unpleasant.

But there'd been no joyous explosion of feeling,

188

either. No sharp surge of desire, no quickening of her heartbeat, no blazing heat deep within her body.

Stop it! Stop thinking of Slade. Feelings for Preston would come in time. When her mind was finally cleared of all thoughts of Slade, things would be all right.

She would do her best to honor the commitment she was about to make. And in time she would learn to respond to Preston.

It was that, or be forever condemned to memories of a dark-haired man who could set her soul on fire with a single look. Memories of what could never be.

Her gaze again went to the pale-haired man standing at the window. Rubbing her damp palms against the skirt of her gown, she swallowed back a lump of apprehension and called to him softly.

"Preston."

He whirled, delight evident on his face. "Glory, dear! I didn't hear you come in. How very good to see you."

Crossing the room quickly, he came to a halt directly in front of her. With one swift movement, he clasped her hands in his, bringing them both to his lips. A small kiss was brushed against her knuckles.

Glory smiled tremulously. "It's . . . it's good to see you, too."

Preston tucked her hand possessively into the crook of his arm, drawing her across the room. He waited until she was settled on the small brocade-covered loveseat and then took his place beside her. Turning at an angle so that he could scrutinize her face, Preston placed one arm along the back of the settee and leaned slightly toward Glory.

She could feel the heat of his arm against her back. If she relaxed her ramrod stiff spine one inch she would be leaning against its hard length. She steadfastly held her erect position and offered Preston a fleeting smile before lowering her head to watch her fingers pluck nervously at the lace-edged handkerchief clutched in her lap.

Preston edged closer. The sleeve of his linen coat brushed against one bare shoulder. Glory tensed. Leaning closer still, Preston reached out with his free hand to still her fingers.

"Your letter was a delightful surprise, Glory. I was very pleased to receive your message."

"Oh? Were you?" she asked with a little choking gulp. The air seemed to go no further than her throat. She wished he'd chosen the long sofa to sit on. He was so close. If she had just a little more space, maybe she wouldn't feel as though she were suffocating.

"Yes, I was. I'm sorry I was gone all day. Business, you know."

"Of course." Glory fidgeted, her fingers fluttering weakly against the restriction of Preston's hand.

"Had I known your sweet little note was waiting, I would have gone home much sooner."

"I . . . I'm sure you would have." She gazed apprehensively at the long, slim fingers intertwined so intimately with her own.

"Do you want to tell me what you wanted?" Preston questioned softly. "Or shall I try to guess?"

"Yes . . . no . . . I mean—"

"That's all right, dearest Glory. Perhaps I can make this easier on both of us."

"You can?" she asked with a catch in her voice. She for one wasn't so sure.

"May I be so bold as to presume that your summons means you've considered my proposal and come to a favorable conclusion?"

"Well . . . I have been . . . thinking about what you said." The words came much harder than she'd expected.

"You know how very happy such an arrangement would make your father . . . and me."

"Yes, I . . . I suppose it would," Glory said lamely.

Preston smiled at her uncharacteristic shyness. "And today you made your decision?"

"Well . . . I did come to a sort of . . . conclusion . . . concerning the matter." Glory was growing more miserable by the minute. Dear Lord! Was she doing the right thing?

Suddenly the memory of Joella in Slade's arms seared across her mind. Slade's lie pounded in her head.

Yes. Yes, of course she was doing the right thing! She had to put Slade behind her. Nothing else mattered!

Glory's chin tilted bravely. She blinked twice to clear the mist from her eyes. Her mouth trembled ever so slightly and she ran the tip of her pink little tongue over her dry lips. Drawing a deep, fortifying breath she resolutely met Preston's gaze.

"And what might your final answer be, Glory?" he inquired softly.

"The . . . the answer is y-yes," she managed to whisper. Glory fought the choking feeling that caused her voice to crack badly with each word.

191

Filled with elation, Preston forced himself to remain calm. Only the sharp glitter of his clear blue eyes betrayed his euphoria. "You've made me a very happy man, Glory dear. In more ways than you could ever imagine."

Once again Preston lifted Glory's hand to his lips, turning it over until her palm was upward. He lowered his head. The spun-gold hairs of his mustache prickled against the tender skin. His breath fanned warmly across her palm. The kiss he pressed into its center did nothing more than send tiny cold shivers down her spine.

The next light kiss was placed on her wrist, the next on the point of her shoulder. Glory sat frozen as Preston's face came nearer and nearer. She fought the impulse to turn her head away. Squeezing her eyes tightly shut, she allowed him to claim her lips. Hot tears scalded the back of her throat.

The grain of ice that had formed in her heart that morning behind the Silver City Saloon grew and grew. Chilling tentacles speared through Glory's slim body, bringing a coldness far greater than any caused by the frigid winds of winter.

As Preston deepened the kiss, a tiny tear seeped from beneath her starred lashes, glittering like a small, cold diamond in the lamplight before trickling slowly down her cheek.

Slade heard the news from his first customer, Mrs. Fain's words plummeting him to the depths of despair. When she'd gushed on about what a lucky catch the Colonel's sweet little daughter had made,

Slade had barely been able to nod his head. Later, he had no memory of what he'd said, but evidently he'd managed to mumble the appropriate words because his customer had beamed at him in response.

When Mr. Cranford arrived just before lunch to start his shift at the store, Slade grabbed his hat and gratefully escaped to the only solace he knew . . . Joella's.

"Good heavens above, Slade!" she exclaimed at her first sight of his haggard face. "You look like death warmed over." Joella glanced around the almost deserted saloon, then pulled out a chair and quickly sat down at the table with him.

Slade raised a half-empty bottle and waved it at her. The liquid sloshed against the glass. "Want to join me for a drink?"

"Good Lord, no! Not at this time of the day. It's barely three o'clock. Slade, what's wrong with you? Has something happened to one of the kids?"

He shook his head morosely.

"Morgan? You've heard something about Morgan?"

"No. No, not that." Slade raised the shot glass and stared blankly into the amber depths, pain twisting in his gut because the color reminded him of Glory's eyes. With a quick flick of the wrist, he downed the fiery liquid.

He waited for the longed-for numbness to appear. Nothing. No matter how much he drank, the pain of losing Glory would not abate.

Joella watched her friend in growing alarm as he continued his uncharacteristic behavior. In exasperation, she finally yanked the bottle out of his reach.

"If you think I'm going to sit here and watch you get stinking drunk, you're wrong. Now, get out of that chair and come with me. We're going upstairs and get to the bottom of this." She rose and stood glaring over him until he shrugged despondently and pushed himself slowly to his feet.

"Come on," Joella instructed in a stern voice as she turned and walked toward the staircase at the back of the room, casting one quick look backward to be sure that Slade was following.

Once inside Joella's sitting room, Slade slumped into the big, overstuffed chair. Joella shook her head in dismay. Balled hands on her slim hips, she stood over him, her mouth a thin determined line.

"Now, Slade Hunter, you're going to tell me what's wrong or else—"

A knock on the back door interrupted Joella's discourse. She frowned, glancing in the direction of the unexpected sound.

With a warning shake of her head, she whispered, "You'd better step into the bedroom, Slade. Just to be safe. I'm not expecting any callers. It could be anyone."

Slade was well aware of the constant danger Joella lived under. No matter how miserable he himself was, he wasn't about to put his friend in jeopardy.

He uttered not a single protest, simply rising and walking on silent feet to the small bedroom alcove. Reaching up, he closed the heavy brocade curtains across the opening, careful that the wooden rings slid as silently as possible along the length of the long polished pole.

As the folds of the deep crimson fabric settled into

stillness, Joella crossed the room to the back door. Hand on the brass knob, she hesitated. "Yes? Who's there?"

"It's me, Preston."

Preston! Whatever did he want at this time of the day? And suddenly the wheels began to turn inside her head. Joella cast a sharp glance at the draperies which cloaked her bedroom. What but trouble with Glory could throw Slade into the depths of despair he was presently wallowing in? And Preston and Glory were tied together in many ways. If she let Preston in, she might be able to solve the puzzle of Slade's misery.

Joella rolled her eyes in aversion. If she had her druthers, she'd never again put up with Preston's wily ways. But her concern for Slade was stronger than her dislike of the man waiting on the other side of the door.

Reluctantly, she turned the knob and pulled the door open. "Won't you come in, Preston?" she invited with a forced smile.

Preston strode into the room, his walk cocky, his face wreathed in a self-satisfied smile. In the center of the parlor, he pivoted on one booted heel, clasping his hands behind his back. One hand still held his broad-brimmed hat, and he nervously tapped it against the back of his superbly fitted trousers.

"Good afternoon, Preston. What can I do for you?" Joella inquired as pleasantly as possible.

The hat stilled and Preston rocked on the balls of his feet. "I believe the issue is more what I can do for you."

Not again. Joella edged toward the big chair in the

center of the room, effectively placing the bulky piece of furniture between herself and the man. "And what might that be?"

"Things are coming to a head, Joella. Moving very fast. I wanted to . . . ah . . . tell you something before you heard it from the town gossips. To be sure you understand."

"And just what is this 'something' I need to understand?"

"First, I want to assure you that what I'm about to tell you will have absolutely no impact on our relationship—"

"*Our* relationship?" she repeated in surprise. "I wasn't aware we had a relationship."

Preston moved toward her. Joella shifted so that the chair stayed between them.

"Now, Joella, honey," Preston appealed. "I know it's a lady's way to play a little hard to get. But enough is enough. You know as well as I do that we were made for each other. How often have I told you you're the most gorgeous woman I've ever seen? I've wanted you since the first day I laid eyes on you."

"So you've said on several occasions." Her tone was only slightly amused. "And I believe I've told you just as many times that I'm simply not interested."

"But you don't understand, Joella. Things have changed."

"What things would that be?"

"Finances. I've just sewed up a deal that will put me on secure footing for the rest of my life."

"How nice for you."

"No. How nice for us."

Preston moved too quickly for Joella to compensate, feinting to the left and then back to the right as she rounded the side of the chair. His hand closed over her wrist and he stepped so close she was enveloped in the spicy aroma of his expensive cologne.

"Let's stop playing these games, Joella, honey. I'm in a position to give you anything you want. Just name it."

He maintained his steely grip on her wrist, pulling her resolutely into his arms. She knew there was no sense struggling. Besides, her curiosity was aroused. She wondered about the windfall he spoke of. It must indeed be something extraordinary to bring on such a euphoric mood.

"What do you say?" His arms wrapped tighter around her slim body.

Joella tilted her head back, trying to hide her distaste as she scrutinized the handsome face leaning over her. "I think I'd have to know a little more about this 'deal' of yours before I could make any decisions. Just what is it, and why is it so important?"

"Who's the richest man in the county?"

Joella shrugged. "I don't know. Colonel Westbrook, probably. Why?"

"Right. But before long it's going to be me. What would you say if I told you that I'll soon have access to his fortune?"

"How are you going to work that?"

"By marrying his daughter."

Joella didn't know whether to laugh or slap the smug look from his face. "And *that* piece of news is supposed to make me fall into your arms. What makes you think I'm interested in sharing any man? Especially you?"

Preston's face grew grim. "You'd be wise to reconsider, Joella. I'm going to be one of the most influential men in this county before long. The wheels are already in motion. And, just remember this, with the Colonel's wealth to back me, there's not anything I can't accomplish."

"And just how are you supposed to have time for me if you're a married man?" Joella's eyes were disdainful, her stance haughty.

"That won't have anything to do with us. Glory will stay at the house in Sivells Bend. She won't be any bother. I'll buy you any house you want, furnish it with the very best. You can give up these crazy hours . . . stop working so hard."

"And what if I like this work?"

"All right, all right. I'm not hard to get along with. Keep the Silver City if you want to. I won't insist that you sell it. You can still own the place; you just won't have to spend your time here. Hire a manager you can trust. Whatever. I don't care. Just so long as you're available for me when I want you. I'll make you happy—give you anything you want. Just name it, honey. I'll see that you get it."

"And you really believe your sweet little bride isn't going to mind you straying from your marriage bed?"

"How will she know? Besides, you know how girls of her social status are." Preston snickered derisively. "Just a tad on the icy side. She'll be glad to be left alone. And I intend to keep her pregnant on a regular basis. That'll take care of that. We'll have all the time we could wish for. Don't worry, I'll be coming into town on a regular basis."

"You've got it all planned out, don't you? You're so damned sure that you can handle the Colonel's daughter . . . and me, too. Has it ever crossed your mind that I might not be willing to participate in your shabby little scheme? Or that Miss Westbrook deserves a husband who loves her and is loyal to her?"

"What are you talking about?" Preston's brows drew together in consternation. "Let's stop playing games, Joella. Come here, I'll prove to you how right we are for each other."

Before Joella could react, Preston pinned her arms to her sides and crushed his lips cruelly against hers. His tongue thrust against her lips, forcing her mouth open so he could stab with rapier swiftness into the sweet depths. His hand crept from her arm to cup her breast, kneading it with strong squeezing motions.

She moaned in protest, twisting away to gasp for breath. "Stop it, Preston!" she demanded in an enraged tone.

"Don't tease me, Joella. You know you like it." He struggled to maintain his hold, forcing more kisses on her.

Suddenly the drapery separating the living area from the bedroom was thrown back with a vicious jerk. The walnut curtain rings clacked harshly against one another. Preston caught a blur out of the corner of his eye, but before he could figure out what was happening, Slade had crossed the room and clapped a hand on Preston's shoulder.

Surprised at the sudden appearance of an unexpected third person, Preston released his hold on

Joella. She judiciously used the opportunity to escape quickly to the far side of the room. Slade spun Preston around and delivered a roundhouse blow to his chin before Preston knew what hit him.

"Get your hands off her, you miserable son of a bitch! Jesus Christ, you have Glory! What the hell else do you want? Aren't you ever satisfied?"

Preston staggered backward, one hand wiping away the trickle of bright red blood that seeped from the corner of his mouth. "Now, see here—"

The words barely cleared Preston's mouth before Slade lunged forward and slammed him against the wall.

"Shut up! How dare you come up here with your lousy bragging and your filthy little schemes? Good Lord, man, you've got an angel and you're going to shame her like that!" Slade's fist slammed into Preston's stomach.

Preston slid down the wall, his feet splayed out and his butt hit the floor with a resounding thud. He stayed slumped against the wall for a moment, then carefully raised his head. Groaning loudly, he shook it to clear his befuddled brain. Finally he looked up, eyes full of malice as he glared up at the dark avenging man standing over him.

"Who the hell do you think you are?" Preston demanded, his voice halting, almost garbled. "What right do you have to interfere?" He stopped to draw a ragged breath. "And what in the hell are you doing up here anyway?"

"Visiting with a friend, if it's any business of yours. I can't stop Glory from making a fool of herself by marrying you. Not with her daddy so damn eager to sell her soul to a bastard like you. But I can save Joella—"

"Save Joella?" Preston repeated in a dazed tone.

"That's right. You're not going to have both of them. I'll see to that. Now get out of here, you slimy bastard, and don't ever come back."

Preston rose painfully to his feet. Once upright, he swayed slightly, then spread his feet wider to maintain his equilibrium. With slow deliberate motions he brushed at his rumpled clothes. Finally he cast a murderous look in Slade's direction.

"I'm going, Hunter. But I promise you'll be sorry for what you've done. I don't forget easily. I'll get you—one way or another—if it takes me forever. You just better get used to looking over your shoulder day and night."

Slade lifted one dark eyebrow in jeering disregard of Preston's threat. "I'm really afraid. Can't you tell?"

"It would be wise of you to be very afraid." Preston's voice was low, menacing. When he finished with Slade, he turned his furious gaze on Joella. "And, you, you lying little bitch. I won't forget what you've done, either."

The line of Slade's mouth hardened again. "This is the last time I'm going to tell you . . . get the hell out of here. And I'm warning you, if you ever dare come near Joella again, you'll answer to me."

Preston's puffy, discolored lower lip made the sneer on his face almost comical. His gaze raked the two figures, pure hate glowing in the cold blue depths of his eyes. Finally, he turned and stalked toward the door, staggering once as he made his way across the room. Grasping the knob, he turned it viciously and jerked the door open. As he stepped through, he repeated his earlier threat.

"I'll get you one of these days, Hunter. That's a promise."

"Then you'd better do your best the first time, Harper, because the next time I catch you around here it'll give me great pleasure to kill you."

Chapter Eleven

"I swear, Glory, I'm so sore I can barely wiggle. Don't bother to ask me to go riding with you again tomorrow, 'cause I'm not going." Lydia pushed an errant strand of light brown hair out of her eyes and kicked her heels into the flanks of her bay mare. She winced when her abused muscles protested at the small movement. "No, I simply will not go again," she repeated with even stronger emphasis.

Glory turned in the saddle, bracing her hand on the broad, smooth rump of her mount. She drew back on the reins to slow the strawberry roan gelding, who snorted and tossed his head in protest. Frowning her surprise at her friend's grumbling, she waited until Lydia's horse drew alongside. "For pity's sake, Lydia," Glory chided. "What's the matter with you? You used to love to go riding."

"I still love riding," Lydia protested. "But six days in a row is too much! And we've been out practically all day each time!" She shook her tumbled curls in emphasis. "Enough is enough. You're going to have to stay home someday. You can't avoid Preston forever."

Glory gave a small huff of denial. "I am not avoiding Preston! What on earth gives you that ridiculous idea?"

Lydia's eyes narrowed. "What would *you* call it when you're gone every day from sunup to sundown? If we're not out riding, we're at my house."

"Well, mercy me, Lydia! I didn't know you minded my company so much. I . . . I'll just find something else to do tomorrow."

Much to Lydia's dismay, Glory's eyes began to fill with tears. Mouth pursed in concern, Lydia watched Glory pull a hanky from the pocket of her blue serge riding skirt and snuffle softly as she swiped it across her eyes and nose.

"Oh, dear," Lydia wailed, immediately contrite at the unexpected results of her tirade. "I'm sorry, Glory. Really I am. I never meant to upset you."

Glory's head jerked up. She dabbed her misty eyes again, repocketed the crumpled hanky, and then gazed at her friend, a trembly little smile on her lips. "I'm not upset. I . . . I'm taking a cold, that's all," she said, sniffing loudly.

Refusing to be fooled by Glory's forced cheerfulness, Lydia replied, "It's been almost a week. How long are you going to keep playing this game?" Sadness mixed with exasperation in her voice.

"I don't know what you're talking about." Glory's gaze shifted and she stared somewhere over Lydia's

204

shoulder, as if she couldn't quite bear to utter such an obvious lie while looking straight at her friend.

"Oh, yes, you do. You haven't been yourself since you told Preston you'd marry him. It was a mistake. I *knew* it would be."

"Don't be ridiculous."

"Well, you can keep fooling yourself if you want. But I for one know better. If you're so happy about this upcoming marriage, why don't you want to be with your fiancé?"

There was no way to answer that question satisfactorily, so Glory simply ignored it. Quickly turning her attention to the ground, she concentrated on guiding the big gelding around a large outcropping of rocks and down the sloping banks of a lazy creek.

"Well?" Lydia prodded, following close behind her.

"It's not exactly that I don't want to see Preston—"

"Yes, it is!" Lydia protested. "Why are you lying to me? I know you better than anyone, Glory. I know how much you love Slade—"

"I don't *want* to love him anymore!"

"All right. Even if things never work out for you and Slade—and I'll be the first to admit I thought it was impossible—it's time you admitted that you don't really want to marry Preston. That won't cure your problems. Why do you keep hiding from the truth? Honestly! You make me so . . . so damn mad!"

Glory looked up in shock. Although not above uttering an imprecation or two herself, she'd never before heard Lydia swear.

"It's wrong, Glory. You may be fooling yourself

205

and your family and Preston, but you're not fooling me. What you're doing is wrong. For you, for Preston, for everyone!" Now Lydia was almost in tears. Jerking her horse to a halt, she slid from the saddle, stopping only long enough to loop the reins over the branch of a small wild plum tree before stomping off toward the creek.

Glory quickly dismounted, secured her gelding, and followed Lydia to the mammoth fallen tree trunk where the young woman now sat, hunched over, elbows on her knees, chin in her hands. The heels of her brown leather boots beat a frustrated tattoo against the rotting bark.

Glory propped herself against a huge, skyward-jutting branch, and waited. Lydia continued to stare straight ahead. Uneasy with Lydia's uncharacteristically morose mood, Glory's restless fingers smoothed her skirt, then flicked some dust from her sleeve. Finally, she leaned over and snapped a scrawny, dried branch from the limb, filling the uncomfortable silence by plucking the long-dead leaves from the branch's brittle length and then shredding them one by one.

Finally Lydia gave a great sigh and cast a concerned glance at Glory. "What *are* you going to do?"

Glory shrugged. "Make the best of it, I suppose. I knew it wouldn't be easy to forget Slade, but I'll manage somehow." Her fleeting smile was resigned, passive. Even the tone of her voice was different, sad and submissive—not at all reminiscent of the feisty, headstrong young woman Lydia was used to.

"Oh, Glory! You're not really going through with

this crazy thing, are you?"

"What else can I do? I really do believe it's for the best. And the rest of the family is happy about our engagement. Papa's ecstatic, and Mama's got the dressmaker bringing in mountains of sample materials and patterns every day."

"But you're not happy. And what about Slade?" questioned Lydia. "Hasn't he tried to contact you at all?"

"No, and I hope he won't." Glory's reply was a bit too quick to be believable.

"But when he hears about your engagement—"

"I'm sure he's already heard by now. If he wanted to stop me—" Breaking off, she shrugged her shoulders forlornly. "It's better this way." The words were low, sorrowful.

"But surely—"

The growing thunder of hooves interrupted Lydia. She turned and shielded her eyes against the sun to watch the approaching rider. "Who is that? Can you tell?"

"No," Glory answered, squinting to gaze at the figure drawing nearer and nearer. A flowing gray cloak enveloped the rider's body, its deep hood completely shadowing the face.

Alarmed at the rider's frantic pace, the two young women glanced toward their tethered horses and exchanged worried looks. A growing awareness of the war was beginning to impact even lazy afternoon outings. Suddenly their safety seemed not quite assured, and they nodded in mute agreement that it might be wise to leave before the stranger got any closer. They quickly headed up the grassy bank to where the horses were secured. As if perceiving their intent, the rider turned and cut across their path. Within seconds the intimidating figure had jerked the snorting horse to a halt and dismounted in one smooth movement.

"Wait! I have to talk to you," a voice called out. The concealing hood fell back, revealing a cascade of bright golden hair.

"You!" Glory gasped in shock.

Lydia simply gaped.

"Miss Westbrook—"

Glory spluttered in anger. "What are you doing out here? No one knew we were going to be here today. And they wouldn't have told *you* anyway!" A sudden realization angered her further. "You . . . you followed us!"

"Yes, I did," Joella said with an emphatic nod. "It was the only way I could get you alone long enough to tell you something of great importance. I'm quite sure you wouldn't relish the idea of me knocking on your door—"

"You wouldn't dare!"

"Don't worry. This way suits me better, too. It's much safer for both of us. Now, if you'll just calm down, all I want is a few minutes of your time—"

"You can't be serious! There's nothing you could say that could possibly be of interest to me." Glory tipped her head obstinately and proceeded to cut a wide circle around the offensive figure, intent on reaching her horse and putting as much distance as possible between herself and the detestable Miss

208

Ashland.

"Are you so sure you don't want to hear what I have to say?" Joella said softly, almost tauntingly. "Don't you harbor even one little ounce of curiosity about what Slade was doing at my place that morning?"

Furious, Glory whirled. "I *know* what he was doing there! I have no interest in hearing the sordid details. And I'll thank you to leave me alone!"

Joella's gaze raked the small, proud figure up and down. She sighed deeply and shook her head. "I don't know why I even bothered." Casting her eyes heavenward, she continued. "What on earth am I doing out here, chasing some hard-headed heartless little snip? Slade Hunter deserves better than that."

"What!" Glory sputtered. "Deserves better! How dare you—"

"I dare because it's true. Why? Does the truth bother you, Miss Westbrook?"

If looks could kill, Glory's gaze would have dispatched Joella instantly.

"I came looking for a woman worthy of Slade's love. I evidently made a mistake. You're nothing but a spoiled, self-centered child. I can't imagine what he sees in you," Joella said.

Hands flying to her face, Lydia gasped at the harsh words. Her gaze swung immediately to her friend. Bright spots of color bloomed on Glory's cheeks as Joella continued.

"Slade needs a woman . . . a *real* woman. Someone who would give him the chance to explain before childishly jumping to conclusions. Someone who'd

209

love him so much that she'd trust him no matter how bad things looked. What a shame that you're obviously not that kind of woman, Miss Westbrook — especially since he loves you so desperately."

Stunned, Glory could only stand and gape at the mocking woman. Despite a raging anger, a small flame of hope flickered deep inside her at Joella's last words.

Joella turned her back on Glory as if in dismissal, tugging at the knotted ties of her cape. It slipped easily from her shoulders, revealing a dark green riding skirt and matching jacket. Even those functional garments molded her sensuous curves in a most disturbing manner. Once again a cold fury burned within Glory as she thought of Slade sampling those charms. Her nails bit into the tender skin of her palms as she watched Joella catch the cape as it slithered from her slim form and then drape it over her horse's saddle.

Once the hindering cloak was disposed of, Joella faced Glory again, feigning surprise that she still stood there.

Knuckles propped against her curvaceous hips, she tilted her head. "You might as well leave, Miss Westbrook. I obviously made a mistake in trying to talk to you." Her green eyes were filled with contempt as she gazed coldly at Glory. She gave a little dismissing flick of her hand. "Go back to your big fancy house and your rich ol' daddy. I've cleared my conscience. At least I made an effort to set you straight."

"Oh!" Rage was building fast in Glory's eyes. She

clenched her fists tightly at her sides, not wanting to listen to the woman's contemptuous words, but unable to make herself turn and walk away.

Lydia stood frozen in place, her astonished gaze flicking back and forth between the two inflamed adversaries. Tension sizzled in the warm September air as Glory glowered and Joella continued to smile disdainfully.

"Slade won't grieve for you forever," Joella taunted in a sultry voice. "Oh, I admit I've never before seen anyone in quite as much anguish over losing a woman. But there'll come a day when he needs someone . . . when he'll crave the warmth and love you refused him. And, I promise you, Miss Westbrook — there'll be plenty of women who won't turn down such a man. I know I wouldn't."

The words sliced through Glory's heart with rapier swiftness. The thought was devastating; the pain total, absolute. Her face puckered, her lips trembled, and fat heavy teardrops gathered on her lashes.

Lydia gasped. "You're awful!" she cried out in defense of her friend. "How can you be so cruel to her? Can't you see how unhappy Glory is?"

A small breeze ruffled Joella's sun-kissed hair. She tossed her head, shaking the long tresses out of her way. "Is that so, Miss Upton — that is the correct name, isn't it?" Lydia nodded mutely. "Ummm. Why do I find it so hard to believe that Miss Westbrook has tender feelings for Slade after what she's done?"

"She *does* love Slade!" Lydia protested vehemently, stomping her foot in angry punctuation of the statement. "She always has!"

211

Raking Glory with an appraising gaze, Joella assessed the situation. Was her ploy working? Was Glory getting mad enough to stay—first to fight, and then hopefully to listen to what Joella had to say?

Joella crossed her arms under her breasts, pushing their lush fullness upward. She stood hip-shot, nonchalant, looking so irritatingly cool and at ease that Glory longed to scratch her eyes out.

"You may very well hate me, Miss Westbrook. You may even want to blame me for all this misery you're so delightfully wallowing in . . . it makes little difference to me."

Glory's eyes flashed with amber fire. She stood straighter, prouder, more determined with each word she heard.

Joella raised a delicate eyebrow at the subtle changes. "Tell me, Miss Westbrook, do you love Slade Hunter or not?"

Glory stood mute for a long, long time. The fury and frustration built higher and higher until finally she exploded. "Yes!" Glory screamed the word, venting her raw emotions in the single syllable.

Joella smiled again; this time there was something other than contempt on her face. "Good. Now, perhaps I can persuade you to sit down and listen to me. Surely, your feelings for Slade warrant a few minutes of your time? It might be the most important time you ever spent."

Angry, confused, intrigued, hopeful, Glory responded to the challenge. Head high, spine ramrod straight, she marched back to the fallen tree and flounced down upon its weathered length.

Joella inclined her head politely in the opposite direction. "If you'll excuse us for a few minutes, Miss Upton? What I have to say is highly confidential."

Shocked beyond words that Glory would actually stay and talk to the woman, Lydia could only nod mutely. With a toss of her head, she stomped out of hearing distance and plunked herself down on a rock. Joella ignored the glare of righteous indignation Lydia cast her way, turning to follow Glory's path. Within a matter of seconds she, too, was seated on the toppled tree.

"I'm listening," Glory declared in a clipped, no-nonsense tone when Joella was finally settled.

Casting a wary glance at the young woman, Joella contemplated what she was about to say. It was a risk — a great risk. Afraid that any more consideration on her part would only further confirm the foolishness of what she was about to do and make her unable to do it, Joella haltingly began her story.

"My better judgment tells me not to do this, but sometimes a person has to follow their heart, not their head. And there's always the fact that Slade trusts you — that's got to count for something. So . . . all I can do is hope I won't come to regret my sympathetic impulse."

"Miss Ashland, would you please say whatever it is you have to say?" Glory beseeched through clenched teeth.

Joella squirmed around, adjusting her seat on the hard, bumpy surface of the tree to a more comfortable position. "You're right. Time to get on with it. First of all, I want to assure you that there's nothing

213

personal between Slade and me—at least nothing romantic. We're friends. Good friends. And that's all. Oh, I won't deny that the thought of that relationship becoming something more hasn't crossed my mind a time or two."

Glory's eyes narrowed dangerously in response to the last remark.

"But much to my regret, Slade's heart doesn't seem to have room for more than one woman. I can only hope the fact that the woman he loves is you won't condemn a good man to eternal unhappiness."

A strange numbness filled Glory. Everything felt so alien, so unreal. Was this really happening? What was she doing sitting here, sharing a length of weatherworn timber on the edge of a deserted prairie with the town's most notorious woman? The whole scene was something out of an over-staged theatrical melodrama.

But it wasn't make-believe. They weren't surrounded by stage props. Overhead a hawk circled lazily, riding the warm air currents in the azure sky. A small breeze rustled the tall tufts of dusty green grass along the creek, whose muddy water flowed silently, eternally toward a meeting with the Elm Fork of the Trinity River. And next to Glory, swinging one slim ankle in a slow arc, sat Joella Ashland!

Glory blinked in an effort to reclaim reality, forcing her attention back to the situation at hand. Staring at the tightly clenched fists in her lap, Glory drew three deep breaths. When she felt she could speak rationally again, she looked at Joella. "Why are you doing this? Why would you go to all this

214

trouble for me? It's obvious you don't like me."

Joella shook her head. "I'm not doing it for you. I'm doing it for Slade. And you're wrong. Although the way you've hurt Slade makes me mad as hell, I don't dislike *you*. Everyone makes mistakes. Lord knows I've made enough of my own." Her voice grew wistful, her eyes misty. "I wish someone had taken the effort to talk to me in the past like I'm trying to talk to you. I was once faced with a very difficult decision and . . . and I've never been able to shake the feeling that I made the wrong choice. Maybe you'll be smarter than I was."

"Please—"

"Well! Back to the subject at hand." Joella straightened her spine, squared her shoulders, and put the past behind her once again. "The point is, Miss Westbrook, that Slade Hunter loves you more than you'll ever know. He's a kind man, a generous and giving man, a brave man. He's been a friend to me in many ways that I can never repay. If he wants you that desperately, I'm compelled to try to soothe the trouble between you."

"All right, Miss Ashland. Even if I could accept friendship as your motive, that still doesn't explain what Slade was doing at your saloon—in your private quarters—at that time of the morning."

Joella shook her head wryly. "You have no idea what kind of man you're dealing with. Slade's been going out of his way to help human beings that have no earthly means of helping themselves. And in doing so he has risked his life more than once."

"What are you talking about?"

215

Joella's mouth thinned in frustration. "So help me, if it turns out I've been wrong to trust you, and you run and tell the authorities, I'll . . . I'll—" She threw up her hands in exasperation. "Lord! How I hope Slade hasn't misjudged you! He's so damn sure that under all those spoiled little rich girl trappings there's a woman of substance and principle. Dear God, let him be right!"

"If you don't tell me what you're talking about I'm going to scream." Glory delivered the statement in deadly earnest.

Joella was faced with the ultimate decision. Either she had to tell Glory the whole truth or give up her rash undertaking. She might as well get on her horse and ride back to town as try to pass off some half-baked excuse to the suspicious woman beside her.

"All right, all right," Joella said in a weary voice. "Are you aware that there's an underground movement to help runaway slaves reach safety up North?"

The question was not at all what Glory expected. What a strange thing for Joella to be bringing up, she thought. What on earth did that have to do with anything?

"Well, yes, I suppose so." Glory tilted her head, a thoroughly perplexed look on her face. "I guess it exists. I mean, I heard rumors about it last year at school. One of the serving girls disappeared and they said she'd run away and gone North. But . . . but I don't understand. What does any of this have to do with Slade?"

"Oh, the organization exists all right. And, what's more, there's a similar association right here in

216

Texas—"

"What?" Glory exclaimed.

"It's true. It's much smaller, and so far it's only managed to smuggle a dozen or so runaways out of the state. But it's better that way, safer, much safer. There's only a handful of people who know about it. And the authorities don't even suspect it exists. We want to keep it that way."

Glory gazed at Joella in shocked disbelief. "You can't possibly mean that Slade is involved in such goings-on!"

"Why not, Miss Westbrook? You're bound to be aware of his feelings about slavery."

"Yes, of course—"

"Then why is it so hard to believe that he'd be willing to help some poor wretch find his way to freedom?"

"But . . . but it's against the law. If anyone finds out, he'll be in trouble! Why, they might even put him in prison!"

"That could very well be true if some irate slaveowner didn't save the court the trouble of holding a trial . . . by shooting him down for aiding and abetting the runaways."

"Oh, no!"

"Oh, yes. And you'd better think long and hard about that if it ever crosses your mind to divulge what I've told you."

Horror on her face, Glory shook her head vehemently. "I wouldn't do anything to hurt Slade!"

"What about your friend, Miss Upton?" Joella asked, nodding her head toward the rock where Lydia sat, chin in hand, watching and waiting.

217

"What are you going to tell her when she asks what I had to say?"

"Why, I'll . . . I'll tell her the part about Slade and you not being . . . not being involved—"

"That's all?"

"Of course. But you're wrong about Lydia. I could tell her all of it. She'd never do anything to hurt anyone, especially Slade. She's always liked him a great deal. But I promise I won't say a word about the other things you've told me."

"Well, that'll have to be good enough, I suppose. At least now you understand what Slade was doing at the saloon."

"I . . . I don't know—"

"Damn, girl! Where are your brains? He'd just got back in town after escorting two men to the next rendezvous point. He was checking in with me . . . letting me know that everything had gone all right."

Glory's mouth fell open. She stared at the woman with a whole new attitude. "You mean that *you're* involved in this, too?"

"Good Lord, yes! I'm the one who recruited Slade to help. We've been working together for almost a year."

The breath whooshed out of Glory. Her mind whirled with the implications of Joella's disclosure. Was what the woman really said true? Slade and Miss Ashland involved in smuggling runaways out of the state? Heavens above! Wild emotions chased each other across Glory's face as she considered the significance.

"But . . . but if what you say is true, then that

218

means Slade didn't — "

"No," Joella stated softly, knowing exactly what Glory was referring to. "He didn't. He wouldn't."

Joy flashed in Glory's eyes, then shame at how badly she'd misjudged Slade. He'd practically begged her to listen to his explanation that morning! But she'd been so sure he'd wronged her, so self-righteous in her conviction, that she'd refused to afford him even that small courtesy. How could she ever make amends for being so stubborn, so foolhardy? Would he be willing to forgive her?

But what about this foolish crusade Slade was involved in? Could she simply ignore the fact that he was participating in a scheme that was in direct opposition to her upbringing? Was helping the run-aways the same as stealing from the slaveowners — men just like her father? Could such actions ever be justified?

Then Glory remembered her own repugnance to the comments Preston had made that afternoon at Sivells Bend. And what about the rumors of abuse that periodically surfaced regarding slaves? Just because her family didn't mistreat their slaves didn't mean that a few others might not do so. It was all so confusing! If there was truth to such tales, could . . . could Slade's actions be laudable rather than dishonorable?

"But why didn't Slade ever tell me?" Glory's words bespoke her bewilderment.

Joella could almost decipher each disturbing thought as it raced across Glory's stricken face. She sighed and proceeded to put the poor girl out of her misery.

"Slade's too honorable to betray his vow of silence. Even if it meant losing you and being unhappy the rest of his life, he would never reveal his knowledge of the organization. Too many other people would be endangered by such a disclosure."

"But *you're* telling—"

A bittersweet smile tugged at the corner of Joella's mouth. "Yes, I am. But no one is in danger except Slade and myself. You don't know who the other contacts are. And I assure you there's no record of who they are, so even if I were to be discovered, those people will still be safe. I'd never tell, no matter what the authorities did to me."

Glory kept silent, watching the woman with growing respect.

"If you tell the authorities about me, you also endanger Slade. And somehow I can't make myself believe that you'd do that. Besides, would you have believed Slade if he had come to you with such a tale?"

"I . . . I really don't know," Glory admitted shamefully.

Joella shrugged as if to verify the truth of her words. "Slade would never have put me in that kind of danger. Not even to keep you. But, think of this, Miss Westbrook, what do I have to gain from this situation? Absolutely nothing. I've placed my safety in your hands. That ought to convince you of the truthfulness of what I've said."

Everything Joella said made absolute sense to Glory. How could she *not* believe the woman's sincerity?

"Yes. Yes, it does," Glory agreed in a meek little voice. "Does . . . does Slade know you were going to contact me?"

Joella shook her head emphatically. "No. I didn't tell him, in case I couldn't reason with you. Why get his hopes up for nothing?"

"What . . . what can I do?"

"What do you want to do?" Joella asked her softly.

Her eyes full of yearning, Glory answered firmly. "Talk to him. Apologize. See if we can somehow keep our love alive despite my foolishness."

Satisfied that Glory meant what she said, Joella nodded thoughtfully. "Very well. I'll do whatever I can to help you."

Glory reached to touch Joella's hand in gratitude. "Thank you, oh, thank you so much." Suddenly she frowned. "But what should I say? Oh, dear! And when will I have a chance to talk to him?"

"You won't have to say much of anything. Just tell him you love him. That's all it'll take. As for the opportunity, I think I can provide you with that."

"You can? How? Where?"

Joella eyed Glory speculatively, assessing the mettle of the young woman. "How badly do you want to see Slade?"

"I'll do anything—"

"All right. I have an idea," Joella said. "I can send Slade a message telling him to stay in town tonight. He'll think nothing of it, since I've made the request several times before when we were expecting refugees. He'll stay at the store all night. All you have to do is

221

get there."

Even as she said the words, Joella could see the determination gathering in Glory's face. She knew without a doubt that Glory was going to do it. Come hell or high water, Glory was going to the man she loved.

Chapter Twelve

The velvet shroud of the night closed around Glory as she slipped through the back door and then carefully pulled the door shut behind her. The click of the latch made her heart leap into her throat, where it beat in wild syncopation with her breathing for a long moment.

Pulling the dark merino cape tightly about her body, Glory rounded the corner of the house on tiptoe, darting from trellis to tree to hedge until she reached the street.

Late that evening the wind had shifted. It now came from the north, reaching fingers of cooling air across the gently rolling prairie land to pluck the heat from the night. The clean scent of coming rain curled across the land as scattered gunmetal gray clouds scudded across the starless sky, playing peek-a-boo with the pale moon.

Should she continue to hug the shadows of houses

and foliage, working her way slowly over the half-dozen blocks she had to cover to reach Slade's store? Or should she strike out boldly down the edge of the road and hope that the prudent folk of the town had long ago taken to their beds? Casting a baleful eye at the angle of the moon in the indigo sky, she calculated the hour at well past midnight. Except for the area around the saloon, surely her path would be deserted.

A little thrill of fear blossomed in the pit of her stomach. She didn't relish spending time alone in the darkness. No doubt about it. Quicker would be better.

Pulling the hood of her cloak lower over her face, Glory hunched her slim shoulders tighter against the night's chilly breezes and struck out for town. Her black kid slippers made only the tiniest sibilant whisperings as she hurried past the shuttered and silent houses.

An owl hooted softly in the distance. Glory's head jerked up at the sound and she stopped to scan the terrain with wide, anxious eyes. The eerie lament rode the night wind, then faded into oblivion.

Funny, she thought, how the two large windows framing the entryway of the Benson house—darker slashes against the ghostly white facade of the building—suddenly reminded her of unblinking eyes, probing, searching, seeming to follow her stealthy progress in the inky blackness. She suppressed a shiver and pulled her gaze away from the disconcerting sight.

How very peculiar the vast empty reaches of the

night made her feel, smothering her in its stygian center, then fading away into the nothingness of far universes.

Lord, how she wished Lydia were with her! How much easier that last trip to town had been with her friend by her side. But, alas, Lydia was safe at home, snug in her pink canopied bed . . . while Glory, trying gallantly to suppress the fright that suddenly bubbled and boiled within her, hurried through the ominous black of the night.

Stop that! Glory chided herself silently. There was no sense dwelling on such matters. They would only sharpen her apprehension. She was going to complete this journey, be it through the very pits of hell! Nothing, no one was going to stop her. Least of all her own silly imaginings.

Glory quickened her step as a strong gust of wind whispered through the treetops, sending them dancing as if to music. Splatters of silvery moonlight appeared and disappeared beneath her feet as overhead the leaves parted, joined, and parted again to nature's rhythmic zephyr.

Slade, Slade, Slade. The pattern of her footsteps called his name, blending with the heavy beat of her heart to urge her onward. Past the huge sprawling homes lining Pecan Street, past the more modest dwellings bracketing Rusk, right to the edge of the town's market square.

Glory stopped dead in her tracks, her mouth a small round O of apprehension as she stared at the gaping ebony maw of the alley entrance. In the distance, thunder rumbled. Lightning darted between heaven and earth, momentarily rimming the clouds with silver. No. She shook her head emphatically. She might have been brave enough to enter that forbidding hole in the bright of day, but nothing would induce her to do so now.

A shudder rang through her as she envisioned the night inhabitants of the passageway. Spiders . . . rats. Ugh! No way! She'd bluster her way through a chance encounter with humanity first.

A fat raindrop splashed against Glory's hand as she hurried on to the intersection. She dried the dampness with the edge of her cape, oblivious to the dozen or so that spattered her cloak with coin-sized circles of moisture as she turned left on Boggs Street.

The chilling night air carried the sound of a rinky-tink piano from down the street. Light spilled through the multi-paned window as well as from the open entrance of the Silver City Saloon, bathing the far end of the block in golden patches of illumination. Her slippers going whisk, whisk, whisk against the weathered boardwalk, Glory quickly passed the deserted businesses bordering the south side of the courthouse square, drawing nearer and nearer to the only source of light and sound on the street.

Prudently she slowed her pace, creeping along next to the rough-hewn walls. Suddenly there was a crash, and then the clink of broken glassware. A roar of laughter rang through the night. Glory's heart fell straight to her toes. Fear flooded her, setting her blood surging wildly.

With a frightened gasp, she pushed herself into the narrow niche of a doorway, hugging the wall with all her might. The laughter echoed loudly and finally died. The piano continued its merry recital. In a moment or two the low babble of voices began again.

Glory drew a deep breath and peeped carefully around the corner of her hiding place. Just then the saloon's swinging doors were slammed outward and two burly men stumbled through, arms about each other's shoulders. The doors flapped back and forth, each agitated swing slower than the last, and finally ceased their motion. With vigilant eyes, Glory watched the drunken pair weave their way across the street to be swallowed up by the raven shadows of the courtyard square, their loud, off-key singing the only evidence of their continued existence.

Glory waited for the hammering of her heart to slow. When no one else emerged, she gathered her courage and once again began her trek. Trying hard to stay within the shelter of the deepest shadows, she inched her way along the saloon front. At the window, she stopped to peep around the edge, watching through the wavy glass in fascination as the establishment's inhabitants went about their nightly rituals.

When Glory finally felt reasonably sure that no one else was preparing to leave the saloon's raucous interior, she tiptoed to the edge of the boardwalk and stepped down onto the street's dusty surface. A jarring clap of thunder echoed through the night skies. Yanking her skirts high, she fled past the saloon and across the intersection as though the devil himself was nipping at her heels.

Safe on the other side of the street, Glory once again melted into the shadows on the boardwalk.

The rollicking tunes from the Silver City Saloon trailed her down the street, fading slightly with distance but still discernible in the crisp night air. Slipping carefully by the deserted entrance of the Davenport Hotel, she continued on her way, past a long length of windowless wall, past Mr. Morgerson's dime store, determinedly making her way to the last establishment on that block — Hunter's General Store.

Where the south and west walls of the building came together, the corner was blunted, making the diagonal entrance of the building visible from Commerce Street as well as Boggs. Glory rounded the corner and stepped gratefully into the niche that sheltered the barred double doors of wood and glass.

She'd done it! Relief flooded through her. Pushing the suddenly stifling hood from her head, she leaned weakly against the angled partition. Now for the next step.

Shielding her face with a hand on either side, Glory peered into the inky void behind the small window. The cloud-shrouded moon offered no help. The interior was black as the bowels of hell. Glory gulped hard. Her eyes fluttered shut as a thousand questions filled her mind.

What if Joella hadn't sent the message? Even if she had done as she promised, what if something else had kept Slade from heeding the plea to remain in town? And worse, even if he was here, what if he didn't want to see her?

She pressed her nose harder against the glass, her rapid breathing creating a patch of mist on the window. Squinting her eyes, she stared intently into the shrouded depths.

Glory tapped lightly against the glass. She waited. And waited. Nothing.

Oh, damn and double damn! She furtively darted a quick glance around the edge of her shelter. A sudden whoosh of wind spattered random raindrops over the dusty weathered boards beneath her feet. The next gust tugged a curl loose and whipped it across Glory's eyes. Sharp zigzags of lightning sizzled across the sky. Quickly brushing the tendril aside, she used the heavenly illumination to continue her perusal of the square.

Good! The streets were still deserted.

Her verified solitude gave her one last surge of courage. She rapped again, louder, longer, her knuckles smarting from the contact. The glass rattled, a distressing clamor in response to her brave assault. Again she waited, growing more disheartened by the minute.

But wait! Was something moving inside, stealthily making its way through the charcoal gloom? Her heart lodged in her throat, its frenzied beat echoing through her body, clamoring for release at each pulse point.

The specter drew nearer, filling the small window. There was a distinct click and the rasp of metal being drawn from its nesting place. The door eased open.

"Who's there?"

"Slade—" The word was a sigh, a promise, a plea.

"Glory!" Flinging the door open, Slade emerged from the shadows. "Sweet heaven! What are you

229

doing here?"

Sweet heaven was right. He was practically naked! The only garment he wore, firm-fitting trousers, rode low on his hips, the top button forgotten in his haste to dress.

"My God!" Slade muttered. "Do you realize the danger of being out alone at this time of night? What on earth can you be thinking?"

His strong fingers closed over her wrist and he fairly yanked her off her feet as he hauled her into the gloomy shelter of the store. He continued his dark mutterings all the while, but few of the words penetrated her reverie.

". . . traipsing around town in the middle of the night . . ." The door was firmly closed. ". . . some people don't have the sense God gave a goose . . ." The bolt was slid into place. ". . . if anyone ever needed a keeper!"

Barely able to make out Slade's movements in the darkness, Glory simply stood patiently where he'd left her. As soon as the door was secured, he whirled, grabbed her, and began to haul her into the blacker area at the back of the store.

She found it impossible to decipher the meaning of the death grip he had on her arm. Was he glad to see her? Or mad?

"Ouch!" Glory protested loudly as her ankle came into contact with the corner of a storage crate. Slade slowed not a whit.

Mercy! she thought as her skirt brushed along an object of such size that it could only be the long counter that separated proprietor from customer.

230

How in the world had he managed to avoid running smack into it in the pitch dark?

Once behind the counter, Slade came to a sudden stop. Glory crashed into him, her hands clutching at him in surprise. Her breath caught in her throat when they contacted the smooth, bare expanse of his back. His flesh felt like heated satin under her fingertips.

She couldn't see a thing, but she heard the grate of a knob as it was turned, the click of a latch as it retracted, the tiny groan of protest the hinges made as a door swung inward.

Once again fingers of steel closed over her wrist and she was jerked forward. The door thudded shut. Almost instantly she was hustled across a small open space and thrust downward by two firm hands. The backs of her legs struck a hard horizontal barrier, and before she could catch her balance, her derriere bounced against a thin mattress. Grabbing a double handful of blanket, she managed to keep from falling backward.

The rasp of a match echoed in the stillness. A single flame burst into yellow brilliance. The feeble light illuminated only the broad planes of Slade's face, leaving his eyes in eerie obscurity. Cupping a protective hand around the match's flickering glow, he bent low and touched it to the wick of a stubby candle on the table near the head of the bed.

The tiny fire flickered and caught. The shadows retreated a modicum, and the room went from obsidian to charcoal gray.

Slade loomed over her, hands clenched at his sides,

a scowl on his face. At first full sight of him, Glory forgot the danger, the shadows, and the possible foolhardiness of her crusade.

The pale glow of the candle flame burnished his sleek tanned skin the color of heated cognac. Thick ebony hair fanned across his muscular chest, narrowing as it traveled down his corrugated stomach. It lovingly bracketed the tempting dimple of his navel, and then, now only a thin line, continued its path down . . . down . . . to finally disappear beneath the gaping waistband of his britches.

"What in hell do you think you're doing?" he demanded, his voice thick with emotion.

Glory quickly raised her eyes to his, a blush beginning to warm her cheeks before she realized he was only asking why she was there. Refusing to show any weakness, she first unhooked her cloak, letting it fall from her shoulders, and then primly placed her hands in her lap. Drawing herself up straight and proud, she met his gaze unwaveringly.

"I came to apologize—"

Slade's mouth gaped open and he simply stood and stared at her for a long minute. Finally one hand was raised to ravage his already tousled hair.

"Damn," he muttered softly, and he began to pace the narrow space between wall and bed.

"Are you angry that I came?"

He cast a devouring look her way. She was a small, still figure, watching him with childlike expectation. Lips slightly parted, eyes large and luminous. He could drown in the sweet intoxicated depths of those sherry orbs. He longed to twine his fingers in the wild disarray of curls that framed her face. He ached to taste the sweet wine of her mouth once again. She was so beautiful, so innocent, so tempting.

Angry? What possible answer could he give? Yes, he was angry with her for coming—although perhaps frightened was a better word for what he felt. Would she never learn the folly of indulging in such dangerous escapades? But angry with her for being there? No. How could he be when his heart had ached for the sight of her since that morning at Joella's—

Joella! Christ, he'd completely forgotten his reason for staying the night at the store. What if the messenger showed up now? How would he explain?

His fingers raked once again through the thatch of sable hair, then over his whisker-shadowed chin. He suddenly halted in front of her, reaching to grab her hand and pull her to her feet.

"Come on. You've got to go home. I'll . . ." Did he dare leave? Yes, he had to. He couldn't possibly send her into the menacing night alone. Surely the messenger would wait a few minutes, if he came at all. "I'll walk you home. Hurry." He dropped her hand and made a grab for the shirt hanging on a peg by the door.

"No. I'm not leaving," she said, reaching to stop his hand.

Whirling, Slade grabbed her shoulders. "You don't understand. You've got to go. I . . . I may have to leave—"

"No," she said with a shake of her head. *"You* don't understand. You won't have to leave. No one is coming. We planned it this way."

Completely befuddled, Slade gaped at her. "W-what? We? Who? Planned what? What in the world are you talking about?"

"This. Us. Joella knew it was the only way we could be together."

His breath whooshed out. "Joella? But . . . but how, when?" His grip tightened and he frantically searched her eyes. "What do you know about all this?"

"Everything."

Chapter Thirteen

"Everything?" Slade repeated in a whisper.

Thunder rumbled, closer now. A flash of blue-white light flickered through the burlap draped across the small storeroom window. And then again. The storm was almost there.

"Yes."

Rain spattered fitfully against the windowpane. Once again the skies grumbled their protest.

"But . . . but how?"

Glory tenderly took Slade's hand and led him back to the small cot. "Let me explain," she said when they were sitting side by side. And she did.

When the story was finished, Slade wearily leaned his spine against the rough wall. "I'm sorry you got dragged into this, Glory. It's not safe for you to know. That's just one more reason why this thing between us was doomed from the beginning—"

"Doomed?" repeated Glory in shock. "You can't mean that. If I'd thought that for one minute, I wouldn't be here."

"But it's bound to make a difference in how you feel about me. From your family's point of view, I'm little better than a criminal for helping those poor souls escape."

Glory placed a soothing hand on his arm. "Slade, listen to me. Maybe I can't give my complete approval regarding this situation — after all, the whole idea is very new and strange to me. But I do think I understand your motives. Despite my personal feelings, I believe with all my heart that your reasons are honorable."

Slade raised hopeful eyes to Glory's face. "You do?"

"Of course. You wouldn't be the man I love if you didn't heed your convictions. I can't fault you for that." For a minute Glory didn't think Slade was going to relent.

Then suddenly a wide smile of relief lit up Slade's features, and he wrapped his arms gently around Glory, pulling her back against the velvet steel of his chest.

Lord above! What a quandary they were in. True, Joella had kindly stepped in to solve the initial problem for them, but there were still so many knotty issues.

Slade could think of no way to win the Colonel's approval. Perhaps after all this crazy war business was over and done — but certainly not now.

And what about Preston Harper? It mattered not that Glory had accepted his proposal before she knew the truth about him and Joella. She was still caught fast in the devious bastard's cruel web. A gentleman might be persuaded to shoulder the blame and find an acceptable excuse to bow out of such a situation, thus leaving the lady's honor unblemished. However, despite his outward trappings, Slade knew Preston to be no gentleman. And the undeniable fact that the Colonel was one hundred percent in favor of the marriage hung over their heads like Damocles' sword. Slade knew full well that Westbrook would employ every devious trick in the book to accomplish his own selfish aims. Slade considered warning Glory about Preston's devious nature, but he finally pushed the thought aside after deciding she had enough to worry about at present.

Unconsciously Slade stroked Glory's arm, as if to reassure himself of her presence. His weary mind balked at dissecting the further problems he faced—the possible consequences of Joella's disclosure, his constant concern about Morgan. Then there were the escalating pressures of the League.

Knox had been almost surly earlier that afternoon when Slade had declined to attend an emergency meeting called for that night—something of "utmost importance" was about to take place, Knox had intoned dramatically. They needed every man in attendance.

But Slade had been just as adamant about not going. His first commitment that night was to Joella and the cause. But, of course, Slade had been unable to reveal the real reason behind his refusal. And eventually Knox had stomped out of the store, his anger barely concealed. Slade had spent the rest of the day wondering if Knox had contacted his father. Slade almost hoped Anson had chosen to visit Mrs. Stafford rather than attend the League meeting.

Right now Slade didn't want to think of any of those things. Not with Glory here, soft and warm in his arms. He simply wanted to cherish the moment, for such opportunities had been few and far between. He hugged her tighter and let his numerous worries seep slowly away.

Glory felt so at peace in Slade's embrace. She exalted in the protective weight of his arm about her shoulders. Snuggling her cheek closer against the broad expanse of his chest, she smiled at the faint, reassuring thud of his heart under her ear. One small hand was curved around the gentle slope where throat and shoulder met. A tiny movement caught her eye and she tilted her head to further investigate the gentle throbbing in the hollow of his throat. Mesmerized, she shifted her thumb and laid the sensitive pad against the intriguing tick. Soon she felt the soft pulsing increase.

The dark haze of hair covering his chest tickled her wrist and she slowly skimmed her hand downward, savoring the intriguing texture with her palm. When her fingertips grazed the hard copper nub buried in the hair, Slade drew a sudden harsh breath and his hold on her tightened. Intrigued, she repeated the gesture, drawing an agonized groan in response.

"Sweet Jesus in heaven above, Glory! I'm dying for want of you." Slade's voice was a ragged velvet murmur.

The soft stroking of her arm ceased. He shifted his weight, grasping and turning her effortlessly until

238

they were face to face, with her half lying across him, her breasts nestled against the hard planes of his bare chest, legs curled beneath her on the bed. They were so close she could feel the syncopated hammering of their heartbeats.

His hand skimmed up her shoulder, sliding around her nape and into the thick curls at the back of her head. Tightening his fingers in the long tresses, he exerted gentle pressure, pulling her head back until their gazes locked.

It was like looking straight into his soul. The smoldering fire in Slade's eyes set Glory's heart singing. The raw passion glimpsed in those ebony pupils, so dilated that only a tiny rim of gray was visible, sent molten heat searing through her veins. Blood surged through her body until every nerve ending was tingling with desire.

She could feel Slade's growing fever in his breath, hot and teasing against her skin, as he showered kisses across her throat, under the gentle curve of her jaw. The tiny nips of his strong white teeth on her sensitive skin were sweet agony.

Nibbling his way to her ear, he buried his nose in the silken locks, breathing in the woman scent of her until he was dizzy with the sweetness. When he finally took her earlobe into his mouth to suck and nip, Glory shivered with pleasure. And then he flicked the moist tip of his tongue across the rim of her ear.

"Ah," Glory moaned softly, arching reflexively, pressing forward for greater contact with the heated steel of Slade's body. Her arms went tighter about his body and her fingers lovingly traced the great slabs

239

of muscle that coiled and flowed under the bare, bronzed skin of his back.

The grip of his widespread fingers against the base of her skull chained her to him. When she thought she could stand no more, Slade lowered his head, fitting his mouth perfectly over hers. At first the pressure was gentle, almost reserved, his lips barely brushing against the sensitive surface of hers. And then he expertly increased the force, moving, blending, molding the kiss until the exquisiteness of the union drew tiny mewing sounds from deep in Glory's throat. His tongue traced the edges of her lips, the soft inner linings, the serrations of her teeth. Finally, he delved into the honeyed recesses of her mouth, savoring the taste of her with each rapier stroke.

Neither heard the escalated clashes of thunder now grumbling across the land. The lovers' ears were attuned only to quick gasps of breath, velvet moans of desire, soft little sobs of passion. Nor did they see the increased frenzy of the lightning as it danced beyond the curtained window, for they had eyes only for each other.

Glory groaned at the sweet thrust of Slade's tongue. Hers met his in joyous dance. The finest wine was tasteless compared to the intoxicating flavor of his mouth. Her nipples tightened, thrusting against the hair-roughened expanse of his chest. She moaned a protest at the separating cloth of her bodice, craving more, needing more. Twisting sensuously, she rubbed against him, increasing the frustrating tactile pressures.

Filled with equal frustration, Slade moaned deep in his throat. "My sweet Glory, my precious love.

You set my soul on fire. I can't get enough of you."

She knew what he wanted. She wanted it more. "Touch me," she breathed against his lips.

With a long, deep sigh of desire Slade slipped a hand between them, blindly fumbling the row of tiny buttons open as he deepened the kiss. Once the last button was undone, he thrust the edges of the shirt-waist aside. His knuckles brushed the generous swell of bosom above Glory's chemise, and Slade moaned softly.

Once again his fingers fumbled between them, seeking the tiny satin bows that secured her chemise. Finding the first prize, he grasped the ribbon between forefinger and thumb and pulled the loops free. Then the next. And the next. At last! His trembling fingers whisked the dainty lace-edged garment aside.

Releasing her mouth, he drew away to look in awe at the splendid sight of Glory's naked breasts. The fever in her blood had tinted the pert, puckered tips a deeper shade of coral. Gently, almost reverently, he reached out, feathering his palms across the pearled nipples, his touch light as a butterfly's wings on a magnolia petal. Elation filled him as they tautened even more under his hands.

Glory sucked in a deep breath. Nothing but his touch could cool her fevered flesh.

"Slade," she pleaded huskily. "More. Please."

Slade's worshiping gaze flickered to Glory's face. His heart soared, becoming a wild thing within him, when he saw the desire etched in the sherry depths of her eyes. Drawing a ragged breath, he turned his face heavenward for a long moment, as if in supplication.

Then once again he lowered his eyes, his gaze hungrily devouring the rich fullness of her breasts.

The wildly gusting wind plucked at the ill-fitted windowframe, whispered through the narrow crack under the door to the alley, causing the candle flame to flutter. Answering shadows danced through the room and across the lush bare expanse of Glory's bosom. Where the light touched her skin it was palest golden-apricot. Her breathing was shallow, rapid, causing the twin mounds to tremble and heave. Tawny shadows flowed into the deep valley between her breasts.

"Oh, God." His words were a chant, a prayer, a benediction. "You're so beautiful, my love, so very beautiful."

Slade circled one breast with thumb and forefinger, pushing upward until the firm swell of her breast came to rest against his palm. For long moments he pleasured himself with the satiny feel of her skin, the lush full weight against his hand, the intriguing sight of her nipple swelling in response to his manipulations. Cupping his hand against the sensitive underside, he lifted her breast. With a sigh he took the proffered treasure within the sweet, heated depths of his mouth, gently raking his teeth across her exquisitely sensitive nipple.

Glory's hands skimmed up Slade's back to tangle in the thick black hair at his nape, pressing him closer, closer yet. She writhed as his tongue traced circles around the throbbing bud of her nipple, her fingers tightening in his curls. When his lips clamped tightly around her flesh and she felt the suckling pull of his mouth deep in her womb, she cried out with pleasure.

Slade finally ended the glorious torture by shifting until he could draw his legs up onto the bed. Twisting their bodies in unison, he lowered Glory until her back was pressed into the mattress and he was stretched out beside her. As soon as he held her as tight as possible against the length of him, he proceeded to once again plunder her mouth with long, deep strokes of his tongue.

Moaning, she arched against him, rocking in timeless rhythm. The hand that had been finessing her throbbing nipple swept down her side and grasped the rounded flesh of her buttocks tightly, pulling the delta of her desire against the straining bulge of his manhood. In answer to the heated tempo of his body, she bent her leg and arched her back to press harder against him in innocent invitation.

Outside, the heavens opened up, unleashing torrents of rain upon the land. Water pounded unheeded against the roof, gushed from the eaves, ran in rivulets over the small window. And all the while the lightning danced to the thunder's beat. Inside their warm shelter, Glory and Slade were caught in a storm of their own making.

The palm of Slade's hand was almost as hot as his breath against her throat. It skimmed down her body, stopping only long enough to pull the restricting material of her skirt upward. And then his hand was stroking the curve of her leg, the soft slope of her hip, the sensitive skin of her inner thigh. He pressed his palm against her heated center. But it wasn't enough, not near enough.

Long, slim fingers plucked at the ties to her pantalets, pulling them free, pushing the fabric down her legs, freeing her feet, discarding the scrap of cloth in a forgotten heap on the floor. Mere heartbeats later, his hand again sought the secret treasure of her body, brushing lightly across the silky, tangled hair, seeking, finding, caressing the silken petals of her womanhood.

And then he parted the flower, his fingers delving, rhythmically stroking the satin recesses of her soul. She shivered with delight, and bent her leg, giving him freer access to the prize he sought. Her soft moans, the gentle thrashing of her head told more completely than words ever could what pleasure he was giving her. His long fingers continued to stroke, building a fire inside Glory that threatened to consume her very soul. She sobbed aloud when his thumb rotated softly against the hard little nub hidden deep within the petals.

Slade raised his head and gazed at Glory. Eyes almost closed, breath rapid, she had given herself up totally to the exquisite feelings he was creating for her.

"Do you like that?" he whispered against her mouth while continuing the searing manipulation.

Her voice was ragged, hoarse when she answered. "Yes, oh, God, yes."

Arching against his hand, she moaned in response to the frissons of heat and sensation that blossomed beneath his touch, then spread like the ripples on a pond throughout her entire being.

"Tell me what you want," he entreated. "Tell me how you feel."

She groaned, raking her nails across his bare back.

"I . . . I think I shall die from the pleasure of your touch."

His heart sang with joy at the words. He ached to give her even greater ecstasy. He wanted nothing more than to touch and kiss and taste her loveliness forever. But his body was afire, the blood pooled heavily in his loins. The throbbing pressure of his manhood, straining hard against the restraining cloth of his trousers, clamored for relief. Soon it would be too late to turn back.

He stamped one last, long passionate kiss across her swollen mouth. Drawing a ragged breath, Slade buried his head against the curve of her neck.

"Glory, Glory," he whispered, his breath ragged against her shoulder. "This isn't the way I wanted it to be for you. I wanted everything perfect. Not . . . not like this. We need to stop."

She heard the anguish in his voice, felt the fierce throbbing of his heart, and then he groaned and stilled his hand.

"No!" she protested, wrapping her arms hard about him. "Don't leave me. I want you. I've loved you for so long. Please."

She tangled a hand in his hair, drawing his head upward until she could gaze into his eyes. Her passion raged stronger than the storm outside.

"It's not fair to you," Slade whispered, his eyes full of self-condemnation. "You deserve better — all the wonderful things that belong to a woman's wedding night. A fine big bed, silken sheets . . . the best of everything."

Glory smiled lovingly and shook her head. "Those are only *things*, Slade. Being with you has made me realize just how unimportant mere material possessions can be. Do you honestly think that those things are what matter? You forget — I have the most important thing of all."

"I . . . I don't understand — "

"Don't you know? I have your love. I'm surrounded by it. I can feel it wrapped all around me, singing in my veins, flowing over every inch of my soul. No fancy trappings could make this night any better."

Slade sucked in a hard breath. "Glory, are . . . are you sure?"

"I've never been more sure of anything in my life, my darling. I'll prove it."

With one quick movement, she slipped from his embrace. On her knees, she gathered her skirt in both hands and lifted one slim leg over his, reaching for the floor. Another second and she was standing beside the small cot. Slade rolled to his back, watching her every move with eyes the color of smoke.

With deft, precise motions Glory began to remove her rumpled clothing. There was a beatific smile on her face, the glow of soon-to-be-consummated love in her gaze.

Slipping the disheveled shirtwaist off her shoulders, she let the garment slide down her arms and fall in a forgotten heap on the floor. The chemise soon followed. One quick maneuver at the waistband of her skirt and it slithered down her legs. Daintily stepping out of the puddle of material at her feet, she stood proud and straight before him.

Slade gasped at the sight of his beloved.

Glory tilted her head proudly, sending cinnamon

tresses cascading down her back. Her breasts were high and firm, pearl-tipped with tight coral buds. Beneath their proud thrust, her body slimmed to a tiny waist, then flared softly into lush curved hips. Her legs were long and slim, perfectly molded, cradling a ginger veil of hair at their apex.

Slade's breath wedged in his throat. He felt the sting of joyous tears against the back of his eyelids.

She was glorious.

She was his.

They needed no words when she held out her hand to him. He rose like someone hypnotized, peeling away the only garment he wore in one quick motion, then he discarded the trousers across a packing crate.

A sudden flash of lightning stroked his body with silver, save for the dark thatchs of hair. The bulging muscles beneath his rock-hard buttocks bunched and slid with satin smoothness as he turned toward her. The proud thrust of his engorged manhood brought a gasp to Glory's lips.

She had never considered that a man's body could be beautiful, but she thought Slade's so now. The broad, sinewy shoulders. The massive chest, crowned with its dusting of ebony hair. The firm waist and flat, corrugated stomach. The slim hips that cradled the essence of his maleness.

They loved each other with their eyes, each sweeping look building the flames of desire higher. Of one mind, they stepped together, embracing each other tenderly. The feel of flesh against flesh was sweet agony. The musky aroma of their passion was intoxicating.

Slade's hair-roughened chest abraded the rigid

points of Glory's nipples. She sighed and shifted in his arms, rubbing the sensitive peaks against the soft, warm hair.

Hands skimmed over silken flesh and heated hollows.

Lips sought succor.

Tongues touched and tasted.

At last Slade cupped his palms against Glory's buttocks, tilting the warm, moist center of her desire against the pulsing throb of his passion.

"Now, please," she murmured against his heartbeat.

"Yes," he sighed.

And he took her hand and led her to the bed, lowering her gently to its surface. With one graceful movement he was braced above her.

"I love you, Glory."

"I know."

"In my heart, you're my wife. No preacher's words could make that any truer."

Sweet joy filled her as she felt the trembling probe of his shaft, poised delicately at the entrance to her soul. "And you, Slade, are the husband of my heart. I will have no other." She reached a slim hand between them, grasping the tool of her pleasure, gently guiding him into the silken sheath of her body.

Her touch was like sweet fire on his aroused flesh. When she raised her hands to cup his face, pulling his lips down to hers for a long, long kiss, he at last began to thrust ever so gently into her, shallow, tempered strokes that stoked the inner fires.

"Ahhh," he sighed. "You don't know how long I've dreamed of loving you like this."

His tongue thrust into her mouth in rhythm with his quickened beat. Each stroke took him a little deeper, stopping just short of the final thrust that would make her his forever.

She sensed he was holding back, but she wanted him, all of him. She would surely die if she didn't have him. Her hands curved around the steel strength of his buttocks, pulling him closer, urging him onward. Her body rocked against his, pulling him into the heated depths of her body.

He gave her what she wanted, sweeping aside the barrier of her innocence with one long thrust into her welcoming softness. He drank the small moan of pain from her lips, then raised his head to watch her eyes widen with surprise as each subsequent stroke brought deeper pleasure.

"You're mine now, Glory. Mine forever."

"Yes, oh yes," she answered, and her breath sighed out in a rapturous moan.

Slipping his hands under her hips, Slade increased the tempo of their joining, thrusting, meeting, burying himself in her sweetness. Stars danced before her eyes. Fire licked through her body with each beat. His mouth ravaged the hollow of her throat, the tender spot behind her ear, and then he claimed her lips. He drank the nectar of her mouth like a starving man. She wrapped her legs around his hips, her body matching his beat for beat as they traversed a star-kissed universe.

And then the magic began, deep, deep within the very pit of Glory's soul. Ripples of rapture flowed through her body, small tremors of ecstasy that grew and grew and grew until she thought she would die from the thrill of it all. Slade wrapped her tightly in his arms, crushing her against him. Sobbing her name, he showered her womb with his love as wave after wave of pleasure took them.

Chapter Fourteen

By the time the lovers left their secret bower, the night's violent storm had thundered its way out of the county and south to Dallas. A soft, clean breeze soughed its way across Gainesville as the town lay huddled in deep slumber under the deep predawn darkness.

Hands laced tightly together, Slade and Glory made their careful way from the market square to Pecan Street. Despite Glory's protests, Slade insisted on seeing her right to the back door of the Westbrook mansion. Right at the moment he cared not a whit if the Colonel caught them. Making an "honest woman" of Glory would be a privilege.

Parting was hard, but not as hard as it would have been had they not had such sweet memories to keep them company through the day. A dozen heated kisses, each more breathtaking than the last, and they finally managed to say good-bye, vowing to meet two days hence at an old abandoned homestead several miles outside of town.

The coming day was inching pale fingers of coral and pink and gold into the eastern sky when Glory at last slipped through the door. One last wave and the door eased shut. Then Slade made his way back to town, so elated that he scarcely heeded the abundance of mud puddles dotting the town's rutted streets.

Once back in the store, Slade straightened the back room, then prepared a bit of new merchandise for display. But he was far too happy to stay cooped up all day, and as soon as Mr. Cranford arrived he left the store in the old man's capable hands and went to fetch his horse from the livery stable around the corner.

It was indeed an absolutely glorious day, perhaps made even more so by the joy in Slade's heart. No clouds marred the brilliant blue sky of mid-morning as Diablo ambled his way along the muddy roads. Slade wore a wide smile, his mind filled with memories of the night he'd shared with Glory.

This morning he felt such contentment, such sheer bliss, that everything seemed possible. They *would* work things out. Somehow they'd manage to dissuade Preston about the marriage. The crazy war would end. The Colonel would see reason. And he and Glory would be married. Not one negative thought would stay in Slade's mind after such a wondrous night.

The whole world appeared clean and crisp, the dirt and drudgery of the terrible times confronting the state momentarily washed away in the cleansing waters of the storm. Slade was positive that nothing could spoil his good mood . . . but that was before he arrived at the farm and found Knox with his father.

Slade heard the loud voices before he even opened the door. "What's going on?" he asked as he hung his hat on a peg.

Anson sneezed, blew his nose loudly in a crumpled handkerchief, and then answered Slade in a raspy voice. "Nothing much, Son. Just a small difference of opinion."

"Anson, you gotta change your mind—" Knox pleaded, completely ignoring Slade's arrival.

"Look, Knox, I'm not going to argue about this with you. I'm not going back out there tonight."

"But—"

"But nothing. I don't intend to impose on Mrs. Stafford's kindness two nights in a row. She stayed with Jeff and Paula last night. Enough is enough."

"That ain't no excuse!" Knox argued. "If you wasn't so dang blind, you'd know the woman's sweet on you. She'd watch them kids every night if'n you only asked her to."

Anson snorted gruffly in response to Knox's statement. If there was anything but friendship between him and Mary, it was nobody else's business. "But I won't ask."

"I was counting on you, Anson—"

"Dammit, Knox! You *counted* on me last night . . . and look what I got for my efforts! The worst cold of my life. I'll be lucky if the damn thing doesn't turn into pneumonia."

"Ah, come on, ol' buddy. How was I to know we'd get hit by the biggest rainstorm we've had in ages?"

"The fact still remains that I spent three hours at Rock Creek last night—three hours sitting in that miserable cold rain waiting for your 'great scheme' to get underway. And what came of it all? Nothing. Not a damned thing!"

"Now, Anson, I explained all that—"

Anson sneezed three times in quick succession. "Explained! Ha! You never even told us what we were doing out there! All the whole bunch of us got for our time and misery was a good soaking. Too bad the six of us who showed up weren't smart enough to stay home like the rest of the League members. I wish I had! And, what's more, I intend to keep staying at home until I understand what the hell is going on."

Knox spread his hamlike hands wide. "I thought I'd made it all perfectly clear. I intended to explain everything just as soon as enough men arrived so that we could carry out the plan—"

"Plan!" Anson barked sharply. "What damn plan? I don't like all this secrecy crap. Not one bit. I thought we were all in this thing together—that the League would work as a unit to help each other. I've always taken pride in belonging to the League, but this just doesn't set right with me. Why all this huggery-muggery all of a sudden?"

"Is this the same meeting you were badgering me about yesterday, Knox?" Slade asked.

"Yeah," the big man answered, his booming voice

more than a tad sullen.

Slade shook his head. "And he didn't tell even *you* what was going on?" he asked his father. Slade had been irritated at Knox's big show of secrecy yesterday, but he was really surprised to find out that he'd played the same game with the elder Hunter.

After Anson had sneezed his way through a negative answer, Slade turned a baleful eye on Knox. "I think you'd better do some explaining, Knox, or it appears the Hunter men might have to call it quits with this League business."

Knox slumped heavily onto the sofa, his long, heavy legs sprawled out in front of him. Slade looked in distaste at the mud still caked on the man's shoes. Evidently Knox hadn't even taken time to change clothes after spending half the night out in the rain. What could possibly be *that* important?

"All right, all right. I'll tell you."

Running his hand across his thick black beard, Knox sighed loudly. His brows drew together, two bushy black slashes on his low forehead. Anson and Slade were well respected by local Union sympathizers. Having their support would almost guarantee the willing participation of a good many other League members. Finally, Knox made his decision. After all, telling them about the plan might be the best way to convince the Hunters to join him that night.

"We were going to raid the arsenal at McKinney," Knox said after a long pause.

"What!" The word exploded from Slade's and Anson's mouths at the same instant.

"Yeah." Knox nodded, the dark thatch of beard bobbing against his chest. "Now you see why I didn't want to tell anyone last night . . . at least not until the whole group reported in and we were ready to go. No sense getting everyone agitated before time to mount up and ride."

"Why in hell would you want to do a thing like that?" Slade demanded. "And what in the world makes you think that those men would have gone along with your crazy scheme anyway?"

Crazy scheme? Christ! Knox grimaced, realizing immediately that he'd made a dire miscalculation by confiding in the two men.

"They'd have gone," he answered sullenly. If the Hunters weren't aware of just how easily some men's emotions could be played upon, he wasn't going to argue the point now. Not with their dander up like it was.

Knox rubbed his neck, seeking to ease the headache that was forming at the base of his skull. He wished that Dunlap and Simmons were there to plead their cause. They'd know how to convince Anson and Slade of the importance of the raid. They'd certainly persuaded Knox fast enough.

Knox shot Anson's son a quick look of irritation. Damn! Why'd Slade have to show up? He was sure Anson alone would have been easier to convince. Knox dropped his betraying gaze back to the hands crossed atop his prominent belly and went on with his explanation.

"We couldn't hold the raid unless we had enough people. That was one reason for not telling anyone

256

what we had planned. If they knew about it, they might not come. After they all showed up we were going to explain to everyone at once."

"Who's 'we'?"

"Me and Dunlap and Simmons . . . one or two others."

"Since when are those Kansas Jayhawkers running the show?" Anson demanded loudly. The words brought on another fit of coughing.

"They ain't running the show, Anson. You know better than that." Knox's voice was wheedling, placating. "It's just that I can trust them not to lose their heads at the thought of a little fight. That's all."

"Oh?" Anson's voice was bitter. "And you think I would?"

Knox rose quickly. "Now, wait a minute. It 'pears you're taking this all wrong. You know that ain't the case—"

Slade's quiet voice cut the tension-laden air. "I think it's more the fact that you knew Pa and the others might not want to participate in your crazy scheme if they had much chance to think about it. That's why you didn't tell them ahead of time."

"Now, Slade," Knox whined. "You're surely not thinking right about this whole thing. Granted, some of them fellers are peace-loving, all right, but I'm positive they'd have agreed to the plan when they heard the whole story."

"I thought 'peace-loving' applied to all members of the League."

Knox frowned at the interruption. "Well, sure. But we gotta think about our own safety. You don't

257

believe for one minute that a Southern militia is going to protect our interests if things get bad, now, do you? We gotta be prepared to take care of ourselves."

"That still doesn't make it right to sneak around and concoct some crackpot scheme without the knowledge and consent of the whole organization, Knox," Anson protested.

"All right, all right, I see your point. But you got to consider how dangerous it would have been if word had leaked out about our plans . . . why, the militia woulda been all over us in no time flat! I had our safety to think about."

Slade's long stride covered the short distance from parlor to kitchen and back again. He made two more rounds, mulling Knox's words over in his mind, before coming to a stop before the big man.

"It doesn't appear you had anyone's safety in mind when you contrived such a ridiculous scheme. Good God, Knox! Men could have been killed!"

"Nah, Slade. You're wrong," Knox denied quickly. "Nothin' like that would have happened. We had it all planned out perfect. Going under cover of night like that, we'd have been able to pull it off without a hitch. It was just our bad luck that that damned storm blew in and ruined the whole thing—"

"I'd be more inclined to consider it a stroke of good luck, myself," Slade said in a cutting tone. "Tell me, Knox, what would have happened if the raid had gone as planned?"

"Why, nothing," Knox answered with a shrug of his huge shoulders. "All we was goin' to do was store the ammunition and gunpowder . . . kill two birds with one stone, so you might say. The militia wouldn't have it to use against us in the future, and we'd have had possession in case we needed it to defend ourselves someday."

"Defend ourselves? Against what? Who?" Slade demanded. "We're damn well not going to fight the Union Army if it shows up."

"Yeah, but what if the damned secesh turn against us 'cause of our Union beliefs? Just what are you gonna do if *they* attack us?"

"What the hell are you talking about, Knox?"

"You better wake up and see the real world. Our good Southern neighbors—" He slurred the word contemptuously. "—don't like having loyal Unionists around. More than one of those sons-a-bitches would be willing to put a knife in a Union back at first opportunity. I say we oughta get them first!"

"Get them?" Slade repeated in a bewildered tone. "Get them how?"

"Don't you ever think about making the first move? That it might be smarter to just shoot the bastards before they can shoot us?"

"Goddamn, Knox! You can't be serious. Do you hear what you're saying?"

Suddenly Knox's mouth snapped shut. He'd said far too much. Dunlap and Simmons would be furious if they found out.

Crossing his arms over his chest, Slade rocked on his heels, eyeing the big man with a sudden, uncomfortable feeling of distrust. Something was wrong. Very wrong. Everything he'd been told on the night of his initiation had proclaimed the peaceful aims of the League. Nothing had ever been said about raids, or storing arms and ammunition. Slade didn't like the sound of all this one bit.

Just what the hell was going on? Had the League itself changed direction? Or could the idea possibly have been Knox's alone? How much influence did Dunlap and Simmons have on Knox's actions?

One look at his father assured Slade that the elder Hunter felt the same way. It was one thing to believe in nonviolent resistance and quite another to actually plan an armed attack on a military site. Slade wanted no part of such things.

"Now, listen, fellers," Knox entreated. "I'm sorry. That was a stupid thing to say. I didn't mean it. I just got all riled up—lost my head. Just forget I said anything. Okay?"

"Christ, Knox!" Anson swiped a nervous hand across his mouth. "You had me scared there for a minute. You can't go around saying things like that. Someone is apt to think you're serious."

"Nah! You know me better than that. I just get so frustrated sometimes." He darted a glance at Anson and Slade, his eyes shifting nervously. "You won't go telling someone else about all this, will you? No sense in stirring things up for nothing, is there? I'm sorry I ever brought any of it up." Boy, was that a true statement! "And if you feel that strongly about the raid, we'll just drop the whole idea right now. I give you my word."

Anson scrutinized his friend. "I could never be a party to bloodshed and thievery, Knox. You should have known that, after all these years. Are you positive you're ready to give up this harebrained scheme of yours?"

"Sure, sure. Whatever you say. Honest, we just thought it would be smart to have some extra weapons—just in case."

Lumbering toward them, Knox's broad face was a study in acquiescence. Right now he'd agree to anything. He had to convince them that he hadn't meant what he'd said. And he had to be sure they wouldn't spill the beans about the planned raid. He'd make whatever promises it took to ensure their silence.

Knox was nervous as a bear with his paw poised over a trap. Sweat dappled his forehead. He needed to talk to Dunlap and Simmons. Maybe they should postpone the raid—at least long enough to let the Hunters, with their high-falutin' principles, feel secure again.

Yeah. Let it all blow over for a few weeks; then they could follow up on their plan. A small niggling voice inside Knox's big shaggy head questioned his participation in something his friend Anson was so adamantly against. But he pushed the disturbing thought away. There were things of far more importance than friendship to consider now . . . things such as power and money—lots of money. Damn but he was tired of just scrapping by!

Ah, well. Let the high and mighty Hunters keep their lofty ideas. There just might come a day when Anson and his son would be sorry they hadn't participated. And that day might not be so far off, either. Once Knox and his cohorts had enough arms and ammunition, they'd put the damn secesh in their rightful place—six feet under, that's where!

His obvious poverty had sown seeds of discontent and grown into a long-smoldering desire for a better life. And very soon indeed Knox had agreed with Dunlap and Simmons that armed insurrection was the only answer to the problems besetting the Unionists. If he could line his pockets in the process, well, so much the better. He'd be long gone to California before anyone realized what had happened.

Knox had been willing to cut his old friend in on the deal. But, if the Hunters were going to stand on principle, so be it. Soon Knox would be having a high ol' time, enjoying the best of everything—wine, women, good food—far away from Texas and the war.

He eyed the father and son with mild contempt— and maybe more than a little fear. Let the dang fools try to feed themselves on honor when things got real bad around here! If they didn't want a share of the expected booty, that would just mean more for those who did.

At least he could count on their overvalued honor to keep them quiet about the scheme, once he had them believing he'd given up the idea.

Knox shrugged inwardly, pasted a huge, innocent smile on his face, and promised his friends that he'd never bring the subject up again.

The memory of Knox's ill-advised plan continued to plague Slade. Did some of the League members really plan to take up arms against their neighbors?

The rumination was almost too disturbing to consider.

Slade was grateful when the appointed day to slip away and meet Glory finally arrived and he could busy his mind with happier thoughts.

On the afternoon of their planned rendezvous, Slade arrived at the old house over an hour early. He tethered Diablo in a little copse of trees behind the dilapidated barn, where the horse would be out of sight. The house itself was cradled in a little valley and ringed by the thick patches of trees that characterized the area south of Gainesville known as the "Cross Timbers." It sat far back off the road, and although it was doubtful anyone would ever come close enough to notice anything, Slade didn't want to take any chances.

When his mount was settled, Slade untied a large bundle from behind his saddle and carried it inside. The farm had been deserted for some months now. It was his intention simply to leave the supplies he had brought today.

Slade longed to shower Glory with all the luxuries of the world. But if this was all he could give her for the time being, he at least wanted the place to be pleasant. First he gave the two-room house a quick sweeping. Afterward, he pulled the abandoned bedstead into the sunniest corner of the biggest room and spread it with the blankets he'd appropriated from the stock at the store. Topping it all was a brightly patterned quilt.

A trip to the creek provided him with water for several old crocks. With silent thanks to the former owner for taking the time to plant flowers across the front of the house, he gathered a double handful of still-blooming chrysanthemums and carried them inside. Their bright yellow and copper blossoms lent an air of gaiety to the rooms, a spicy fragrance to the air.

When things were as nice as he could make them under the circumstances, Slade took up vigil at the front window. He didn't have long to wait.

At first sight of Glory, Slade was out the door and running down the front path to meet her. Before she could dismount, he reached up and encircled her waist, hauling her down and into his embrace in one strong movement.

"Lord, honey, I've missed you so much!" Slade breathed in the sweet fragrance of Glory's hair, hugging her tight, raining kisses across her laughing face.

"I missed you, too."

"I've found a safe place for the horses. Come on, I'll show you." Hands linked, they took Rosebud to join Diablo.

"Would . . . uh . . . would you like to go inside?" Slade asked after Glory's horse was taken care of. He suddenly felt almost shy in the bright sunlight.

"Yes. Of course I would." Glory gifted him with her loveliest smile and hooked her hand through Slade's arm.

Slade grinned broadly. Silently they climbed the small grassy incline between barn and house. Just as they reached the doorway, Slade stopped and swooped Glory up in his arms. She let out a whoop of laughter and flung her arms around his neck.

264

"What are you doing?"

"This may be the closest we get to a honeymoon for a long time, so I'm going to carry my bride across the threshold."

Glory laughed with delight and began to teasingly nibble at Slade's ear while he tried to maneuver his way through the narrow opening without bumping either her shins or her head.

"Oh, Slade, how wonderfully thoughtful you are!" Glory exclaimed when he lowered her to her feet inside the neat little house. Tears misted her eyes as she touched a finger tenderly to a bright yellow blossom and then turned on tiptoe to press a kiss on his flushed cheek.

"I . . . uh . . . wish things could be nicer—" Slade explained in a choked voice.

"Hush! Everything is wonderful! No woman ever had a lovelier greeting. Thank you."

Slade's hands slipped up Glory's arms, bringing her closer to him. Putting her arms around his neck, Glory molded her soft curves to the lean contours of his body. His hands caressed the small of her back, tracing small, nervous circles against her sensitive skin. The mere touch of his hand sent a delicious warmth shivering through her blood.

Slade nuzzled the side of Glory's neck. "Ummm, you're so soft, and you taste so good." He nibbled delicately at her earlobe.

Tilting her head, Glory allowed him better access to the sensitive area. When his hot, moist breath fanned across the shell-like opening of her ear, tingles danced down her spine and she arched into his hardness. Trailing his fingers across her throat, he levered her chin upward with one strong fingertip. His gaze seared through her, and then his lips descended to claim the sweet prize of her mouth.

Glory's heart skipped and capered within her breast as the pleasure of Slade's nearness seeped through her soul. He rocked his head, changing the pressure of the kiss . . . hard then soft then hard again.

Finally, he drew just far enough away to allow him to whisper against her mouth. "You've filled my every thought this past few days. I've been half crazy with the memory of your sweet love. God, I never dreamed anything could be so soft, so warm, so giving."

The adoring words rainbowed through Glory's mind. She drew back and gazed into eyes the color of thick smoke, so full of love for him that she could scarcely breathe.

Once again he took her mouth, teasing the sensitive inner lining with his hot, slow tongue. Glory writhed under his exquisite torment. Holding on to him as if the world were about to dissolve beneath her feet, she matched each thrust and parry, building a fire within Slade that threatened to reduce him to ashes.

They progressed across the room to the bed in a deliciously tormenting dance of seduction—holding, turning, touching, pressing—each slow inch of the journey only heightening their desire. At last they fell upon the bed, wrapping themselves in the all-consuming pleasure of their love.

Button by tiny button Slade undid the bodice of

Glory's gown. As each fastening was released, he pressed a blazing kiss on the bared skin. She tangled her fingers in his sable hair and urged him closer. He nuzzled the hard bud of her nipple through her chemise. She moaned and arched against him, hating the restrictive clothing that separated them.

"Off!" she moaned softly, tugging at the offending material of his shirt. "Take it off. I want to feel you — all of you."

They parted long enough to quickly remove their clothes, discarding the garments in forgotten heaps on the floor in their haste. Sunlight blazed through the window, bathing their bodies in molten gold, and they gazed at each other with the adulation that only lovers know.

Taking her shoulders in a gentle grasp, Slade lowered Glory to the bed. She lay back against the soft blankets, gazing upward with awe. God! He was so gloriously masculine. Hard work-honed muscles rippled under sleek, tight skin. Buttery sunlight glinted off the crow's wing blackness of his hair-dusted chest. She tugged impatiently at his shoulders.

"Wait. Just let me look at you first," he said with a sigh. "You're so beautiful. I'll never get enough of looking at you."

Glory watched Slade through lash-shadowed eyes. Never had she felt so cherished. She wished they could live in this golden world of love forever.

Slade's touch was almost reverent as he traced a fingertip around Glory's pale coral nipple. He worshiped her with his eyes, his hands, and his lips, learning every inch of her body, every texture, every taste.

"Look at me," he said when at last he lowered himself over her. "Let me see the pleasure in your eyes."

Lifting love-drugged eyes to his, she opened herself to him, joyously accepting the blending of their bodies, arching against him as the hard length of his manhood gloved itself in her velvet warmth.

Chapter Fifteen

Long minutes later, when the lovers were momentarily sated, they lay side by side under the light blanket Slade had pulled over their sweat-sheened bodies. Glory snuggled into Slade's warmth, wishing they could always be together like this. A small heartfelt sigh escaped her lips.

Instantly alert to her change in mood, Slade turned his head to look at her with concerned eyes. "What's wrong, Glory? You're . . . you're not sorry, are you?" The terrible thought twisted in his guts like a white-hot knife.

"Oh, no!" Glory quickly protested. "I'll never be sorry." She raised herself enough to plant small, loving kisses along the line of his jaw, then over his chin. Finally, she kissed his mouth tenderly. "Please don't think that—"

"Then what is it? I *know* there's something. Strange, isn't it? You're so much a part of me—I can feel that something's bothering you. Please tell me. I don't want you to be unhappy."

She stroked his cheek. "I'm not. I promise you. I was just wishing we could be together every day. That's the only thing that brings me any sorrow . . . being away from you."

"I know. I feel the same way. Ah, Glory, what are we going to do? Honey, is there any chance your father would listen to reason?"

She shook her head emphatically. "Please stop worrying about that, Slade. Papa's a good man. He loves me dearly. I'll find a way to talk with him soon—"

"I don't think it'll help," Slade muttered, remembering his last angry confrontation with the Colonel.

"Yes, it will. You don't know him like I do. He's really an old dear."

Slade's mouth thinned in mute dispute. Never in a million years would Slade agree with that rose-colored judgment. Glory simply couldn't see past the father she loved to the true man beneath the surface. Slade just let her talk; he had no heart for trying to open her eyes to cruel reality.

"I know how Papa's mind works. I just have to wait for the right opportunity. But, believe me, now's not the right time."

"Why?"

"Something peculiar is going on. Papa's been preoccupied the last few days—much more than usual. It's almost like he's worried about something."

A sudden rush of fear stabbed through Slade. That damn crazy raid Knox had talked about! Surely the Colonel couldn't have caught wind of that! No. No, of course not. What a foolish thought. Knox had obviously been very careful about who he told.

But what about Knox's ugly threat to shoot someone . . . How many others might be feeling the very same way? The Colonel would surely be a prime target of anyone bent on retaliation. Was Westbrook in possible danger? If so, did that mean his whole family was in jeopardy?

The thought sent Slade's stomach plummeting. It took all his willpower to try to evaluate the problem in a rational manner.

Sure, the plans for the raid had been real enough, but Knox had sworn it was just his anger talking when he'd threatened more. And he *had* promised to forget the raid and the threats of violence. Knox's word was good. Wasn't it?

Damn! The whole situation was becoming unthinkable!

While Slade's mind fought with demons, Glory continued her discourse. "Papa goes to General Bourland's almost every day . . . sometimes twice a day. And I'm almost positive Preston has been going with him. But there's one good thing that's come of all this—"

"What's that?" Slade asked, struggling to overcome his nagging worries.

"At least Preston's hardly ever around." Glory lovingly traced the line of Slade's mouth with a fingertip, then trailed the digit down his throat and through the maze of springy hair on his chest. There was instant arousal in his manhood when her palm grazed over his nipple.

"And why is that?" Slade asked in a husky voice,

having to concentrate hard to keep his mind on the conversation.

Glory ceased peppering kisses across Slade's chest long enough to answer his question. "He's been too busy trailing after Papa to pay much mind to me. Even when he stops by the house, he and Papa stay closeted in the study for hours. So, it looks like I won't have to worry about him for a while. It'll give me time to think of a plan—"

"What kind of a plan?" Slade asked warily, instantly on the alert despite the distraction of her caresses. He was all too aware of Glory's penchant for trouble.

"Ummm, I don't know," she replied, her breath warm against his skin. Right at the moment she was too busy watching the fascinating way Slade's body reacted to her touch to spend precious time worrying about how to deal with Preston Harper. "But don't worry. I'll think of something. All I needed was some time, and now I've got it."

Much as Slade longed to turn his full attention to Glory's tempting ministrations, he was still troubled by the lingering memories of Knox's revelation. Whether there was much truth to the threat or not, Slade felt compelled to warn Glory of the danger— no matter how remote the possibility.

"Honey," he said hesitantly, reaching to still her questing fingers for a moment. "I want you to promise me something."

"What?"

Slade slipped a finger under her chin and tilted it so he could see her eyes clearly. "Uh . . . just be careful, really careful. Don't go slipping around places you shouldn't be. That little excursion through the alley is a prime example."

"Oh, pooh!" Glory declared in a saucy tone. "I wish you'd quit worrying. Lydia and I were perfectly safe." Turning her head, she took a playful nip at the bulge of muscular arm pillowing her head before trailing butterfly kisses across the sun-bronzed expanse of his shoulder.

Slade squirmed, trying to ignore the distraction of her warm lips against his naked skin. "Listen to me, Glory. I'm serious." His voice was just a touch huskier than before as he continued his plea. "I don't want you going to town alone anymore, or slipping out late at night. Please. It's important. All I'm asking is that you be aware of the possible dangers out there. We are at war, after all."

"Are you worried about Papa again?" Glory questioned, raising her head to gaze at him in puzzlement. "I was careful when I left. I told you Papa's busy. He'll never know I was gone."

"No, that's not what I'm talking about."

Slade knew he couldn't possibly tell her what was prompting his worries. There had been enough problems created by her knowledge of Joella's organization. There was no way he could reveal the existence of the League to her—for her sake as well as for the safety of the other members of the association.

God! What a muddle this was becoming. How could he convince her to be properly cautious when he couldn't tell her why?

"Just . . . just be careful. That's all. It's bad times out there. You never know what might happen."

He'd said all he could say under the circumstances.

Hopefully some of it had sunk in. Finally, somewhat more at ease because he'd at least cautioned her, he pushed the disturbing thoughts aside and gave himself up to the tantalizing temptations of her honeyed mouth and silken touch.

"You're right—I suppose we should all be careful in time of war," Glory mumbled softly against the velvet texture of his skin. "If it'll make you feel better, I promise I'll be good. But it's only fair that you promise, too."

Far, far back in the gray subconscious, something nibbled at the edge of Glory's mind . . . something she was going to tell Slade.

But the thought drifted right out of her head when Slade groaned softly and shifted to stamp a passionate kiss across her lips, his hand caressing the satin smoothness of her stomach. Shivering with anticipated delight, she rolled to her back, waiting breathlessly for the rapture she knew his caress would bring.

Over the next two weeks, Slade and Glory rendezvoused as often as possible at the old house. Little by little they added to the stock of items left behind after each visit—a kerosene lamp, several bottles of wine, tins of biscuits, matches and kindling so they could use the fireplace on the increasingly more frequent chilly afternoons.

The little house was their haven—a sanctuary of peace in the whirlwind of disaster that was fast overtaking the people dear to them and the land they loved. Even though they were filled with a happiness that grew stronger with each passing day, Slade

274

feared that the gap of dissension separating the Union sympathizers from their Confederate neighbors was about to become a chasm of monumental size.

He expressed his concerns to Glory saying that Gainesville, perched on the very edge of the frontier, faced danger on many sides. Commanches and Kiowas still ruled the rolling prairies to the west; the no-man's-land of Indian Territory lay to the north, separating Confederate Texas from the threat of Union-held Kansas. But, he explained, the greatest danger Gainesville would face came not from the Union or the Indians, but from the internal conflict seething beneath the surface of the placid little town.

Even as Slade held Glory, the events he'd worried over were quickly unfolding.

"Well, I must admit, you certainly chose your spy well, James," Colonel Westbrook complimented Bourland after being told of Colonel Chance's gleaning from Dr. Childs the information necessary to spring the trap on the unsuspecting Union sympathizers.

"Yes, I owe you my congratulations also," Preston concurred. "I must confess that I was more than a little doubtful about Chance's ability to pull it off. It's hard for me to believe that Childs would confide so much in a man so well known for his Southern sympathies. But I'm absolutely delighted that he was trusting enough to do so."

"Thank you for the kind words, gentlemen," Bourland replied, his cold blue eyes warmed just a bit by their compliments. "And now, what would your suggestions be? Do you think we have enough information to set the trap? Chance has now been initiated into all four degrees of League membership. He's been given the passwords, signs and grips—"

"Not to mention the membership list," Preston interrupted with a decidedly wicked chuckle.

"Ah, yes. How wonderfully convenient for us," the Colonel said smugly. "The only problem I can see is that some of the names we were most interested in are not on the list. What do we do about that?"

Preston leaned forward to tap a long gray ash from his cigar. With a shrug, he answered, "We simply add whatever names we wish to the list. No one will ever know the difference. What does it matter if some of them never actually swore allegiance to the organization? They're still Union sympathizers. That makes them equally guilty, doesn't it?"

Preston knew exactly what name was going to go on the very top of the list—member or no member. Slade Hunter was going to pay dearly indeed for his interference.

Bourland and Westbrook were quick to agree with Preston's sentiments.

"Fine," Preston continued. "It appears to me that it's just about time to call in the militia. As for myself, I believe it would be wise to keep the closest units on alert until we're ready to cast our net. Perhaps we should start by sending word to some of the units. They can start moving this way. What do you think, Robert?"

"You're absolutely right. After all, it'll take a considerable amount of manpower to make all the

276

arrests at the same time. Once we're ready, we want to make sure that we have enough men to carry out the plan."

"Very well," Bourland agreed. "Shall we set a tentative date for two weeks hence?"

"Excellent," said Preston.

"Agreed" came Colonel Westbrook's comment.

Late Saturday night Johnny Dunlap, Curtis Simmons, and Knox Coleman sat hunched over the rickety table in Knox's small house. Two empty bottles stood on the table alongside one that would soon be just as dry as the others.

Knox drained the last amber drop of whiskey from his glass and plopped it back on the table. "I'm tellin' you, if the Hunters don't go, then a lot of others won't go, either." His words were slurred. "And ol' Anson ain't going to go; not to mention that snot-nosed holier-than-thou boy of his. You can damn well write them off."

"All right, Knox," Johnny Dunlap soothed. "Why don't you just forget the Hunters? We don't need them anyway. Now concentrate, Knox. How many men do you think you can rally for the raid on the arsenal?"

Knox slumped lower in his chair. His brows furrowed as he struggled to mentally enumerate the men who would probably be willing to go. His head hurt abominably from all the whiskey he'd consumed, but he tried to concentrate on the promised rewards rather than the chastisement he'd received at the hands of his erstwhile friends.

Finally, he belched loudly, then ventured an answer. "Guess I can get a dozen together. Maybe a few more."

"Good men in a fight?" Simmons asked sharply. "Decent shots? They got enough arms and ammunition to back us up?"

"Yeah," Knox mumbled.

The Kansans exchanged questioning gazes across the expanse of dirty wood. Dunlap lifted a bony shoulder, then nodded his head in reluctant assent. It certainly wasn't the amount of manpower they'd hoped for, but time was running short. It was now or never. Finally, Simmons returned the nod, the brow bisected by the pale scar tugging upward in a wary arch.

"All right, let's do it. Start getting the word out," Dunlap instructed. "We'll ride for Sherman late Tuesday night."

Outside, a shadowy figure knelt just to the side of the dirty window. The wavering glow of their kerosene lamp starkly highlighted the faces of the three men at the table. Their words had been quite clear through the thin walls of Knox's ramshackle house.

Carefully Preston's spy drew away from the window, picking his feet up ever so slowly, then setting them down with extreme care. It wouldn't do to be caught by the trio he'd been spying on. While Knox, in his inebriated state, didn't offer much of a threat, the other two were known for their quick tempers. Rumor had it that the big guns on their hips were heavily notched.

Dreams of the sizable amount of cash Harper had promised for any information about the Hunters or their friends whirled in his head as the man made his careful escape. What luck that he'd followed a wild hunch and trailed the Kansans that night — straight to Knox's, straight to a veritable gold mine of information. Why, Harper might even be willing to pay double for this startling piece of evidence.

Avarice was the man's stalwart companion as he galloped through the black night, eager to claim his reward.

Chapter Sixteen

Glory paused at the top of the sweeping staircase to peer cautiously over the carved banister. Good! The entry hall was deserted. She raised the hem of her riding costume and began her descent, the plush carpeting on the steps cushioning her boot heels. At the bottom of the stairs she hesitated again to verify her solitude and then began to tiptoe across the highly polished parquet floor.

She managed to make it as far as the passageway leading to the kitchen before her father's voice rang out from the study. "Glory! Is that you out there?"

Damn and double damn! "Yes, Papa."

"Come in here, my dear."

Glory dropped the hem of her skirt and turned toward the half-open study door, her heels clicking loudly now that she had no reason to be stealthy.

"I'm coming," she said with a loud sigh.

Just outside the entrance, Glory paused and forced a pleasant smile to her lips, hopefully evoking the perfect picture of a sweet adoring daughter. The well-oiled hinges of the huge double doors made not a sound as she placed the flat of her hand against the middle panel and pushed the door open.

"Yes, Papa? Did you want something?" Glory inquired sweetly when she stood facing him across the massive oak desk.

The Colonel shifted his fat cigar to the other side of his mouth, signed his name at the bottom of a letter with a flourish, and then gazed up at his eldest child from under bushy gray brows. Blowing out a blue-gray cloud of smoke, he scrutinized her riding outfit with a frown.

"Just as I thought," Colonel Westbrook remarked with a shake of his head. "You were going out again, weren't you?"

"Well—"

"What is all this sudden passion for riding, Glory? Your mother says you've already been out several times this week."

"Why, nothing really, Papa," she answered meekly. "It's just that I was cooped up for so long at the school." Glory made a small moue. "I'm sure you can understand how I feel. It was so busy, so crowded in the city. I never got the chance to ride like I was used to doing here."

Glory quickly rounded the desk to perch on the arm of her father's chair. Slipping her arm around his beefy shoulders, she pressed a kiss against the silver-tipped hair at his temple.

"Harummph," snorted the Colonel in response to her artful cosseting. Determined not to lose sight of what he'd called Glory in for, he continued to shuffle through a stack of papers.

"After all, Papa dear," Glory continued, "it will soon be turning cold and then I won't be able to get out at all. It's been wonderful to have the freedom to ride over the open countryside. You don't know how much I hated being closed up at that school . . . all those stuffy old rules!"

"That's all very well, Glory, but your mother has been a mite worried about you being gone such long hours."

"But, Papa—"

"I think you'd better stay home today and spend some time with your family. And besides, Preston will be joining us for the evening meal. So you really wouldn't have time to do much more than mount up before you'd have to head back for home."

"But, Papa—"

"No buts, my dear. No riding today. Now be a good girl and run along so I can finish this work before dinner."

Disappointment surged through Glory. She'd been counting on seeing Slade today! But she recognized that special tone of voice that meant her father would brook no further argument from her. Well, there was nothing she could do but obey him.

"Yes, Papa," Glory acquiesced in a disheartened voice.

In a morose mood, Glory wandered from the room. Without the promise of seeing Slade, the whole boring afternoon stretched endlessly before her. What was she to do to pass the weary hours?

Just then Sara passed through, her arms laden

with clean linens. The girl's appearance evoked a remembered promise. Glory had pledged to show Sara the schoolbooks she'd brought with her from New Orleans. Glory had no desire to keep them as mementos; she had only carried them home after recalling Sara's secret hunger for knowledge.

Although still sad at being unable to see Slade that day, Glory brightened somewhat at the thought of presenting the playmate of her youth with something the girl would treasure greatly. The afternoon seemed not so bleak anymore.

"Pssst! Sara, wait up," Glory called out softly as she hurried across the broad entry hall to catch her childhood friend.

Turning at the sound of her name, Sara smiled when she spied her mistress. "Yas'm, Miss Glory? Do you need somethin'?"

Placing a silencing finger across her lips, Glory drew Sara away from the entrance to the study, knowing full well that her father, like almost all slaveowners, frowned on education of any sort for slaves. Whispering, the Colonel's daughter and the small brown girl made plans to meet in the garden as soon as Sara had finished her chores.

Then, feeling at least somewhat appeased about her lost afternoon, Glory went upstairs to fetch the books from her room.

It was sunny and unseasonably warm in the garden that afternoon. Only the smallest breeze wafted across the land, and Glory's light shawl was more than enough protection against the faint chill in the air. Not knowing how soon Sara might come to join her, Glory settled herself on a small maple bench in a sunny spot of the veranda.

The gazebo where she planned to meet Sara was visible from where she sat, but it was in shade at this time of day and Glory had decided to wait in the sunshine until the slave girl could slip away. Nearby, the French doors leading to her father's study were open to admit the fresh air. Occasionally she could hear the familiar squeak of his chair.

Making herself comfortable in the same corner of the bench where she'd spent many enjoyable childhood hours, Glory opened one of the books and began to leaf through the pages in search of particularly interesting pictures to share with Sara. Glory had been there almost half an hour when she was startled out of her reverie by an excited voice coming from the study.

"Robert, I'm so glad to find you in. Just wait till you hear the news!"

Preston! What was he doing there so early? Dinner time was still hours away.

Oh, bother! Glory sighed in exasperation. If Preston spotted her, he would probably expect her to spend the rest of the day with him, and her pleasant afternoon with Sara would be ruined.

Quickly she decided to avoid that irksome possibility by quietly slipping away. The coward's way out, she supposed, but she couldn't bear the thought of spending the day with him. She knew she had to find a way to tell Preston that their engagement was off . . . and soon. It wasn't fair to keep him dangling. After all, it wasn't his fault that she loved another.

She frowned in distaste at the thought of the unavoidable chore, well aware of how unpleasant it might be.

I'll worry about it later, she assured herself, giving her head a little shake. She simply wasn't up to it now.

Glory was in the process of carefully and silently gathering up the stack of books when Preston's next sentence froze her where she stood.

"Those goddamned Unionists have planned some sort of raid on the arsenal at Sherman for Tuesday night." His gloating laughter hung in the air. "Can you believe it, Robert? The ignorant fools are playing right into our hands."

Oh, my God! Glory's mouth dropped open in shock. The Unionists! Oh no! Did that mean Slade? No, surely Preston couldn't be talking about Slade.

"Where'd you come by that news?" Westbrook inquired in an excited voice.

Glory listened in horror as the tale of spying and intrigue unfolded.

"Well," Glory's father said, his tone extremely pleased. "Looks like we've got the League right where we want them, all right."

"We'd better get word to Bourland as soon as possible," Preston continued. "With the raid planned for Tuesday night, we're going to have to schedule the arrests for Monday at the latest. We could warn the arsenal and most likely thwart their plans for the raid, but you know how slow the military moves at times. I hate to take the chance of waiting too long. I believe tomorrow's our best bet."

"I certainly agree" came the Colonel's reply. "You're absolutely right, Preston. It's vital that we move fast. Do you think we should go ahead and arrest the ones we can get to now?"

"No. I don't want any warnings. We'll wait until we can get them all at once."

"Good thinking," Westbrook replied.

Preston continued. "Now, to accomplish our plan we're going to have to get busy. The militia will have to be notified so they'll have sufficient time to get to town and get in position. I want enough men in Gainesville to make sure those damned Unionists don't have a snowball's chance in hell of escaping."

The appalling words assaulted Glory's senses. The League . . . Unionists . . . alert the militia . . . arrests!

Slade! Oh, dear God above! Slade might be in terrible danger! She had to warn him!

In a swirl of skirts, Glory abandoned the books on the bench and ran for the stable.

"Jedediah!" she called out as she charged through the entrance and into the shadowy confines of the large frame building. "Jedediah, where are you?" Glory stomped her foot in frustration. *Drat the man!* Where had he got off to?

"Yas'm?" came Jedediah's voice at last.

Glory's head whipped around at the sound and she finally spied his woolly head peeping out from the last stall. "Hurry!"

"Yas'm, I'm coming." The old man shuffled toward Glory. "What you be needin', Miss Glory?"

"Saddle Rosebud. And be quick about it!" she

instructed in a breathless voice.

"Yas'm."

Pacing the straw-covered floor, Glory waited impatiently while the man hurried to do her bidding. Within minutes, he had boosted her up to the back of the horse and Glory was thundering across the open field behind the stable.

Glory agonized over which way to go. Finally she gave in to the compulsion to swing first by their place of rendezvous, particularly since it lay between town and the Hunters' farm. They had earlier agreed to wait only an hour past each appointed time of meeting, but Glory fervently hoped that Slade might have stayed a little longer today.

Although his absence was expected, Glory was still disappointed when she found no sign of Slade at the house. She pushed the unreasonable irritation from her mind. It was, after all, considerably past time for their meeting.

With a jerk of the reins, Glory turned Rosebud back toward the road. There was nothing to do but head for the farm.

Please, please let him be at home! The thought hammered through her mind as she turned the strawberry roan in the proper direction. Long streamers of cinnamon hair flying wildly behind her, Glory urged the gelding to greater speed.

The dirt road under Rosebud's hooves blurred before Glory's eyes as her valiant steed answered the call for haste. Birds took startled wing from the thick foliage bracketing her path. Hunched anxiously over Rosebud's straining neck, Glory paid scant attention to them or to the curious young raccoon who paused in the middle of the road at the sound of her approach. Bright black eyes peered up out of his little masked face, then he emitted a high-pitched squeak of alarm and scuttled from under the flying hooves. His angry chirring went unheard as she thundered on her way.

Vastly disappointed that Glory had not shown up for their meeting, Slade had returned to the farm in search of physical exertion to take his mind off the situation. He was chopping firewood at the edge of the woods in the field on the far side of the Hunter house when Glory pounded down the road.

At first the ring of his axe as he split the logs into quarters covered the muffled tattoo of hoofbeats, and he continued the rhythmic arc and descent of his tool until distant frantic calls finally caught his attention.

Instantly alarmed, Slade left the axe buried in the heart of the fat oaken log he'd just started working on. Raising a hand to shade his eyes against the sun's brightness, he whirled around, searching for the source of the cries.

Slade's heart thudded sharply against his rib cage when he recognized the small figure atop the great galloping horse. Snatching up the faded blue shirt he'd discarded while working, he ran toward the fast-approaching rider.

Glory was off her mount and clutched against the bare bronzed expanse of Slade's chest before Rosebud had even come to a complete halt. Like a frightened child, she wrapped her arms tightly about his neck, her face pressed into the hollow of his shoulder. Her fingers scrabbling for a tighter hold on his perspiration-sheened back, Glory gulped in great drafts of air and fought to still the erratic beating of her heart.

"My God, Glory, what's the matter?" Slade questioned in alarm. "What's wrong? Tell me!" His hands moved soothingly over the smooth plane of her back, stroking her lovingly as he sought to calm the dreadful trembling in her body.

Winded, Glory only managed to gasp, "They're coming!" between frantic gulps for air. She clung to Slade even tighter.

"Sweetheart, please, you've got to tell me what's happened. You're not making any sense." Slade's strong hands closed over her arms. Still holding her steady, his grip firm and protective, he stepped away to gaze into her anxious face.

Glory finally nodded understanding. She closed her eyes for a moment of composure while drawing in a great long breath to calm the fear still racing through her body. Somewhat more composed, she tried again.

"I . . . I heard Preston and Papa . . . in the study." She gulped for oxygen again. "Something about a raid on the arsenal . . . the Unionists." Slade swore violently and Glory's eyes grew even larger and more frightened. "Oh, Slade! They're calling in the militia. They're going to arrest everyone!"

"Goddamn Knox! The stupid bastard!" Slade rasped harshly. Keeping his arm protectively around Glory's shoulders, he reached to clutch Rosebud's

drooping reins. "Come on, let's go to the house."
Glory only nodded mutely.

Winded horse and frightened woman in tow, Slade
led them away from the stump-scattered edge of the
woods. Glory stumbled when a large clod crumbled
beneath her foot as they crossed the field and Slade
tightened his hold on her.

At last they reached the house. Slade looped Rosebud's reins once around the hitching post and then he
led Glory up the steps, across the small porch, and
into the house. When he had her settled on the sofa,
he slipped his shirt on, leaving it unbuttoned in his
haste, and went to pour her a glass of water. Tumbler
in hand, he returned to sit beside her.

"Thank you." Gratefully accepting the glass, Glory
raised it to her wind-parched lips to drink.

"Are you all right?" Slade questioned, anxiety
strong in his voice.

Glory nodded. She set the glass on the small table
at the side of the sofa and then clutched her trembling hands tightly in her lap.

"Sweetheart, start at the beginning again and tell
me everything you heard," Slade instructed in a
gentle voice. "It's very important that you not leave
anything out. Do you understand?"

"Of course."

Half an hour later Glory had told Slade the whole
story, including the previous time when she'd overheard her father and Preston talk about the Unionists. Slade's face grew stormier with each new
revelation and Glory's astonishing tale was punctuated with his frequent bitter curses.

Running his hand raggedly through his ebony hair, Slade tried to absorb the shocking news Glory had just imparted. A quick glance at his mother's clock over the mantel affirmed how little time they had.

Think! He had to have a plan! What to do? What to take care of first?

Glory watched a gamut of desperate emotions play across her beloved's face as he tried to puzzle his way through the problem. Suddenly a frightening thought ripped through her mind.

"Slade, I . . . I'm well aware that you have strong feelings about the Union. But that League they keep talking about . . . you're . . ." She swallowed back a choking lump of fear. "You're not mixed up with it, are you?"

Slade's eyes grew stormier. The muscles at the corner of his jaw bunched alarmingly.

"Oh, no! Please tell me you're not—"

"Honey, it's nothing. Really. The League isn't what they're making it out to be."

"Then what is it?" she cried. "Oh, Slade, I'm scared. I don't understand any of this."

"Neither do I," Slade muttered under his breath. Leaning forward, he propped his elbows on his knees and cradled his whirling head in his hands.

"Slade." Glory's voice was thick with concern. "I've got to know what all this means. Please. Just what is this League?"

Slade shook his head tiredly. "It's only an organization of Union sympathizers; just people banded together for a little moral strength."

"But why? What do they do?"

"Well, for one, we all vowed not to take up arms against the Union if the fighting actually gets this far. And another aim was to work for a peaceful settlement of the innumerable problems created by this damn war, not only during the fighting but when it's all over."

"Then why . . . what about the raid on the arsenal?" Glory's confusion was evident in her voice. "That's certainly not peaceful."

"No, it damn sure isn't." Slade expelled a long sigh. "I don't know, honey. I just don't know. Knox Coleman mentioned the raid once. But when Pa and I absolutely refused to have anything to do with such a crazy scheme, Knox promised us he'd forget the whole thing."

"Then what Preston said really is true? The League is going to raid the arsenal?" Glory asked.

"No, honey, not the League. A raid on the arsenal would be tantamount to armed insurrection. That would be absolute insanity. I cannot believe the League would participate in such an act. But it is true that Knox is a member of the League."

"Along with a lot of other people around Gainesville?" Glory asked reluctantly.

"Yes. I've heard the membership may be as large as seventeen hundred in this part of Texas."

"Seventeen hundred!" Glory gasped. "So many!" The number was incomprehensible to her. The faces of friends, neighbors, townsfolk flashed through her mind. Who among them belonged to the clandestine association? "Who are they? No! No, don't tell me. I don't think I want to know."

292

"I couldn't tell you if I wanted to. I don't know who all the members are. I've only met a few. Lord!" Slade slammed his fist against his knee. "How did this ever happen! I'll admit that Knox is often hot-tempered. And he gets these crazy ideas sometimes. But usually they just blow away when he cools off. He was pretty heated up that day, but I thought it would be like always before—"

"You really thought he didn't mean to go through with it?"

"Of course. He promised to forget the whole thing." Slade raised troubled eyes to gaze at Glory. "But you've got to believe me; it isn't the League behind this stupid scheme. They don't operate like that. Sure, maybe there're a few other League members involved," he said reluctantly, thinking of Dunlap and Simmons. "But they're acting as individuals, not as representatives of the League."

"But why were they going to do that? Raid the arsenal, I mean. What was the purpose if they don't want to fight?"

"Knox said it was just so they'd have ample weapons if the Confederates hereabouts turned on us. Just a safety factor, that's all. He said they were going to store them away—"

"And you believed him?"

"I had no reason not to. We've known Knox for a long time. God, I honestly thought he was just spouting off. I never dreamed this would get so out of hand. Or that just being a member of the League would put people in jeopardy."

"And . . . and you're a member, aren't you?" It

wasn't really a question. The disturbing flutter of her stomach somehow confirmed the truth of her statement.

"Yes, I am."

"Oh, Slade! Why? Why did you have to join them?"

"Because Pa had joined. And belonging to it changed him somehow . . . It gave him something to look forward to. He'd been so depressed since Mama died."

"But why did you have to join?"

"Several reasons, the least of which being there was really no reason not to. But it was mostly Pa, I guess. He'd been so remote, so uninvolved with life for such a long time . . . thank God that's changed lately. He's been spending more time at the farm next door—I'm grateful for that. Mary Stafford seems to be a good influence on him. But back then I felt so responsible for him. I wanted to be sure that whatever he was involved with was worthwhile, safe. Ha!" The caustic retort exploded from Slade's throat. "Great job I did, huh? I not only didn't watch out for Pa like I intended but I got myself caught up in this damn mess, too." Bitter lines bracketed Slade's mouth.

"But, if you didn't know—"

"No, I didn't. I swear I didn't." Slade's hands clenched, the knuckles standing in ridges under the smooth copper skin. "And I still say that the League itself had no part in the plot. Knox and the others are working on their own. I'm positive they are."

Glory lay a soothing hand against the taut muscles

in Slade's arm. "Then you mustn't feel guilty. You did the best you could."

Slade gave a small, harsh laugh. "I wish it were that easy. But wishing won't solve the problem. If Bourland's got wind of the League, we're in big trouble. We couldn't have found a worse enemy than that man. He hates the Union with a passion. They say he's even turned his house up at Delaware Bend into a veritable fort, complete with stores of gunpowder, lead, extra rifles. God, there's even rumors about an underground escape tunnel. He intends to fight this war to the bitter end."

Abruptly Slade jerked his head toward Glory. "Good Lord, just how much do you think they know? Are you sure you've told me all the names they mentioned? Think hard, lives could very well be hanging in the balance."

"I think that's everyone. Dr. Childs. And his brother. Chance—but he's on their side. I don't remember any other names."

"All right. Okay, let me think. So they know about the League. But that doesn't mean they know who all the members are. Maybe there's hope after all." Slade's mind was awhirl with fragmented plans. "But I've still got to start warning people. Hell! I wish we knew who they planned to arrest."

"They didn't name any more names. Really. They just kept saying that they were going to arrest all the Unionists."

"Well, regardless, the first thing I've got to do is warn Pa—"

"Where is he?" Glory asked, suddenly aware that

they were indeed alone in the house. She glanced worriedly about the room. There was no sign of Slade's family. "And Paula and Jeff?"

"They all went over to the Widow Stafford's. Pa's excuse was that he planned to do a little mending on her barn in return for her help with the kids."

"Help?" Glory asked blankly.

"Yeah. She's been so nice about watching them when we both have to be gone—it's been a little tougher trying to handle everything now that Morgan's gone. She's a very thoughtful lady—always doing a little something extra if she can. Like bringing that big pot of chicken soup when the kids were sick. Actually I think Knox was more than a little right when he said that she's sweet on Pa . . ."

Glory watched in surprise as Slade jumped to his feet and began to pace the room. "Knox! Jesus! I've got to warn him, too." Suddenly he returned and sat down beside her, gathering her hands in his. "I'm sorry, Glory. I should be thinking about you, too. You didn't take any chances coming here, did you?"

A sinking feeling in the pit of her stomach made Glory squirm uncomfortably. She didn't dare tell him she'd left home after express orders from her father to stay at the house all day. Slade had enough to worry about. No sense in adding the extra burden of wondering what kind of trouble she'd be in when she returned to town.

She'd just have to hope that her father had gotten so caught up in Preston's news and their plans that he hadn't missed her. And if he had . . . Glory shrugged mentally. She'd worry about that later.

Right now the most important thing was to see that Slade and his family were safe.

When she failed to answer immediately, Slade's grip tightened on her fingers. "Honey . . ." His apprehensive voice penetrated her reverie.

Glory quickly lowered her guilty gaze. "No, everything's fine. Please, darling, you mustn't worry about me. Just do whatever you have to do. I'll be all right."

Expelling a slow breath of relief, Slade slumped back against the sofa. "Thank goodness."

His troubled gray eyes searched her face lovingly, as if to imprint her features indelibly on his mind. He was filled with an unexplained sadness, a feeling that the safe, secure world that they had known was about to crumble beneath their feet.

With a soft moan, Slade pulled Glory into his arms. His lips claimed hers, branding her with his burning love. Lacing his fingers through her disheveled hair, he chained her to him, desperately seeking sustenance from her closeness. If possible, he would have climbed inside her skin and become totally one with the woman who had filled his dreams and his heart for so long.

Who knew what lay ahead of them? Or how long it would be before he held her like this again?

In response to his unquestionable need, Glory's arms slipped inside Slade's open shirt, going tightly around his waist, her fingers digging into the hard, muscular strength of his back. Her mouth parted beneath the fire of his kiss and she gladly gave herself up to his fierce caress. Her shuttered eyes sheened with moisture as he whispered love words against her lips.

By the time he ended the fiery kiss and simply held her cuddled against his chest, the hot, unshed tears were prickling the back of her throat. Glory could feel the thunder of his heart beneath her ear, and her heart cried for a time, when they would never have to leave each other again.

Pulling gently away, Glory cupped his face between her hands and pressed the softest of kisses on his lips. Quickly his hands covered hers, pressing them against his skin. He turned his head, placing a kiss in the palm of first one hand and then the other.

"Go home, Glory. Be very careful, darling. I'll get in touch with you as soon as I can—"

"But how? What are you going to do?" she asked in alarm, loath to leave him.

"First, I'm going to ride to the Stafford farm and talk to Pa. I want him to take the kids and get away from here right away. And then I've got to warn Knox. I know a few others that I can warn. But he'll know more names than I do."

Glory simply sat and watched Slade's face with huge, frightened eyes as he outlined his plans.

"I have to hurry, darling. Time is running out. Come on. Rosebud should be rested enough by now. You'd better go."

Every ounce of her rebelled at the thought of leaving him, but she knew she had no choice. "All right, I'll go. But promise me one thing."

"What?"

"I understand that you have to warn your family.

298

And I even understand that you feel compelled to warn Knox and the other members that you know. But you're not responsible for everything. Let some of them help you. Knox can ride to warn the men he knows. And if you can persuade your father to leave town, then I want you to promise me that you'll go with them—just until this is over."

"Glory, I can't do that. I want Pa and the kids on the road away from here first. Then I'll go warn the others—"

"Then promise me you'll catch up with your family afterward."

"I can't leave everything here . . . simply turn my back on the rest of them. Don't you understand that?" Slade asked imploringly.

Sick with fear, Glory protested. "Slade, listen to me. I simply can't ride back to town and sit there not knowing if you're safe or not. Please, you've got to give me some assurance—"

"Sweetheart, I'll be careful."

"No!" she said vehemently. "Careful isn't good enough. I know you better than that. I know your penchant for putting other people's safety first. Just look at that slave-running thing with Joella. You *aren't* careful, and I know it!"

"Honey—"

"At least tell me you'll stay away from the store—and away from the farm! If they know about you, those are the two places they'll check first." Her face brightened suddenly. "I know! You can stay at the old farmhouse. It's so far off the road that hardly anyone knows about it."

Slade considered the idea. "Well, I guess I could. You're right. As thick as the woods are around that area, any unexpected visitors would have to come in the front way. And I'd have a clear view of their approach to the house. That would give me plenty of time to get out the back."

"Yes, of course it would! Oh, Slade, please say you'll stay there. There're enough supplies to hold you for several days and I can bring out more later."

"No! I want you safe at home. I'll take some things from here. There'll be plenty. Surely this will all blow over in a day or two. In the meantime, I want you to stay in town and stay out of trouble. I'm not promising anything if I don't get the same from you. Agreed?"

"Yes," Glory answered with great reluctance.

Chapter Seventeen

"Pa! Where are you?" Slade called loudly, kicking Diablo in the flanks as he rounded the corner of the Stafford barn. Relief flooded through him when he spotted his father and Mary Stafford on the widow's porch.

In response to Slade's cry, Anson Hunter hurriedly set the glass of lemonade Mary had just served him down on the edge of the table, rose from the rocker he'd been sitting in, and watched the horse and rider pound across the yard. More than a little alarmed by Slade's uncharacteristic behavior, he waited for his son to dismount.

"What's wrong?" Anson asked as soon as Slade was near enough to hear.

"I gotta talk to you. Where's Jeff and Paula?" Slade asked in an urgent tone as he took the steps to the porch in one bound.

"I sent them inside to get a plate of cookies, Slade," Mary answered. "Is something wrong?"

"Uh . . . Mary, could I ask you to keep the kids

occupied for a little while. I . . . I need to talk to Pa in private. It's important."

Concern filled Mary's hazel eyes, but she quickly nodded assent and went into the house. The minute the door was closed, Slade drew his father aside a few steps and told him the reason behind his frantic ride.

"Jesus Christ!" Anson muttered under his breath when he heard the startling news about the raid. "What in hell's got into Knox? I never figured he'd go through with that scheme of his."

"Neither did I," Slade said as he paced the porch's weathered boards. "We could be in big trouble, Pa. We don't have any way of knowing whose names they have. It's for damn sure, if they're condemning people simply because of their Union sympathies, we're going to be right on the top of the list."

"I know, Son. Damn! This is unbelievable." Anson's smoky gray eyes, so like his son's, were brooding and apprehensive. He frowned harder and raised his gaze to Slade's face. "Who did you say told you about all this?"

Slade nervously slapped his dusty hat against his leg. He pointedly ignored his father's question. "Pa, there's apt to be real trouble. You've got to take Jeff and Paula, and get away from here. At least for a while."

"But, Slade, I don't see how I can do that. What about the store? And the farm?"

"Be sensible, Pa! What about the kids' safety? We've got to consider that first."

"But maybe they don't know about us — " Anson's brow furrowed. "After all, how do we know this information is genuine?"

302

"It is," Slade declared emphatically. "You've got to get the children away from here."

Anson crossed his arms across his chest, heels wide apart, legs braced in a familiar stubborn stance. He shook his head. "I'm not leaving my home on that flimsy piece of evidence. I want to know who told you."

"Pa—"

"I'm not budging until I know, Slade."

"Shit!" It crossed Slade's mind to lie, but he could think of no name that would evoke the necessary belief from his father. And right now he didn't have time to argue. "Glory."

"Glory?" Anson repeated blankly. Then a sudden light dawned in his eyes. "Glory Westbrook!" Anson gazed at his son as if he'd lost his mind. "Are you crazy? Why on earth would you believe anything Colonel Westbrook's daughter said? And why in hell would she tell you anything anyway?"

The stubborn jut of Slade's chin confirmed his anger at Anson's attitude. "She told me because she loves me. Because she cares what happens to all of us—"

"Slade, Slade," Anson said wearily. "I thought that was all over. I thought you gave up that foolish idea after the Colonel sent her away."

"Well, you thought wrong, Pa," Slade answered in a gritty voice. "I never gave up loving her. I never will. And she feels the same way."

"Don't be a fool, Son. She's engaged to Preston Harper—"

"I know all about that. You don't know what really happened. If you did, you'd understand. You'll

303

just have to believe that we're going to work it out." Every ounce of Slade's being spoke determination. "I love her. I'm not giving her up, Pa."

"Christ, Slade. Don't you know you're heading for heartache? She's not our kind."

"I love her," Slade repeated stubbornly.

Anson paced the porch in agitation. "And what if she's just setting you up? Didn't it ever cross your mind that she could be lying to you? What if this 'warning' is false—some sort of ruse to get the League all riled up?"

"Don't talk about Glory like that, Pa," Slade lashed out angrily. "You don't have any idea what she is, who she is. You've got no right—"

"I've got every right! You're my son. I don't want to see you hurt."

"The only thing that will ever hurt me is losing Glory. And she feels the same way." Slade stared his father down. "She's not lying."

"All right, all right," Anson finally said in a weary voice. "Maybe she was totally sincere when she told you about all this. Maybe she really is trying to help us. Even if her motives are pure, you've got to consider where the information came from. This could still be some crazy sort of scheme. Who knows what Westbrook and Harper have in mind? It could all still be a lie."

Slade shrugged. "I don't believe they'd go to all that trouble just to spread a rumor. And why bring Glory into it? They don't have any idea that we're seeing each other. But even if it were possible, what would be the point, Pa?"

Anson pushed his fingers through his graying hair.

"Hell, I don't know. Maybe they're trying to spark the League into doing something. How can they go arrest people on the basis of some fool rumor? Nothing's really happened." Anson searched his mind for a plausible explanation. "Maybe they're trying to trick us into making the first move . . . into staging some sort of attack."

"Pa—"

"That's it! That's the answer. We can just ignore this. If the League members don't know, if they don't do anything out of the ordinary, that should put a stop to whatever Westbrook has planned. Goddammit, Slade, barring people like Westbrook and Bourland, those folks are our neighbors, our friends. They won't arrest us for something we haven't done."

"Don't you see, Pa?" Slade's voice was full of anxiety. "It doesn't matter at this point. It's wartime. Everybody's all heated up. They won't care whether something has actually been done or not. Just the threat of danger will be enough. Those people are scared—scared that the Union army might come marching into town any day now, scared for their families, scared for their very lives. They're not going to listen to reason. All it'll take is a spark and the town could go up like a powder keg. You've got to get Jeff and Paula out of here! It's our only choice."

Anson rubbed his brow, shaking his head from side to side in denial of the unthinkable situation. "But what if none of that happens?" he asked in an almost pleading tone.

"What if we both got arrested?" Slade asked, his eyes as bleak and stormy as a winter sky. "What would happen to the kids then? Can we afford to

305

take that chance?"

Anson slumped wearily against a support post, his shoulders sagging in resignation. He slowly shook his head. "No. I guess not. You're right, Son. For Jeff and Paula's sake, we can't take a chance on that happening. But where can I send them?"

"No, Pa. Not send them. Take them. You've got to go, too. If they know about the membership, they'll have your name. You've been a member much longer than I have."

"But I should go with you to warn the others. You'll need help."

"Knox will help me. Somebody's got to stay with Jeff and Paula. I'm not leaving Cooke County—not while Glory's still here. That leaves only you to get the kids out of here."

"But if all this turns out to be real, you'll be in danger, too, Slade. You can't stay at the farm, either," Anson protested.

"I don't intend to. I've already picked out a safe place where I can hide out. I'll be all right. Believe me. I won't go back to the farm or to town until Glory sends word that it's safe. Now, we've got to decide where you and the kids are going to go."

Suddenly the door creaked open and Mary slipped through. The portal closed behind her and she joined the men at the edge of the porch.

"Don't worry," she said. "Jeff and Paula are busy at the back of the parlor. They didn't hear a thing." Her twisting fingers belied the calm facade she was trying to present. "But I heard. I'm sorry. I didn't mean to. I just did."

"Mary, you don't need to get mixed up in this,"

306

Anson said softly.

"That's where you're wrong, Anson," she answered, her gaze firm and determined despite the fear that lurked in its depths. "I *am* involved, simply because I care about what happens to you and the children."

"We'll be all right, Mary. And you won't have to worry. I'm hoping there's nothing to all this, but if there is, I'm sure they won't be bothering you since you have no strong ties with the Union—"

Mary's mouth thinned to a stubborn little line. "And what do you intend to do to ensure your own safety, Anson Hunter? And that of those two darling children waiting inside?"

"Well . . . I . . ." Anson's words faded away. He didn't know what he was going to do. Everything they had was tied up in the farm and the store.

Slade answered instead. "I want them to leave the county—as quickly as possible."

Mary nodded. "I think you're right."

"And just where are we supposed to go?" Anson inquired, frustration thick in his voice.

"To Dallas," Mary answered with quiet determination.

"Dallas?" Anson repeated in bewilderment. "But we don't know anyone in Dallas."

Shrugging her plump little shoulders, Mary turned a resolute gaze on Anson. "No, but I do. I have a younger sister who lives there. We'll simply load up the children and go for a visit."

Anson's mouth gaped open. "Mary, you can't be serious."

"Oh, but I am. And when we return, no one will

be able to say you were running away from anything. It's none of their business if I invite some friends to travel with me."

"Mary," Anson said with a stunned shake of his head. "You'd do that for us?"

"Of course I would, Anson." She cocked her head slightly to the side, one slim brow arching toward blond hair that was sprinkled with gray. "Why would you doubt it?"

Reaching to give her hand a quick squeeze, Anson replied, "I shouldn't be surprised. Not after all you've done for us in the past. You're a very special woman, Mary Stafford."

"Well," she countered, a wry smile playing at the corner of her lips. "I suppose that remains to be seen." Her eyes were soft, misty with unspoken affection for the man before her. "Now," she said sharply, suddenly all business again. "We'd better hurry. There's the wagon to pack, and we must go by your house and pick up some clothing for the children."

"Yes, of course," Anson agreed.

"Slade, would you turn ol' Bessy out of her stall in the barn? That mule's smart enough to forage for herself for a while. She won't stray far."

"Sure, Mary." Slade threw her a grateful smile. "And thanks. I can't begin to tell you how much I appreciate your help. I don't know how we'll ever repay your kindness."

Mary simply returned his grin and gave a little flip of her hand, as if to flick away the compliment. "Anson, you ready the wagon. I'll get the children." With that, she disappeared into the house.

In record time, Anson, Mary, and the two children

were aboard the wagon and ready to leave. Mary recited her sister's name and address to Slade one last time and Slade assured them that he'd write as soon as things were calm again.

Anson flicked the reins over the backs of the horses and the wagon rolled down the red dirt road in the direction of the Hunter farm. Waving one last time, Slade quickly mounted and galloped toward Knox Coleman's homestead.

Hauling Diablo to a halt in front of Knox's small cabin, Slade scrambled down and raced to the door. The flimsily constructed panel quivered under the pounding of his doubled fist.

"Awright! Awright!" Knox's angry voice filtered through the barrier. "I'm coming, for gawd's sake. Keep your pants on."

Slade took a step back as the door was thrown open and Knox's big bulk filled the entranceway.

"Slade!" Knox said in surprise, reaching to pull his drooping suspenders up over his shoulders. Once they were adjusted, one big hand moved downward again to scratch the mound of belly hanging over the almost totally obscured waistband of his pants. "What the hell's going on, fella? It sounded like an army out here—"

"Army, hell, you dumb son of a bitch! That's just about what you're going to get if you don't get your butt in gear." Slade stormed into the little house. "I can't believe you could be so stupid!"

"What are you talkin' about?" Knox asked, a perplexed look furrowing his brow.

309

"Lord almighty, Knox! You know what I'm talking about! How could you do it?"

"Do what, Slade?" Knox's words stumbled over the tail end of Slade's tirade.

"The goddamn raid, that's what!" Knox's face first registered shock and then a sullen guardedness as Slade continued. "You promised Pa and me, Knox! You promised."

"I think you've made a mistake—"

Slade whirled, his face furious. "No! You've made the mistake! And because of your bungling stupidity we're all in danger. They know about the raid on the arsenal."

Knox's mouth fell open; his eyes were large and full of confusion as he gazed at Slade. "Wh—what are you talking about?" A fat stub of tongue licked nervously at the thick lips buried within the bushy mustache and beard.

"The raid, Knox, the raid. The one you promised to forget about," Slade said, his voice so thick with sarcasm that it could be cut with a knife. "Bourland knows all about it. Not to mention Westbrook and that bastard Preston Harper. The militia is moving toward town right now—"

"Militia!" The word exploded from Knox's mouth as if he'd been socked hard in the gut.

"Right," Slade continued bitterly. "Militia. Coming to arrest the members of the League."

"Arrest? Militia?" Knox repeated stupidly. "No, sir! Not Knox Coleman. They ain't gonna do no such thing to me. I ain't hanging around for no militia to come arrest me, you can bet your ass on that!"

The big man moved with surprising speed. Within

seconds he'd pulled an old valise from under the sagging bed. The bedstead creaked in protest when the bag was tossed upon it.

Knox turned and began grabbing garments from the pegs on the wall, then shoving them in great rumpled wads of material into the gaping maw of the bag. A small tin followed the clothing, the few coins it obviously contained clanking against the sides of the box when he dumped it on top.

Knox smashed the contents down and then raised up to look around the room. "Now, let's see, what else do I need?"

"Knox, we don't have time for that now," Slade protested as he moved to confront his erstwhile friend over the battered iron scrollwork at the end of the bed. "Just take the bare necessities in case you can't get back by the house. Right now we've got to get on our way to warn all the people we can."

Knox shook his great shaggy head belligerently. "Don't be a fool, Slade. We can't take the time to do that! What if the militia arrives in the meantime?"

Knox lumbered off toward the rickety kitchen cupboard. The door slammed against the wall and he began to paw through the contents on the bottom shelf.

"Where the hell is it?" he muttered under his breath. "I'm sure I had some more ammunition in here somewhere."

Knox was reaching toward the top shelf when Slade's hand clamped on his arm in a viselike grip. Slade jerked and Knox spun like a top, slamming against the wall in total surprise. Despite his greater bulk, Slade's sudden show of force effectively intimidated the bigger man. He cowered against the rough surface of the wall, eyes round and worried as he gazed down into Slade's blazing eyes.

"You gutless bastard!" Slade roared, his fingers tightening on the front of Knox's shirt. "How can you stand there and say such a thing? You're the one that's brought all this trouble down on our heads! And you intend to run away and leave the others to face this alone? Like hell you will!"

"Now, Slade, I didn't mean—"

"You *did* mean it!" Slade gave the fabric a vicious shake; a seam parted with a loud purr. "Well, I say you're not going to get away with such cowardly tactics! Do you hear me?"

Knox's big hands scrabbled at the shirt collar that was tightening in a most uncomfortable manner across his throat. "Yeah, sure, Slade. Anything you say."

A sickly grin peeked through the black thatch of hair covering Knox's face as he tentatively tugged at the clenched fists under his chin. Finally, Slade untangled his hands from Knox's shirt front. With one last piercing gaze, Slade dropped his hands and backed away.

Pulling a deep draught of oxygen into his laboring lungs, hands clenched against his sides, Slade waited for Knox to make the next move.

Knox shuffled sideways, seeking to put space between himself and the furious man facing him. His tremulous grin widened as hamlike hands fluttered to smooth and retuck the rumpled shirt.

Slade watched every move, his muscles coiled like steel springs. An angry tick worked at the corner of his jaw. His raw nerves ached for action. All it would take was one wrong move, one wrong word from Knox.

But Knox was smart enough to read the fury in Slade's eyes. The big man had no intention of goading him into another display of wrath.

"Calm down, Slade. Just calm down," he pleaded in a wheedling voice. "I'll help. I kinda lost my head for a minute or two. Just give me a minute to think about this."

Slade didn't say a word. He was still trying to subdue the anger surging through his system. Watching Knox with ice-cold eyes, he simply waited for him to continue his speech.

Adjusting a sagging suspender, Knox ambled back in the direction of the bed with its open valise. He stuffed the few dangling articles into the recesses of the bag and snapped it shut. His mind was scrabbling for a means of escape like a rat in a trap.

A small glimmer of hope flickered deep in his selfish soul. If he could only separate himself from Slade, he'd have the opportunity to escape. Sure. All he had to do was convince Slade to ride one direction in warning and assure him that he'd spread the alarm the other way. Once out of sight he could high-tail it for safety, and the others be damned!

Knox smothered the sly grin playing at the corners of his mouth and turned back toward Slade, his plan formulated. Slade listened intently, nodding on occasion, watching with cold, appraising eyes as Knox outlined his scheme.

"You ride east, Slade, and alert Sawyer and Hoskins and Davis. Each one of them will know

313

other names to give you. Then you can all fan out and spread the word. Tell 'em to meet up at Rock Creek tonight. We can make further plans then. I'll ride west and do the same thing. Agreed?"

Slade nodded his head.

"Fine, fine," Knox boomed in response, appearing his old jovial self once more. He plucked his heavy coat from a peg and pulled it on, then grabbed up the bag. "We'd better get going."

Slade agreed. The two men moved quickly across the room and out the front door. Knox turned toward the small shed where his horse was stabled. Slade mounted Diablo to continue his grim journey.

Chapter Eighteen

It was dark by the time Glory returned to the house on Pecan Street. Leaving her lathered horse to the care of Jedediah, she hurried toward the house, praying all the way that her absence had not been noted.

But, alas, her prayers went unanswered. Colonel Westbrook descended on her like a hawk on a mouse the minute she slipped through the back door.

"Where in hell have you been, girl?" he demanded, his face deep purple with fury.

For a split second Glory cowered back against the door, quite disarmed by the wrath in her father's voice. She swallowed hard and steeled her nerves for the confrontation, deciding that in this instance a strong spirit and a lot of courage would serve her better than daughterly meekness.

"Out riding, Papa," she answered in a voice she hoped didn't betray just how trembly she felt inside.

If possible, the Colonel turned a darker shade of purple. His cheeks puffed out and his eyes rolled wildly as he fought for enough breath to continue his tirade.

"I told you to stay home!" he bellowed, stomping back and forth. "Didn't I?"

"Yes, Papa."

"How dare you disobey me! Whatever could you have been thinking of? There's trouble afoot today and there you are, out all alone. Anything could have happened. I've been worried about you, not to mention your poor mother!"

Trouble! How well she knew. "I'm sorry, Papa. I didn't mean to frighten you or Mama. I only meant to take a short ride. I planned to be back for mealtime. Truly I did."

Beyond her father's pacing figure she could see Violet huddled at the far side of the kitchen. Violet's eyes were large and round with apprehension for the young woman who'd been her charge for so many years. Never had the slave woman seen her master in such a fit of rage at his beloved daughter.

"Well, you weren't! Mealtime passed hours ago, Glory. And what about the embarrassment I felt when it was time to sit down to eat and you were nowhere to be found? We had a guest—or did you forget that as well as the time?"

"No, Papa, I was—"

"And poor Preston! What about him? I can just imagine what he's been thinking! What kind of wife could he expect from such a willful girl?" The Colonel stopped long enough to poke his big cigar emphatically in her direction. "These antics are not to be tolerated at your age, Glory. You're not a child anymore, you know!"

"Yes, Papa."

"I suppose it's all my fault—at least your mother seems to think so! She says I've let you have your own way far too often."

"Yes, Papa."

"Well, I can tell you right now, my girl, Preston will put a stop to such nonsense. You can't expect to be pampered and spoiled all your life."

"No, Papa."

When the Colonel turned to begin another lap of his furious march across the room, Glory and Violet exchanged hurried nervous smiles. Glory waggled an eyebrow to let the concerned woman know she was all right, knowing from past experience that Violet would try a diversionary tactic soon if her father didn't calm down shortly.

Between the Colonel's circuits, Violet shook her head and pursed her lips as if to chide Glory for being foolish enough to spark her parent's wrath. Glory shrugged slightly and blinked her eyes, indicating that she had survived her father's anger before and she would again.

Oblivious to the signals being passed, the Colonel continued his pacing and ranting. Finally, he spun on his heel and headed for the hallway.

"Come along, Glory!"

"Yes, Papa," she replied softly. She gave Violet the most convincing smile she could muster, and then followed her father down the hall and into the study.

He stood guard at the door until she had crossed the room and was standing before his desk. She jumped when the doors banged loudly shut. Clenching her hands within the folds of her skirt, she waited for him to take his place across the wide, polished surface.

When the Colonel finally rounded the desk and faced his apprehensive daughter again, Glory had successfully managed to quell the frissons of alarm that had raced through her body at his first appearance. Holding herself straight and tall, she savored the few seconds of peace and quiet, knowing full well it wouldn't last long.

"Well, Daughter, I hope you're suitably sorry for the bother you put us all through today."

"Yes, Papa, of course I am. I'm sorry for upsetting you. I-I wish it hadn't come to that."

That at least was true. She fervently wished that she wasn't caught in the middle between her love for Slade and her love for her family. But wishing would do no good at this point. She was forced to do the things she'd done.

"You owe Preston an apology, Glory. I'd like to hear one immediately," her father said sternly.

Glory's stomach plummeted. She'd never considered having to face Preston so soon.

"Now, Robert, don't be so hard on Glory," Preston's eloquent voice purred from the far corner of the room. "It's quite understandable that she gets bored occasionally and needs a breath of fresh air."

Managing a weak smile, Glory turned in Preston's direction. She hadn't expected him to be quite so understanding.

"Thank you, Preston. I'm sorry. I really didn't mean to be so late." Her befuddled mind searched for a plausible excuse. "Rosebud . . . uh . . . Rosebud stumbled in a gopher hole. He limped quite a bit at first and I was so afraid that he was badly hurt that I . . . I decided not to ride him until I could tell what was wrong. So I walked for a long while—"

"Really, Glory!" her father exclaimed. "I'm appalled. Surely now you understand why I cautioned you about riding out alone. Don't you see what could have happened?"

Preston's smooth voice overrode the Colonel's grumbling. "What a very clever young woman you are, Glory. Many females would be down right addlebrained if faced with an emergency situation. How very commendable of you, my dear, to put another's well-being ahead of your own."

While he talked, Preston moved slowly toward her, a slight smile on his inscrutable face, his Nordic blue eyes strangely cool and calculating. Somehow his words of commendation were more disturbing to Glory than her father's chastisement.

It almost sounded as if he were referring to a person rather than Rosebud, she thought. *No, surely not*. There was no way Preston could know where she'd been that day or who she'd talked to. No way at all.

Glory was at least partially right in her assumption. Preston wasn't *sure* where she'd been or who she'd seen, but he was quite sure Glory had been in pursuit of something more than an afternoon of pleasant diversion.

By sheer accident, Preston had been standing at the French windows when Glory galloped across the back pasture on Rosebud's back. For some unexplained reason he'd made no remark to the Colonel. Later, a casual exploration on his part had revealed the abandoned books.

What haste had caused Glory to leave them in such haphazard disarray on the bench, forsaken to the fingers of wind that ruffled and dog-eared the corners? Why had she left still others tumbled on the porch, one facedown, pages bunched and creased?

Could she possibly have overheard the conversation he and the Colonel had just had? Preston could think of nothing else that would have precipitated her rash flight.

Where had she gone in such a desperate hurry? And why?

A dark, forbidding thought had begun to form in the deep recesses of Preston's mind. That humiliating afternoon at Joella's—Slade Hunter's words: *You have Glory . . . She's an angel . . . I can't save Glory.*

The puzzle pieces were beginning to fall into place. Hunter had stopped him from having Joella. Could he possibly have a hold on Glory, too? The thought was untenable.

Standing in the waning afternoon light, a spark of cold, calculated rage had begun to blossom in Preston Harper's icy heart. All this he'd withheld from the Colonel as they went about their business. They'd made a quick visit to Bourland's, messages had been sent to the necessary military units, key figures in town had been alerted.

Preston spearheaded the details of the scheme with his usual cool-headed competence. But deep inside was a growing rage of determination to rid himself of Slade Hunter once and for all. The man had thwarted the prospect of an arrangement with Joella; he would *not* allow him to upset his designs where Glory was concerned. Too many of his plans hinged on his continued close association with Westbrook, and marriage to Glory would secure that.

Preston had reached the limits of his tolerance. Perhaps Glory would bear closer watch in the future. Whatever her proclivity, he would not allow her to make a fool of him. And Slade Hunter was as good as dead.

Glory paced the floor of her darkened bedroom, worrying about Slade's safety, wondering if he'd been able to warn his friends. Again and again she padded to the window, pulling the curtain aside to peer into the night. But the gale-force winds continued to drive the rain hard against her windows, and water ran in such torrents down the glass that she could see little more than an occasional flash of lightning.

In the wee hours of the morning, she finally climbed into the big feather bed and pulled the covers snug around her ears. Thoroughly exhausted, she dozed fitfully till just before daylight, then fell into a deep sleep.

In the small, abandoned house, far off the traveled pathways, Slade lay awake. He thought about his family, relieved that they were far away and safe, then wondered fretfully if Knox had been able to reach more members than he had. Finally he pushed the troublesome thoughts from his mind and turned on his back, trying to cease his restless tossing.

Hands under his head, he watched the waterfall of

rain on his narrow window and remembered the times he'd shared the lonely bed with Glory . . . how comforting it had been to hold her close, soft and warm and loving in his arms. At last his eyes closed in slumber.

Chapter Nineteen

The clamorous tolling of bells awakened Glory. Almost instantly she was out of her bed and across the room. Heedless of the fact that she wore only her long cotton nightgown, she yanked the French windows open and stepped out onto the narrow balcony encircling the upper story of her parents' house.

Puddles of water, left behind by the night's violent storm, stood on the painted wood floor. They chilled her bare feet and drenched the hem of her gown as she crossed the cold boards.

Glory hurried to the banister, her nightdress slapping wetly against her ankles. The loud ringing of the bells finally ceased, but it brought no peace. The clanging in Glory's ears was instantly replaced by an incessant rumble from the direction of the street, intensifying Glory's feeling that something was dreadfully amiss.

Leaning far out over the railing, Glory tried to see

what was happening. A nippy little breeze plucked at her tumbled hair, blowing strands across her face. Even in her precarious position, the view was still obstructed. Glory brushed the hair from her eyes and stretched her body further. Now she could see a slice of the street in front of her house between the jut of a corner cupola and the lush polished greenery of a huge old magnolia tree.

"Heavens above!" Glory whispered, shocked at the sight that greeted her. Normally a quiet, residential road, Pecan Street was now filled with a bevy of humanity: soldiers in bedraggled uniforms, weapons on their shoulders; sodden men on horseback; farmers atop rickety mud-splattered wagons.

On the far side of the street, the driver of a sleek carriage called out in anger, issuing sharp instructions for the rabble to clear the way so he could pass. The crowd simply ignored him and continued its mindless ebb and flow toward town, pushing, shoving, grumbling all the way.

Panic frissoned through Glory, every nerve ending set on edge by the unaccustomed chaos below.

"Slade!" she groaned aloud. "I've got to get out of here and find out what's happened."

Never in her life had Glory dressed so speedily. Within minutes she'd washed her face in cold water and piled her hair into a haphazard topknot of tangled cinnamon curls. Next she pulled on plain cotton underthings and a simple dark frock. Lastly, she slung a cape around her shoulders and tied a wide-brimmed bonnet atop her head.

Her clamped jaw warned of Glory's determination as she marched the full length of the hallway and swooped down the stairs. But this time she made no effort to hide her movements. It simply didn't matter anymore. Nothing—no one—was going to keep her from going to town.

Once down the stairs, Glory crossed the entrance hall unobserved. Grasping the gleaming brass knob of the front door, she gave it a hard twist. The door sprang open.

"Oh!" Glory cried in surprise when she almost charged straight into Lydia.

"Glory! Thank goodness!" Lydia exclaimed, lowering the hand she had raised to knock. "I kept waiting and waiting for you to come. I was so worried. But it got so late, and finally I couldn't stand it anymore. I had to come."

Glory slipped through the doorway. A quick pull closed the door securely behind her.

Lydia backed up a step or two in surprise. "What are you doing? Oh, Glory, where are you going?" Lydia asked in alarm when Glory's attire finally registered on her mind. But in her heart she already knew the answer.

"To town, of course," Glory replied in a do-or-die voice as she crossed the broad porch and began to descend the front steps.

Lydia cast her eyes heavenward. "I knew it. I just knew it!" With a small moan, she skipped down the steps, hurrying to catch her friend.

"My pa warned me to stay away from there,

Glory," she hastened to explain as she followed Glory down the long walk leading to the street. "I've never seen this many people in Gainesville before. Don't you think just this once we ought to think before doing something crazy?"

Nearing the gate, Glory stopped long enough to turn and grasp Lydia's fluttering hands in her own. "Listen, Lydia, you don't have to come with me. I don't want to put you in danger. But I have to go. You must understand that."

"But, just take a look, Glory," Lydia begged, pointing toward the milling crowd. "There's *hundreds* of soldiers in town . . . and strangers! People I've never seen before. It's not safe out there!"

"It doesn't matter. I have to be sure that Slade's all right," Glory declared with a vigorous shake of her head. And then a sudden hope flared in her eyes. "Did your pa know what was going on?"

"Not much, I'm afraid. He just said something about a lot of people being arrested and some sort of rebellion in the county. That's all I know."

A lot of people! Glory's heart thumped hard against her ribs. The League! It had to be the League members. Dear God! Hadn't they gotten the word out?

"But the bells . . . why were they ringing?" Glory persisted.

"Pa said it was to call the menfolk to town—" Lydia paused, wrinkling her brow as she searched for the memory. "A committee . . . they're getting together some sort of committee to form a citizen's court."

"Court!" Glory repeated. "What for? Who's on this committee?"

"Pa didn't know any names," Lydia admitted. "But I'm sure I can find out tonight." She cast a hopeful glance Glory's way.

"No," Glory said with an emphatic shake of her head. "That's not good enough. I can't wait that long. If I don't go, I might never know if Slade's safe."

"Oh, surely the news would get around. We'd hear something later today or in the morning—"

Glory frowned deeply. "Heavens above, Lydia, do you think I can stand to wait that long? And just how would I find out? I certainly can't ask Papa. He wouldn't tell me even if he knew." The fire in her eyes bespoke a will of steel. "No, I have to go and find out for myself."

"Oh, dear!" Lydia muttered, her cornflower-blue eyes as big as saucers. "I was so hoping that if I came over I could convince you to be sensible for once."

Glory gave Lydia's hands a reassuring little squeeze. Finally releasing her hold, she raised her shoulders in a shrug and tossed her head. "Mercy me, Lydia. Why ever should I start being sensible now? It would surely ruin my reputation." Her gently teasing words were delivered with a heartbreaking attempt at a smile.

"Oh. Well. I guess you're right," Lydia replied, trying hard to match the forced humor in Glory's voice. "In that case, I . . . I'll go with you."

327

"Oh, Lydia, no one ever had a sweeter friend than you." Glory hugged her quickly. "But I don't think you should go. It wouldn't be fair for me to get you involved in something this . . . this . . ."

"Dangerous?" Lydia supplied the fateful word in a halting voice.

Glory responded with another lopsided grin. "I suppose so. But I still have to go."

"I know you do," Lydia replied softly, the breath she'd been holding whooshing out in a rush. "That's what frightens me."

"Don't be afraid for me. Please. I'll be all right."

"I'll try."

"I know!" Glory declared in a falsely bright voice. "Why don't you slip around to the kitchen and find Violet or Sara? Stay with them while I'm gone. I'll be back as fast as I can." Her voice grew hushed, her smile trembly. "I may be in dire need of a friend if . . . if the news is bad."

"Oh, dear!" Lydia clasped her hands against her bosom. "You don't really think that Slade's been arrested, too, do you?"

"I'm praying he hasn't. Surely he paid attention to my warning—"

"Warning?" Lydia repeated in surprise. "What warning? About all this?" she asked, her arm sweeping out to encompass the chaotic throng still traveling the street. "But . . . how did you know?"

"I'll tell you everything later, Lydia. Just be patient. Right now I must go."

"All right, but you be careful!" Lydia instructed in

a fierce, protective tone. "I'll be here when you get back. And hurry!"

"I will."

With that, Glory passed through the small picket gate dividing the Westbrook grounds from the street and slipped into the crowd. Within seconds she was swallowed up and swept away.

Resolutely, Glory fought her way through the crush of bodies clogging the street. Oblivious to the sucking red mud that tugged at her small kid boots, she struggled toward town. The constant babble of voices set her teeth on edge.

Glory's nose wrinkled in distaste as she pushed farther into the crowd. A dozen aromas enveloped her. The pungent odor of horses that had been ridden hard and far, the acrid gunpowder smell of recently fired rifles mingled with that of wet woolen clothing, the raw stink of unwashed bodies, and consumed liquor. And over it all, the caustic reek of fear.

The hitherto solitary figures and occasional pairs of men Glory slogged through the mud with began to link up, forming into groups of fours and fives, then tens and twenties. The larger the groups, the more vocal they were. The chants grew louder, harsh cries demanding action, justice, revenge. Against what exactly, Glory did not know. And after viewing the wild fanatical gleams in many of their eyes, she was sorely afraid that the increasingly inflamed mob members were not much better informed about what was going on than Glory herself.

Panic had a stranglehold on the town. As they neared the market square, the ranks of soldiers grew more numerous, more watchful. Guns were gripped with white-knuckled intensity. The militiamen's voices became louder, harsher, more hysterical as they were obliged to order the panicked people to move on, move back, move away.

As she pushed through the thickening mass of humanity converging on the already crowded town square, Glory began to hear frightening snatches of conversation, rumors of attacks, raids, shootings. Once she stood stock-still in her tracks, shocked into immobility by the unbelievability of what she was hearing. She gaped at a man who excitedly informed his neighbor that a vigilante group was forming outside the town. Any minute now, the agitated man swore, the dreaded Union League was going to thunder into town to rescue their imprisoned comrades.

Glory started to protest the fellow's irrational statement but instantly gave up the thought when he brandished a pistol and vowed to shoot the bastards on sight. Moving quickly away from the disturbing scene, she fleetingly wondered how many innocent people might suffer if he carried through his threat.

The closer Glory moved to the east side of the square, the madder things became. Trying to fight her way through the shoulder-to-shoulder crowd proved impossible. She could barely manage to work her way around the perimeter.

The crowd surged and seethed like cornered mustangs. The usual friendly atmosphere of the small

330

frontier town had been completely enveloped by a relentless fear that swept through the town like a prairie grass fire. Glory struggled to keep her feet under her as she was jostled like a leaf on the wind.

"Please, have you heard who's been arrested?" she requested time and again.

"Don't know no names, lady, but I hear they's got a lot of men in that there storeroom."

"The Childs brothers been arrested. And some others. Lock and Morris, I think."

"I hear the blacksmith's locked up. You know, that fellow John Crisp."

"And Scott and Fields."

Some names Glory recognized, others she didn't. The tales got wilder, sometimes the responses made no sense at all. But she breathed a silent prayer of thanks that so far no one had replied "Hunter." She clung to the hope that Slade and his family had escaped.

Rumor after rumor rippled through the crowd. Fifty arrests. No, eighty! A hundred! Hysteria spread like cholera.

The mob ebbed and flowed, finally breaking apart just enough to allow Glory to slip through the middle and squeeze forward. Filled with trepidation, she bravely approached one of the soldiers guarding the east side of the square.

"Please," she implored. "Could you tell me who's in there? I'm looking for a friend—"

Concerned eyes looked down at her from the old soldier's weathered face. "Now you listen here, little lady, this ain't no place for a woman," he scolded in a gentle voice. "You best run along home before things get too rough."

"But the names—surely there's a list," Glory insisted.

"There ain't no list that I know of, miss. They're bringing them in faster than we can keep track of 'em. Go home, please. It ain't gonna do you no good to hang around here. You're apt to get hurt."

"But—"

Suddenly a loud cry went up from one side of the swirling mass of humanity filling the square.

"Give 'em to us!"

"Hang the bastards!"

"Teach 'em a lesson. Ain't a goddamn Unionist gonna threaten to shoot my family!"

"Let's hang them! Hang them all!"

"Get a rope!"

The crowd roared its approval.

"Please, miss," the soldier pleaded above the din of the voices, apprehension etching harsh lines across his face. "Move on. It ain't safe here."

"Hang 'em!"

"Get the bastards!"

The mob pushed hard against the ring of soldiers and Glory's man turned quickly to shove back a pair of encroachers. "Here now! We'll be having none of that!" he yelled at one burly man, using his gun stock to hold the line. "Get back in your place. Move back! Move back!"

The big man snarled a curse and tried to slap the

soldier's gun away. Lightning fast, the militia man stepped back and whipped his gun to the ready, aiming the barrel straight at the surprised man. "I told you to move back." There was a cold steel warning in his command.

Grumbling blasphemies under his breath, the big man quickly took a few hasty steps backward, nearly sending Glory sprawling. The world rocked precariously and her heart leaped to her throat as she envisioned herself trampled beneath the feet of the hysterical throng. With quick reflexes, she barely managed to keep her balance by grabbing hold of the coat sleeve of yet another man.

Upright again, Glory breathed a ragged sigh of relief. Then her huge, frightened eyes searched for the soldier's familiar face.

The crowd was growing uglier, but the soldier risked one last glance in Glory's direction.

"Get out of here, miss, while you still can!" he shouted before turning his attention back to the shoving, shouting mass confronting him.

For once Glory had the good sense to listen and obey. Her boots slipping sickeningly in the mud, she swirled and, with fear-driven strength, pushed her way out of the crowd.

When she at last reached relative safety at the edge of the boardwalk, she leaned tiredly against a support post, pulling in great gulps of air in an effort to slow her pounding heart. Turning her face against the pillar, she fought an almost overwhelming desire to give in to the tears of frustration that scalded the backs of her eyes.

Oh, Lord! All this miserable trying, and she hadn't learned a thing. Not one useful thing.

Pushing away from the post, she set her weary feet in the direction of home. But just then, above the sea of bobbing heads, she caught sight of Mr. Cranford's tall, lean form. Perhaps there was one last hope.

Glory hurried down the south side of the square, skipping between and around the smaller groups of men straggling along the boardwalk. The closer she got to Hunters General Store, the less congested it was.

Halfway down the block, she had a fairly clear view of Slade's hired clerk. He'd dragged a large wooden crate just outside the front entrance of the door and was standing atop it to better peruse the turmoil taking place on the square.

"Mr. Cranford, Mr. Cranford!" Glory called as she drew near.

In response to hearing his name called, the old man's gaze searched the crowd. She knew when he spotted her by the way his brow arched. A few more steps and she was standing at the side of the crate looking up.

Mr. Cranford's usual jolly smile was missing. "Miss Westbrook, what on earth are you doing here?" Worry furrowed his forehead as he gazed down at her.

"I need to talk with you. Please."

"Of course." Cranford quickly stepped down from his perch and led the way into the store. Once inside, he pushed the double doors shut to block out the growing noise. He turned to face her with sharp blue eyes full of concern.

"What can I do for you, Miss Westbrook?" he asked in a solicitous tone.

Glory pulled her thoughts away from memories of the last time she'd been in the store—the tender, loving hours she'd shared with Slade. She gulped hard and turned her attention to the task at hand. "Slade. Have you heard from Slade?"

Cranford frowned slightly. "He sent a message two days ago, asking me to watch the store. Said something about going out of town."

"Oh. That's good." Glory breathed a long sigh of relief at the news. That was one worry off her mind. Now, if she could just find out if Slade was all right.

"Any . . . anything else?" she asked hesitantly.

Scratching his thinning hair, Cranford gave Glory a speculative look. "Well, just that he didn't know when he or his pa would be back. Said I should just do whatever I have to. Told me to keep it open, if possible. Close up for a while, if I had to. You wouldn't know anything about that, would you, Miss Westbrook?"

"What?" Glory's head jerked up in alarm. How much did Cranford know? Was he aware of the League? Or possibly even a member himself? Did he know Slade and his father belonged? She didn't dare ask those questions. There was always the chance he knew nothing of their affiliation with the clandestine organization. Better safe than sorry. "Oh . . . uh . . .

335

no. Of course not. I was just worried about him . . . that's all."

"Would you like to leave a message for him?" Cranford asked kindly. "I mean, just in case I hear from him again any time soon."

Glory gave him a trembly smile. "Well . . . uh. I suppose I could do that."

What could she say without betraying that she did indeed know where Slade was?

"Good."

"Yes, of course I'll leave a message," she finally declared. "If you do hear from him, just tell him that I inquired as to his well-being . . . that I sent my regards."

"That's all?"

"Yes."

Cranford plunged his bony hands into the pockets of his pants and rocked back on his heels. He gave a sharp nod in the direction of the street. "You worried about what's going on out there?"

Glory's fingers clutched a wad of skirt fabric. "Well . . . yes . . . of course. Anyone would be, I suppose."

"Ummm." Mr. Cranford eyed the milling crowd through the front window for a long moment. "You weren't expecting to hear that Slade was locked up with those others, were you?"

"No! Of course not!" she protested, too quickly and too loudly.

"My, my." The old man shook his head slowly. Finally, he looked her in the eye again and forced a reassuring smile to his lips. "Well, just in case the thought crossed your mind, you can quit worrying, missy. I've been watching since all this started up this morning. I haven't seen hide nor hair of any of the Hunters."

Glory's lashes swept down in relief. When she opened her eyes again, they weren't quite so filled with apprehension. "Thank you," she whispered.

"Tell you what, little lady, why don't we just assume that everything's all right? At least until we hear different? Think you can do that?"

"Yes. I'll try," she replied softly, nodding her head. "But—" Lord! She hated to say the words out loud.

"But what, Miss Westbrook?" the old man asked in a gentle voice.

"Will . . . will you keep . . . uh . . . watching? I mean, shouldn't the concerned citizens of the town know what's going on?"

That's all she could manage. There was no way she could say "keep watching just in case Slade's arrested."

Such awful words. The mere thought of speaking them aloud made her stomach lurch.

Cranford nodded sagely. "Don't worry, Miss Westbrook. I'll be here every day—whether or not I can open up the store for business."

Glory's grateful smile lit up her face. "Do you suppose I could come back every day or so? Maybe you could tell me what's happening out there." She gave a flick of her head toward the street. "I hate not knowing."

337

It wasn't so much for herself that she wanted to know. She knew how hard it would be on Slade to hide out in the little house in the Timbers, never knowing what was going on in town. If he got too anxious, he might be foolish enough to come to town. Glory had to prevent that at all costs. If Mr. Cranford could keep her informed, she'd be able to sneak off occasionally to tell Slade what was happening.

The old man considered her question for a moment and then replied, "Yes, of course. But you must be careful coming to the square. Folks are getting awful riled up out there."

"I know," Glory said, recalling the harsh words and angry shoving between the nice soldier and the big, burly man.

"I hear there's over seven hundred soldiers in Gainesville now—and more coming. They've sewed up the whole town."

"What?" Glory asked abruptly, trying to understand what the elderly gentleman had just said.

"The soldiers. They've been setting up barricades, so I hear. Not supposed to let anyone in or out. Bourland's orders, I think."

No one in or out of town? Glory shivered with icy fear. No. No, she couldn't think of that now. Just be glad that Slade was safe. Later she could worry about slipping out of town. Surely the soldiers wouldn't try to detain Colonel Westbrook's daughter.

Forcing a smile, Glory prepared to take her leave from Mr. Cranford.

"Thank you for your help," she said. "I'll be back as soon as I can to find out what the military has planned."

"I'll be here," Cranford assured her. "You be careful going home. And even more so coming back. All right?"

"Yes. I will. I promise."

With that, Glory slipped out the front door of the store. One quick look at the frenzied crowd and she prudently turned left onto Commerce Street, deciding to take the longer way home because it would get her off the square faster.

A cacophony of sound followed Glory for a long way—the harsh challenges and demands of the maddened mob. But despite this disquieting accompaniment, Glory's heart was a bit lighter as she headed toward the sanctuary of home.

At least for the time being, Slade was safe.

Chapter Twenty

It was a considerably bedraggled Glory who returned home that afternoon. Lydia, true to her word, was waiting in the kitchen. Violet and Sara clucked and hovered over their young mistress, whisking away the damp, stained cloak, the mud-encased boots, the drooping bonnet.

"Land sakes, girl!" Violet scolded in her loving way. "You're gonna catch your death of cold. Miss Lydia, now you see to it that Miss Glory gets right out of those clothes and into something dry. I'll be right up with a nice pot of hot tea." With a flap of her apron, Violet shooed the two young women toward the stairs.

In the sanctuary of Glory's bedroom, Lydia took her usual place on the big feather bed while Glory shed her disheveled clothing and wrapped herself in a warm flannel robe. First Lydia demanded to be told about Glory's discovery of danger to the League and her warning to Slade and his family. Then she listened in shocked silence while Glory recounted the tale of her visit to town.

"And then what happened?" Lydia asked in a breathless voice.

"So I told Mr. Cranford I'd be back as soon as I could and I came home."

"Mercy!" Lydia leaned against the headboard, terrifying scenes of what Glory had just described filling her head. The panic, the milling people, the soldiers with their guns at ready. It was almost too much for Lydia's gentle soul to assimilate. "You don't really think that the . . . the mob will hurt those people, do you?"

Glory sighed. "I don't know," she replied in an equally worried voice as she settled on the end of the bed, tucking the skirt of her robe around her chilly feet.

"But they're our neighbors!" Lydia protested.

Glory frowned. "I know. It's difficult to describe the way things were. It was almost like being in another world . . . a peculiar foreign place filled with strangers. I don't know how to explain it. The buildings, the trees, all those things looked like my home, my town, but the people were . . ." She trailed off, trying to find a way to illustrate the eeriness of her venture to Lydia.

"Yes?" Lydia prompted.

"The people—they . . . they weren't themselves. It was like being picked up by a tornado and set down among people of a totally different culture. Mr. Cranford was the only one who seemed normal. The rest of them—" Glory shuddered. "Their eyes were wild . . . like those unbroken mustangs they brought through town last week, or . . . or maybe a pack of wild dogs. It was scary, Lydia—scarier even than the guns and soldiers and noise."

"What do you think will happen next?" Lydia squeaked in a frightened voice.

"I don't know. I just don't know. But I do know that if I were locked up in the storeroom, I'd be very, very afraid." Glory delivered her discomfiting statement in a shaky, subdued voice.

"Oh, my!" Lydia gasped.

Just then a knock sounded on Glory's door.

"Come in," she called.

The door swung open and Violet entered, a large tray balanced against her middle. Setting it on the writing table, she hurried over to Glory and placed a pink palm against the girl's forehead.

"Well, at least there's no fever," the slave woman declared with a worried shake of her head. "Now, I want you to drink every last drop of that tea, do you hear me? And stay warm and quiet for the rest of the afternoon. If you do, I'm sure you'll feel like coming down to dinner tonight. Then no one will know—"

For the first time since the bells' hectic pealing had propelled her out of bed, Glory thought of her family, especially her father. Did he know she'd gone to town?

Turning a worried gaze on Violet, she tried to voice the disturbing question. "Did . . . did Papa—"

Watching the play of emotions on Glory's face, Violet knew at once what was bothering the girl. "No," she assured her, "your father went to Colonel Bourland's early this morning. He hasn't returned yet. And your mother spent the better part of the day in bed with a nervous headache."

Glory sagged in relief.

Bracing her folded hands against her hips, Violet gazed sternly down at Glory. "You listen to me, Miss Glory. You done got away with sneaking out once. But you best be smart and stay home from now on. If'n your papa gets wind that you've been down there with those crazy folks in town, he's gonna—"

"I know, Violet," Glory said with a sigh, feeling like a tiny frightened rabbit caught in a trap. "I don't mean to do things to make Papa mad, but sometimes a person has no choice. Sometimes you have to do something regardless of who it might worry or what might happen to yourself." Her chin tilted upward and the amber lights in her eyes shone with unwavering determination. "I'm going back."

Violet's full bottom lip stuck out stubbornly. "Miss Glory—"

"It's no use arguing, Violet. I have to go. If you can see your way to help me keep Papa from finding out, I'd be much obliged. But I'm going regardless. The only thing that'll stop me is for Papa to lock me up."

"Um huh!" Violet said with a troubled shake of her head. "And that's just what that man is apt to do if he finds out."

"I'll just have to take that chance."

A loud sigh of capitulation escaped Violet's lips. "All right, honey chile. I'll help if I can. I don't have to like it. No, siree! I sure don't have to like it. But I'll do what I can."

A great diversity of moods permeated the group

343

that sat down to supper around the Westbrooks' big polished table that night. A subdued and worried Glory found herself ensconced between an exceptionally jovial Preston and a very discomfited Lydia.

Glory breathed a prayer of thanksgiving that she'd prevailed upon her friend to send a message home and stay the night. Perhaps Lydia's presence would protect her from having to field another evening's worth of hints about setting the wedding date. As a gentleman, Preston could hardly expect her to neglect a guest in order to listen to his entreaties.

For the first few minutes, the only sounds to break the quiet of the room were the movements of the two serving girls as they circled the table presenting first one course, then another. Violet's unobtrusive comings and goings between the kitchen and the dining room were barely noticed by the family after all these years. Placing each successive dish on the sideboard, Violet left the serving to her subordinates. Her authority in the house was so well established that she had only to quirk a wing of dark brow at one of the young slaves to prod the girl into greater efforts.

The two men were in a splendid mood, and almost immediately the Colonel and Preston fell into a lively conversation about the effect of the approaching war on the cost of goods in the state. The turmoil in town seemed to have had no effect on them at all. In fact, Glory thought they seemed inordinately pleased. She surmised that some recent business deal must have gone well.

While she failed to see how they could be so jolly when the town suffered from such madness, she did feel relief that she could obviously quit worrying that her father might have heard about her furtive expedition to the square.

Preston and the Colonel seemed to be the only two in the room in good spirits, Glory noted. Across the table from her, Mary and Helen were uncharacteristically subdued. An afternoon of peering out the parlor window to watch the strange goings-on in the street had unsettled her two younger sisters. Lydia was quieter than usual. And after one look at her mother, Glory knew immediately that Mrs. Westbrook was struggling to appear her usual gracious self. Eventually the talk turned to the day's events, and Glory was even more convinced that her mother was upset when Mrs. Westbrook rebuked the Colonel for discussing such an unsettling topic at the supper table and then pursued the conversation herself.

"Robert, dear," Mrs. Westbrook commented in her soft, refined way, "I'm extremely concerned about subjecting the girls to such disturbing events as those we witnessed today. Might you not consider returning to Sivells Bend, at least until things are back to normal?"

The Colonel stroked his chin in contemplation, gazing at his two younger daughters with a sudden awareness. "Well . . . perhaps you're right, my dear. While I can't leave at this time, I can certainly make arrangements for a militia unit to escort you and the girls to the plantation house, if you'd feel safer there."

"Oh, yes, Robert, I would," Mrs. Westbrook answered in a relieved rush of words. "Today has been most unsettling, and I'm very much afraid it's going to get worse."

Preston and Westbrook exchanged a quick glance. "Very well, my dear. I'll take care of it first thing in the morning. I should have thought of it myself. I'll probably feel better with the four of you out of all of this—"

"Four?" Glory asked quickly. "Oh, no, Papa. I don't want to go."

"But, Glory," Mrs. Westbrook protested gently, "Gainesville is hardly a seemly environment for a well-bred young lady under the present conditions."

"Mother, I'll be perfectly fine here. There're plenty of servants to protect me. And Papa will be home. And don't forget, I have several appointments with the seamstress. You know how much Mrs. Williams depends on those fees to support her family." Glory cunningly appealed to her mother's tender nature. "I'd hate to let the poor woman down, what with money getting tighter and all."

"I don't know—"

"I'm afraid I have to agree with your mother, Glory. My current . . . uh . . . business dealings are apt to take a great deal of time. I may even have to go out of town for several nights at a time—"

"But, Papa, Lydia's family will be here," Glory hastened to assure. "I can always stay with the Uptons if you have to be away. Can't I, Lydia?"

Glory's gentle kick to her shin prodded Lydia back to reality. The mouth that had dropped open as she listened to Glory's hasty expostulations snapped shut and she hurriedly replied in the affirmative. "Yes, yes, of course Glory can stay with us—all the time if she wants to. You know my parents would be pleased

346

to have her, as always."

Surprisingly, Preston intervened on Glory's behalf. "Mrs. Westbrook, let me assure you that the town is well protected by the military. There are upwards of eight hundred troops here at present. With that many men, there's hardly worry about danger. And I, of course, will be happy to do what I can to doubly ensure Glory's well-being."

"Ummm—"

It was plain to see that Mrs. Westbrook wasn't entirely happy about the arrangements, but she did realize that very soon her daughter would be given into Preston's safe-keeping for good. If he felt it was all right for Glory to stay in town, then she supposed she shouldn't interfere.

"Very well. Mary, Helen, and I will leave in the morning. But, Glory," she turned a stern eye on her frequently wayward daughter, "you must promise to stay in the house, or at the Uptons', and obey your father at all times."

Lowering her eyes demurely, Glory crossed her fingers in her lap and answered with all the sincerity she could muster, "Yes, Mother, of course I will."

That issue settled, the family and their guests turned their attention to the meal once again. Glory even experienced a return of appetite now that she had assured her continued stay in town. She was contemplating a second helping of roast beef when Preston spoke again.

"I hope some of those frocks you're commissioning will be trousseau items, Glory." The corner of his mouth quirked up in a teasing smile.

The quiet statement quickly disbursed the glow of

347

self-satisfaction Glory was feeling. She toyed with the food on her plate for a moment, and finally pushed it to one side in disinterest. "T-trousseau?"

"Of course. For our wedding."

"Oh. Well, yes, Preston, I will talk to Mrs. Williams about t-that." Glory suppressed the twinges of remorse at having to tell still another fib.

To hide her discomfort, Glory quickly reached for her glass. Tipping the crystal goblet up to take a sip of rich ruby wine, she once again agonized over how she was ever going to manage to break her engagement. She certainly couldn't do it now. Without Preston's reassurances, she'd most assuredly find herself in exile at Sivells Bend, with no way to get to Slade. No, she certainly couldn't broach the sensitive subject now.

Later, she vowed as usual, once the turmoil in town was over with, she'd have the necessary talk with Preston.

But Glory had barely settled the hopeful thought in her mind, when Preston dropped a bombshell in their midst.

He patted the snowy linen napkin primly against his pale gold mustache and then turned in his chair so that he was almost facing Glory. "I have a surprise for you, my dear." A satisfied smile wreathed his face as he leaned nonchalantly against the deeply carved back of the chair and waited for her response.

What now? Unable to help herself, Glory exchanged a quick look of annoyance with Lydia before turning her attention to Preston. "Oh?"

"A wedding present. Something I'm quite sure you'll be pleased about."

"A w-wedding present?" Glory stammered. Her hands nervously twisted the napkin in her lap.

Preston nodded regally. "Something you can take to your new home at Sivells Bend. Something to keep you company and make you feel more at home."

Glory smiled weakly. "How . . . how thoughtful of you, Preston. Am I . . . uh . . . supposed to guess what this g-gift is?"

Preston chuckled. "No, my dear. You'd never guess in a million years."

"You're absolutely right, Preston," the Colonel boomed from his place at the head of the table. "You'd best salve her curiosity. Go on, tell her." Glory's father beamed in her direction.

Preston bestowed another smug smile upon her before elucidating. "I've prevailed upon your father to sell Sara to me."

Crash! The bowl Violet was carrying smashed against the floor, potatoes splattering the floor in white, fluffy globs. Every head in the room turned to stare at the visibly trembling woman in the doorway.

Eyes huge and shocked, shaking hands pressed hard to still the instinctive cry of protest, Violet stood mute. She didn't even move when the two younger slaves scurried to clean up the mess she'd created.

Glory's fork clattered sharply against her plate as a sick dread swept through her. She finally dragged her eyes from the slave woman's stricken face and glared at her father.

"Papa," she protested vehemently. "You can't do that. You can't sell Sara. She's like family!"

"Now, Glory. Don't get so riled up," the Colonel

349

soothed quickly. "You're reacting before you even think about what's been said. After all, Sara will still be with the family."

"What are you talking about?" Glory asked, her mind so filled with concern about what Violet must be going through that little of the conversation was penetrating.

"Why, she'll be with you. Preston has promised that he won't take her until after the wedding."

"That's right," Preston confirmed.

Glory's father spread his hands wide. "So, you see, you're upset for nothing. Sara will stay right here until it's time for her to accompany you to your new husband's home."

Violet gave a choked little cry. Tears formed in her eyes and she whirled and ran from the room.

"Violet!" Glory called out in dismay, but the woman never looked back. Long after Violet was gone, Glory continued to stare at the spot where the black woman had been. When her unbelieving gaze met her father's once again, she was still feeling as if her heart had dropped to her toes.

"I was sure you'd be so pleased that I agreed right away when Preston approached me with the idea."

"R-really, Papa," Glory pleaded. "I know you were only thinking of me. But . . . but I'd honestly prefer that Sara be allowed to stay here with Violet and Jacob." Her attempted smile left a great deal to be desired. "Let's just forget all about this—"

"It's not possible, my dear," Preston interjected smoothly. "The papers have already been signed. Sara belongs to me now. I'm quite sure you'll be happy with your gift once you think about it."

Glory raised her stricken gaze to Preston's cool blue eyes. The cool, calculating look in them left no doubt in her mind that he had no intention of backing out of the deal.

Oh, Lord! Glory moaned inwardly. Sara would be taken away from her family whether or not Glory married Preston. But to give up Slade, even for Sara's sake, was unthinkable.

What in God's name was she going to do now?

It was only the lack of sleep from the previous night that allowed Glory to sleep any during the long night after Preston's announcement. That and the comfort of having Lydia near in the darkness.

The two young women had talked late into the night, trying desperately to find a way for Glory to escape the trap closing around her. But the wee hours of the morning had found them still without a solution to the problems. Finally Lydia dropped off to sleep and soon afterward Glory's weary eyes fluttered shut.

The morning was a repeat of the day before; gloomy gray skies to match the mood of the restless, panicky people roaming the streets, an unnamed fear riding the chill winds that buffeted the town.

Mrs. Westbrook and her younger daughters left for Sivells Bend at first light. The Colonel departed the house shortly thereafter. At supper last night, Glory had shrewdly thought to plant the idea that she would be going home with Lydia for the day.

Glory's first concern that morning was Violet. She'd been unable to find her after the disastrous supper. And the thought of the gentle servant fleeing to the sanctuary of her family's quarters with such suffering in her heart filled Glory with anguish. Glory could not even envision how terrible it must have been for Violet to have to tell her husband and her daughter of the terrible deed.

As soon as she was dressed, she sought Violet out. The black woman's eyes were puffy and red from weeping.

"Oh, Violet," Glory cried. "I'm so sorry for all of this. I had no idea." Glory flew across the kitchen and wrapped her arms about the sagging shoulders of the woman who had provided such comfort for Glory many, many times in the past. "I promise I won't give up. I'll talk to Papa again. Surely there's something I can do to prevent this."

Violet only nodded mutely and swallowed back the flood of tears which threatened once again to break free.

"How are Jacob and Sara taking all this?" Glory asked gently, guiding Violet to the old rocker by the kitchen fireplace.

The woman sagged tiredly into its comforting depths, her hands twisting nervously in her lap. "Sara's all right. As long as she'll be with you, she says she doesn't mind so much. Jacob . . ." She shook her head and reached to swipe an escaped tear from her burnished cheek. "Jacob's ol' heart's near broke. You know how he dotes on that chile."

Glory could think of nothing to say, so she simply reached to pat the slave woman's trembling hand once again.

Turning tear-sheened eyes toward the young

woman hovering at the side of the rocker, Violet continued. "It's not that we didn't expect Sara to grow up and go away some day . . . But not so soon. She's just a baby! And I always hoped the master would find a suitable mate for her and bring him here and . . . and then we'd always have our family together."

Guilt flooded through Glory. It was all her fault! If she hadn't agreed to marry Preston in the first place, he'd never have thought of buying Sara. She didn't want to marry Preston, but how could she save poor Sara from a life of exile from all she'd ever known?

A very contrite Glory knelt, clutching the curved wooden arm of the chair in a fierce grip. "I promise, Violet, I'll do everything I can to stop this. I'll talk to Papa again. Please don't cry anymore. I won't give up until I find a way. I promise."

A tiny spark of hope flared in Violet's black eyes. With every fiber of her being, Glory prayed that she'd be able to keep her vow.

Later that afternoon, when Lydia set out to return home, it was surprisingly easy for Glory to leave with her and then slip away in the direction of town. Taking the same circuitous route she'd followed on her return trip the previous day, Glory made her cautious way toward the congested center of town. The belligerent milling mob filling the courthouse square paid no attention to the slim figure that slipped through the store entrance.

"Ah ha," said Mr. Cranford with a worried smile, "so you came after all."

"I said I would."

"Yes, I know. But the situation is becoming more difficult by the minute. I was hoping you had changed your mind."

"More difficult?" Glory repeated, casting a quick glance out the window. "What's happening? Oh! Slade hasn't—"

"No, no," Mr. Cranford quickly assured her. "Put your mind at ease. "The only thing I've heard about the Hunters is a rumor that they went to Dallas with the Widow Stafford. That being the case, we can surely assume that they're safe."

The knot in Glory's stomach eased a bit. "Then what do you mean? What's more difficult?"

"Early this morning they convened a citizens' court to try the prisoners. Young has been appointed to oversee the proceedings, and another twelve men have been appointed to the court."

"Who?"

"Montague, Barrett, Long, Doss . . ."

Glory listened with growing concern as Mr. Cranford recited twelve names. "But seven of those men are slaveowners!" she protested. "That gives the Southern side an unfair advantage."

"Aye, it does. And to make matters worse, they've decided on a simple majority vote to convict."

"Why, all those seven have to do is vote together and the defendants'll have no chance at all!"

"True enough, Miss Westbrook, but I can see no way to rectify the situation. The trials have already begun."

"But what are the charges?"

"Disloyalty, treason, conspiracy, insurrection—

"There's been no insurrection!"

354

"They have witnesses who swear that one was planned," Cranford countered.

With a sickening certainty Glory knew who at least some of those witnesses were. Hadn't she heard their names from her own father's lips? McCurley and Chance.

She struggled for understanding. Had Knox Coleman's foolish plans precipitated this disaster? Or could the poor men presently ensconced in that wretched jail perhaps be the innocent victims of a few overzealous slavers?

Bourland. Preston. Her father. Was there any possibility that they were justified in their actions? Or had the unsuspecting members of the League been doomed to imprisonment because of the less than honorable designs of those men? Was there any validity in bringing such dire retaliation down on the heads of neighbors and friends? Who else would suffer in this dreadful web of revenge and deceit?

No! her heart cried. Her father couldn't deliberately have done such a terrible thing. There had to be a reasonable explanation. There had to be. The court would look at all the evidence and find out that a mistake had been made. Justice would win out in the long run.

Finally Glory turned her attention back to the waiting man. "It's . . . it's so hard to believe that this is happening."

"There's more, Miss Westbrook. They've already tried Henry Childs and his brother Ephraim, and several others. They've all been found guilty—and condemned to death by hanging."

The strength seeped right out of Glory's bones and

she stumbled to a barrel, collapsing upon it just as her weak knees gave way. "Hanging! Merciful God!"

Glory's mind struggled for comprehension. What kind of trial could be held in such haste? Had the men even had benefits of counsel? Tried and condemned in a matter of hours! How had such a travesty of justice happened?

Rushing to her side, Mr. Cranford expressed his concern. "I'm sorry, my dear, I should have told you in a gentler manner. Forgive an old man's foolishness. Could I get you a glass of cool water?"

With a fluttery hand, Glory waved his effusive apologies away. "No, no. I'll be all right. It was just such a shock." Clasping her hands tight in her lap, she begged him to continue his story. She needed to know everything she could possibly find out before making the trip to Slade's hideout.

Chapter Twenty-one

It was ten agonizingly long days before Glory managed to see Slade. Getting away from the house was easy; getting out of town was another story.

With her mother and her younger sisters gone, Glory had only her father to deal with. Luckily, he was gone almost constantly. He accepted without question the alibi Glory used to cover her continued trips to town. He had no reason to doubt that she was spending those hours with Lydia; after all, such visits between the girls had been the standard of behavior for many years.

And, if the truth be known, the Colonel was glad to have his daughter safely occupied. He and his colleagues certainly had enough worries. The continued arrests and subsequent trials were keeping them busy from sunup to midnight.

If Violet suspected that Glory wasn't spending all her time at Lydia's, at least she never questioned her. The black woman had her own troubles—the impending loss of her young daughter had pushed most other concerns from her mind. Although Glory promised daily to resolve the problem somehow, Violet's only response was a trembly smile that never touched her eyes.

Jacob was even worse. It broke Glory's heart to confront the familiar figure; he looked like he'd aged ten years in the past week. And poor Sara crept about the house like a little lost kitten, trying her best to appear pleased about the coming change in her life.

Glory kept hoping that a good long talk with her father would make him change his mind. But so far, she'd been unable to catch him alone long enough to even broach the subject. He routinely left before she awoke and didn't get home each night until long after Glory had given up and gone to bed. Still, Glory clung to her hopes, vowing to pursue the matter with him at the first opportunity.

To make matters even more difficult, the situation in town had gone from bad to worse. Every passing day made Glory just that much more anxious to see Slade. Her flight to his assuring embrace would have been accomplished far sooner had it not been for the continued upheaval in the town.

Glory's first two attempts to leave Gainesville had been thwarted when the seasoned soldiers standing guard duty on the road refused to let her pass without the proper documentation. Finally, frustration had driven her to take desperate measures.

Early one morning, after checking to make sure her father had left for the day, Glory went into his study, where pen and ink and his special letterhead were all available for her taking.

Immediately Glory set to work. The first four attempts wound up as crumpled balls in the wastebasket. But her fifth effort pleased her. Not too long, not too short, the words at least read like something her father would have written. She spent several long minutes practicing his signature on scrap paper before she finally applied it with a flourish to the bottom of her fake pass.

"There," she said to herself, "that ought to do it." Sufficiently satisfied with her morning's labors, she tucked the paper in the pocket of her riding skirt and ran for the stable.

At the edge of town, fate intervened in her favor once again. This morning, the guard on the small back road was young and inexperienced. All jumpy nerves when she first approached, raw relief filled his eyes as soon as he realized the rider was only an innocent-looking young woman. He barely glanced at the paper once he learned he was dealing with Colonel Westbrook's daughter, so eager was he to please.

"Why, thank you, sir," Glory murmured, quickly refolding the bogus pass and putting it back in the pocket of the dark-blue skirt. Then she put on her brightest smile and fluttered her lashes at the boy, who turned a lovely shade of pink.

"My pleasure, ma'am," he squeaked, his young voice changing from soon-to-be-adult bass to adolescent soprano. The color in his face darkened another shade in embarrassment and Glory quickly suppressed a nervous giggle at his plight.

"My, don't you get lonely, staying out here all day?" Glory asked sweetly.

"Oh, no, ma'am," the lad answered fervently. "I'd a sight rather be out here than back in the middle of town —" His words tumbled to a stop and he blushed again, aghast at the thought that the lovely lady might construe his avid response as a form of cowardice. "I mean . . . uh . . . I ain't used to all that hullabaloo, like what they got going on. Being from a farm and all, I never been around this many folks before —"

"Oh, I know exactly what you mean," Glory assured him, striving to put the young soldier at ease so she could finish her line of questioning. "All that noise, and the crowds! It's more than a body should have to deal with. You're lucky you were assigned guard duty out here."

"Yes'm, I surely am." The broad grin that split his hairless rosy-cheeked face bespoke his relief at her understanding.

"We're so lucky to have fine soldiers like yourself to protect us," she cooed.

The young man's recurring blush took on shades of the sunrise. "Well . . . uh . . . yes'm."

Glory plunged ahead. "Do you have to stay out here long?" She delivered the words in a tone of deep concern.

"Till nightfall, ma'am," the boy answered, shuffling nervously from one foot to another.

Thank God! thought Glory. She'd be returning long before then.

With a few pleasant parting words and one last brilliant smile, Glory took her leave of the enraptured young man. As she rode away, reins clutched tightly in her hands, she fought the overwhelming

360

impulse to race madly across the countryside. It took all her willpower to keep Rosebud at the same sedate canter until she was far out of the soldier's sight.

Once free of such restrictions, she slapped the reins across Rosebud's neck and tapped her heels into the roan's soft flanks. Rosebud responded magnificently, stretching his muscular neck forward, surging ahead with each long stride. Glory only slowed the reckless pace when it was time to leave the road and strike out through the thick stand of timber surrounding their hideaway.

Drawing to a halt at the crest of a small hill, Glory's eager eyes scrutinized the cabin. There was no sign of life, and for a moment her heart sank. But she quickly rationalized that things were as they should be. Slade had promised to be careful so that no wandering rider might suspect his presence in the small, abandoned house. She pulled a long shuddering breath deep into her lungs and once again prodded Rosebud into movement.

She made the approach to the house in a slow and obvious manner, so that Slade could be sure who was coming and know that it was safe to show himself. It seemed to take an eternity to descend the gentle slope and cross the sparsely timbered field cradled at the bottom. Her heartbeat increased with each step. *Slade, Slade, Slade,* it crooned.

She drew nearer and nearer and still Slade did not appear. The excited expectancy she'd felt all morning began to fade to dismay and disappointment. Tendrils of fear were beginning to creep into her mind when the door was suddenly thrown open and Slade emerged. His eager stride devoured the distance separating them. In seconds they were in each other's arms.

"Glory, darling! God, how I've missed you." Kisses were rained across her upturned face. His strong arms wrapped about her, holding her tightly against him, savoring her warmth and softness after the endless empty days without her.

Threading her fingers through his raven hair, Glory pulled his dear face down to hers, drinking in the sweetness of his taste. Her heart sang with joy as his lips claimed hers and his tongue slid into the soft, warm recesses of her mouth. Her hands clung to his nape, prolonging the fiery kiss until they both gulped for breath.

"Hold me, Slade, just hold me," she pleaded, snuggling deeper into the sanctuary of his arms, seeking to use his beloved nearness to blot out all the ugliness she'd witnessed.

Slade gladly complied, settling her tighter against him, his strong hands gliding gently up and down the expanse of her back. His moist, warm breath fanned across her temple, seductively stirring the baby-soft strands of hair. Turning her face into the sheltering hollow between shoulder and throat, she breathed in the soothing, familiar aroma of the man she loved.

They stood thusly for a long, long time under the soft gray-blue skies. A playful breeze set the few remaining chrysanthemum blooms at the front of the little house to dancing. A mockingbird called in the distance. And in Slade's arms, Glory's world once again righted itself.

"Are you all right?" he finally asked in the sweetest, most caring tone.

362

The lump of emotion in her throat made it hard for Glory to answer, but she nodded her head, bumping the top of it gently against the underside of his chin in the process.

"Come on, sweetheart," he instructed, keeping his arm tight around her shoulders.

Grabbing the gelding's dangling reins, he led the way to the back of the house. "Go inside. I'll be right there. I just want to put Rosebud in the barn with Diablo."

Glory was reluctant to leave him, but after one last kiss she gave in to his tender urgings and went inside. Peace enveloped her. She wandered about the rooms, touching the sparse furnishings, lovingly running her fingers over the bright splashes of color in the quilt spread across the bed.

Beside the small table in front of the window, Glory bent to sniff a bouquet of late blooming wild asters. Lost in thought, she pulled one dainty lavender blossom from the crock and twirled it aimlessly between her fingers as she stared out at the tall autumn-yellowed grass.

Slade perceived her pensive mood the minute he slipped through the door. Crossing the room on cat-quiet feet, he cupped her shoulders in his strong hands and pulled her back against him. Glory sighed and leaned her head against the comforting expanse of his chest.

"Is there bad news?" he whispered hesitantly against her ear. "My . . . my family?"

She heard the apprehension in his voice and turned quickly, winding her arms tightly around his waist as she gazed up into worried gray eyes.

"Oh, no, darling," she said with a vigorous shake of her head. "Nothing like that. There hasn't been a word about any of them. I'm sure they're still safe and sound in Dallas."

"Good." The word was carried on a deep sigh of relief. Dark lashes dropped over his eyes, and when he opened them again, the fear in their silver depths had eased a bit. "In that case, maybe I can go home soon."

"No! You mustn't!"

Glory's explosive words shocked Slade. "But why? What's wrong? I thought things were better."

"Oh, no, Slade, you're wrong. They're worse. Much worse."

Placing one finger under Glory's chin, Slade tipped her head up until he could gaze searchingly into her anxious eyes. "Sweetheart, you've got to tell me what's going on."

"Yes. Of course," she answered, sadness tinging her voice.

Cupping his hands to her lips, she brushed a quick kiss across his knuckles and then pressed the warmth of one palm lovingly against her cheek.

"Come on," she said. Threading the fingers of one hand through his, she tugged softly in the direction of the bed. "Let's sit down and I'll try to tell you everything that's happened."

Slade followed Glory across the room to the bed and they sank down on the edge of the sagging mattress, their bodies snuggled against each other shoulder to hip. Her hands instinctively clutched at his again.

"I'm listening, Glory," Slade prodded gently after

364

several minutes had passed and she'd made no effort to speak.

Glory gave a long, weary shake of her head, cinnamon curls sweeping her shoulders with the movement. "I don't know where to start. It's awful, Slade. Just awful."

"What's awful, honey?"

"The town, the crowds."

"Yes."

"They've gone crazy. I've never seen so many people in Gainesville before. The town's full of soldiers. Mr. Cranford said there's over eight hundred—"

"Cranford's all right?"

"Yes. He goes to the store every day, although there's not much business going on. Most the time he just checks on things, then he locks up again and goes to the courthouse for the day's trials. He feels rather bad about doing that—not keeping the store open, I mean—but he believes it's more important to know what's happening."

"He's right. I don't care about the store now. I'm just glad the old man's safe. I couldn't help but be afraid he might get hurt if the soldiers came looking for me." Slade frowned. "Trials, did you say?"

"Yes, I'll tell you about that in a minute. But first you've got to realize that you're not out of danger. The soldiers haven't been looking for you, not yet anyway." Glory's fingers tightened almost painfully on his. "But that doesn't mean they won't, Slade. You've got to understand how things are now."

"I'll try, darling. Tell me."

"Everybody's scared of everybody else. Neighbors

365

have quit speaking. People are hiding in their houses, loaded guns at their side at all times—"

"Good Lord!"

"There's more, Slade. Much more." Her voice choked with emotion, Glory continued her fearful story. "A citizens' court was appointed the day after the arrests. They began holding trials immediately—"

"These trials . . . Cranford's the one who's been telling you about them?"

"Yes, I've been sneaking away to meet him at the store every few days."

Visions of Glory making her way to town day after day chilled Slade to the bone. He'd worried about her before; now his worries mushroomed to suffocating fears for her safety. Later, he vowed, he'd convince her not to take such chances, but right now he needed to hear the end of her story. "Go on. Tell me the rest."

"Most of the time the prisoners are just brought out, the charges against them read, and then they're found guilty. There's no one to dispute the charges or speak in their defense—"

"Guilty?" Slade repeated in a confused tone. "Guilty of what?"

"Conspiracy, insurrection, treason."

"Treason? Ridiculous! There's been no insurrection, no conspiracy! How can they accuse men of such charges without irrefutable proof?"

"They have witnesses."

"Witnesses? For God's sake, who? And what could they possibly say to support such charges?"

"Most of the time Chance is the witness."

"You mean the mail carrier?"

"Yes. Or McCurley. And at times the testimony of a prisoner has been used against another one. Mr. Cranford says a man by the name of A. D. Scott confessed that the League had plans to take possession of the county and kill all those who didn't favor their purpose—"

"That's not true! I never heard of any such plans!" Slade cried.

"Could some of them have planned things the others didn't know about?" Glory asked.

"No!" Slade was quick to retort, but his mind overruled his heart. "Oh, hell, I . . . I suppose so," he finally conceded, as the bitter memory of Knox's betrayal filtered through his mind once again. "But surely every League member won't be painted with the same tar brush. I'm positive that most of them hadn't the least idea—"

"I'm very much afraid everyone's in trouble— whether they knew or not. There doesn't seem to be any distinction in the way they're being tried."

"What about Knox Coleman? Or two guys named Dunlap and Simmons. Were any of them arrested?"

"I don't think so. I don't remember hearing their names in connection with the trials."

"I should have guessed," Slade said bitterly. "Go back to the beginning. Tell me who's been tried, and anything else you can think of."

He listened in growing horror as Glory continued her explanation of what was happening in the courthouse.

"Court was convened ten days ago. Out of those trials, seven men were found guilty and hanged—"

Slade bounded to his feet, turned, and gave her an

367

incredulous look. "Hanged! My God! When you said they'd been found guilty, I thought you were talking about time in prison. I never dreamed they'd hang them! And for something that didn't even happen? How can they do that!"

"Oh, they're doing it all right, Slade. They're doing it."

He raked an agitated hand through his hair and began to pace the floor. "Hasn't anyone tried to stop them?"

"Dr. Barrett's been trying. He and a couple other jurors have threatened to walk out—to break the jury. But they haven't so far. Barrett keeps begging the other jury members to put a stop to this madness. He's been trying to get them to agree to a two-thirds vote rather than a simple majority. Maybe he's finally succeeded."

"Christ! I can't believe this," Slade rasped. "Go on," he said wearily. "Tell me the rest."

"Mr. Cranford told me that the jury had decided to recess last Saturday. It seems they planned to take a week off and then reconvene and turn the rest of the people loose. But news must have leaked out about their plan and someone didn't like it all. Just as the jurors were preparing to file out they were met by a lynch mob."

Slade whirled and stared at her. "A lynch mob?"

"Yes. They told the jurors that all the prisoners would be put to death unless the court agreed to hand over twenty more men . . . they even had a list of names already prepared."

Slade whispered a ragged oath.

Glory continued. "The jurors argued with the men

and finally it was settled that fourteen names would be chosen by the mob leader."

"And?" Slade asked in a fearful voice, pausing in front of her, eyes wide with apprehension.

"They gave those men to the mob and . . . and they hanged them, too."

Slade slumped to the edge of the bed, numb with shock. "Hanged," he repeated in disbelief. "Twenty-one men dead in less than two weeks because of this insanity . . . how can this be? This can't be happening."

"But it is. It's all true. And no one knows what's going to happen next."

Slade jerked upright. "Austin. Someone should send word to the capital. Those maniacs have got to be stopped!"

"It's too late, Slade. It'll all be over before anyone could make the trip and bring help back."

"There's got to be something . . . somebody who can do something." His shoulders sagged as the enormity of it all washed over him. "Maybe I should go—"

"No!" Glory cried, clutching at his arm in desperation. "Don't even think that. You can't go anywhere! Don't you realize how dangerous it is out there?"

Memory of the terrible dreams that had haunted her nights since the first hangings flooded through her—unspeakable visions of Slade being taken out to the big old elm tree on the banks of Pecan Creek, his life being snatched away in the blink of an eye. The tears that had been gathering behind her eyes broke through, coursing in hot rivulets down her ashen cheeks.

Glory's agonized sobs cut Slade to the very depths of his soul. He turned and swept her into his sheltering arms.

"I'm sorry, darling. I won't go anywhere. I promise. Please don't cry. It's all right. Shhh. It's all right." He rocked and crooned while she clung to him and cried like her heart would break.

At last Glory's tears subsided. "Oh, Slade, it's not all right," she at last said with a soft hiccup. "I'm not sure anything will be all right ever again."

Chapter Twenty-two

"Shhh, my darling," Slade crooned, rocking Glory in his arms. "You're safe with me. I won't let anything harm you."

"Hold me, Slade," she pleaded. "Tighter. Make everything else disappear. I need you so much. Being with you is the only thing that wipes out the madness of the world."

"It's all right, darling."

"No, no, it's not. I'll never understand how people can do such horrible things to one another. Why do they think war is such an exciting thing? How can they be so blind to reality? All the patriotic songs, the rallies, the boastful speeches . . . never do they touch upon the horrible reality of war, the ugliness, the death, the heartache. It was easy to believe in honor and state's rights when the war was far away. But now all that ugliness is right here at home and I hate it! I hate what it's doing to Gainesville, to the

371

people, to us."

"Sweet love, some things you can't change. Put it all out of your mind. Don't think of anything but how much I love you."

"Oh, darling, what would I do if I didn't have you?" Her voice broke at the awful thought.

"Don't think such things, Glory. I'll always be here for you."

"The world we knew is disappearing, Slade," she whimpered. "I'm so afraid it will soon be gone forever. Nothing will ever be the same."

"It doesn't matter, my love. We won't let it hurt us. We'll build a new world, a wonderful shining world just for us."

Like two lost souls they clung together, each of them drawing on the strength of the other to alleviate the fears in their hearts, the sadness in their spirits. Slade's strong arms embraced Glory, tucking her tighter against his hard, bronzed body, offering her the shelter and warmth and reassurance she so desperately needed. She strained against him, turning her face upward like a flower seeking life-giving sunshine.

With infinite tenderness Slade took possession of her mouth. With a sigh, Glory gave herself up to the wonder of his kiss, the enticing way his strong white teeth nipped lovingly along the rim of her pouty bottom lip, the velvet smoothness of his tongue as it slid across the silken inner lining of her mouth. The cares of the world began to melt away under his limitless proficiency. The sweet taste of his mouth was ambrosia to her starving heart.

Slowly lowering their entwined bodies, Slade maneuvered until they were stretched out on the soft quilt, the gentle give of the old feather mattress scooping them together from head to toe.

Exalting in the delicious sensation of her breasts crushed against his chest, Glory hugged Slade to her, her hands skating lovingly across his back. He wedged his knee between her legs, the pressure of his warm, hard thigh against her femininity sending shivers of longing singing through her body.

Edging aside the short jacket she wore, Slade's fingers eagerly found the pebbled hardness of Glory's nipples, plucking and kneading them until her breath came in staccato gasps.

"I want to see you, touch you, taste you, all of you," he whispered urgently, the eyes that bored into hers a passion-clouded silver.

Deftly, Slade unfastened the tiny row of pearl buttons running down the front of Glory's shirtwaist. Pulling the material out of the waistband of her skirt, he thrust it aside with quick, eager movements. One tug at each tiny blue satin ribbon and the dimity chemise parted, baring her straining coral-tipped breasts to his hungry gaze.

With a soft groan he lowered his head and captured one throbbing bud in his mouth. From under sheltering lashes, Glory watched the rapturous sight of his raven's wing hair brushing against the pale cream of her bosom. A heated tugging began deep in the depths of her stomach, an age-old echo in response to her lover's adoring ministrations.

The moist bud of her nipple puckered in the chill

373

air as Slade lifted his mouth. Glory's small moan of protest turned to a throaty purr of pleasure when he began to rain kisses down the plump, round contours of her breast, one hand gently kneading the sensitive underside. Instinctively her back arched, offering him greater access. Her fingers threaded through the thick, dark waves of hair bracketing his bronzed face, gently urging continuance of the sensual kisses and strokes.

A wondrous flood of desire flowed through Glory. She longed to fill Slade with equal pleasure. Bravely, she drew her fingertips caressingly across his sculptured back, raking her nails teasingly across the fine-woven cotton cloth of his shirt, over the bulge of his shoulder, down, down, down until her questing hand brushed the nub of hard male nipple beneath the pale-blue fabric.

Glory smiled with satisfaction at Slade's sharp intake of breath. His head arched back, silver gaze shuttered by fans of thick, dark lashes, as he pressed himself against her trembling hand.

Capturing her mouth once again, he delivered a kiss that was long and thorough. Slade's hand crept up to cup hers to his hair-roughened chest for one last, long moment. Then, palm to back of hand, fingers entwined, he began to slide her hand down the granite firmness of his stomach. Each successive inch of descent caused her heart to beat faster. When the exquisite journey was over, her palm was pressed firmly against the irrefutable evidence of his desire.

"Oh, God, Glory," he groaned. "Do you feel how much I want you? How desperately I need you?"

"Yes," she sighed, relishing the burning desire he felt for her. "Love me, Slade, love me. I need you, too."

With a minimum of motions the lovers divested themselves of their restrictive garments, tossing them heedlessly to the floor in their eagerness to look at and touch and pleasure each other.

Warm sunlight streamed through the window, bathing them in its heavenly glow. Facing each other, they knelt and let their hungry eyes feast.

Never had Slade seen anything so beautiful as Glory enshrined in the golden sunbeams. Threading his hands through the long tresses cloaking her ivory shoulders, Slade lifted the silken mass and then let it shimmer reverently through his fingers, a ruby-highlighted waterfall.

Glory's eyes praised the firm masculine lines of Slade's body. Intrigued by the way the sunbeams glinted in the dark whorls dusting his chest, she lovingly ruffled her fingers through the sun-warmed hair.

"You're so lovely," he said. "Just looking at you makes my heart want to leap from my body. And touching you . . . sometimes I think I could die from the joy of it."

She smiled and leaned forward, testing the way his hard, copper nipples felt against her tongue. Slade gasped in response, his hands going to her shoulders to steady her. The low moan elicited from him by her heated mouth sent delight flashing through Glory. She braced her fingertips against the firm flesh of his thighs and raised her head to smile at him.

"I love you," she said softly.

"Sweet heaven, Glory, you must know I love you more than life itself."

She raised her hands to cup his face. Slade caught them and drew them to his lips, turning each palm upward to press a kiss into the center.

A shiver of ecstasy ran through Glory as Slade gently grasped her shoulders and slowly lowered her to the bed.

Kneeling over her, Slade scattered primitive, scorching kisses down the sweet slope of Glory's throat, across the pouting coral-tipped breasts, over the satiny expanse of belly, against the soft nest of ginger curls.

She sobbed with pleasure as his knowing fingers stroked and caressed each sensitive area. A pearly earlobe, her nape, the exquisitely tender flesh along her rib cage, the silky skin of her inner thighs, the responsive dip at the back of her knees. Every inch of her body was worshiped by touch or tongue or strong white teeth that bestowed baby-gentle nibbles in the most delectable manner.

Then he braced himself over her. She arched toward him, eager for the sweet joining. She fit him like a glove, welcoming the thrust of his love with equal ardor. Their bodies blended, merged, melded, a mating of rapturous giving and sharing.

The gentle, slow rhythm renewed itself, each stroke becoming stronger, longer, deeper. The whispered love words became sighs, delighted gasps, soft cries of completion.

Afterward, Slade rolled to his side, pulling Glory

into his arms, holding her tight against him so that the beat of his heart was echoed in her own. Lovingly he laced his fingers through her hair, brushing the desire-dampened strands from her face, peppering her temple and cheek and chin with butterfly kisses.

She moaned a soft protest, then purred with contentment when his mouth captured hers once again. Desire temporarily sated, they sealed their love with angel-soft touches and sweet teasing sips. Little by little their breathing slowed, their heartbeats slackened, and love's sweet lethargy overtook them. Limbs entwined, they slept while heaven's golden rays poured warm blessings over them.

Glory was just as reluctant to leave Slade as he was to have her go. But it was getting late and they dared not take a chance on worrying Glory's father. She must be free to return with further news of what was happening in Gainesville.

It was a quieter though happier Glory who bid the young sentry on the road "good evening" and stopped to chat for a few brief moments before continuing on into town. The boy shuffled in embarrassment, echoed her parting words in a cracked voice, and then with worshipful eyes watched the pretty young lady as she rode off.

Luckily the Colonel was still away from home when Glory returned, but he had sent word that he and Preston would arrive before dinner. Glory frowned when Violet delivered this news, wishing she wouldn't have to face Preston that night, but on the other hand she was grateful that she'd finally have a chance to talk to her father about Sara. Heads together, the slave woman and her young mistress planned a menu of the Colonel's favorite foods. Step by step, Glory conspired to set the stage for the coming discussion.

When she'd covered every aspect she could think of, Glory left Violet to oversee the cooking. Taking Sara with her, she slipped upstairs to change clothes.

Agonizing in front of the wardrobe, Glory shuffled through the dozens of dresses, discarding first one and then another. She finally chose one she'd previously worn on her father's birthday. Hadn't he remarked several times that night about how lovely she looked and boasted proudly that he had the most beautiful daughter in the county? The teal-blue satin did set her hair and eyes off to perfection; and hopefully the dress would evoke pleasant memories for her father.

"This one," she instructed Sara, handing her the dress.

"Yes'm," the young girl replied, running her hands reverently over the smooth satin before settling the yards and yards of fabric over Glory's head. Her smooth brown fingers quickly fastened the row of tiny buttons and then she went to work brushing and arranging Glory's hair.

At last Glory was satisfied with the reflection in the silvery mirror. "Thank you, Sara. You did a marvelous job."

Sara smiled shyly at the compliment. "Thank you, Miss Glory. Do you need anything else?"

378

"No, that's all. Let's go downstairs. Violet can probably use some help."

"Yes'm."

Sara followed her mistress out the door and down the grand staircase. At the bottom, Sara bade her good-bye and hurried off to the kitchen, and Glory went into the parlor to await the arrival of her father and Preston.

Long minutes later, the sound of the front door opening and the subsequent thud of boots across the polished parquet floor set Glory's heart to thumping. She pasted a bright smile on her face, jumping up to greet her father and her "fiancée" the moment they entered the room.

"Papa! I'm so glad to see you. I've missed you," she prattled on, rushing to press a kiss on his florid cheek.

"Good evening, Glory," Preston said as he followed Westbrook across the room.

"Hello, Preston," she replied before turning her attention back to her father. "You poor dear, you must be tired. May I pour you a drink? And how about you, Preston? May I get you something?"

Both men said yes. Divesting themselves of cloaks and hats, they made themselves comfortable in the wing chairs on either side of the cheery fireplace, which Jacob had moments before lit to ward off the slight chill of the October night.

Reaching for the squat crystal tumblers her father generally used, Glory suddenly changed her mind. Quickly she secured two larger glasses from the silver tray and then poured an extremely liberal portion in each glass. Just a little more insurance. She wanted the Colonel in the mellowest mood possible before she tackled the subject of Sara.

Nervously, she fluffed the curls framing her face, then picking up the two brimming glasses, she turned and hurried across the room.

"There," she said with a broad smile, depositing a glass beside each chair. "That'll help warm you up. Violet said dinner would be served as soon as you were ready."

"Fine, Glory. We'll go in after we finish our drinks."

Glory perched on the edge of the sofa, her alert gaze taking in every move made by the two men. When her father's eyes flickered in the direction of the humidor, Glory jumped up and hurried to fetch it for him.

"Why, thank you, Daughter," the Colonel said, a bit surprised at her perceptiveness.

Why, the little minx, he thought, a paternal smile hovering on his lips. He wrongly concluded that his daughter was cunningly using Mrs. Westbrook's absence as an opportunity to display her skillful handling of the house, that she was trying to impress Preston!

With a flick of his wrist, Glory's father ignited a match. Suppressing the wide grin that tugged at the corners of his mouth, he held the flame to the fat cigar and puffed heartily.

Glory's insides were all aflutter, but she continued to play her role until dinner had been served and the three of them were back in the parlor, the two men

380

full and warm and well brandied.

Glory eyed the clock. It was getting late and she'd accomplished absolutely nothing yet. She had to face the issue. Drawing a deep breath to still the fluttering in her stomach, she broached the issue. "Papa, could I ask you something?"

Crystal goblet in hand, the Colonel glanced up at his fidgety daughter. "Of course, my dear. What is it?" Suddenly aware of the pinched look about her mouth, he frowned and asked, "Is something wrong?"

"Oh, no, Papa," she was quick to assure him. "Nothing's wrong. I . . . I just have a favor to ask of you."

"What's that, my dear?"

"Well, it's this situation about Sara." Her fingers plucked agitatedly at the lace-edged hanky she held. "Please don't sell her, Papa. I'd really be happier if you didn't."

The Colonel's eyebrows rose in surprise. "But, Glory, the sale has been completed. I've given my word. You can't expect me to go back on it. No, my dear, I'm afraid Sara belongs to Preston now."

"But, Papa—"

"Glory, dear, I really do believe you're overreacting to this whole thing. You must realize that Preston has done this for you. You should be grateful for his thoughtfulness." The Colonel's voice took on a sterner tone. "And why all this concern over a mere slave, Glory? Such a tempest in a teapot. Ridiculous, my girl, and totally uncalled for."

"Yes, Papa," Glory murmured dejectedly. It was

hopeless. Obviously she'd get no help from her father. There was nothing left to do but appeal to Preston. What on earth could she say to convince him to listen to reason?

Glory hazarded a quick glimpse at Preston. A small, amused smile played at the corner of his lips as he raised his tumbler and sipped the amber liquid within. Something about his cool, disinterested demeanor set her stomach aquiver once more.

The Colonel noticed the nervous glances Glory was casting Preston's direction and once again misinterpreted the reasons behind her actions.

"Well, if you young people will excuse me," he said, rising from his chair. "It's been a long day and I'm going up to bed."

"Oh, Papa, do you have to?" Glory blurted, jumping up and following him across the room. She was loath to tackle the job of pleading all alone for Sara's return.

Westbrook stopped and turned to pat his daughter's cheek lovingly. "Yes, my dear. These old bones are weary. And it's time the two of you had the opportunity for a few minutes alone." He threw a quick glance Preston's way. "I'll see you bright and early in the morning."

"Fine, Robert. Sleep well," Preston said magnanimously.

"Good night, Papa," Glory called after him in a resigned voice. Head down, she walked slowly back toward the sofa.

"Glory, dear," Preston said softly.

Glory stopped in midstride. "Yes, Preston?"

"Come here."

Reluctantly she crossed the room and stood at the side of his chair. "Can I get you something?"

"No. What I want is right here." With one quick movement, Preston grabbed Glory's wrist and hauled her down onto his lap.

"Preston! Please!" she protested, struggling to rise again.

"Relax, Glory," he instructed gruffly, nuzzling her neck with his cool lips. "Surely you won't deny your betrothed a few kisses. After all, it's been a long time since I had a chance to hold you or kiss you. You can't fault a man for wanting a little affection."

"Please, Preston, you mustn't," Glory sputtered, turning her head to avoid his seeking mouth. "Papa might return—"

"That's a feeble excuse, dear. He's already upstairs. And I'm sure he'd understand my desire to savor your sweetness for just a moment. After all, we will be man and wife before long."

His head dipped and he flicked the tip of his tongue against her lips. She recoiled in alarm. One arm held her firmly about the waist. His free hand crept upward to knead the soft ivory bosom above the low bodice of her dress.

"No! Don't!"

Glory reacted instinctively, jerking back at the same time her hands desperately tried to push him away. It was utterly impossible for her to continue the charade for even one more minute. She *had* to tell him the engagement was off. The thought of Preston touching her in such an intimate fashion after having spent the afternoon in Slade's loving arms was more than she could bear.

All the more determined, Preston tightened his grip. But Glory struggled desperately, finally managing to wrench herself free of his grip. With a muffled sob, she flung herself out of his arms and across the room. Hands clenched tight together in her lap, she sank down upon the sofa and bowed her head, trying to slow the agitated racing of her heart.

When she finally felt composed enough to confront Preston with her decision, she raised her stricken gaze to his. But the angry look on his face stilled her words.

A long, painful silence passed while they sat and simply stared at each other—Glory growing less sure of herself by the minute, Preston's initial shock and confusion at her refusal building within until it became a tight, hard knot of anger.

Finally he cleared his throat and asked, "Would you like to explain these theatrics, Glory?" His calm monotone voice betrayed no hint of how hard he was struggling to maintain his temper.

"Please, Preston. I'm sorry. I know I should have told you sooner—"

"Told me what?" he asked in a voice cold as the winter wind.

"I—I can't marry you."

Swift anger flared hotly in the depths of his pale blue eyes before they once again became hard and remote. "I see," he said. "And is that all you have to say? Do I not even deserve the courtesy of an explanation?"

Glory tried to swallow the lump in her throat. Her voice, when she managed to answer, was nothing more than a remorseful whisper. "Please understand. I'm in love with someone else."

With a steely grip on his emotions, Preston heaved his tall frame out of the chair and stalked to the sideboard. The hand that gripped the crystal decanter was white-knuckled and trembling as he filled his glass to overflowing. The decanter rattled alarmingly as he set it down on the tray. With one quick jerk of his head, he tossed the glass's contents down his throat. The burning liquid did little to clear his whirling mind.

Once again he filled the glass, but this time he left the amber-filled goblet sitting on the tray as he gripped the carved edge of the sideboard hard with both hands.

Head bowed, he fought to control the rage building inside. How dare she! All his plans, all the hours he'd spent wheedling his way into the Colonel's confidence. Did she really believe he'd give up so easily simply because she fancied herself in love with someone else?

What foolishness! What did love have to do with the scheme of things? Love was nothing. Preston wanted wealth and social status and power—and he intended to have them, at any cost.

A sudden flicker of comprehension flared, fueling the cold fury within. Finally he turned and gazed at Glory, his cold, calculating stare raking her up and down.

"Let me guess," he said, sarcasm edging his voice.

"This *lover* wouldn't happen to be Slade Hunter, would it?"

"Preston, we didn't mean—"

"No," he retorted quickly, raising a hand to silence her explanation. "Don't bother. Why should I listen to any more of your lies? I've had suspicions before, but I foolishly thought you too sheltered and innocent to be capable of such duplicity."

Leaning his buttocks against the edge of the sideboard, he picked up his glass and took a long sip of his drink. "It appears that I underestimated Mr. Hunter . . . again."

Glory raised her pleading eyes to his. "Preston, please listen to me. We didn't set out to hurt you. Slade and I have loved each other for a long time. It's just unfortunate that you somehow got caught in the middle—"

Preston's answering look was a strangely discomfiting mixture of sarcasm and amusement. "You really don't expect me to believe that, do you, Glory? This isn't the first time Slade Hunter has set about to thwart my desires."

"What are you talking about?"

Preston ignored her question, his mind besieged with thoughts of vengeance. "Interesting situation we have here, isn't it, my dear? Just what do you propose we do about all this?"

"Well," Glory offered timidly, hope flaring briefly in her heart. "I had hoped you would understand and we could just . . . just call the engagement off. I . . . I thought we might even remain friends."

Preston emitted a short, bitter laugh. "Friends?

Really, Glory, how quaint."

"Preston, please, just consider—"

With a sudden jerk, he drew himself up straight and stiff. His cold, scornful look seared her.

"No, Glory, *you* consider! Consider that I don't take kindly to my plans being disrupted. Consider that I have no intention of becoming the laughing-stock of this town simply because you've changed your mind."

"I didn't mean for things to happen like this," she cried.

"And I don't mean to give up what I've fought for so long. I have every intention of seeing that this marriage takes place."

"You can't make me marry you!"

"Perhaps not, my dear." The smile that played on his lips was wicked. "But have you forgotten I hold the hole card? Do you really intend to save your own pretty little neck if you can only accomplish your goal at someone else's expense?"

"What . . . what do you mean?"

"Sara."

Disbelief flooded Glory's face. "But, surely you wouldn't—"

Once again Preston relaxed against the sideboard, nonchalantly crossing one ankle over the other as he slid his hands into the pockets of his trousers.

"Surely I wouldn't what, Glory?" he asked with a mocking smile.

"But if there's no wedding, there's no sense in you buying Sara. I'm positive Papa will give you back your money."

"I care nothing for the money."

"But there's no reason—" Fear raced through Glory. "Please, Preston, all you have to do is tear up the bill of sale. Why don't you understand? We could never be happy. I don't love you."

"And what made you think for an instant that love is of any concern in this issue? You're the means to an end, Glory. That's all. I intend to have my way. Why not be smart and accept the situation?"

"No!" she retorted vehemently. "I won't marry you. Nothing you could say or do would make me change my mind."

Preston eyed her with devilish amusement. "Are you so very sure about that, my dear?"

He slipped one hand from his pocket and reached for his glass. A flick of his wrist and the tumbler was empty again. With utmost care, he set it down on the sideboard, then crossed the room to gather up his coat and hat.

Eyes wide and uncomprehending, Glory watched him saunter toward the door. "Where . . . where are you going?"

When his long, slim hand was on the knob, Preston turned and pinned her with a piercing stare.

"Home, my dear. I have a busy day ahead of me tomorrow."

"But you can't just walk away and ignore all this—"

"I can do anything I please, my dear."

"That's not fair!"

"In the meantime, I suggest that you rethink this whole situation, Glory. And to show you how chival-

388

rous I can be, I'll even give you a week to contemplate just what might happen to Sara if you choose not to honor our agreement."

"What do you mean?"

"You might consider that comely young slave girls still fetch a good price further west."

"You wouldn't!"

"No?" he questioned with a mocking shrug of his shoulders. "You might be right about that. Perhaps I'll decide that if you choose not to warm my bed . . . Sara can."

Glory's horrified gasp echoed through the room.

An extremely smug smile curved Preston's mouth upward. "Pleasant dreams, my dear," he said softly.

With a turn of the knob he was gone.

Chapter Twenty-three

Glory was sick at heart over her dilemma when she made her usual trip to see Mr. Cranford the next morning. Even the news that court was still recessed didn't do much to cheer her.

"Perhaps there's hope this time," Mr. Cranford said. "I've heard rumors that when they reconvene they'll turn the rest of the prisoners over to the military or set them free."

"I'm almost afraid to believe that could be true," Glory responded in a mournful tone.

She was finding it difficult to feel very hopeful about anything right now. After tossing and turning all night she'd still found no way to extricate herself, much less Sara. The fact remained that Preston owned Sara legally. No one could change that. Preston could do anything he wanted to do with Sara and no one could stop him.

Out of the corner of her eye, Glory caught movement on the square and she turned to gaze morosely out the store's front window. Frowning, she tried to decide if the people seemed a little less hostile this morning. At least there wasn't quite as much pushing and shouting in front of the temporary jail. Perhaps Mr. Cranford was right and the gruesome reality of the hangings had mollified a less bloodthirsty segment of the mob. Her sad, assessing eyes continued to watch the restless milling of the crowd as the old man continued his story.

"As far as I know there've been no new arrests. And, thank heaven, no hangings for two days."

"That's m-marvelous," she managed to say. "Maybe we will see an end to all soon."

"I certainly hope so," the old man answered with an emphatic nod of his gray head. "But I suppose we shouldn't get our hopes up too high, Miss Westbrook. There's a lot of men still in that jail."

"Yes, how well I know," Glory demurred, feeling imprisoned herself. Bars alone did not make a jail—sometimes one's conscience provided its own impenetrable barrier.

Mentally and physically exhausted from her long sleepless night, she slumped dejectedly against a storage barrel. Much as Glory wanted to see the remaining prisoners free, she couldn't help but think about the men who had already lost their lives. Why, some of those men she'd actually known and talked to over the years.

What had gone wrong? How could such a dreadful thing have happened? Fathers, husbands, brothers, sons—all dead and gone.

"Now, don't look so discouraged, Miss Westbrook. The situation *has* improved. There's hope, little lady, there certainly is."

Glory forced a wan smile in response to Mr. Cranford's concern. "You're right, of course. We must continue to have hope."

She appreciated the old man's attempt to cheer her, but under the present circumstances she found it difficult to put much stock in his current news. The thought of further disappointment was almost unbearable.

Mr. Cranford was trying so hard to alleviate her sadness. And deep down Glory wanted to believe again. But did she dare? Things looked so hopeless at this point.

Would anything really ever be right again? Could Gainesville once again be the gentle country town she'd known and loved? Would the fear and distrust and violence that had marked almost every household disappear when the militia marched away? Could neighborly love and friendship and confidence bloom once again? And—most distressing of all— would she find a way to escape Preston's clutches *and* save Sara?

She longed to believe that it was possible. Despite all she'd experienced the last week—the ugly mobs, neighbor turning against neighbor, the all-consuming fear of losing Slade, and now the unthinkable dilemma Preston had created—she still clung to a tiny shred of faith. Deep down she wanted to believe, *needed* to believe that there was a bright future ahead for the town, for herself, for the people she cared about.

A small ray of hope swelled in her heart, a lifeline

in a raging sea of despair. If Mr. Cranford was right about the recent changes in attitude — if the court really did reconvene and set the rest of the prisoners free — then it would be just a matter of days until Slade could come out of hiding. Just knowing he was no longer a fugitive would help. With that worry gone, surely her mind would begin to function again and she could find a way to save Sara.

Why, oh why couldn't Preston have understood? Had she committed such a terrible sin? Was it so selfish of her to want to spend her life with the man she loved? A love such as she and Slade shared was too rare to risk losing. How could Preston be so cold-hearted? She couldn't give Slade up. She couldn't!

Dear God, but what about Sara? That cold calculating look Preston had scorched her with last night had planted a seed of fear in her heart — and it was growing larger by the minute. She knew without a doubt that he was capable of doing just what he'd said. Neither she nor Sara could expect freedom at the hands of Preston Harper.

Freedom! A daring thought streaked through Glory's mind.

Of course! Why hadn't she thought of it sooner? If she couldn't prevail upon Preston to do the honorable thing, then she could damn well make sure that Sara was taken to safety — somewhere far enough away that Preston would never find her.

Glory's mind whirled at the rashness of her plan, but she could see no other way. And why should Sara have to go alone? If Glory was going to do this thing — and she suddenly knew without a doubt that she was—then she'd make sure Violet and Jacob were given their freedom, too.

Joella! She had to get to Joella as fast as possible.

"—Don't you agree?" Mr. Cranford asked.

"Umm? What?" Glory finally responded, her thoughts stumbling back to the present. Her mind had been so busy with the intriguing thought of gaining freedom for Sara and her family that she'd heard practically nothing the man had said the last few minutes.

"I said, perhaps young Slade and his family will be coming home soon. How lucky that they decided to take that trip to Dallas with Mrs. Stafford at this precise time. Not that I think the family had done anything to put themselves in jeopardy—" Cranford was quick to insert in response to Glory's sharp look. "But, it *is* widely known that their sympathies lie with the Union. At least their absence has enabled them to avoid all this unpleasantness."

"Yes. Yes, of course. Very lucky. Surely this will all be over by the time they return."

For the first time that morning Glory felt that there *was* hope, at least about one of the worries that plagued her. Apparently Cranford and perhaps a good many others thought that *all* the Hunters had accompanied Mrs. Stafford to Dallas. What a relief. Now she could turn her full attention to arranging the escape with a clear conscience.

"Well," Glory said, a sudden out-of-place lilt to her voice, "thanks so much for the information, Mr. Cranford. I'd best be on my way. I've held you up long enough, and I know you want to get on over to the courthouse. Maybe the news tomorrow will be even better."

"Let's hope so, Miss Westbrook, let's hope so." Ever polite, the elderly gentleman opened the door for Glory and stood aside so she could pass through. "Now, you be careful; there's still a passel of onery-looking fellows out there. A nice little lady like you wouldn't stand a chance if they took it in their mind to indulge in a little mischief."

"Oh, don't worry. I'll go straight home." Glory's quick declaration was accompanied by her sincerest smile. *After a quick stop at the Silver City Saloon,* she amended silently.

Eager to be on her way, she threw the old man one last smile and slipped out the door.

As usual, Glory hooked a sharp left as she exited the store, hurrying down the boardwalk that edged Commerce Street. But this time she didn't continue straight ahead as she had done on previous days. At the entrance to the alley behind the store she stopped and cast a wary glance around. Most of the people were still clustered around the courthouse.

There wasn't a soul close enough to see what direction she took. She heaved a sigh of relief at her good fortune. Dare she believe that her luck was about to change for the better?

Quick as a wink she stepped into the shadowy recesses of the narrow opening. Paying little heed to the rubble and rubbish lining the narrow lane which wound behind the block of stores, Glory focused her whole attention on reaching Joella.

At the far end she slowed and, pressing her back

against the rough-hewn log wall, she peered cautiously around the edge of the building. The sight that met her eyes made her heart lurch.

A dozen armed men stood at the north corner of the street. Over the steady rumble of the market square crowd she could hear their angry voices. One man argued stridently that the court would be sure all the bastards hanged before they were through. Another shouted back, "Why take a chance? Let's get it over with. Storm the jail and shoot the sons-a-bitches!"

Shuddering at the vehemence of their words, Glory pulled back, wedging herself hard against the sheltering wall. She swallowed hard and gazed longingly at the opposing alley entrance. The saloon was straight across the street — just a matter of feet, but it looked like a million miles.

A clamor rang out from the square and Glory chanced another quick peek. The men had turned their backs to her, their attention riveted toward the courthouse. It was now or never.

Jerking her long skirts high, Glory sped across the street and into the alley. Looking neither left nor right, she didn't slow her pace until she was at the top of the staircase behind the saloon.

Winded, she clutched at the railing and gazed downward with wide apprehensive eyes while her laboring lungs sought to pull in great gulps of air.

I made it, she thought jubilantly when no outcry was raised at her strange behavior. With one last deep breath she turned toward the door.

Glory's first knock was timid. When no one responded, she raised her hand again and rapped her knuckles hard against the wood panel.

A sudden thought flashed through her mind. What if Joella had already gone downstairs? What would she do then? It was one thing to sneak up a back staircase, but quite another to walk blatantly through the saloon's front entrance.

She was contemplating that distressful thought when the door was suddenly pulled open. A sleepy-eyed Joella gaped in surprise at her unexpected visitor.

"What on earth—?" she exclaimed. Her mouth snapped shut on the unfinished sentence, and she reached to grab Glory's wrist and haul her bodily into the shadows of the room.

"Good Lord, girl!" Joella spluttered after the door was safely slammed shut. "Have you got the least idea what you're dong? What if someone saw you come here? Your reputation won't be worth a plug nickel in this town if those old biddies get wind of this!"

All Glory could manage in response to Joella's harangue was a trembly smile.

"And your daddy! I shudder to think what he'd do if he found out. Why, he'd have me closed down and run out of town!"

Glory drew herself up bravely. "I'm sorry, Miss Ashland. I sincerely don't want to cause you any trouble. It's just . . . just . . . there's a real problem and I can't think of any other way to solve it."

Joella shook her head in amazement, the shock she'd felt when she first opened the door beginning to abate. A grudging admiration for Glory started to form. She had to admit the young woman was plucky.

Joella's brows rose upward. "Well, it's too late to worry about propriety now. You might as well sit down and tell me what's on your mind."

"Oh, thank you."

Glory followed the slender blonde across the parlor. She perched nervously on the edge of the sofa while Joella struck a match and lit the lantern, chasing the shadows from the heavily draped room.

Pulling the edges of her lace-trimmed robe together Joella sank into her accustomed chair. "Excuse my attire," she said as she tucked the garment more securely around her legs. "I'm up so late at night that I seldom rise this early—"

"I'm really sorry to have to bother you like this—"

"There's no need to apologize," Joella said, noting the desperate look in Glory's eyes. "It's time for me to be up anyway. Business starts very early these days, what with all the troops and strangers in town. Now, tell me what brings you here. Is there something wrong?"

Glory nodded her head solemnly. "Yes, there is. Something very wrong. Miss Ashland, you . . . you were nice to me once before . . . about Slade, I mean. You did me a great favor. And I simply can't think of any other way out . . . I-I'm afraid I desperately need your help again."

Joella eyed the obviously anxious girl sharply, her brows furrowing. "Is this about Slade? Is he in trouble? Do you know where he is? I haven't heard from him in several weeks, and I know he hasn't been to the store, either."

"No," Glory was quick to assure. "Slade's all right." Noting the profound look of relief that crossed Joella's face at this news, she decided that it would be unfair not to share the whole truth with her. "I saw him yesterday. I can assure you he's in a safe place."

"Well, I'm certainly glad to hear that. I was beginning to get worried when he didn't check in to ask if there were any people to—"

Glory fairly pounced on the thought. "Miss Ashland that's precisely why I'm here—because of the help you've given other people in search of . . . uh . . . well, people who need help in reaching a safer environment."

"Oh?" Joella responded in surprise. "From our previous conversation, I thought you didn't approve of such endeavors."

Glory had the good graces to blush a bit. "I'm afraid I didn't really understand before. I saw the issue from only one side."

"And now?" Joella questioned.

"And now something terrible has happened which has forced me to think about this in an entirely different way."

Gathering her courage tight about her, Glory proceeded to tell her the whole story. Joella muttered a soft, unladylike oath when she heard of Preston Harper's vile threats, but she held her tongue until Glory ended her tale.

Heaving a heavy sigh, Joella shook her head from

side to side. "You were right to believe Preston capable of doing just what he said he'd do."

Glory's face lit up with hope. "Then you think I made the right decision?"

Joella cast the young woman a commiserating look. "You made the *only* decision you could make. Believe me, Preston is a real bastard. I'm glad you came to your senses and broke off the engagement. You wouldn't want to be married to such a man—"

"No, I mean about helping Sara and her family escape," Glory corrected. She smiled gratefully. "Oh, I just knew coming to you for help would be the right thing to do!"

Joella frowned. "Wait a minute, Miss Westbrook. I wish it were that simple."

The happy smile on Glory's face slipped a bit, but she squared her shoulders and plunged ahead. "Believe me, I understand that it'll take some time to make plans. I know you can't just snap your fingers—" The sight of Joella's slowly shaking head filled her with a gut-wrenching dread. "Please, Miss Ashland, you don't have to worry about Preston finding out. I'll never tell. I promise. And I can hold him off long enough for you to make whatever arrangements are necessary. I'll . . . I'll tell him I've reconsidered—that I'll marry him. I can convince him, I know I can."

"It isn't that, Miss Westbrook. I'd be quite willing to chance Preston's wrath. But I'm afraid we have another problem—I have no one left to guide your people to the next safe house."

Glory's expression evinced her bewilderment. "But

. . . but I thought Slade said there were two others who did what he did."

"There were. Both wisely left town when all the arrests began."

"Oh." Glory's face fell. She slumped against the back of the sofa, momentarily stunned at this unexpected news.

"I'm sorry," Joella said softly. "Really I am."

Determination sparked in Glory's eyes. "Couldn't someone else — ?"

"I'm afraid not. Only Slade and the other two men know where the next safe house is."

"But . . . but why?" Glory asked, her mind refusing to accept the futility of the situation.

"Protection for the organization — by keeping knowledge to a bare minimum."

"I-I see . . . but surely there's a way to solve this problem — "

"I'm sorry, Miss Westbrook. I wish I could think of something. I simply see no other solution than to wait. With things as bad as they are, if one of our men didn't accompany the travelers, those at the next station would be afraid to take them in."

Glory sighed.

"It's this crazy League thing," Joella explained. "Cooke County and a good many counties surrounding it are scared out of their wits about what's going on. Nobody trusts a soul anymore."

"I know," Glory answered weakly. "Then . . . then there's no way to get them out of town?"

"Not at this time. My only suggestion is to wait until it's safe for Slade to guide them."

Nibbling nervously at her lower lip, Glory pondered Joella's disconcerting comment. The rumors, the hopes, the memories, the fears of the last two weeks all swirled in her head until she thought it would burst. Dare she take a chance that the rumor Mr. Cranford had heard was correct? Would the jury actually set the remainder of the prisoners free when they reconvened, thus putting an end to this travesty of justice, an end to her worries about Slade's safety?

If the jury did as Mr. Cranford believed they would, Slade could simply return to Gainesville as if everything were perfectly normal. Due to the continuous upheaval of late, many of the town's residents were probably unaware of his absence. Those who questioned it could be placated by a few glowing comments concerning the "trip." A word or two that the rest of his family had elected to stay a little longer would be sufficient to set any curious minds to rest about Slade's solitary return.

With the trials at an end, there would be no fear of reprisal, and everyone would still be too busy thrashing over the awesome events of the last two weeks to connect Slade's arrival with the eventual disappearance of Sara and her family.

Despite Mr. Cranford's certainty that such events were imminent, Glory was still worried about the time element. Only six days remained until Preston's deadline.

Try as she might to find an alternative, she really had but two choices: fetch Slade in immediately, knowing the possible result could be his arrest, or wait and pray the court would be disbanded soon—

very soon.

Drawing a ragged breath, Glory weighed the probability of danger against the days she had left. Six days. Six short days.

But if everything went smoothly, that *was* sufficient time for the jury to reconvene and set the remaining prisoners free. Glory could get word to Slade in a matter of hours. If Joella had everything else ready, they could still get Sara and her family out of town before the sands of time ran out.

Chapter Twenty-four

The Uptons' front gate screeched in protest as Glory pushed it open. Turning to secure the cranky latch, she lifted her hand to wave one last time at the figure on the veranda. "Bye, Lydia," she called happily, and then she turned her face toward the pale October sun.

Glory's muted shadow skimmed the ground before her as she followed the edge of the road leading back to the Westbrook home. A small smile tugged at the corner of her mouth as she watched the dark smudge of plume adorning the shadow-figure's bonnet bob in gay response to her own springy step. It was amazing what a little bit of hope could do to improve one's outlook.

Upon her return from Joella's the previous day, Glory had taken Violet aside and assured the downhearted woman that all would be fine. "I'm not at liberty to tell you anything else now," Glory had said. "You'll just have to believe that I've found a way to solve our problem. Please be patient a little longer.

When the time is right, I'll explain everything." Violet had tearfully accepted Glory's cryptic explanation and promised she would tell no one — not even Jacob.

Last night Glory had enjoyed her first good night's sleep in weeks, and the pleasant afternoon just spent with Lydia had been far more reminiscent of such events in the past than the hurried, worried visits they'd shared of late.

The tiny seed of hope born in Joella's parlor had apparently taken root and was putting forth tender shoots of optimism. Glory knew it wasn't merely her wishful thinking; the town's mood did seem better today.

The community and its inhabitants had evidently benefited immensely from the two peaceful days since the last hangings. Despite the shocking loss of far too many men to the hangman's noose, the remnants of the League had not banded together and stormed the town as once feared. And people were even beginning to question whether such a threat ever really existed.

Another good sign was the fact that security around the perimeter of Gainesville had slackened considerably, and folks were beginning to come and go in a more normal fashion. Despite the continued presence of soldiers, the courthouse square seemed almost blessedly empty. The angry mob that had choked it for the past fifteen days had all but disappeared. Glory wondered if the final bloodletting had left more than a few of the town's population remorseful about their own participation in the dreadful events.

Word rapidly spread through town that the madness was indeed over. The court was expected to meet for the last time on Saturday — just two short days away. Only the formality of dismissing the final charges and the freeing of the prisoners remained.

Glory was blissfully certain that Slade would be back in town by Sunday, and by Monday Sara and her family would be gone. *Ha!* she thought with sweet glee. Then let Preston show up on Tuesday, demanding her answer to his ultimatum! What fun it would be to give him her response and know there was nothing he could do about it. Absolutely nothing. She could hardly wait!

Pleasurably engrossed in her thoughts, Glory covered the distance between the Uptons' home and hers in record time. She was humming by the time she reached the great carved door. Inside, face beaming, she fairly skipped up the stairs.

Once in her room, Glory discarded her light cape and bonnet on the end of her bed and then crossed the room to the vanity. Picking up the silver-backed brush, she quickly set to work putting her wind-ruffled hair in order.

By way of the reflective glass, her gaze fell on the books Violet had stacked neatly on the corner of her desk, and she suddenly remembered she'd never had a chance to show them to Sara. Inspiration blossomed. She'd devote the remaining hours of the day to the young slave girl.

With thoughts of the pleasant undertaking filling her mind, Glory descended the stairs with the intent of searching for Sara.

Suddenly the massive front door was thrown open. Glory jumped when it crashed loudly against the wall. Colonel Westbrook and Preston stomped into the foyer, their angry voices filling the small area.

"Papa!" Glory exclaimed, her startled gaze taking in the high color in her father's cheeks. "Good heavens, what's wrong?"

"More trouble, that's what!" he fairly shouted in reply. "Those goddamn Unionists have gone and done it again."

"Done what, Papa?" Glory asked, apprehension squeezing her heart.

"Shot Young and Dickson, that's what! Ambushed them and shot them dead. Just like those cowardly bastards to do something like that. Well, you can rest assured — they're going to pay for it!"

With that he stormed into his study, leaving Glory to stare after him with wide, shock-filled eyes until Preston's low chuckle brought her back to reality.

"What's the matter, Glory, dear?" he inquired mockingly. "Are you worried about something . . . or someone?"

As she stared at the arrogantly handsome face, a blind hate for the man swept through her. "No!" she fairly hissed at him, jerking up her skirts to race after her father.

Glory found the Colonel behind his desk, digging frantically through one drawer after another. "What . . . what are you doing?" she asked in voice that she barely managed to keep from trembling.

"Looking for my guns."

Westbrook breathed a sigh of relief when his pudgy fingers finally closed over the objects of his search. He pulled the weapons out of the drawer, then looked up. A frown creased his face when he realized his daughter was still standing beside his desk.

"Glory, dear, I think you'd better go on about your business. This is no concern of yours."

"But it is!" she protested vehemently. "I'm not a child. I have a right to know what's happening."

"You might as well tell her, Robert. She'll find out sooner or later."

Glory whirled at the sound of Preston's mocking voice behind her.

"Tell me what?" she demanded, her confused eyes searching his face for a clue.

Preston deliberately prolonged Glory's agony by sauntering from the doorway to the side table where the whiskey was kept. Each movement was controlled and unhurried as he filled his glass.

"Anyone else?" he inquired, holding the glass aloft in questioning manner. When neither Glory nor her father answered affirmatively, Preston raised the glass to his lips and took a slow sip, watching her across the crystal rim.

Biting back the furious words that formed on her tongue, Glory turned once again to her father. "Please, Papa, *what* is going on?"

"I really don't think you should—" the Colonel began again.

"You must be realistic, Robert," Preston interrupted. "Glory's right. This is something she *needs* to hear." The corner of his mouth quirked at the irony of his words. "But perhaps it would be better if I handled the telling."

Before Glory knew what was happening, Preston crossed the room and clasped her hands in his, his face a caricature of concern. Her eyes blazed at his audacity.

She tried unobtrusively to free herself from his grip, but he only held on tighter. His cold blue eyes bespoke his silent amusement at her fruitless struggles. Finally she gave up, willing herself to endure his touch until he'd had his say.

Perhaps it was just as well her hands were securely entrapped, she grudingly decided. If they were free she might very well have slapped the phony look of solicitude right off his face . . . and how would she ever explain such actions to her father?

"I'm afraid I have some rather shocking news for you, Glory," Preston said. "Three men were hunting deer in the brakes of the Red River this morning. They were attacked. One of the men—a fellow by the name of Dickson—was shot and killed."

Frowning, Glory stopped the useless tugging and listened to Preston's discourse. She didn't recognize the name. Why would he consider the news "shocking" to her? And why was he imparting it in such funereal tones?

"The other two men rode for help. One made it to William Young's house. Young gathered a small squad of men who rode for the brakes, splitting up when they got there to search for the murderer."

Preston paused for a long dramatic breath. Glory stifled an urge to prod him to continue. When he at last resumed, he savored each word as it rolled off his tongue.

"According to one of the men who rode out with the squad, Young spotted something as they were about to cross a ravine. Just as he called out 'There they are, boys,' he was shot in the head."

"How awful!" Glory exclaimed.

"Young fell from his horse, causing it to stumble. The horse crashed into the rider next to Young, pushing man and mount over the edge and into the gully—probably saving the fellow's life in the process. The other men in the party dismounted, took shelter, and prepared to fight, but the assailants vanished as suddenly as they'd appeared."

Glory waited for Preston to continue, but he simply stood there, watching her with strange glittery eyes. "I-I don't understand," she finally said, turning a bewildered gaze on her father. "I'm sorry to hear about all this . . . but what has it got to do with any of us?"

Preston's fingers tightened, drawing her attention back to him. "Don't you see, my dear? The Unionists are responsible for these two vicious murders."

"You can't possibly know that for sure," Glory protested heatedly. "Not if they didn't catch any of those men!"

She jerked away from Preston, more than a little surpised that he allowed her to do so. But he made no move to approach her again. Wearing a smug expression, he moved back a few paces and leaned negligently against her father's desk. Glory was positive she caught the beginnings of a smug smile beneath his golden mustache before he bent to smooth the impeccable crease in his tan trousers.

Preston's smug, self-satisfied look sent fear racing through her. *Not again, not again!* Glory's troubled mind begged. Fingertips massaging her throbbing temples, she bowed her head and desperately tried to decipher the import of what she'd heard.

Why did this have to happen just now? Why, oh why couldn't they have waited until those poor souls in jail had been dismissed, until the court had been dissolved? What would come of all this?

Bracing his long, slim hands against the edge of the desk, Preston shook his head in response to her objection. "You're wrong about what we can prove. For once, luck was on our side, my dear."

Each carefully enunciated word brought growing alarm to Glory. Her head jerked upward and she stared into his cool blue eyes. "Luck?" she repeated, her voice raspy with a sudden unexplainable fear.

"Yes." Preston smiled. "The leader was identified."

Glory's heart took a sickening slide to the pit of her stomach. "W-who?"

"Slade Hunter."

Her knees turned to water. She swayed suddenly, her fingers scrabbling for the edge of the desk. A misty darkness surrounded her, seeping through the room like a cold deathly fog while pinpricks of light danced before her eyes.

"Glory!" Her father's alarmed voice sounded far, far away as the mist grew darker.

She was only remotely conscious of strong hands gripping her arms on either side. The next thing she knew, she was slumped in the big wing chair at the side of the desk, her head lolling against the high back. Her father's worried voice echoed faintly above the buzz in her ears.

"Glory! Speak to me, Glory."

The earth seemed to tremble again, and Glory moaned in response.

Westbrook glared at Preston. "Dammit, man, get some brandy! I told you she had no business hearing about all this!" His worried hands continued to pat her cheek and chafe her wrists until Preston returned. "Here, sweetheart, take a little sip," the Colonel urged, pressing the glass to Glory's mouth. "Come on, it'll make you feel better."

She murmured a protest, pushing weakly at his hand.

"Just a sip, Glory," her father encouraged, tilting her head back to pour a small portion of the liquid between her lips. A trickle of the potent brew seared down her throat.

Glory rasped and sputtered, pitching forward to cover her face with her hands as she choked and coughed in reflexive response to the fiery spirits.

Preston clapped her on the back to help clear her lungs, and she all but cringed from his touch.

"You must realize, Glory," Preston said when she'd regained her composure. "I only told you for your own good. I knew it would be far too cruel to allow you to hear the news about your former friend from some stranger. Of course, Hunter and his men will be caught and punished for what they did. A posse is forming even as we speak."

Glory looked up, her terrified gaze going from Preston to her father and back again. Why couldn't the Colonel see what Preston was doing? The naked truth was right there on his face—the sly amusement, the gloating self-satisfaction. The truth was so very obvious; how could her father be so blind?

"Lies!" she shouted at Preston. "All lies and you know it!"

"Now, Glory," her father cautioned, hovering at her side. "You mustn't take on so. You'll make yourself sick."

Glory clutched at the Colonel's coat sleeve. "Papa, you have to listen to me. Preston's lying. Slade didn't have anything to do with the shootings. I know he didn't!"

"There, there, Glory," the Colonel consoled, patting her hand. "I know you don't want to believe that someone you used to . . . uh . . . care for could do such a thing. But these are war times, darling. People do irrational deeds. You'll just have to accept the situation and put it out of your mind."

"No! You don't understand. Slade is innocent. Preston is just using this as a way to get even with him. He wants revenge—"

"But, Glory," Preston protested innocently. "I barely know the man. Why would I go to all that trouble to harm a virtual stranger?"

"Oh!" Glory seethed with anger. How could she tell her father everything behind Preston's plan? Her beseeching gaze sought her father's once again. "Papa, you've got to believe me. He's making all this up!"

"Am I making up the fact that Hunter's brother is a fugitive from the militia? Morgan Hunter was called to serve his country, and instead of doing the honorable thing, he ran away."

"I-I don't know what his brother did. But—"

"The army knows. He's a deserter, a worthless coward. And Slade is a traitor." Preston shrugged. "It appears to me that both the Hunter brothers have conclusively displayed their contempt for law and

413

order and honor."

Glory was furious. "So what if Morgan did leave! You can't blame Slade because of what his brother did. It's . . . it's not fair! Morgan's actions don't make Slade guilty of what happened today."

The Colonel shook his head sadly. "That's not why Slade is considered guilty. There was a witness, Glory. The man identified Slade Hunter without a shadow of a doubt—"

"That's impossible!" she cried. Her gaze flew to Preston's cunning blue eyes. Suddenly she knew exactly who was responsible for the terribly convenient witness. "It's all a fabrication! If you'd check into that man's background, I'm positive you'd find a link with Preston. For God's sake, listen to me!"

When her father reached to pat her hand again, Glory jerked away, jumping up to pace the room in agitation.

Sighing, the Colonel rose and went to his daughter's side. "Why don't you go upstairs and lie down, Glory? I'll have Violet bring you a nice pot of tea. And tomorrow I'll have Jacob take you to Sivells Bend. Your mother will know better how to deal with all this—"

Fighting the hysteria roiling inside her, Glory whirled and clutched his lapels. "Papa, please. If you care anything about me at all, listen to what I'm trying to tell you. Slade is innocent. I swear! Won't you take my word for it? Can't you do something to stop this madness?"

"I'm sorry, Glory. I hate to see you so unhappy. But you're too distraught to realize what's going on and how important it is to put a end to the Unionists'

414

violence before the whole town is destroyed. Everyone's very upset. There's even talk again of lynching all the prisoners—"

"All!" she repeated in shock. "But there's almost a hundred men still in jail. Papa, you've got to stop them! Those people aren't guilty of a crime simply because they're Union sympathizers."

"The militia is trying to keep the mob under control, Glory. That's their job. And it's up to the court to decide the fate of those prisoners."

Glory stared unbelievingly at her father, her mouth agape. "You're . . . you're just going to let the slaughter go on and on! You won't try to help those poor men? You won't even believe me, your own daughter, when I tell you Slade is innocent?"

"I can't do anything to change things, Glory. Don't you understand? You're not thinking rationally. Those people made their own choices. Now they must pay the price. And if Hunter is guilty, he must be punished. The courts will decide."

"He'll get a fair trial, just like everyone else," Preston intoned somberously.

Fair trial! Horrified, Glory backed away from her father's consoling hands. It was useless. Utterly useless. She could expect no help from him. He was too blind, too caught up in his own ambitions and problems, to see how Preston was manipulating the situation to his own benefit.

Well, Preston wasn't going to get away with it! He wasn't! She'd stop him—someway, somehow. Hands clenched tight at her sides, Glory drew a long, shuddering breath.

Although she longed to tell Preston how foul, how

415

unbelievably vile he was, she choked back the scathing words. It was far more important to put her father and Preston off guard immediately. If the Colonel insisted on sending her to Sivells Bend in the morning, she had only one night to formulate a plan, one impossibly short night to follow it through.

Raw defiance surged through her. It blazed in her mind, setting her blood to boil, unleashing a cold clear streak of do-or-die determination.

She *could* do it! She'd get word to Slade. They could leave Cooke County. Go far, far away. It didn't matter where. There was certainly no chance of a life for them in Gainesville.

Glory felt little anguish at the thought of leaving home and family. Slade was her life now. She belonged with him.

But Sara? What about Sara and her family? She couldn't desert them and there was still no one to guide them to freedom. A sudden thought surfaced. Freedom didn't necessarily mean going north! If *she* could get to Slade, so could Violet and Jacob and Sara. She'd simply take them with her!

Glory smothered the triumphant smile that threatened to break forth. The important thing now was to get her father and Preston out of the house as fast as possible. When they were gone, she could start the necessary preparations. And as soon as it was dark the four of them would leave.

Eyes cast downward, she demurely laced her fingers together. "I'm sorry, Papa," she forced herself to say in a meek little voice. "You're right, of course. I was simply upset by all this terrible news. I believe I will go up and lie down."

The Colonel breathed a sigh of relief. "Quite wise, my dear. I'm sure you'll feel better soon." He patted her cheek lovingly. "Now, I want you to stay in your room and rest all evening."

"Yes, Papa." Placidly, Glory turned and began to walk toward the door, fighting the desire to run from the room in search of Violet.

"Oh, just to ease your mind, my dear—" Preston's icy voice sliced through the air. "You don't have to be afraid of being here alone, Glory. I've posted a man to keep watch all night long."

Chapter Twenty-five

Preston's parting words jolted Glory cruelly. She barely managed to keep putting one foot in front of the other until she was out of the room. Once the door was closed behind her, she sagged against the wall and blinked away the tears of frustration.

The bastard! He'd *known* what she would do. He'd planned for every eventuality.

Glory fought the impulse to jerk the door open and scream her rage at her tormentor. Though such actions might be cathartic, they would change nothing. Her energies would be better expended on finding a way around Preston's stratagems.

Think! Her befuddled mind tried to rally to the desperate demand. All the way up the stairs and down the hall to the sanctuary of her room, she analyzed her options. She came up with no answer. No answer at all.

Discouraged, Glory threw herself across the bed,

rolling onto her back and staring blindly up at the lace canopy. She could think of no excuse that would get the four of them past Preston's spy.

Suddenly she gave a gasp and sat bolt upright. *The four of them!* That was it! Preston's man would be on the alert for Glory. No one suspected that Glory planned to take three other people with her. If she blatantly distracted the man, Jacob could sneak up behind and bash the fellow over the head!

Ha! she crowed gleefully. It was a wonderful idea. So simple it had to work.

While Glory waited for Violet to appear with the pot of tea ordered by her father, she set to work packing a small valise with a few items of clothing. For this trip, there'd be no trunks full of expensive gowns, all ruffled and flounced, no high-heeled slippers, no saucy, plumed bonnets. Just the bare essentials in a bag light enough for Glory to handle herself.

A knock on the door sent a flutter of fear to echo in her throat. Glory snapped the valise shut and hurriedly shoved it under her bed. "Who's there?" she called as soon as the ruffled counterpane was smoothed again.

"Me, Miss Glory," Violet answered, her voice muffled by the door.

A relieved sigh escaped her lungs. "Come in."

The panel swung open and Violet entered, loaded tea tray balanced against her hip. "The Colonel said you were feeling poorly. I brung some of my medicinal tea and some of those nice little biscuits you like so well."

"Thank you. Just put them down on the table, Violet."

Glory could hardly contain her elation, but she dared not say anything just yet. With bated breath she watched Violet bump the door shut and then move across the room.

"Now, you drink this while it's hot, honey chile." Violet lifted the china pot and began to pour.

"Never mind that now, Violet," Glory whispered urgently.

The woman looked up, startled at the intensity of her young mistress's voice. "But, Miss Glory, your daddy said—"

Glory hurried to Violet's side. "It doesn't matter. We have to talk. Is Papa gone?"

"Yes'm, he is. Said he probably wouldn't be back till late tonight," Violet answered.

"And Preston?"

"Yes'm, he's gone, too." A worried frown furrowed Violet's café au lait brow. "Chile, are you sick? You look so peculiar. Have you got a fever?" she asked in sudden concern, laying her palm against the high spot of color on Glory's cheek.

"No. I'm fine, Violet."

Glory caught the hand testing her flushed skin and gave it a tug, pulling Violet toward the vanity bench. "Sit down," she ordered. As soon as the startled slave woman complied, Glory drew another chair up so close their knees were bumping.

"Listen carefully, Violet. I have something very important to tell you."

The gilt-edged china cup of tea had long ago

420

grown cold by the time Glory told her all that had happened in the last weeks. A gamut of expressions—shock, anger, fear—raced across the slave woman's face as she listened to the tale. The pinched, desperate look of her mouth eased only when Glory revealed her bold escape plan.

The thought of leaving the only home she had ever known had been traumatic to Violet at first consideration. Running away had simply never crossed her mind. She always had been treated well by the Westbrooks. She never questioned that her life was the same today as it had been yesterday, that it would be the same for all the tomorrows she had left. That was simply the way things were.

But Violet had loved and cared for Glory from the day of her birth. The girl was as much a part of Violet's life as her own child. It had taken only a few seconds for her to make a decision when she realized that leaving would mean still being with Glory as well as offering a way to protect Sara. From then on, she listened eagerly to Glory's scheme.

"Well," Glory said when her story was finally ended. "Do you think Jacob will agree to the plan? And to knocking out the guard?"

"Hummph!" snorted Violet. "If'n he don't, I will. Ain't no good-for-nothing man gonna harm my baby or send her far away from us neither!"

"Good!" Glory threw her arms around the black woman's neck in a quick hug. "We can do it. I know we can! Now all I have to do is figure out how to get us past the sentry. I'm afraid the roads are going to be heavily patroled."

Violet's face lit up. "Jacob knows an old trail what follows the creek right into the Cross Timbers and on down the Trinity. He goes hunting out that way sometimes. It's twisty and rutted and overgrown, but he says nobody uses it anymore at all. They didn't have no guards out there before—"

"Oh, Violet, that's marvelous!" Glory declared, fervently wishing she'd known about Jacob's trail earlier when she having such trouble getting out of town to see Slade.

"Now, what else do you want us to do, honey chile?" Violet asked when Glory had settled down again.

"First off, send Sara to your quarters to pack clothes for the three of you. As soon as possible Jacob can go out to the barn—just like everything's normal—and prepare the smallest wagon. Maybe he can load your things in it ahead of time. Meanwhile, think of some excuse to let the other servants go to their quarters early. Soon as they're gone you start packing supplies for us—food, blankets, water—"

"And my medicines," Violet interjected.

"Yes, that's a good idea. And I'll check Papa's study. Maybe I can find a gun. Now, there won't be much room in the wagon, so we can't take a lot of stuff. And it's important to keep things light because we'll be traveling hard and fast. I'll leave it to you to choose the most vital items."

"All right," Violet nodded sagely, her mind already busy at work.

"Tell Jacob to be very, very careful. Have him get what supplies he can out to the barn before dark. But

422

he mustn't take any chances! The guard has to believe that Jacob's just going about his regular business. If we have to, we can finish loading after we dispose of Preston's man. I'll bring my bag down shortly. We can hide it in a kitchen cupboard until we're ready to leave."

Violet nodded in agreement.

"Now, as for Preston's watchman, just before dusk—" Quickly and concisely Glory outlined her plan.

Shades of pink and coral and lavender were just beginning to streak the western sky when the final steps to Glory's scheme were set in motion.

"Jacob has had more than enough time to get in place, don't you think?" Glory questioned Violet and Sara as she nervously paced the dimly lit kitchen.

"I think the light is just right—dark enough that our watcher will believe I'd try to leave, but light enough that he'll be able to see me without too much trouble."

Mother and daughter quickly agreed. Glory drew a deep breath and prepared to face the task at hand. With one last shaky smile, she tied her blue wool cape loosely over her shoulders and then placed her hand on the doorknob of the back door.

"You two better move back. I don't want to take a chance on Preston's man spotting anyone but me."

Violet and Sara quickly complied, melting into the shadows. "You be careful, Miss Glory," Violet admonished softly.

"I will." She drew a deep breath. "Well, here I go. Wish me luck."

With trembling fingers Glory turned the knob and then slowly pulled the door open. Poking her head through the crack, she looked left and then right with broad exaggerated movements, playing her role to the hilt. Once outside, she closed the door tightly, tugged the hood of her cloak up over her head, and began to descend the back steps on tiptoe.

Was he watching? Lord, she hoped so!

Reaching the ground, she broke into a quick babystep run that carried her to the shelter of a big old magnolia tree. She flattened herself against the trunk and, with embellished sneakiness, peeked around the rough-barked trunk.

Out of the corner of her eye she caught a flicker of movement. Was it the guard? Had he spotted her? If so, she dared not let the man know she was aware of his presence. Keeping her eyes and face totally blank, she let her gaze sweep a broad semicircle once again.

Yes! There he was! A gunmetal silhouette against the pewter sky. Excitement bubbled inside Glory. Preston's spy had taken the bait, precisely as planned.

With emphatic, stealthy gestures Glory sidled around the big old tree and readied herself as if for flight. That's all it took. Instantly, the man was but a few feet from her.

"I wouldn't do that, miss, if I were you." His deep voice broke the night stillness.

"Oh!" Glory cried out, her hood slipping far back on her head as she whirled around in a dramatic display of fright. "You startled me!"

"Mr. Harper left strict orders that I see to your safety, Miss Westbrook," the gravelly voice intoned. "You best go back inside where you belong."

"Well, mercy me!" Glory replied, eyes wide with innocence. "All I was going to do was get a bit of fresh air. Is there any law against that?" She forced her gaze to stay directly on the man's face, fighting the desire to watch Jacob's careful approach.

The guard was fairly young, tall and whipcord lean. His sharp hooked nose underscored the foxy look of his elongated face. His close-set eyes played over a long silken strand of hair that had escaped the confines of Glory's hood and now lay against her heaving breast.

"No, ma'am, ain't no law against it. But I have my orders—"

"But, sir," Glory protested sweetly, "don't you think it would be all right for just a short time. What . . . what if you walked with me?"

Desperate to keep his attention riveted on her, she raised her hand and pushed the hood the rest of the way off her head, allowing the mass of cinnamon curls to spill forth.

The man's eyes widened greedily at the sight. The tip of his tongue darted out to dampen his thin lips. "Well, I . . . uh—"

Wham! Jacob brought the small tree limb down squarely on the man's head. The guard's eyes rolled back and he slid to the ground in a boneless heap.

"Good Lord!" Glory exclaimed in amazement. "It worked. It actually worked!"

425

"Yes'm, it surely did!" Jacob replied, flashing a huge toothy grin.

"Quick! Get the rope and tie him up. Be sure to tie him up good! We don't want him getting loose. And gag him, too."

Shortly the man was trussed up like a Christmas goose, a red bandanna stuffed in his mouth. Then Jacob dragged him to the back of the house and rolled him under the porch. At the sound of their approach, Sara and Violet cautiously peeped out the door.

"Hurry!" Glory called urgently. "Get the last bags."

Violet nodded. In mere seconds she and Sara, arms full of bundles, descended the steps.

Jacob braced himself against the edge of the porch and stretched his booted foot into the black recess to give the slack body one last nudge. Preston's spy gave a long, muffled groan of pain and then settled into silence once again.

"There!" Jacob said, rising and dusting his hands against his breeches. "Our friend should be safe and sound in there fo' the rest of the night. Won't nobody find him till sometime tomorrow."

"Perfect! Now, let's get out of here. I don't know how much longer it'll take us to get to the Cross Timbers on that old road. And be very, very quiet on the way to the stable," Glory cautioned, thinking of the slaves who had already gone to their cabins at the far side of the Westbrook grounds.

Glory and Jacob relieved Violet and Sara of some of their packages and then the four figures hurried

426

silently through the thickening dark.

Afraid a lantern would draw too much attention, they left the big double-wide doors open and worked by moonlight. The women loaded the last of the supplies into the bed of a small work wagon while Jacob saddled Rosebud. As soon as he'd boosted his young mistress into the saddle he climbed atop the wagon and took a seat beside Violet. Sara perched on a box in the wagon bed.

"Lead on, Jacob," Glory called softly. "I'll follow you." She flicked the reins against Rosebud's sleek neck, guiding the big roan to fall in behind the wagon as it rolled slowly out of the barn and across the back field.

The chill air enveloped the brave little band as they rode through the darkness. To Glory, the sounds of their passage seemed alarmingly loud, filling the black velvet night with the soft creak of saddle leather, the jingle of bridles, the low rumble of the wagon wheels. Glory cringed at each new intrusion on the surrounding silence, fear of discovery making her heart pound painfully. Her breath wedged in her throat, while prickles of apprehension scampered up and down her spine. Not until the lights of town grew dim in the distance did she finally stop waiting for the alarm to be sounded.

Under Jacob's expert guidance, the wagon lurched its way down the almost nonexistent path, working its slow way around fat clusters of brush and trees and over ground so rutted and clogged with rocks that it seemed impossible to pass. More than once they all climbed down to help clear the path.

On they rolled through the hushed night, threading their way through the ebony shadows cast by canopied boughs, nerves tightening each time they crossed another silver-bathed clearing.

Once the distant drumbeat of horses' hooves carried to them on the crisp night air, and they sat frozen with fear, not knowing who the riders were or in which direction they were going. When the low rumble finally died away, all four slumped with relief. Finally Jacob clucked softly to the horse and they began again.

Glory felt very small and alone under the star-sprinkled expanse of sky. She urged Rosebud close to the wagon, closer to the comforting nearness of her friends. Like darting fireflies, her mind flickered from one thought to another. The shock of her father's refusal to listen to her plea. Small tingles of regret at having to cause her mother and younger sisters concern. Memories of Lydia, and the knowledge that she'd miss the friendship they'd shared through the years.

But underneath the sadness there was a growing sense of elation — the wonderful promise of a new life with Slade, the pleasure of knowing Violet and Sara and Jacob would be free to pursue their own happiness. As she reflected on her life, she realized just how pampered she'd been. Glory felt a growing sense of pride that underneath that privileged veneer had been the grit to endure the recent challenges.

Her heart beat with a new serenity as she pushed the remaining shadows from her mind and turned her thoughts to the future.

Miles later Jacob broke her reverie, calling softly that they were nearing an intersection with the road. "What you want to do now, Miss Glory? Take the good road or keep going cross-country?"

Pulled back to the threatening present, Glory's fingers unconsciously tightened on the reins and Rosebud pranced nervously in response to her transmitted agitation.

"I think we ought to chance the road. We'll make better time, and speed is essential right now." Rosebud crabbed sideways, giving the little wagon a jarring bump. "Whoa, boy, whoa," Glory murmured, leaning to pat him soothingly. "Calm down. It's all right."

Pricking his ears at the reassuring sound of her voice, Rosebud snorted twice and craned his long neck until he could nuzzle at the toe of her boot with gentle, quivery lips. Finally satisfied, he let Glory turn him toward the road and they moved on.

Although their speed improved once they were on the travel-packed dirt ribbon of road, Glory almost immediately regretted the decision she'd made. She kept telling herself that the prickly feeling of danger running up and down her spine was only due to their increased vulnerability. The old deserted trail had been rough and slow but at least there'd been no chance of running headlong into a troop of militia men or, God forbid, the posse. Trying to hide her growing apprehension, she urged Jacob to pick up the pace.

The moon was still rising when they reached the turnoff to the house. Glory took the lead, grateful to leave the unsettling stretch of public thoroughfare. She felt better when the heavy fringe of trees finally obscured them from the road.

Her heart gladdened when they topped the crest of the hill and she could see Slade's hideaway nestled in the center of the little valley. The air had turned colder while they traveled and she pulled her cloak tighter against the night breeze that whispered across the hilltop.

A tiny sob of relief caught in her throat. It was almost over. Within minutes she would be in Slade's strong arms. By morning they would be well on their way to a new life.

Knowing Slade would be wary at the sight of unexpected visitors, Glory told Jacob to continue the wagon's slow approach to the house while she rode ahead to alert Slade. A slap of the reins and Rosebud broke into a canter, his easy lope eating up the remaining distance.

"Slade!" Glory cried out softly as she drew to a halt near the front door. "It's me, Glory."

As her eyes searched the velvety darkness, the door opened and Slade stepped through. His hair was sleep-tousled and he wore nothing but a pair of hastily donned pants. Moonlight glinted on the gun in his hand as he dropped it to his side.

"Christ, Glory! What are you doing here at this time of night? What's wrong?"

Grabbing Rosebud's reins as Glory dismounted, he quickly secured them around a support post. Then his arms encircled her and he pulled her close, burying his nose in the wild tangle of curls, breathing in her soothing woman scent. Suddenly he tensed and Glory knew he'd spotted the slow movement of the wagon coming their way.

"Don't be alarmed," she explained quickly. "It's Violet and her family. I had to bring them with me."

A million questions filled Slade's mind but he wisely saved them until the others arrived and they were all inside the cottage. Sara had fallen asleep in the wagon. Jacob carried her in and at Slade's insistence placed her on the bed. Glory spread a quilt over the exhausted girl. Slade snagged his shirt from a peg on the wall, put it on, and the four adults adjourned to the other room.

Slade put a match to the small pile of branches in the fireplace and soon a welcome warmth began to fill the room. While they sat at the table and waited for a pot of coffee to heat, Glory told her story for the second time that day.

Filled with a whirlwind of emotions as he listened, Slade paled visibly when he heard about the ambushes. Hot anger knifed through him when they told him of Preston's wicked machinations. He frowned faintly in response to Glory's recital of how she'd lured Preston's man out into the open. And all the while he clutched at the small, warm hand in his as if to reassure himself that she was really safe, really there.

"You're sure, darling?" he asked when she finished. "Really certain this is what you want to do?" Did she realize what she was saying? Was she aware they might never return to Gainesville? That she would probably be bidding farewell forever to her family, her secure way of life?

"Of course I am, Slade," she replied softly, giving his hand a reassuring squeeze.

"Listen to me, Glory. I want you to think about your decision very carefully. You've already done more than your share. I can take Jacob and Violet and Sara on to safety. I promise I'll see they get to where they can live in freedom. I know of places out west where they can build a good life. Maybe you shouldn't go. It's going to be a very hard trip. And we've very little money—"

Glory grinned and reached into the pocket of her skirt. "I thought this might come in handy." Coins clinked loudly in the leather bag she plunked down on the table. "I found it while I was fruitlessly looking for a gun. Papa can afford it," she explained with a mischievous twinkle in her eye.

Slade shook his head in wonder. "You never cease to amaze me."

"Then stop trying to talk me out of going," she teased. "You'll make me think you don't want me."

Slade's eyes grew smoky with passion. "Oh, I want you all right. I want you more than life itself." His thumb caressed her wrist. "I just don't want you to do something you'll regret. I'm sure if you tell your father the truth about Preston, he'd never make you marry him. You shouldn't have to give up everything that matters to you—"

"Slade," Glory said softly, reaching to place a hushing finger across his lips. "You're what matters to me—the *only* thing that matters to me. All the riches in the world would mean nothing if I didn't have you."

Swallowing back a thick lump of emotion, Slade gazed into her loving eyes and finally allowed himself to believe. Raising her hand to his lips, he brushed a gentle kiss across her knuckles. "I'll never question your love again," he whispered. "And I promise we'll never be separated."

Without warning, the front door slammed open and the four around the table jumped at the shock of the unexpected noise.

"I wouldn't count on keeping that promise, if I were you," Preston said menacingly as he sauntered into the room, a gun in each hand.

Violet shrieked and clutched at Jacob, her eyes huge and filled with fear.

Slade's hand instinctively went for his gun but his fingers closed over thin air. He cursed violently when he realized he'd left it lying on the mantel. Quickly he grabbed Glory and shoved her behind him, sheltering her from the lethal threat of Preston's weapons.

Glory gasped audibly. "How . . . how . . ."

Preston's evil chuckle sliced through the stillness. "Call it intuition. I decided it might be prudent to return and check on things. You're quite clever, my dear, but not clever enough to best me. You'd have been smarter to kill the guard, then he wouldn't have heard you speak of your destination—"

"But I didn't!" Glory cried, pressing closer to Slade, her hands clutching him, seeking the reassurance of his granite-hard body.

Preston shrugged, the big guns swaying slightly with his derisive gesture. "Not exactly, but you did mention the Cross Timbers. And since there's only one road out of town in this direction, it was fairly easy to pick up your trail. I've been behind you for quite some time now."

Slade took a step forward.

"No you don't, Hunter!" Preston snarled. "Just stand very still. All of you."

Slade watched the guns sweep back and forth in a tight short arc. Huddled together as they were, there was no way he could charge Preston without putting everyone else in danger.

There was a glint of madness in Preston's cool blue eyes. His usually impeccable attire was mussed and soiled in spots, the golden locks disheveled as though he'd torn at them in frustration.

"What are you going to do?" Glory asked in a quivering voice.

"Do?" Preston repeated, his mustache tugged up at one corner by a demented smile. "Well, after I've safely disposed of the four of you, I'll return to town for a hero's welcome. Won't they be pleased to hear how I tracked down the man responsible for the killing of Young and Dickson? How shocked they'll be to learn his accomplices also included two runaway slaves and that he'd persuaded them to kidnap the Colonel's daughter."

"You'll never get away with this!" Slade said in an angry, grating voice, his fists bunched tight at his side.

"Of course I will, Hunter. It's a wonderful story. The masses love such melodramatics. I'll simply tell them that the three of you were arguing about the fee

434

to be paid for that service, and after you killed your colleagues, I was forced to shoot you to save my own life."

"No!" Glory cried. "Think about it, Preston. If you found us, Papa could, too!"

"I'm afraid not, my dear. He went north with the posse, back to the Red River to look for the assailants. He has no idea that I slipped away from my group and returned to town."

Glory's eyes were wild. "There's still me! I'll tell everyone the truth. Nothing you could do would make me keep quiet. And . . . and I'll tell the whole town how you masterminded the scheme against the League—how you framed those poor people. It's your fault, all your fault those men needlessly died! I'll tell everything, Preston, I swear I will!"

"Of that, I have no doubt," Preston said, tilting his head imperiously. "But my brilliant plan also covers that eventuality. The coup de grace will be when I tell them how hard I fought to save the Colonel's poor kidnapped daughter, but alas Hunter fired one last shot before he died, mortally wounding her. How sad."

"You bastard!" Slade shouted, instinctively tensing to throw himself forward.

Glory felt Slade's spring-steel muscles coil for the fatal lunge. "No!" she cried, her hands clutching desperately at his shoulders. "Oh, God, Slade, don't! He'll shoot you, just like he says!"

At Slade's first motion, Preston instantly moved to the left, raising his guns higher to take deadly aim. Realizing his movement would put Glory directly in

435

the path of fire, Slade forced himself back to stillness.

Squeezing his eyes shut momentarily, Slade drew in great gulps of air, trying desperately to clear the red fog of rage from his brain. Over the roaring in his ears he could hear Violet's soft sobbing; he could feel the heated rush of Glory's panicked breathing against his tensed shoulder. He had to do something. He had to!

"Listen to me, Harper. Think this through, man. You'll never get away with it. If Westbrook suspects one tiny bit that things weren't as you say, he'll never let it go. Despite his obvious faults, he loves his daughter. He'd never give up—"

"He'll never suspect," Preston declared. "I've covered my tracks too well. Now—" He motioned with his gun. "—move on around a bit, away from the table. That's right," he crooned as the four prisoners grudgingly complied. "A little further."

Preston motioned them onward until they were backed into the corner by the fireplace. As they moved, so did he, edging across his side of the room until his back was to the small room behind. When there was nothing but empty space between them, no possible shelter from table or chairs for his captives, he nodded. "Good. Stay right there."

Slade refused to give up. "We were going to leave, Harper. Go far away. Why don't you let us go . . . or at least let the women go. They'd be too far off to harm you."

"Not a chance." Preston gave a slow sullen shake of his head. "What would stop them from writing or

436

returning? No. Glory's refusal to marry me has already caused quite enough delay in my plans. I'm not taking any chances. The power and wealth I've always wanted are within reach at last. While I would have preferred to be the Colonel's son-in-law, I'm quite positive he'll still act as mentor to the grieving man who tried so desperately to rescue his beloved daughter."

"You're mad!" Slade said vehemently.

Preston ignored him. A wicked smile wreathed his face. "Now," he said jovially, "who shall be the first to go?" The deadly click of the guns being cocked vibrated through the air. "Shall we put the old darky out of his misery first? Or will it be the illustrious Mr. Hunter?" Slowly he raised the gun, taking careful aim at Slade. His finger tightened on the trigger.

"Paw!" Sara's piercing scream rang out precisely as Preston fired. His arm jerked upward at the terror-driven sound. A crimson blossom appeared on Slade's left shoulder just as he launched himself in a long, desperate dive straight at their captor.

Glory shrieked as the resultant collision tumbled both men head over heels across the room. One gun flew through the air, discharging when it crashed against the wall. The other was trapped between the desperate adversaries.

The women's terrified cries continued to fill the air. Jacob charged across the room, grabbed up the gun, and pointed it toward the flailing mass of humanity on the floor. "Damn!" he cried in frustration. There was no way he could take aim at the tangled bodies. One moment Preston was on top, the next Slade.

"Shoot him! Shoot him!" Glory screamed as Jacob's wavering hand continued to jerk from left to right in a desperate attempt to get a clear shot. Sara screamed and ran as the thrashing mass of arms and legs tumbled toward her. There were loud grunts and groans, snatches of curse words, the sound of blows landing against muscled flesh. Preston twisted violently and Slade clutched tighter. They rolled again, crashing headfirst into the wall.

Pow! The thunder of gunfire reverberated through the room and the brawling pair collapsed in an immobile heap.

"Slade!" Glory shrilled hysterically, racing across the room and throwing herself down beside the motionless bodies. Her frenzied hands began to push and pull at the topmost man.

Jacob rushed to help. The gun fell from Preston's limp hand when Jacob shoved his inert body off Slade. Jacob kicked the gun far out of reach and then knelt to feel for a pulse. "He's dead," he said, relief thick in his voice.

Slade lay sprawled on the floor. The scarlet stain on his shoulder was now saucer-sized. Glory leaned over the still and pale face, fighting to see through the tears that streamed down her face. "Slade, darling! Please! Talk to me! Say something!" She smoothed a dark shock of hair from his forehead. "Oh, no!" she exclaimed. There was a big, discolored lump on Slade's temple.

Violet shoved past her husband, anxious to get to the wounded man's side as fast as possible. "Quick,

Jacob! Get my medicine chest out of the wagon. Sara, get some clean rags and some water!" Father and daughter scurried to do her bidding.

Glory drew a shuddering breath and raised her hands to dash away the blinding tears. "How can I help?" she asked, her voice low and quivery with fear.

"Never mind his head now. Get a knife. We've got to get his shirt off so we can see what damage the bullet did."

Glory raced to the cupboard, mere seconds passing before she again knelt at Slade's side with a knife in her hand. Slade groaned when she slit the material. Glory bit her lip and kept on hacking at the fabric. Jacob and Sara returned, placing the items Violet had ordered near at hand. As soon as they'd done so, they moved out of the way. Jacob placed a consoling arm around his daughter's shoulders as they watched the women work with huge, worried eyes.

Glory ripped the last of the shirt away from Slade's wound and Violet quickly sponged the area with a damp rag, washing away the congealing blood. Slade groaned again as she gently poked and prodded the lacerated flesh. He protested even louder when she rolled his shoulder upward to peer underneath.

When she'd finished, Violet raised her eyes to Glory and suddenly broke into a broad smile. "It went clean through the meat of the shoulder! He's gonna be just fine. That nasty ol' bump on the head done more damage than the bullet."

Glory pressed trembling fingers against her lips. "Oh, thank God."

"Here," Violet instructed. "Wash his face with this

cold cloth. It'll help bring him around."

Glory obeyed.

"Glory?" Slade moaned softly, his eyelids fluttering.

A wild surge of happiness filled Glory's heart. "Yes, my darling, I'm here. Right here."

"What . . . where . . ." He struggled to rise. "Ouch!" he responded to the painful throb in his head and he raised his fingers to gingerly probe at the egg-sized lump.

"Now you quit that wallering around, Mr. Slade," Violet scolded gently. "You lie still till I get this shoulder bandaged."

"But . . . Preston . . . danger—"

"Shh, darling," Glory soothed, stroking his cheek lovingly. "It's all over. Preston's dead. Everything's going to be fine. Now, hold still like Violet said. She's almost done."

Slade ceased his wiggling and gave himself up to Glory's sweet ministrations.

"All done, Miss Glory," Jacob said with a satisfied nod of his head. "I buried that Mr. Harper so far back in those woods they'll never find him."

Glory looked up from helping Slade load the wagon. "Thank you, Jacob. I guess that takes care of everything."

"Yes. This is the last of my stuff. We'd better get on our way," Slade said, peering toward the east where the dawn's first pale fingers of light were probing the indigo sky.

Hand in hand, Slade and Glory stood at the side of the wagon, watching while Jacob and his family took their places atop the wagon.

"Head 'em west, Jacob," Slade said with a big smile. "We'll be right behind you."

"Sure 'nuff, Mr. Slade," Jacob replied happily. A flick of the reins and the wagon rolled out.

Glory reached to tug Rosebud's lines free. But instead of mounting, she turned toward Slade. Slipping her arms around his waist, she leaned her cheek against him, breathing a prayer of thanks that he was still with her. It could so easily have been Slade who lost his life instead of Preston. The thought sent cold chills through her body.

"What's the matter, darling?" Slade whispered against the crown of her head.

"Nothing. Not one single thing," she murmured against his chest. "I'm just so very, very happy to be with you."

Slade held her tighter and she let the gentle reassuring thud of his heartbeat under her ear hammer away the last remnants of fear. He gave her one last lingering hug before stepping away.

"We'd best be on our way."

"I know."

"Up you go," Slade said, boosting Glory onto Rosebud's broad back. As soon as she was settled in the saddle he mounted Diablo.

His warm silver eyes sought hers. "Are you ready?"

Glory smiled and reached to twine her fingers with his. "I'm ready for anything, darling, as long as we're together."

"Always," he murmured, nudging Diablo closer to Rosebud. One small shift in his seat and he leaned to capture her lips.

"Always," Glory echoed breathlessly when the kiss was ended.

In unison they turned their horses in the direction the wagon had taken. Side by side, they began their journey.

Epilogue

The front door of the store banged loudly, announcing the arrival of two small children. The boy clutched his little sister's hand protectively as they crossed the room to the counter where Slade stood.

Slade braced his hands on the countertop and bent at the waist to peer down at his small visitors. "Well, now, what have we here? Two new customers? Wonderful! If it's anything I love, it's nice new customers for my store."

"It's us, Papa! Adam and Lizzie. We've come to walk you home!" the children squealed in delight.

Slade gasped in mock surprise, playing the game to its familiar conclusion. He rounded the counter and squatted down to scrutinize them intently. "Well, so it is! You've grown so much today I didn't recognize you."

The children collapsed against each other in a fit of giggles.

"And where's that gorgeous mother of yours?" Slade inquired, scooping a child up in each arm.

"Right there!" they cried, pointing gleefully to Glory standing just outside the store entrance.

"All right, you little scalawags," she said with a laugh. "Let your papa lock up."

Slade sat the children on their feet again. They scampered to their mother's side, waiting impatiently for their father to turn the key in the lock.

"There's apple pie for dessert, Papa!" Lizzie declared in her little piping voice.

Slade gave Glory a hug, then linked his hand with hers. "Wonderful! Two new customers for the store and apple pie, too—all on the same day. How lucky can a man get?"

"As lucky as this woman is," she answered with a smile.

"There they go, Lizzie, getting mushy again."

Still giggling, each child took one of their parents' hands and the family headed for home.

Author's Note

Within a three-week period in October of 1862, over forty men lost their lives to the hangman's noose — the biggest mass hanging in the history of the United States. Bourland, Chance, McCurley, Young, and Dickson were real people. To this day, the mystery surrounding the Great Hanging of Gainesville, Texas, remains.

<u>FREE</u> Preview Each Month and $ave

Zebra has made arrangements for you to preview 4 brand new HEARTFIRE novels each month...FREE for 10 days. You'll get them as soon as they are published. If you are not delighted with any of them, just return them with no questions asked. But if you decide these are everything we said they are, you'll pay just $3.25 each—a total of $13.00 (a $15.00 value). **That's a $2.00 saving each month off the regular price.** Plus there is NO shipping or handling charge. These are delivered right to your door absolutely free! There is no obligation and there is no minimum number of books to buy.

TO GET YOUR FIRST MONTH'S PREVIEW... Mail the Coupon Below!